LOST ARROW

3-BOOK EDITION

MARSHALL ROSS

PUBLICNOISE PRESS

For information contact Publicnoise Press at
www.publicnoise.com

Published by Publicnoise Press, LLC

ISBN: 978-1-7324610-3-1

Book layout by www.ebooklaunch.com

For Robin
As everything is.

Acknowledgments

This flight of fancy benefitted tremendously from the freedom afforded me by my partners at the ad firm Cramer Krasselt.

If it's enjoyable at all, the credit goes to the outstanding work of editors Sarah Kolb-Williams and Kathleen Schultz.

My research was inspired and supplemented by the excellent counsel of Richard Brooks, religion professor at University of Wisconsin. He provided invaluable insights into the mindsets of the deeply devout.

And special thanks to Ralph Gerbie, Gary Kurland, Elizabeth Holland, Michael Ross, Daniel Ross, Zach Ross, Craig Likhite, Gary Doyle, and Melinda Hendrickson, who read the earliest of pages and encouraged me anyway.

LOST ARROW

BOOK I OF
THE KALELAH SERIES

The abyss hunkers distant and unknown.

Forever untouched by the warmth and illumination of the sun, its residents are monsters drawn in the dark. Nearly blind, they have no need for color or beauty. With spiny whiskers and weakly glowing orbs, they navigate an endless night, a prison of ink. For eons, the miles of water bearing down on the abyss have been the perfect jailer. Should any of its residents attempt escape, their ghostly bodies, held together only by the pressure bearing down upon them, would simply burst.

The abyss lives by its own rules. But it does live. A miracle that has not gone unnoticed.

At the bottom of this underwater canyon where no light can reach, below the silt and sand, an ancient secret sits dark and silent. Waiting …

1

Sarah Long crushed her cigarette against the side of the red metal pail hanging on the wall behind her and let the butt fall into the bucket. She stepped back to the rail and into the sun and took in the breeze one last time before returning to her desk two decks below.

She smoothed her hair back and started down the drilled-metal stairs. She hated to leave her spot along the portside rail. If she could get away with it, she'd do nothing more all day than lean against the steel guard, smoke, and look out at the water. She grew up far from any ocean, but now she couldn't imagine a day without it. The smell of it. The size of it. The distance-from-home of it. Despite her work schedule in the decks below, she never failed to steal away several times a day to her spot outside with the breeze, the fearless dive-bombing booby birds, and the endless, swallowing enormity of the water.

People on the ship who noticed her fixation with the sea sometimes asked her why she hadn't become a marine biologist. She would laugh and shrug her shoulders. *They think I'm actually a science geek.* But she knew the idea of marine biology would never have crossed her mind, no more than working as an oil company geologist did two years ago when she had finally, after so many delays, graduated from college. Everything in her life so far had seemed to happen without her consent. She never really said yes to geology. It was just a train she got on her freshman year and then never hopped off.

Even the pull of the ocean had become more of a happy compulsion than a determined choice. Being near the water wasn't on her checklist. Her hometown didn't even have a river. But once under the big water's spell, she never wanted it to break. Looking out over the endless whitecaps, she could find, at least temporarily, a kind of peace. She could fall into that shimmering expanse, drown the part of her that needed choking off, and then make it through another day. She wasn't sure where she was going, but she was grateful it was this big ship on a big ocean taking her there.

She wished she could say it was hard work and excellence that had made it happen. But in truth, she owed it all to an accident of birth, a rare bit of luck, and some good old American political payola. In return for huge amounts of donations to political campaigns, Congress had allowed America's oil companies to practically write America's energy policy. And as cover for the politicians whose coffers they filled, the oil companies did their best to hire American. But given the state of math education in the United States, maintaining this tidy little quid pro quo was getting harder and harder to pull off.

Enter Sarah. It may have taken her seven years to finish a five-year program, but her math scores were decent. And the certificate that listed Lancaster, Ohio, as her place of birth, clinched the deal.

And so, Sarah, with a middling resume and middling academic scores, from a middling branch of a state university, but hailing from a place almost precisely in Middle America got a junior research job on the *Lewis*, a large, fan-shaped, Titan-class survey ship with Honolulu as her port of registry. It was a job she couldn't have even imagined—and literally hadn't even heard of—just a few weeks before she got it.

And it was a job right atop the place she needed most, though that, too, was something she didn't know at the time. A place so far from Lancaster it might as well have been on the moon.

Lucky.

When she got below deck, she poured herself a cup of coffee and woke her computer. Mostly what Sarah did aboard the *Lewis* was set up sonar runs that mapped the seabed below the ship. Pretty boring stuff. She would spend her days below deck analyzing sediment scans for the telltale signs of oil, the dark, irregular spots that looked like bubbles trapped between layers of rock. But for the last several days, the ship had been hunting for something else. What it was exactly, Sarah had no idea. Because the ship was in strange waters. Deep waters.

She tapped in the code to pull up the scan in progress. The system was layered with security protocols. Once she had logged in successfully, there were still several steps to get to the actual scan. She answered the double- and triple-authentication questions and wondered for the thousandth time why all this crazy security mattered. Whatever's down there, she said to herself, is going to stay down there. At least that's what everyone onboard had been telling her.

The image began to load. But it was in no hurry, coming up one scan line at a time.

The *Lewis* had been sent to explore the Mariana Trench in the western Pacific Ocean, an abyss nearly seven miles beneath the surface. A place so deep there was no point in finding oil; you could never pump it out. But the *Lewis's* real mission on this particular voyage wasn't oil at all. It was to pay off a debt. Allied Oil, the Houston energy company that owned the *Lewis*, had had a nasty spill off the Hawaiian Islands a few years back. In a deal to keep a certain senator with deep ties to environmental lobbies from punishing the company into bankruptcy, Allied agreed to lend its new ocean floor mapping technology to a joint university team of US and Japanese researchers studying the trench.

The trench—the deepest place on the planet—had been mapped before. There had even been expeditions that recorded video of giant snails and single-cell amoeba more than four inches around.

But geologically, underneath the floor, the trench was still a mystery. And that's why the *Lewis's* new scanner had been drafted to the research team. By combining adaptive radar and artificial intelligence, the scanner could see deeper into water and rock than anything before it: past the seafloor, past the oceanic plate, down even as far as the Earth's soft upper mantle—which promised to yield a whole new field of study.

She watched the progress line slowly crawl its way rightward along the bottom of the image load screen. And then it stopped.

"Great," she said softly.

She watched the pinwheel icon spin as the computer worked to grind through the data. There couldn't be much left to go. She could already see the abyssal ridge, the floor of the crevice, and the first few layers of sediment below. Everything looked like the last two days' worth of scans. Except at the bottom, where the image was still incomplete. That looked different.

What she usually saw were layers of boulders, rocks, sand of various coarseness, the biological remains of dead sea life, silt, and clay. This, whatever it was, wasn't marine sediment. There were long, perfectly straight, horizontal lines that went on for great distances, broken up by small, square shadows at regular intervals.

She took a sip of her coffee and waited for the image to clarify. This had to be some kind of digital dirt in the load. She was sure that once the image was finished, whatever this artifact was would simply disappear. She'd seen squirrelly things during loading before. "The AI thinking," the nerdy guy who trained her on the scanner had told her.

At last, the pinwheel blinked away and the loading continued. Finally, the sluggishness was gone, and the scan lines drew in faster and faster until, after just a few seconds, the image was complete.

But the anomaly wasn't gone. If anything, it'd gotten clearer, more absolutely there and more obviously unlike anything that should be there.

"What the fuck."

She moved to put her coffee down on the desk. Instead, still unable to mentally process what she was seeing—still transfixed by what she couldn't believe she was seeing—she overstretched her arm and the cup fell to the floor with a crash, splashing scalding coffee along with shards of ceramic across her bare left ankle and calf.

She paid no attention to it. Instead she refreshed the screen, gambling the reload would go faster. It did. But the image remained the same.

"Jesus, Sarah, what the hell happened?"

The smash of the mug had brought Scott Bronner out of his closet-sized office. Sarah didn't look away from the screen.

"Nice job," Scott complained, "there's coffee everywhere. You're just gonna sit there?"

"Take a look at this, will you?"

"What? I already saw that video Dalton sent around. It was stupid."

"No. The scan. Something's really strange."

"It's probably the start-up software again. Those asshole consultants—I've emailed them like six times and they never email back."

He was behind her chair and leaning over her to get a look at her screen, a habit that usually made Sarah cringe. *Why always from behind the chair?* But this time she didn't make anything of the creepy move. Something else had her attention. She pointed to the bottom of the image.

"Look at that."

"What is that?"

"I don't know. I refreshed. But it keeps coming up the same."

"These are the right targeting specs?"

"Same we've been using all week. Same depth, same duration, same pulsing."

He traced a forefinger along a section of the image from left to right. "Is this scale correct?"

"Yes."

"My God."

Bronner took a few steps back, but Sarah could feel his eyes still trained on the screen. In a reflection on the glass she saw him make the sign of the cross.

But Sarah didn't feel the need for prayer or protection. She was too fascinated by the thrill of discovery to worry about what the image meant. For the first time in all her studies and the long, dreary routine that had become work, she saw something in a sediment scan that made her heart beat faster. It was a feeling she wasn't willing to surrender just yet.

Though, days from now, she'd wish the image was just another routine scan, with nothing about it the least bit noteworthy.

And nothing the least bit terrifying.

• • • •

The message came on quickly and flared with the colors of emergency. It blinked furiously: red, then yellow, then red, over and over. At the same time, a small metal needle punctured the seal on a round, polymer vial containing a light blue liquid. Another needle pierced through the seal of a second vial, the contents of this one green, almost chartreuse.

Machines tilted the vials to pour their luminous contents into yet a third, empty vial. The two liquids mixed loosely, holding fast to their original hues until the cocktail was sonically blended to a softly transparent cyan. The vial was flash heated and then distilled to a vapor.

The gas was collected and swept up by a miniature fan, which directed it into a larger chamber containing a precise and delicate mix of nitrogen, oxygen, argon, and carbon dioxide. The new element swirled with the older tenants.

The chamber was now another weapon in the arsenal of emergency management. Until the moment the new gas was introduced, the chamber's contents had kept their human beneficiary in a deep, almost deathlike sleep. But once altered, it took only a few moments for the new gaseous cocktail to trigger in its recipient precisely what the emergency warning system required.

A pair of eyes opened. The blinking message that proclaimed emergency was aligned perfectly to be the first thing the eyes saw and at just the distance to be in perfect focus.

The message was read.

It all happened exactly as programmed, exactly as planned. Except the planners never imagined an emergency quite like this.

2

The VP's room was large, plain, and orderly to an extreme. Unlike Sarah's workspace, which was just a desk shoved under some stairs, Mike Henderson's office had a window and a door leading directly to a deck overlooking the water. She stared out at the ocean as Henderson studied the printout she and her boss had brought to his attention. Though he was not the captain, Henderson ran the ship, hence his room with a view. Sarah was grateful for the calming sight of the water but she desperately wanted a cigarette.

She hadn't played this right. The last three hours were spent below deck confirming the data. Scott wanted to be absolutely sure that what they had was, in fact, a scan image. As soon as he was satisfied, the two of them rushed to Henderson's office. There'd been no time to grab a smoke on the way. She was nic-fitting badly and starting to fidget.

Henderson made a note on the margin of the image. A flush began to bloom red around his neck.

"If this is some Photoshop bullshit, someone's gonna get fired," he said with a drawl, looking over his glasses at her and Scott sitting in the straight-backed aluminum chairs at the front of his large oak desk. "And by *someone,* I mean you two. No way am I sending this to corporate."

"Mike, I'm not a child and this isn't a joke," Scott answered quickly. He flashed Sarah a look that said *let me handle this.* Typical.

Scott Bronner was tall, lanky, and paler than it would seem possible for a person who works on the open seas. He complained to her incessantly about "guys like Henderson." Guys who spent their days, he said, dealing with corporate BS and treating it like it mattered. What she thought he really hated about the Hendersons of the world was that they always ended up in charge, and guys like Scott Bronner never did.

Sarah was nervous. She didn't know Henderson personally, but everybody on the ship knew his story. Ex-navy. Twenty years out of the service and he still wore his hair military short and his shoes polished bright. He was XO of a surveillance ship in the nineties and had been part of a contingent of senior officers who stepped in some sort of political dog pile she'd never really understood, except that Henderson had gotten a whole lot of it on the bottoms of his shiny shoes. Up close here, face-to-face, she understood why Henderson made people nervous. For one thing, he was huge. His desk was taller than normal desks; sitting in front of it, her knees together, she felt tiny, like a little girl called to the principal's office.

"It's straight off the machine," Bronner argued, pointing to the VP's computer to emphasize the point. "You can go in the system yourself. It's real. There's something down there."

"Besides," Sarah blurted, "I suck at Photoshop."

Scott gave her another look.

"Yeah?" Henderson challenged as he got up from his chair, the red in his neck growing hotter and moving now to his cheeks. "Suckin' at Photoshop never stopped the *National Enquirer* from showin' us pictures of Bat Boy and Clinton's dick."

"You have to trust me on this," Scott said, turning in his chair to follow Henderson as the VP paced by the window, smoldering. "I wouldn't be here if I hadn't checked Sarah's work. This isn't some idiot game, Mike, this is … something." He paused like he was searching for the right words. "This is exactly why we spent a hundred million dollars on the scanner. To find something like this."

"Really, Bronner—somethin' like *this*?" Mike whirled back around from the window, pointing to the scan on his desk. "Are we a university? Are you a wreck-divin' arche-fuckin'-ologist, Bronner? We're an oil company and you're an oil hunter. So tell me, what did we find down there in that godless crack? And if it ain't oil, cousin, I don't need a second look."

That seemed to take the steam out of Scott's argument. Now he looked cornered. "I don't know," he said. "We have to get closer to find out. That's why we need your help."

"You don't know? Don't sell me that shit. You know plenty. You know the only thing that matters here." He put his giant hands on the big desk and leaned in toward Scott. Sarah could smell his aftershave. "This ain't anythin' we're lookin' for."

"It's a ship," she interrupted, shocked by the sound of her own voice. "Why are we pretending it isn't? It's so obvious. It's a giant ship. Look at it. What else could it be?"

The room went dead.

Scott winced. Henderson said nothing, though now his neck and cheeks were screaming red. But why all the speaking in code? It *was* a ship. She was sure of it. And she knew Scott thought so too, even if he didn't have the guts to come out and say it.

"Let's not all go off looking for Bigfoot here," Scott weaseled. "Like we discussed earlier, Sarah," he lied, "it could be a hundred things. It could be crystals."

Crystals? she thought. Is he high? And she doubted Henderson would ever go off looking for Bigfoot. There was nothing about him that seemed even the slightest bit indulgent. The short-cropped hair, the starched shirt, and the desk with no clutter beyond some neatly stacked papers and a few office accessories lined up with military precision. He didn't seem like a nut-case fiction kind of guy to her. No, Henderson seemed more like a policy manual kind of guy to her. A beat-you-dead-with-a-policy-manual kind of guy.

"Okay, Bronner," Henderson said, playing along like a henchman sharpening his blade. "Let's go with crystals. Yeah, I like that—*crystals.*" He gave the word a mocking flourish. "Except that's total horseshit. Not that I give a damn one way or the other. Look, I don't want to be here one minute longer than I have to.

So *we* don't want to be here, get it? This ain't our shit. Why am I gonna do anythin' more than I have to out here?"

"What if there's something in it we'd want, I mean, something *corporate* would want?" asked Sarah.

Henderson lifted an eyebrow toward Scott. It looked to Sarah like a cue to get the girl under control.

That was not going to happen. "Something incredible is inside that thing, I know it," she plowed on before Scott could talk over her again. "You don't build something like that without, I don't know, some big purpose."

"Yeah, to die at the bottom of the fuckin' ocean," Henderson teased.

"At this point it doesn't matter," Scott squeezed in with something that almost sounded like authority. "We have to send this to Hawaii. We have to send it all. And I have to copy corporate. That's the deal. I brought this to you because we need to get closer to this thing and my pay grade isn't going to make that happen." He paused for a minute and softened his tone. "Mike, you know I could get fired for sitting on this, right?"

"I think you're gonna get fired if you don't."

"I'm going to ask for a submersible," Scott said.

She watched as Henderson mulled over the idea. His mouth curled slowly to a small smile. The flaring red in his face throbbed on. "And I think, bubba, they'll send you back a nice little note with flowers and birds on it, and that little Hallmark card is gonna say, 'Congratulations, Asshole, you're dead.'"

"You could turn your back on this?"

"Hell yes. Because my bosses, who are also your bosses, are in the oil-pumpin' business. Not the what-the-fuck-is-that business. Think about it. If you were a suit, what would you do with this? We're only scannin' the damn Trench to pay a fuckin' bill. It's already costin' us a fortune and a whole lot of time. There's no payday for us out here. Jesus, Bronner, it's the deepest place on the whole damn planet. Even if it was oil, which it clearly is not, what could we do with it? Seven miles down, for Christ's sake. Meanwhile, the South China Sea is gettin' drilled like a whore on Saturday night, and this thing"—Henderson pointed to the printout again—"doesn't look like money, Einstein. It looks like the kinda thing that *costs* money, and more."

Scott pushed his chair back and stood to face Mike Henderson. "So you're not going to tell me what you think this image is?" he pressed, but not very hard.

"Oh, I'll tell you. I think it's somethin' you forget to report. I think it's somethin' you delete from every damn drive linked to that scanner the second you leave this office. I think it's somethin' you get as far the fuck away from as you can."

Scott gave Sarah a look that said *let's go*. He picked up the scan from Henderson's desk. "Okay, Mike, thanks for your input on this," Scott said as they both started for the door. "I'll let you know what we do."

She paused at the doorway to watch Henderson turn back to the window, crimson-faced. The view had lost its sun. His window now looked out upon a gray ocean and a sky darkening with gray-black clouds. "Shut that fuckin' scanner down for repairs," he called in a voice edged with dread.

3

Seven miles below the surface, Analyst Trin could already feel the nausea. Kneeling before his prayer glass and whispering the First Commitment, his body began the inevitable convulsions that signaled the start of another square in his patchwork life. After the trauma of awakening from a Skip, most people's second activity is to vomit. The first is always to pray. His day would require three more prayers before he could rest. But Analyst Trin would get no rest for quite some time.

When his retching was finally over and he could stand without needing the wall to steady himself, he pulled on the dark blue jumpsuit of his rank and peered into the mirror. This would have been E Two, the second Epochal Check, and so five thousand years would have passed since he had zipped into his M-suit, swallowed the met-tube, and closed his eyes. He could find no signs of gray in his dark brown hair, nor any change in length. It was still cropped short along the sides and just slightly longer at the top. Standard service cut. He saw no change on the dark skin of his face.

His light green eyes seemed to have kept their color. There were no lines at the corners of his lids, nor along the stretch of his forehead. He stepped back from the mirror for a wider look. He'd been thin and fit at the start of the Skip, and he appeared the same now.

He turned and pushed open his pod's door to the short hallway lined with two dozen other pods. The hallway's empty darkness was a surprise. In training, and during his first actual Waking, the hallway was always lit brightly, loud and bustling. He walked the thirty yards ahead to the main doors that separated his cluster of pods from the cavernous stem of Leaf Six. The huge guide ship was arranged in an overlapping pattern of leaf-shaped structures, with four leaves on each side of the central hull. When it wasn't buried beneath the sea, its great leaves swept back, layered, and lit by a thousand glowing windows, a guide ship appeared like a glittering, triangular metropolis.

The stem of each leaf was a city unto itself. Tall, vaulted ceilings of gray steel and brass filigree canopied an enormous concourse lined with offices, stores, and service outlets. At the start of a Waking, a stem was at its busiest. Thousands of people rushed to their posts and were happy to do so. Though Skips are completely without memory and go by in what seems like a blink of an eye, no one took lightly the inherent dangers of Skipping. Disease, system failures, and causes never truly identified always took their toll. At least ten people from every Skip never woke. So, in that early time before work and routine had reasserted their dulling influences, the stem was always filled with the excited din of a thousand greetings and well-wishes.

But now, as Trin took his first cautious steps forward, except for the emergency lights on the floor, the stem was dark and silent.

He stopped at the threshold and looked down both directions of the stem, but he saw no difference in either direction. The bright spots that glowed like perfect yellow jewels embedded in the metal panels of the floor vectored to vanishing points at both ends and were swallowed up by a black nothingness that seemingly went on forever.

"Good luck, assholes," he whispered into the void, careful to keep the words below a volume the microphones could record. "Another training exercise. Another total fucking waste of time. You know this will only take me a few minutes."

When he was just eight months old, still an infant with his dark hair in short, fine tufts on his wobbly baby's head, he began speaking in full sentences. By his second birthday, he was reading at the level of a ten-year-old. At age four, he reprogrammed the nanny bot to serve him candy for breakfast. He remembers all of this. He remembers, too, the sense of wonder from others. From everyone. There seemed to always be a crisis level of urgency spinning around him. What makes him tick? How can he do what he does? And how much can he do? But for him there was no urgency, no crisis. He didn't need to understand why he was the way he was. He understood that to Them—which was everyone—his brain was some kind of miracle. They said so. And often. But he wasn't interested in that. He was interested in math. He was interested in chemistry and physics and the inner working of magnetic drives. But They were clearly in charge, his genius apparently doing nothing to change the legal powerlessness of children.

And so an endless battery of testing would become the paintbrush that would color all his earliest memories. Can you do this? Can you do that? And every time he could, which was nearly every time, the ante of challenge was upped once more along with the enthusiasm of his benevolent tormentors, who would leave each session giddy with plans for the next. His parents, themselves constantly agape at his remarkable precociousness, had no strength of will to keep him from the probing curiosity of these insistent bench markers, the doctors, teachers, and Keepers forever marveling over his odd leaps of progress. What pains in the ass.

Classmates, always years older, tested him as well in the cruel ways children do. But like everything else for him, mastering the tricks of charm and the skills it took to win the occasional tussle came quickly. He finished his compulsory seventeen years of school in just ten. A dozen careers opened up to him, but he turned them all away to join the service. He craved the anonymity of a system designed to make him exactly like others, a mere member of the rank, a cog of common training, subject only to the same common tests.

It was his first wrong answer. A face too young to hide, his difference was instantly spotted. And the special challenges, along with the custom-made measuring sticks, emerged again. Despite the annoyance, Trin flew through the training academy and was made the youngest analyst in the entire Guide Service.

That was five thousand years ago. *So why another damn training exercise?*

. "Hello?" he called out to no one. *Aren't we past this ... shit?*

Forbidden as they were, his curse-filled thoughts flowed freely. He had read the Plan enough times (once, which was enough) to know that Profanity is expressly prohibited. Human thought and language is a sacred gift, not to be sullied by obscenity. Blah, blah, blah. But he loved the way the scandalous words felt, the way they burst from his thoughts like black and glorious birds taking flight. He didn't see anything blasphemous about a particular sound or paring of characters and graphlets. *Shit* was the absolute perfect expression for the moment, simple and precise to his feelings. *Shit, shit, shit.* Lamir's favorite of the forbidden.

Lamir. A puppy of a boy. His eyes were big, brown, and dancing and almost too big for his head. He was small for his age, nearly a foot shorter than Trin. Yet the two boys were inseparable: Trin always taking the first step and Lamir always following dutifully.

When the two were very young, Trin would read aloud to Lamir. But having long since outgrown stories fit for his age, Trin soon sought and found more interesting fare. The kind of literature his parents had thought they kept well hidden. That's when the swearing began. Like everyone's parents, his were outwardly observant. And, like most people, once inside the relative privacy of their homes, they colored outside the lines of orthodoxy. Soon after he could walk, Trin discovered his parents' hiding places for wine, sex-beam

19

plays, and story files with language the Keepers would be quick to condemn. He never cared much for the wine. The beam plays frightened him at first. But he instantly embraced the look and sound of the forbidden words that spiced the stories his parents thought were out of reach of so young a boy. He would read quietly behind the closed door of his room, keeping the stories safely on the glass rather than pulling them to the air where more innocent tales could be shared. Every time he'd come across a forbidden word, he'd pause, and before *shit* or *fuck* or *bitch* even left his lips, Lamir, his big eyes widening even larger, would begin to laugh and Trin, laughing too, would have to hush him up for fear they'd be caught.

His eyes misted. Lamir, like his parents and so many others he knew and loved, was millennia dead, dust long scattered. The swear words, the wrong words, were theirs, learned and practiced and laughed over together, remnants of a childhood cut short by a mind that would be allowed no time for youth. And this was how he could still keep Lamir alive, how he could still keep the two of them laughing in his room in his parents' house, joyfully struggling to keep a boy's secret. He just had to say the words.

After a half-mile walk in the dark, he reached the point where the stem of Leaf Six met the much larger main stem that ran nearly the entire length of the ship. Darkness, pinpricked only by the dim spots of tiny emergency lights, glowered from all directions. And still not another soul in sight. *Crap.* Ridiculous as it seemed, there was no denying the slow creep of fear. A guide ship was nearly two miles wide and more than four miles long. So far, he'd seen no one, heard no one. The hum of the air units offered some mild comfort. *The ship is working*, he told himself.

His mind replayed the last hour. He was awoken. His M-suit had been powered when he peeled it off. His prayer glass had glowed its usual blue-green holographic image of the Chief Keeper chanting. His washbasin had filled and emptied on his command. Everything *inside* his pod was working as it should. It all added up to some kind of drill. Nothing real was going on. But still, most tests made clear what they were testing. This one hadn't revealed anything yet.

He kept walking toward his post, working to push the dread away as he went. *This is an exercise*, he kept telling himself. *A fucking stupid exercise, but an exercise.* His stomach, though, was stubborn and continued to make a different, colder calculation. His fingers trembled as he swept them across the flora scanner that granted access to the Command Center.

The doors slid open and the blast of light from inside was so bright he had to put his arm across his face to shield his eyes. At last, something as it should be. But this was just a tease of normality. When his eyes adjusted to the glare of the Command Center's overheads, he could see just one person in the room. And now there was no getting around it. This was no test. And no good.

"Analyst Trin," a clear voice called from the far corner. "May God ease your new start."

"Thank you, sir." In an awkward reflex he added, "May God ease yours as well."

"I hope He will, Analyst. But I'm still waiting. Would you mind stepping over to your post, please?" It wasn't a question.

Captain Jan Argen, olive skinned, with dark hair and a build just shy of muscular, moved with the easy confidence of someone who always knew he'd be in charge. Command presence. He was making his way to the scan desk, the analysts' station, straight and taller than his actual height. But Trin thought he detected worry in the captain's eyes, which did nothing to calm the tremor in his own hands. His eyes swept the room again. Still no one else. The Keeper's chair was empty.

Where's the Keeper? The Command open, without Phetra? Fuck.

"Analyst Trin, I need you to help me get a better understanding of some data."

"Yes sir." He sat at his glass. "Can I ask, sir, about the Waking? I haven't seen anyone else but you. E Two's not a big check, sir, but it's big enough. At least half the ship should be up."

The captain moved closer. "What you need to know now, analyst, is that you and I are chasing a bug."

Bug. Trin kept quiet the *fuck me* that wanted out. "Yes sir."

Argen kept things businesslike and routine, but Trin could see it was work. Argen was using the language and posture of command, the kind of thing Trin had seen plenty of in Academy. But there was something quaking underneath, the same cold-stomach warning Trin was feeling.

"More than likely, this is nothing," Argen said, keeping his shoulders straight. "And once we know it is, you and I get ourselves a meal and we tuck back in for another couple thousand or so. I've already read the message that got us out of bed. It's in my private files. But I want you to go check the source. Go deep and tell me what you find, if anything."

This was all standard shit, he knew it. The captain was just reading from the book, going through the motions. Trin cursed the shaking in his hands. It took longer than it should have, but he managed to activate his earpiece, slip light tips on the ends of his fingers, and tap in his security code so he and the *Kalelah* could communicate. Usually he loved the moment when signals from the earpiece and the finger lights reached into his mind and touched the clusters of neurons that connected him directly to the systems his rank could access. The *Kalelah* was the only intelligent being who could care less about how smart he was. The *Kalelah* was just glad to have someone who could understand. There was an eagerness there in the code that Trin could feel. And one he was usually glad to embrace. But in this moment, that satisfying rush when he made connection, the usual gooseflesh on the back of his neck, the strange pleasurable tingle of electricity in his brain—all of it was absent.

He was too scared to make a note of any of it. Working hard to keep his thoughts from jumping around like the inside of his guts, he asked the ship to provide the alarm status. The answer prompted more queries, and soon he and the *Kalelah* were moving deeper and deeper through the file. Underneath the back-and-forth of his communication with the code, he kept the tiniest hope alive that this was a test after all, an elaborate drill, made convincing even to a mind like his by the captain's heretofore hidden acting skills and the *Kalelah*'s complicity. At any moment, people would leap from clever hiding places and scream, "Surprise!" But no one startled him out of his dread. No one frightened his hands into stillness. Instead, like watching his own part in a dream, he heard himself say, "Sir, I've got something."

"Tell me."

"I know this makes no sense, sir. But there's a ping detection." Trin's mind was racing through the possibilities and stoking the fire of his worries. "Based on what the *Kalelah*'s telling me, we've been scanned, sir."

"Detail it," the captain shot back.

"X band. Very high frequency, upper eights. Super clean color. But no way that's right. So yes, of course, it's got to be a bug, because—"

Argen cut him off. "How long?"

"Sir?"

"How long was the *signal*, Analyst? Was it a blip, a flash? Air it, please, and graph it out. My math's not as fast as yours."

Trin broke the data free from the privacy of his glass and threw it to the air between them. It was bigger now, easier to manipulate, a sparkling beaded curtain of digits suspended from an invisible rafter. With a glowing index finger, he traced a line to translate the numbers and graphlets for Argen. "Two hours, from these coordinates and at a consistent pace."

The captain didn't wait for Trin's next move. He walked into the data himself, his shoulders pushing aside whole columns. *The captain getting his math fingers dirty? How bad is this?* Argen poked at a few equations, grabbed whole strings at a time, and, coming up with nothing, he threw a fistful of fiery threads away to reset to their original positions and backed out of the floating math. "Could it be random radiation? A solar flare?" he asked quickly.

"Could be and should be, sir." Trin highlighted and graphed another detail of the data. "But it's so fucking steady. Sorry, sir, my language. I'm a little nervous."

The captain let the urgency go from his voice. "You can do this, Analyst," he said in a way that felt like an apology for his earlier trampling into Trin's domain. "You've done it a thousand times in training. Take a breath and run the numbers. That's why you're here."

But Trin didn't want a breath, he wanted different numbers. "I mean, look, these patterns just repeat and repeat. It's machine steady. No variation. Doesn't look anything like a solar event or ambient radiation. It can't be, obviously, but I'd swear it was tech."

The captain took another step back to survey the entire float. "There's a triggering error here somewhere, Analyst. We just have to find it."

A detail in the corner of the projection caught Trin's eye and his stomach went to ice. "Sir, the time counter."

The captain followed Trin's gaze to the corner of the float where the time counter flashed. He squinted at the numbers, as if he wasn't quite sure of what he was seeing. When he finally spoke, his voice was soft, almost sad. "E Thirty-Seven? That can't be right."

"I hope not, sir. Epochal Check Thirty-Seven would be an awfully long time from now." Trin struggled to keep his voice from trembling.

The captain tightened his expression. But Trin knew he was doing it for him, playing the part of staying cool when clearly something was seriously fucked up. *Let's not scare the kid. Well, too fucking late for that.*

"Estimate it," the captain said. "How long from now?"

"Something like one hundred and twenty thousand, sir. Years, I mean. Epochal Check Thirty-Seven won't happen for another one hundred and twenty thousand years."

The implications of Trin's math hung in the air, even more worrisome than the projection floating between them.

The captain leaned against the metal post that secured a nearby workstation to the Command Center's glossy white floor. It was just for a moment, and just a little bit, but it looked to Trin like Argen's shoulders sagged.

"Well, if that's true, if the counter is correct ..." The captain sighed. "We've overslept a bit, haven't we?"

"That's fucking crazy," Trin whispered, too frightened to speak in a full voice. "Isn't it?"

After what seemed like a long time, the captain put a small smile on his face. He pushed away from the metal post, stood straight again, and looked across the CC like he'd just seen someone he'd been meaning to speak to. But there was no one else. He and the captain remained the only two people awake.

"You were quite the standout at Academy, weren't you, Analyst?"

Trin said nothing. He just stared at the data hovering ominously, waiting for them to somehow change or waiting for his eyes to stop screwing around and make things right. But the message from the blue-white graphlets and numbers remained stubborn and merciless.

"So let's go with your assessment, then," the captain continued. He looked back at Trin with a look of determination.

"That's fucking crazy."

4

Argen sat in the small antechamber off the Command Center that served as his personal conference room. His eyes were fixed on a small window that had no view. When the ship was buried and still, the eight-inch glass ports that served as windows to the outside world were shuttered and sealed by another three inches of armor spun from strands of alloy shield that webbed the hull like the silk of a titanium cocoon.

The blocked window seemed fitting. Just another form of blindness. So, he sat in the little room, a full two hours after he'd been awakened by a frantic alarm, thinking about how much in the dark he still remained. That was why he had taken the chance on Trin. He couldn't risk going to the next step, whatever that might be, without more information. The kind only someone with Trin's skills could decipher.

Yet waking Trin had carried its own risks. To reach down so low in rank with an alarm firing had been a dramatic breach of protocol. Still, if this was something other than a glitch, he'd want some time on his own before things went sideways. Trin would get him the certainty he needed, and even if he asked questions—as a kid with Trin's brains would no doubt do—Trin couldn't demand answers. But others on board could do more than that. And would.

The scenarios running through his mind offered little comfort. If the ping was real, if the ship really was scanned, then the *Kalelah* had already failed in its mission. A Halfborn population in possession of that level of technology, and everything that went with it, was completely discordant with the Plan. And a failure of this magnitude would set a terrible chain of events in motion, a scenario he loathed to even contemplate. He knew of only one instance of *Correction*. And the people of that ship were broken in the process. Mistrust, disappointment, and shame spread throughout the crew. They could no longer serve. But neither could they stop. There's no retirement from the service. Where could you go? Your home world has moved on without you for thousands and thousands of years. How could you ever belong again, a stranger so out of time?

And besides, a crew that's failed its mission would never find a welcome home. *We'd be pariahs, untouchables. No prayers could ever redeem us. Even God would turn His back on us. Maybe He already has.* In the end, all they'd have would be each other. And once shrouded in such calamity and sin, could that ever be enough? The ship he knew of, the ship that lost control of its planet and failed the Plan and God, had become a ghost, a lost city cruising deep space without purpose. Eventually it turned its remaining weapons upon itself and that was it. Two worlds lost in one

29

mistake. *Is that what's happening here, to us, to me?* The thought that the *Kalelah* had failed so early in its time cut like a knife.

His mind jumped back to the present. The time clock. Another impossibility. In a strange way, it was the one thing that gave him hope that everything happening here, the alarm, the ping, were all just a series of glitches. The brilliant Trin would find them and reset the code and they'd both go back to nothingland. After all, he consoled himself, no ship had ever slept so long. If the *Kalelah* had—if 120,000 years have passed since they began their last Skip—how was it possible that he and Trin and God knows who else were even *alive?*

The *Kalelah* was not an old ship, that was true. And that might have made it feasible. But no M-suits had ever been tested for so long a Skip. When he wakes the ship, he wondered, or *if* he wakes the ship—he hadn't gotten that far yet—how many would never open their eyes? More than the usual ten or so? More than a hundred? Could thousands already be gone? He couldn't believe he'd ever learn the answers to those questions because he couldn't believe they'd slept from Epochal Check One to Epochal Check Thirty-Seven, a jump of 120,000 years. But, truthfully, he didn't know. Until he had confirmation of the bugs, he didn't know. So he sat there in the antechamber waiting for Trin to come back and say he'd been wrong about the ping, that it was a sun flare's interference after all. He pictured Trin's glowing fingertips happily tracing in the air a picture of the sustained burst of radiation that had taken on the appearance of a scan, triggered the alarm, and zapped the time counter senseless.

Another hope, though a much less likely one, was that Trin would tell him the computer had brought up a memory from somewhere deep in the code and mistook it for a real-time danger. The code was old, as old as time. A ship could be newly built, but the code that dictated all its automatic functions and responded to human command was always a progeny of the original, like bread from a mother dough. At every Epochal Check, the code would upload to deep space everything it had encountered since the last contact. At the same time, it downloaded already-ancient updates and messages waiting from across the known universe.

Over the long span of deliverance work, the code had become nearly a living thing. So sometimes when the ship slept, it dreamt. No one knew why. The code didn't shut its eyes and swallow a met-tube like all the rest. For the code, time didn't fall into a black hole and speed along too fast to even be felt. The code was aware of every passing increment. It kept working: running the compression systems, leveling the temperature, spinning the gravity shells, ordering the cleaning bots from this place to that, checking the core for any troubling changes, monitoring the seed stores and the farms, and keeping the 22,342 M-suits functioning properly. And all the while, it kept time. Was it simply bored without the myriad requests of its human masters? Was it lonely—and so it imitated the one thing that might keep the ship from being just a machine?

But if the ping was a dream, a coded memory replayed as real, why dream of X band? That was the sliver in his mind that kept his stomach roiling. That was the single fact with the power to break the back of

31

the bug hypothesis. The Guide Service didn't use X band. Nothing used X band. Certainly nothing the *Kalelah* could be picking up on this planet. It roused something he'd been trying to push back, to deny, questions that kept pressing to be answered: Were these two failures separate—two random bugs that just happened to occur at the same time—or were they connected? Had one led to the other? And if the time counter was right, why were the checks, so many checks, missed? How had they gotten from E One to E Thirty-Seven without ever Waking? Another sliver.

The last hope was that the real bug was in his head. His Skip was malfunctioning, and instead of being a dreamless, timeless wormhole to the next check, it had twisted itself into a tangled nightmare of a ship on the cusp of destruction. If it were true, if his Skip had gone bad, he'd be glad to trade this failure for all the others.

He was sitting there looking at the window, seeing nothing, wishing for dreams, when Trin entered the room.

"Sir."

"I've been praying for some good news, Analyst Trin."

"I'm sorry, sir," Trin answered darkly. "I can't find shit, anything. There's no bug. Least not one you can track." Trin's voice cracked. "I—I think this is real."

The captain looked at the analyst and for the first time he saw the cocksure facade of the young and profane officer melt away entirely, leaving just a terrified eighteen-year-old kid. He wondered what Trin saw.

"Go get yourself some food, Analyst Trin," the captain said gently. "The *Kalelah*'s nap time is over."

5

When she had finished her prayer, she told the view glass to show her the stem. The image she received was dark and lifeless. That was good. But she had little time to waste. She was banking that when Argen sent the wake hails, she'd be at the top of the list. That would give her just enough time to make her way from her pod in Leaf Three to Tanter's pod in Leaf Four.

She had no idea how far-reaching Argen's hail would be. It wasn't likely Tanter would make the short list, if short-listing was in fact the direction Argen took, but it didn't matter anyway. At some point Tanter, a gossipy third-class engineer, would be hailed. And Tanter was a problem. There'd been no opportunity to get him under control prior to Skipping, so this was her chance. Her last chance. And if God was on her side, which she knew He was, she'd make it to Tanter's pod and set things straight with no worries. It disgusted her that the Circle needed Tanter's help at all. He was an animal. You could tell in Chapel that the verses meant nothing to him.

Like too many people on the ship, Tanter spoke the words like the ship's computer repeated a command. He was just following a code, a ritual. But balding, round in the middle, and known for trying too hard with any woman willing to give him more than a passing word, Tanter was easily cowed. God had given the Circle that at least. It took only a small step closer than professional, a little more scent in her hair than usual, and the slightest touch on his arm to persuade the soulless, thin-lipped petty officer into giving her time alone in the code room. An hour was all she needed.

Three's stem was as dark as her glass advertised, a relief. Argen was short-listing instead of Waking the entire ship. He was taking things in steps, gathering the Leadership first. If God kept her from being seen going in the wrong direction, she'd know she was on the right path. But, of course, she knew it already. She had always known it.

She followed the glowing specks of lights down the empty stem, whispering the Watcher's Prayer as she walked. It was a good quarter mile before she reached the intersection to the main stem that would take her to Leaf Four. But when she heard the footsteps, she stopped. From what she could tell, there were at least two people moving toward the same intersection. If they saw her, she'd have no choice but to join them on their way to Command. That would take her in the opposite direction of Tanter's pod. And this was her last opportunity.

The footsteps were coming toward her from the right. Quietly, she sidestepped her way to the right-side wall of her corridor. There was no nook to hide in, no doorway to slip through. The shops and offices that would normally be open were all shut. She'd passed the last toilet facility several hundred feet ago. Her only cover were the bumps of the pilasters supporting the softly arched metal beams of the towering ceiling. It was hardly cover at all. She held her breath and tried to flatten into the shadow coming off the tall half column. She thanked God for the dark of the stem and for Argen's decision to stagger the Waking.

The footsteps drew closer. Still, if anyone was to turn her way, the column's slim shadow wouldn't be enough to hide her. She'd be seen, clinging to a wall like a spider trying to hide in plain sight. How would she explain her odd behavior? She didn't have an answer for that. She pushed herself harder against the wall and remembered that the path she was on was His, not hers. As the footsteps entered the intersection she closed her eyes, imagining that her own blindness would keep her from view.

The other newly awoken people walked quickly, probably anxious to learn why they were up when the rest of the ship seemed to still be sleeping. They passed through the intersection without a glance in her direction.

When she felt safe enough to open her eyes, they had progressed too far for her to see who they were, but no matter. God had helped, as she knew He would. When they were out of hearing range, she entered the main stem and turned right toward Leaf Four. But she kept to the walls this time where the shadows were deepest and walked as quietly as she could. It wasn't long before she got to Four and then to Tanter's pod. As she now expected, no one else was up and out. She let the door to the pod detect her aura and the seniority of her rank. She made a mental note to scrub the stem cameras and the entry records of Tanter's pod. Not that it was a critical precaution. She'd be in charge of any investigation that might come about. But sloppiness was an ugly weakness.

When the door slid open, she found the engineer still very much asleep. The rest was easy. There are more than a dozen ways to die in a Skip. She made the gentlest choice she could for Tanter. God, says the Plan, has given us dominion over all the animals in the universe. But it reminds us, too, that He expects kindness in our ways with them. The engineer deserved less than he received.

6

Scott Bronner couldn't sleep. He got up out of bed, put some pants on, and went out on deck. It was warm and the waters were calm. The clouds had hung in and blocked out the moon and stars and so the dark was a thick wool blanket pulled over the eyes of the night. He walked the deck slowly, keeping a finger on the railing while he adjusted to the seamless black. After a half-turn around the ship, he spotted a tiny red glow ahead. Sarah. He stopped next to her left.

"Can't sleep either?" he said.

"Can't sleep usually."

He leaned on the railing and tried to look out into the night but there was no seeing. "Not much of a view tonight. How long have you been out here?"

"A couple hours. You still mad at me?"

"It doesn't matter. Henderson is going to be Henderson. In the end, he won't listen to either of us."

They stood awhile looking out into nothing.

"I've never found anything before," Sarah said into the black.

"Sarah, most geologists spend their entire careers not finding anything of scientific importance."

"No. Not that. I never cared about that. I mean, I've never found anything that made me want to *keep* looking. Never. This is the first thing. The first thing in my entire life."

Scott tried to see her face, to catch maybe just a glimpse of what she sees out there in the water for hours every day. But there was only the soft, amber glow as she drew on her cigarette. It revealed nothing.

"Next time I need you to follow my lead," he said. "No more talk of a ship and who might have built it and why. Not to others, anyway. We're going to have to be smarter about this. Henderson will be working against us now. And, you know, we're just the geeks. They already think we don't care about the business side of what we do. They don't think we even understand it. We have to use that against them. Play their game. Be the first ones to deny it's anything other than a natural phenomenon. It's crystals—diamonds maybe—it's gas, it's oil—"

"Crystals? Even I knew that was stupid."

He sighed quietly. He liked this new Sarah. Or maybe he liked suddenly having something between them, this scan. She needed him now. They were partners. But she worried him now, too. The things she says ... they could get them both in trouble.

"It was the first thing that came to my mind," he finally said.

"Henderson's not so scary. I've seen worse."

"Henderson? I'm not scared of Henderson. But he's a bully. And there's only one way to deal with bullies."

"Punch them in the face?"

"Not my style."

"So it's a matter of style?"

"Listen, I've been doing this a long time. I hate the oil companies. But they own this place. I mean the *whole* place. I'm here because they'll be here too, no matter what I or anyone else does. And I want a seat at the table so maybe, maybe what they do won't always be so one-sided. And this thing down there." He paused for a minute. "I think it might be something, I don't know, something important. I feel like there's a message in there for us. The minute I saw it on the screen I had the same feeling I used to have in church. Awe."

"You looked a little scared, if you ask me."

"In the Bible, awe was always mixed with the terrifying."

"Huh. I didn't take you for the religious type."

"I'm not. At least not anymore."

For the first time in the conversation, she turned his way. "What changed?"

"I did. I was supposed to go to seminary school. But then I discovered rocks. Broke my mother's heart."

"Rocks don't ask much of a person," she said, turning back to the water.

"No. Maybe that's why we get along so well," he joked.

She didn't laugh.

"Anyway, I don't want to lose this thing down there," he continued. "I don't want to lose the idea that maybe all the oil I've helped pump can finally add up to one little thing that doesn't hurt. Does this make any sense to you?"

"So we're not deleting the files?"

"We're not deleting the files."

"Thank you," she said, as much to the sea as to him. She crushed her cigarette under her foot, bent down to pick up the stub, and walked back toward her quarters. "And by the way," she said over her shoulder, "I'm not a geek."

Scott tried to watch her walk back across the deck, but it was still too dark to see her.

7

The briefing room was opposite Argen's antechamber and connected to Command by a secure vestibule. To make it through the vestibule, one's body needed to contain a minimum number of cells matching the DNA associated with that body. Nobody, except the *Kalelah*, knew what the number was for any given individual on record. A mere stolen hand, say, or a retina, wouldn't likely open the door. Therefore, it was nearly impossible for anyone unauthorized to enter. With the ship mostly still sleeping, there were plenty of other places the Leadership could have met. But other than personal pods, the briefing room was the only place on the ship that wasn't automatically monitored and recorded. Argen didn't know how this particular briefing would go, and the last thing he wanted was a permanent record of him saying or doing something regrettable. Though it seemed, with every passing minute that ticked by without Trin finding a bug, regret would be something with which they'd all become mightily familiar.

"Good Waking, all," Argen said when he entered the room. "We'll get started just as soon as we're complete."

Only two chairs remained empty. His and XO Laird's. Finally, a bit of good news. It meant at least five people so far had made it through the incredibly long Skip. The benefit of a new ship perhaps.

Chief Smenth Ganet, Dent Forent, the ship's Guide Lead, and Keeper Phetra were all seated.

"There's nobody working the kitchens, Captain. And you have the balls to say 'Good Waking,'" Dent Forent grumbled as a way of saying hello. Forent, a big ball of a man with very white hair, a close-cropped beard, and an indefatigable smile, overfilled the chair just to the left of Argen's.

The captain shook Forent's big, stuffed hand. "Good to see that at least your appetite is normal, Mr. Forent."

"That's about all that is. Even the chief here doesn't know what's going on." Argen gave Ganet a nod and a look that he hoped would say *just give me a minute.*

The Keeper sat directly across from Argen's chair as she always did in this room. If she was wondering why the Leadership was awake while the rest of the *Kalelah* appeared to sleep, it didn't show. She sat calmly waiting for her cue to say the opening words that reaffirmed their mission to God's Plan. As Argen sat, she gave him a small smile. Despite her sixty-one connected years, in the right light Phetra still reflected the charms that had made her beautiful before so many millennia had come between her and youth. Her hair was still the rich auburn it was when she was in her twenties, her eyes still glowed an intense shade of blue, her skin was still smooth, and she could still wear her gold Keeper's wrap as tightly as a woman half her age. Phetra had her followers, in prayer and otherwise.

Argen turned to the chief at his right. "I'm going to need your help, buddy. Hang with me when the onslaught starts. This will all make sense. I think."

Chief Smenth Ganet was the first person Argen would have woken if Ganet could do what Trin could. He was just two years younger than Argen. The two had trained together and rose through the service together. They were close. If Argen had his way, Ganet would be XO. A commander in rank with a spotless record, Ganet had all the qualifications needed. But Argen hadn't built this team. He inherited it when Captain Rojasan drilled a test craft into the side of a mountain. Rojasan was a legend, the most experienced captain in the service. The fact that it was ridiculously risky for a man of Rojasan's rank to fly an experimental craft was overlooked. Rojasan loved to fly and the service loved him, so he got what he wanted. Even in death. His prerecorded succession plan followed the expected path when Rojasan posthumously promoted then Executive Officer Argen to Captain Argen.

But the old legend bent convention when he elevated Laird to replace Argen as XO. She was Commander Laird then, Deputy CAG and several levels below the obvious next in line to assume the lofty post of XO. But Laird was a standout talent, her record as spotless as Ganet's. She wore the Plan on her sleeve, too, practically defining the phrase "God-fearing." The orthodoxy liked her. Given all that and their overflowing respect for the old man, there were no objections to Rojasan's untraditional request from the grave. So Laird had become XO, and Ganet was left to choose between taking an XO job on another ship or accepting the underpowered post of chief to stay with his best friend. He chose his friend.

He leaned in to Argen so the whole table wouldn't hear. "You woke Trin … *alone?*"

"No choice."

"She won't be happy."

Argen looked at his friend. "Has she ever been?"

"Good point."

Argen turned back to the doorway that opened to a view of the entrance vestibule. "Seen her yet?"

"Not yet. But don't sweat it, lover boy, she'll show up," his chief said with a lightness Argen knew was designed to take the tension down a notch. "This was just a catnap."

"I don't know. I have a bad feeling about M-suit failure."

Ganet scoffed. "Now I'm worried you really are in love, Captain. Suits don't fail. Bodies fail. Cellular breaches are brought on by Waking, not sleeping. And like I said, this was just a—"

"Not hers in particular," Argen interrupted. "*All* the suits."

That should have been a show-stopper. But Ganet kept quiet any alarm bells that might have been ringing in his head. "What are we talking about here?" he said evenly.

"Has anyone seen the XO?" Argen asked the rest of the group.

Before any of the others could answer, she stormed into the room, looking athletic, dark, and angry.

"Why is a junior officer up and working without my orders?"

She's seen Trin, he thought. *And here we go.*

"Good Waking, XO," Argen answered coolly. "May God make it as pleasant as possible, given the circumstances."

"God will do as He deems worthy, Captain. I'll ask again. Why is Analyst Trin at his post? Alone? Without proper supervision?"

Right on script, Argen thought. But he met her dark glare with a practiced, steady calm. "I'll let you all know what's going on, at least as much as I can figure, as soon as the Keeper gets us started. And, XO, I'll make sure to record your complaint in the ship's log."

"Complaint?" Laird echoed incredulously as she took her seat. "As long as you're making an entry of this, call it what it is. A report of a gross violation of protocol. That way our two accounts won't be at odds. We wouldn't want a break in Leadership *unity*, would we?"

Argen saw Ganet shake his head, the chief's resentment towards Laird still seemingly present and accounted for after the last Skip. Time, even lots of it, doesn't heal all wounds.

Laird's fits could be amusing sometimes because they were so predictable. Someone would do the wrong thing or say the wrong thing and Argen would game out in his head when the storm would blow in. But this kind of fit, directed at him, at the ship's captain, was just the kind of entitled tantrum to press Ganet's buttons the quickest, not that Argen could blame him. She'd been bumped three levels, and when it happened she acted like it was overdue. If she had just acknowledged the fact once, just once, maybe Ganet would feel better about it. Not good. But better. A simple *Hey, I know Rojasan screwed you* might have made all the difference. Maybe Ganet could deal with her piety and her obsession for the rules, respect them even, if she just once did what Ganet surely would have done if the tables were turned.

Luckily, Forent broke in before things got too heated. "Someone woke up on the wrong side of the bed," he interrupted with a conciliatory smile. "I'd offer you some coffee, XO, but alas, the ship has not quite had hers yet. Apparently, we are to wait for our meals. And I do hope not too long. So perhaps the Keeper can say her words now?"

Forent was always a quick draw, and the distraction seemed to help Ganet cool down a bit. But the real storm hadn't hit yet.

Argen nodded and Phetra rose and said the Second Devotional. "God speaks, the Plan records, and Humankind follows. We start this work ever mindful of its end. As the universe spreads, so must the sustenance of Faith. To dry ground we bring water. And to the Halfborn we bring God." As she sat, she added, "Whenever you're ready, Captain."

He wasted no time. "An alarm woke me just a few hours ago. I kept you sleeping until I could confirm that it wasn't merely a glitch. That's why Analyst Trin is also awake; I think you'd all agree he has an extraordinary talent for—"

"But what he doesn't have, Captain," Laird cut in, "is the rank to work autonomously or to challenge your decision to keep us all sleeping."

"Waking anyone outside a normal check schedule is no small thing. You know the risks as well as anyone, *Hanta*." Using her first name in public, something he knew she hated, was his subtle way of reminding her the difference between their ranks. "If someone were to die coming out of a Skip for the sake of a false alarm, I think you'd have a bigger axe to grind than just my breaching the chain of command." He addressed the whole table again. "The alarm that woke me was a scan alert."

"Sir, did you say *scan* alert?" Ganet asked.

"I did."

"We're still beneath the floor," Ganet said. "What's here for the *Kalelah* to scan?"

"The ship didn't initiate the scan. She received it."

"Received it?" he said incredulously. "From where?"

"You mean from *what*, chief," Forent jumped in again. "From *what*. And that's the proof it's a glitch. There is nothing on this planet to initiate a scan, other than us."

"The scan came from outside the ship, from up top," Argen countered.

"And it wasn't ours," asked Ganet. "Another Guide, maybe?"

"No. This was X band, and no trace of our signature in the signal. It was an unknown scan. The *Kalelah* had never seen it before."

"Impossible," Forent insisted, his round, kindly face now looking annoyed and dismissive. "Evolution doesn't work that way, Captain, you know that. It's slow. That's why we Skip it out. And we haven't even started the process of influencing the population, whatever's left of it. E Two is more of a survival check than a real intervention. We're not guiding on this check. We're *counting*. The creatures we've put up top, if they've managed to make it to the next stage, are still mastering the trick of sharpening sticks. They're hunters and gatherers and more the latter than the former. They're still in the middle of the food chain. It takes complex societies with agriculture and cities to develop truly complex tools. The idea of these primitives in possession of scanning technology is—"

"I'm not finished," the captain said. "There's another factor here, and I know this will sound even stranger, but according to the *Kalelah*'s time counter, we're not at E Two. We're at E Thirty-Seven."

The table went silent.

"If we can't locate a bug, if we can't be absolutely sure that we've got a triggering error," Argen continued, "then we have to consider this event as real. And we have to get eyes and ears up top."

"That's going to make a lot of noise, Captain," Ganet said. "And if this isn't a bug, they apparently have their own eyes and ears."

"God only knows what they have," added Laird with what almost looked like a smile.

"I don't even want to think about that," said Ganet.

Forent waved away the comment with a swipe of his enormous hand. "So, don't. All this worry is contingent on the scan being real," he said. "Which it isn't. Captain, I assure you, this is all completely … impossible. You're talking about the *Kalelah* sleeping for, what, a hundred thousand years?"

"One hundred and twenty thousand," Argen clarified.

"Fine, one hundred and twenty thousand. It might as well be a million. It's barely worth contemplating. The odds are … I don't have the skills to even figure that out."

"Whatever the odds, we can't ignore the possibility."

The table turned to Keeper Phetra. Her earlier equanimity was less composed. "If it has happened, and the population we put up top have gone unchecked for all that time, then our mission has taken a gravely dramatic turn." She was looking at the big, round guide lead, but Argen knew she was speaking to him.

8

A 747 from Honolulu en route to Manila was skirting some storms to its north and bent its normal flight path just south enough to pass over the Mariana Archipelago. Its MARSAT system sent a series of pings upward to handshake with communication satellites circling the Earth. Most of its 230 passengers were asleep. It was dark, and a layer of cloud floated between the plane and the ocean surface.

On the water below, a small silver orb no bigger than a man's fist gently bobbed on the waves. If you were in a boat just twenty feet away, you would likely never have noticed it. There was no moon at all. And even if there had been, any reflection the little orb might throw could easily have been mistaken for a flash of quicksilver or a jumping fish.

As the plane flew overhead, a small metal probe emerged from the orb. When the plane was gone, the probe retracted into the orb and the small silver object sank into the sea, falling and falling until it neared a perfectly round opening in the seabed floor. Five inches from the opening the orb stopped its fall, hovered for a bit, adjusted its position, and disappeared inside the hole. Seconds later the hole disappeared.

The captain of the 747 was chatting with an attractive flight attendant who stood guard over the serving cart she had placed to block the entrance of the cockpit while its door was open. The copilot was asleep in business class. The navigator read a book as a means of ignoring the ridiculously obvious flirtations happening over by the serving cart. No one and no machine aboard the flight from Honolulu to Manila noticed the orb.

Minutes later, a soft ding announced a float next to the bed where Captain Argen lay. He turned to read it.

"What do they know?" she said from the foot of the bed, pulling her jumpsuit up around the curves of her hips.

"No details. But Ganet wants me in the CC. Scout read is back." He sat up, watching her dress.

"From the surface?"

"Yes, sent it right after … the briefing." The word *briefing* had an underscore of reproach and not just a little hint of a wound still smarting.

She sighed. "I was doing my job."

"No, I understand. I just think it's great the way we're able to collaborate in those moments. Especially under the current circumstances. It's impressive, actually."

"You went straight to Trin, Jan. How did you expect me to react?"

"Differently."

She turned to him as she pulled the zipper of her suit upward. "You know that's not possible."

"Knowing and believing are two different things."

"So, you believed I could be unfaithful? That I could ignore the vows I took? The same vows you took?"

"Let's call it something else. Hope. I was hoping for some understanding."

"Understanding? You mean *slack*, don't you? You were hoping for some slack because we're sleeping together."

"Well, when you say it like that, I guess it does sound kind of insane. And here I thought that incredible head was you trying to get on my good side, *XO*."

She didn't answer for a long time. "Will you do your duty?" she finally said.

"I always do my duty."

"What I'm talking about takes a particular courage."

"I'm ready to do what I think is right, if that's what you're asking."

"It isn't. I'm asking if you're ready to do what God thinks is right. Are you?"

"We're not at that point yet, Hanta. There's too much we don't know."

"We know enough. It's a yes-or-no question." Her voice quieted now but held steady. "Will you do what God demands of you?"

"This isn't that simple."

"Of course it is. Everything is."

He had gotten up from the bed and was pulling his own suit around his shoulders. He looked back down at the bed and then at her. She was facing him, dressed and pinning her hair back. The tiny beads of sweat that earlier had dotted her forehead were gone. The flush in her cheeks had all but disappeared. The heaviness in her lids and the wet hunger of her lips were now just things to remember, fragments of warmth he could pull up to his chin when the cold of living so far from life kept him awake and shivering in the night.

He smiled sadly. It was always the same after. Once she was done, she was done. Like a switch. He always marveled at the women she could be. Just two minutes ago he was holding the woman who could tease and laugh and make him believe the other, this relentlessly determined one—this always certain one—was just an act, a facade of cool, a job. But the two versions of Hanta Laird were equally convincing. And he was sure right now at this moment that it was, in fact, the other version that was the real act. The one who wanted and maybe even loved him—she was the ruse. It's a remarkable skill, he thought. He envied her ability to separate these two women completely, to let each inhabit her fully, with a purity he couldn't help but desire.

"Yes. Or no," she asked again.

"I always do my duty," he said, knowing she wouldn't believe him. And somehow, unexpectedly, wanting her all the more for it.

9

Exactly two hours after Sarah Long dropped her coffee mug, and before she and Scott Bronner told their boss they'd be sending their data to Allied Oil, the image of a four-mile-long ship in the shape of an arrow was projected on six flat-screen monitors that lined the walls of a conference room two stories below ground.

A distinguished-looking man, Johnathon Lee sat quietly thinking at the end of a long table that faced the screens. He absently spun a fountain pen around the end of his left hand and back between his thumb and forefinger. The pen would stop for just the briefest of moments, and with a slight push it would start its aimless orbit again. Round and round, round and round. The rest of the people in the room, all but one of whom were men, said nothing. They watched the man at the end of the table, the man spinning the pen around his hand and looking at the image on the screen of the thing that could not possibly be but was.

"I've just heard three different people present three different explanations for what we have here but only one possible course of action," Lee said. "Why aren't we discussing any reasonable alternatives?"

The room was still for a moment, and then a small man in a dark suit sitting at the opposite end of the long table closed the binder he had in front of him and looked straight down the table. "Because, Mr. President, there are no *reasonable* alternatives."

The pen stopped spinning.

10

Mike Henderson stood on the forward deck of the *Lewis* holding his right hand to his forehead to block the sun's glare as he watched the helicopter heading toward his ship. There were only two possibilities for how the Pentagon could've gotten hold of that scan. Either that shit-for-brains Bronner sent it, or he hadn't needed to. Mike wasn't sure which was worse. But he was sure that things on the ship were about to go fubar very fast.

The short email from Houston explained nothing and told him everything:

Mike,

US military will be joining the *Lewis* en route tomorrow morning at 8 GMT. Cooperate completely. They'll brief you. Sorry I can't give you more details.

—Lindsey

As the chopper got closer, Mike made his way to the winding metal stairs along the port side of the bridge that would bring him to the helipad. He knew how the military worked, so he also knew how this would go down. The senior-ranking person in that helicopter would be polite, professional, and courteous. He or she would not ask that Mike give up his tidy office. But there would be no doubt that in just a few minutes, Mike would be giving up the *Lewis*. He would be paid, and he would be allowed to be helpful, but to a limit. Some things he would be told. Most things he would not. None of that made him happy, but he understood it. What worried him now, with an Osprey landing atop the bridge, was that damn thing seven miles below him. Whatever it was, it seemed to be every bit the mess he'd thought it would be.

He studied the horizon ringing the open water around him. Clouds from the west, but no ships. Not that that mattered. He knew this helicopter touching down now was not the last of the heavy equipment headed his way. This was the command-and-control party. The other parties would be coming soon. And the sight of this roaring monster landing on his boat made him feel like a war would be coming with them.

He braced as the twin rotors stirred the dirt on the pad into a spinning storm. The force of the machine was overwhelming. He'd been out of uniform for a long time now and he'd forgotten how loud these things were. He put his fingers to his ears, but when the door flew open and the Osprey's stairs began to lower, he dropped his hands to his side and noticed his shoulders pulling back a notch straighter. Old habits.

Three men in uniform descended the stairs first, two with sidearms holstered, one an officer carrying a metal briefcase. Last to leave the helicopter was a man in a dark suit. Clearly civilian, much shorter than the others, but without doubt the man in charge. The officer carrying the case approached first.

"Mr. Henderson? Tom Riley from Mount Taos Command. Thanks for letting us come aboard."

"I didn't think I had a choice, Major, but welcome to the *Lewis* anyway."

The major simply nodded. "Thank you. This is Deputy Defense Secretary Len Wilson. We'll be briefing you now if you've got the time."

He shook hands with Wilson. "I have a feeling my schedule's been cleared. Office is down one deck."

They made their way down the spiral stairs and through the bridge to Henderson's clean office with the large desk and the one window and a view of the billowing gray clouds moving in from the west. It felt strange taking his seat behind the big desk, in a position of authority, when he already knew the truth about to be made plain. But there was nowhere else to sit except for the two armless aluminum chairs Bronner and Sarah sat in just yesterday. A deal is a deal, he reminded himself: a chair for a ship. He took his big leather seat and left them the hard, metal guest chairs.

The deputy started talking almost before Henderson's ass hit the cushion.

"Mr. Henderson, how often do you meet with your geologists?"

"Often enough, I guess. We're oil hunters, Mr. Secretary. And they're the ones who do the huntin'. So, we stay in touch."

"I'm not the secretary of defense, Mr. Henderson. I'm just a deputy," Wilson said in what sounded to Henderson more like a push for precision than any attempt at humility. "Are you aware of any recent findings?"

"Actually"—Henderson smiled to keep his neck from blooming—"the *Lewis* is sort of on loan at the moment, gentlemen. We've been invited to help with a bilateral study of the trench. Pretty boring work, in my humble opinion. But I don't make the rules."

Wilson gave Riley a look and the major pushed the twin buttons on the clasps of his metal case. The spring-loaded hasps swung up and hit the lid with the bang of gunshots.

"We're aware of the US-Japanese mapping project, Mr. Henderson, and why the *Lewis* is here," Wilson said. "So, naturally, we also know you're operating an experimental scanning technology."

Henderson could feel the heat on his neck.

"I'm going to be straightforward with you, Mike," Wilson said, his new informality doing nothing to make the words sound any warmer. "Allied Oil's scanner was partially funded by the DOD. And, as is the case with all strategic technologies the DOD helps fund, we've been keeping tabs on your scanner. *Our* scanner, I guess I should say." Wilson smiled now. "After all, we're partners." But just as quickly as it came, Wilson's smile left him.

Henderson stayed quiet. He knew what was coming next.

"We see what your geologists see."

And now the heat on his neck made a path upward to his face. He'd gotten his answer to whether Bronner had sent the scans.

"We know that so far no communications about the object on the seafloor at coordinates seventeen point seven-five zero zero north by one hundred forty-two point five zero zero zero east have been sent, either to the research team on Hawaii or to Allied Oil," Wilson continued, sounding bored with what Henderson knew was just a necessary game. The deputy secretary paused for a moment and gave the slightest of glances in Riley's direction. "We're going to need your signature on a document, Mike. In fact, we'll need the signatures of your entire team. Everyone on board." Wilson took the document Riley produced from his case and placed it on his side of Henderson's desk. "This particular nondisclosure document, Mike, is a very serious contract. It makes sharing any information about the object a federal offense."

"You mean treason," Henderson said.

Wilson smiled again.

"We're going to need your computers, phones, tablets, and any peripheral drives," Riley added.

Henderson looked down at the paper as Wilson slid it across the big surface of the desk. He knew the answer, but he couldn't resist asking the question, just so they knew he could play the game too. "How 'bout I send this off to our attorneys for review? They're from New York. Big fancy outfit. They can be a bit …

particular. I'm sure it won't take long to get y'all the answer you want."

Wilson's smile vanished. Henderson held his gaze for as long as he dared. Riley cleared his throat. After a minute, Henderson reached to his breast pocket for his pen.

He knew the game.

11

Just hours after everyone aboard the *Lewis* had signed their name on a piece of paper identical to the one that now carried Mike Henderson's signature, a dot appeared on the horizon. It was slow moving and remained just a shimmering mark where the water met the gray-washed sky for much of the day. Bronner and Sarah stood on the deck watching the speck in the distance slowly grow.

There wasn't much else for them to do. The scanner was taken over by one of the helicopter's crew who seemed to know more about how to operate the device than they did. All communications with Hawaii or the mainland were cut off. Their phones were gone, their computers confiscated. No Facebook. No Twitter. It was as if the people aboard the *Lewis* had all simply vanished. And so, Scott and Sarah leaned against the railing, waiting for something they couldn't even guess about.

"Henderson did this," Bronner said.

Sarah lit a new cigarette with the stub of the one she was working on and just kept her eyes on the dot that was undeniably taking on the dark silhouette of a ship. First a helicopter, now this. And Bronner was like a little boy in search of his mother. He wasn't handling this well and had become whiny, which was just a few degrees more annoying than his normal complaining. But he'd become weirdly clingy, too.

"He sent the DOD the image. He did it to get Allied out of it. To get him out of it. Now it's the government's find. And you and I will never know what's down there."

Before she could tell him to chill out, a big Southern drawl boomed from behind them.

"It was never your find, Mr. Arche-fuckin'-ologist," said Henderson as he walked up to the railing from the main staircase. "I told you this thing was a mess in the makin', didn't I? Run away I said, right? Except it was too late. Wasn't nowhere to run."

He told them as much about his conversation with Major Riley and the deputy secretary of defense as he thought he could, given the paper he'd just signed, and when he was finished, he brought a pair of binoculars up to his eyes and studied the smudge looming on the gray-black edge of the water and the sky. He took the glasses away, pressed the meaty part of his left palm up to his eyes, and drew the binoculars up again.

"I'll be damned."

"What?" Sarah said.

Henderson gave Scott the binoculars. "Look through here. You see some letters on the bow? What do you see?"

"A-G-E-R-2."

"What's A-G-whatever—what is that?" said Sarah.

"I'll be damned," Henderson said, looking out to sea as the ship grew.

"You said that already. What's out there?"

"A ghost."

"A ghost?" she repeated.

"You ever hear of the *Pueblo* Incident?" he said. "The ship comin' our way is the USS *Pueblo*. AGER-2. She started as a cargo ship, but then she was a spy ship. The North Koreans captured her. Sometime in the sixties."

"We got it back though, right?" asked Scott, giving his new worry voice a nice workout.

"Nope. It's moored in P'yŏngyang, I think. Like a museum, a trophy for the Dear Leader."

Sarah took another drag. "What the fuck is it doing here, then?"

"That's a damn good question."

Scott kept the binoculars up as he watched the ghost ship steam closer. "I don't think we're going to get off this boat."

12

The *Pueblo* was nearly 180 feet long, a good fifty feet longer than the *Lewis*, several decks higher and nearly twice as wide at her center. As the ship pulled alongside the *Lewis*, it plunged the smaller boat into shadow. The two vessels, one flying the blue and white flag of the Korean People's Navy, put their drives in neutral and idled in the open waters at a safe distance.

Henderson found Len Wilson on the bridge. "That's a damn strange boat out there, Mr. Wilson. Damn strange. You mind fillin' me in some?"

Wilson's face didn't show any of the worry that Henderson was feeling. "There are a lot of strange things in the world, Mike. This is just another."

Henderson walked to the large port-facing window Wilson stood looking through. "Well sir, seein' as we don't exactly have diplomatic relations with North Korea, hangin' out in the ocean together with guns and soldiers runnin' around like we're about to start some sort of military exercise seems a bit more than just run-of-the-mill strange. Where I come from, this crazy boat here falls nice and clean into the category of *damn strange.*"

"What do you know about the *Pueblo*?"

"Not everythin'. But enough to start figurin' my history books might've been a little off."

"History and the truth have never had much in common." Wilson put down his coffee cup and turned to face Henderson. "We're about to do something from which the United States will want some distance. And the *Pueblo* is here to offer some ..." The deputy secretary of defense paused, looking for the right word. "Confusion."

Mike's neck was hot. "I thought the *Pueblo* is docked somewhere in P'yŏngyang, givin' us the finger."

"And it is, in a way."

"'Cept here it is."

"Yes and no. P'yŏngyang is just a show city, a facade designed to create an illusion of culture, peace, and progress. While the real people of North Korea starve, the government gives the news cameras P'yŏngyang, a beautiful city with bright lights and people who can keep their pants up without string. Nothing about it is real. So, when the *Pueblo* was caught spying, we let the DPRK have another fiction. We gave them a victory. They could claim the capture, build a fake *Pueblo*, and we'd get our crew back."

"And a ghost ship in the bargain."

"I don't think anybody at the time thought that far out, but yes. The *Pueblo* has become a convenient asset for this particular moment. Should something about what we're doing out here get out, there'll be satellite records of the *Pueblo* where it shouldn't be."

"But the North will have their own sats of the *Pueblo* sittin' pretty in the harbor."

"Like I said, Mike. Our goal is to add a little confusion. It'll be our word against theirs. The US against a lying, lunatic dictatorship. People will believe what they want to believe. They always do. A little confusion is all we need."

"All we need for what? Who's on that ship out there, Mr. Wilson? Who's going down in the trench to look at that thing that would need a cover like the *Pueblo*?"

"No one's going down to look at anything, Mike."

13

The stem of Leaf Three was filled with people, autocarts, and the rush of a Waking's first thrilling hours. Cyler tried to tiptoe herself above the throng to get a better view. Before the Skip, the two had agreed to meet at the top of Stem Three before reporting for duty. More than two hours had passed since the hail. She was excited to get back to her post in the labs, but first she wanted to see him.

They'd met just a month before the Skip after E One. She was with a friend at a small café not far from the labs and complaining about a ridiculous timeframe she'd been given to turn around a population analysis. The job would take at least a week of overtime. And then an air note floated down between the two women with a simple equation and threads to two reference papers. She turned around to look for the sender but saw only a dark-skinned boy at a table two over from hers.

"I'm pretty sure that'll work," the boy said.

She turned back to the note still hovering above the table. "You sent this?"

"You were talking fast and I couldn't really hear all of what you were saying. Otherwise I could guarantee it."

Who is this kid? "You could guarantee it. Guarantee what? You don't even know anything about … um … my God." The math hanging there in the air was so simple she couldn't believe she didn't think of it. But it would do the trick. It would cut her workload by days. She looked back to the sender. He was so young. Except for those eyes. And his smile held the unmistakable hint of trouble. "How did you do this?"

"I was listening to what you were saying and it just popped into my head."

"You always eavesdrop on other people? It's very impolite."

"No. But I couldn't help it this time. Blonde hair."

She blushed, partly because he embarrassed her. And partly because she found his bombastic flirtation unexpectedly welcome. "And this just popped into your head?" she said.

"Yeah. You know—" He snapped his fingers. "Pop."

"Uh, okay, thank you. I think." She looked back to the float.

"So, you agree?" he called.

She looked at her friend and rolled her eyes.

"He's cute," her friend whispered.

"He's what, ten years old?" But she looked back over her shoulder. "Agree with what?"

"That it'll work."

"Uh, yes. I guess it will. I mean, it should. I'll give it a try. Thanks again."

"Then you'll be free tomorrow night."

She blushed again. "Sorry?"

"You'll get the work done like"—he snapped his fingers again—"and be free to meet me tomorrow night."

Her friend laughed. "Oh, no, he's coming over."

He walked over to their little table, looking taller and older than when he was sitting. "I'm Trin," he said, holding out his hand, a bright smile on his face. His eyes stayed straight on Cyler's, like there was no one else there.

She shook his hand. "Nice to meet you, Trin. I'm Cyler, but you probably already know my name. This is Reni. How old are you?"

He gave Reni only the slightest acknowledgment. His eyes went back to hers. "Same as you, a bit more than five thousand."

"Very clever. I mean *connected*. How old are you, really?"

"Connected, I'm eighteen. And you're about twenty-three."

What doesn't he know? "About."

"A difference of five years. Divided by five thousand. That's …"

"I get it."

"So, what do you say? Now that you'll have all this new free time."

"Say to what?"

"To dinner. Or something. You know, whatever older women like to do." He smiled again.

Reni kicked her under the table. She glared at her friend. "Okay, Trin, dinner. But just dinner." She was sorry the second the words fell from her lips. It was the eyes, though; she couldn't stop herself.

And that was it for Cyler. Despite his age—and worse, his swearing, a sinful habit that troubled her greatly—she fell hard. And every moment she could escape the lab she wanted to spend with him. The weeks before the Skip were the happiest she had ever known. At night, before going to bed, she would kneel at her prayer glass and fill her Fourth Devotional with so much gratitude she nearly cried.

But now she was desperately worried. She had heard this Waking had not gone as usual. There were rumors that instead of the usual ten or twenty casualties, this Skip's death toll had climbed to the hundreds, maybe more. She didn't believe the numbers. People always got a little weird after a Skip. But she'd seen several emergency crews in her own pod section loading carriers with gurneys draped head to toe. And now Trin wasn't answering any of her messages and wasn't where they agreed to meet.

It was time for her to get to her own post, so she turned toward the main stem that would take her to the guide labs and started to make her way. She considered the speed walks, but she wanted to go the slow way just in case Trin would show.

That's when the sirens started. A loud, repeating sequence of a long piercing tone followed by three short bursts filled the concourse with the desperate, screeching wail of emergency. The laughter, the hugs of reunion, the cooking in the stalls, all of it froze as people looked to one another for answers or bent away from the shock, holding their ears.

After a minute or so, when the sirens didn't let up, the hesitation that comes from wishful thinking gave way to the months of training, and people began their swift but orderly move to the strap-down stations. Cyler wanted to make her way to Command first to see if Trin was there. Whatever was happening, she didn't want it to happen not knowing where he was, if he was safe. If he awoke. But she knew that Command would be the first area to lock down in an emergency. There'd be no getting near someone who could tell her anything about Trin, so she found the nearest safe wall and strapped in.

After ten minutes of the sirens' scream, the noise stopped and Argen's voice filled the concourse.

"Ladies and gentlemen of the *Kalelah*, this is the captain. Our scanners have detected an oncoming disturbance in the waters above our ship. We expect it to be brief but powerful. We do not anticipate any damage and we have no worries for your safety. But please remain in straps until the all-clear signal. Thank you."

Thirty seconds later, there was a sound like someone taking a deep, long breath. It held, waiting to exhale; then, after what seemed like an eternity, the breath went out, erupting into a roaring concussion, like a mountain shattering.

Cyler's vision vibrated, the taste of copper soured her tongue, and she felt a current running through the wall behind her. She wanted to bend down, to wrap herself in her arms, sink to the floor, pull her knees to her chest. But the straps were pulled taut and kept her pinned to the wall to face the growing roar like some offering to an angry altar. Her mouth opened to a scream but she made no noise that she could hear. The straps, the fear, the volcano yell smothered her completely. She tried to breathe but could not. Sweat rolled down her forehead, stinging her eyes. But she wouldn't shut them. She had to see that the walls were not crumbling, that others were still standing.

And then the lights went out.

14

The *Lewis* sat in the disappearing shadow of the big navy ship as the sun went down. The albatross and brown boobies that usually circled above had vanished with the sun, and the air was quiet and still. The earlier commotion atop the *Pueblo* of orders barked and cranes rolling into position had stopped some time ago. Everyone aboard the neighboring hulk, the true number of whom could not be discerned, had all gone below deck. And so, with the sky growing dark and the big ship silent and unmoving, it truly seemed a ghost. Only the yellow dots of light from the ship's few portholes offered any relief from the dreadful silhouette backlit by a dying sun.

Sarah turned her gaze to the open waters stretching beyond the starboard length of the *Lewis*, hoping the ocean would do its usual work of drowning her thoughts. But this night, with the big, dark ghost ship haunting her, the waters offered no solace, no cover. Lancaster, Ohio, and the back bedroom of the cramped brick bungalow she grew up in, and Jack, and the smell of his Old Spice, and the horrible feel of his callused hands, his mocking nickname for her, "Blon-dee," that always felt like a warning, and the things she wrote in a letter she never sent—none of it would stay under.

Jack. He and the questions he planted in her head, like thorny weeds you can't grab hard enough to pull out by the roots, were the phantoms who howled and shook their chains loudest that night. Was it because she was the youngest of her mother's two daughters? Was that why he had picked her? It started when she was only ten. Why did he wait until then? She was hardly more a woman at age ten than she was at age, say, nine and three-quarters. And he had been in the house for years already. What suddenly made a difference? Something she said, something she did, something she wore?

Her bedroom. The bedroom. Her sister in the next bed, huddled and shaking under the blankets, pretending to sleep. And just past her, the only wall in the room that wasn't taken up by doors or windows. When the moon was right, as it was that night, the poster she'd hung there long ago glowed as if lit by the sun. It was a cheap reproduction of a softly painted beach scene, a little girl in a white dress reaching for the string of a red balloon that had gotten away from her. The girl had bright eyes and a smile. Before that night, Sarah never imagined anything but a happy ending to the girl's chase. A lucky gust of wind, or a running jump that united the girl and balloon again so neither would be without the other, the girl's smile vindicated. The poster had always been a sweet story of together-ness.

But shame has a way of twisting every plot. After that first night, the idea of the balloon and the little girl in the white dress reuniting became just another of the dashed hopes of children. So, in the next scene, the one no one painted because it was just too obvious to be worth the bother, the balloon accelerated its escape, as if it had found the companionship of a little girl chafing and distasteful all along, and so became like all runaway balloons, a tiny red dot in the sky, and then simply gone. Like the little girl's smile.

She thought about the ship below. Another balloon that would never be caught.

The air around her became oddly charged. The thin hairs of her arms stood and tingled, though she was not cold. Her hair, too, became softly flyaway, as if blown by a secret breeze that couldn't elsewhere be perceived. She looked to Henderson and Bronner down the railing to see if they felt the strange static too. And then the ocean seemed to take a giant breath. The stillness became absolute, and, like a world turned upside down in a madman's painting, lightning flared from deep beneath the surface of an otherwise calm sea.

It came on bright and fast, a shock of the senses. And as if to confirm without doubt that the storm below was no natural twin to the type that gathers and bursts from above, the lightning didn't wink out in a flash. It dimmed from its initial angry explosion, then lingered, suspended in the liquid sky, illuminating the waters so completely Sarah could see down a distance past reckoning. A horror and a beauty. Her forehead began to sweat. Somehow, this too was her fault. A familiar shame, that same ugly shroud from Lancaster, wrapped her up in its black, scratchy wool. She rocked gently on her heels, her own arms pulled tightly around her while the ocean shone like a starburst in the darkness.

After what seemed like many minutes, the fire itself began to speak and a softly distant rumble, like a faraway thunderstorm, broke the stillness. The two ships swayed gently on shallow waves brought about not by the wind but by a force none of them could say aloud. Several minutes more and it was suddenly over. The sea went back to its natural color of night and the sound of clouds crashing faded to nothing. Sarah's chest heaved and her silent tears became a sob. Bronner moved closer and put his arm around her.

"Don't," she said and stepped away.

Henderson turned from the railing and took the stairs that led down to his office. She and Bronner stood at the railing in the dark as the pieces of the puzzle fell into place without a word between them. They stood there, together and alone, knowing what had happened but understanding nothing.

• • • •

In the morning, she woke with something like a hangover. She had no recollection of even going to bed. She put on the clothes she'd worn the day before, then took the stairs to the deck for the day's first cigarette and to see if there was any action on the deck of the bigger ship. But the *Pueblo* was gone.

The emptiness off the *Lewis*'s port was a surprise. And even though the *Pueblo* was a hulking menace of a ship, its cargo the nightmare of an ocean boiling and burning from within, there had also been a kind of security in having it so close. What could possibly be more frightening than a ship that could wield such dark power? What would dare challenge such a devil? She looked in all directions but could see no trace of it. She remembered what Henderson had told her about the mysterious ship and the things he learned from Wilson. She looked to the gray-splashed sky and imagined a satellite somewhere too far away to see, giving credence to what could never make sense. She lit a cigarette and sucked in the thick, white, dependable smoke that tasted as it always did despite how much was now, again, forever changed.

A booby dove hard and fast into the water just twenty yards from where she stood. Maybe it saw the glowing, flashing fiery water the night before. Maybe it was as panicked as she was by the sound of thunder from the sea. But the bird seemed no different from the day before. Like the thousand other times she'd witnessed, it hit the water with barely a splash. And like a thousand times before, it resurfaced and launched itself from the peak of its own barely visible wake, the water as solid as tarmac to the bird. She saw a glint of a small fish in the brown bird's beak. She envied the ignorance. Or the facade of it. Or simply the rule of hunger. She took another drag and heard the opening of a steel door behind her.

Major Riley came out to the railing and lit a cigarette.

"Are you here to apologize?" Sarah asked.

"Why would I do that?"

"You destroyed the object, didn't you? Last night. You dropped some sort of bomb."

"And if we did, what difference would it make? An exploratory mission was never going to happen. Seven miles is a long way down. In many ways, the bottom of that canyon down there is farther than the moon."

"But someday it might not be. Someday we could reach it. And what we'd find would probably teach us more about us than the moon ever could."

"Maybe. But that someday isn't today."

"You could've waited. It's not going anywhere."

"You know that for sure?"

"It's buried in the bed."

"Without evidence of wreckage. Which is about all we know for certain."

"And that makes it something dangerous?"

"Anything could be dangerous." He looked her up and down, a crooked smile in the works.

She turned away back toward the ocean. "That must make things easy for you," she said.

"Just clear. I know you and Bronner think this is some big discovery from another world and in it will be all the mysteries of the universe solved and everyone'll live happily ever after."

"What if we're right?"

"Are you willing to bet the United States on it? Are you willing to bet the planet on it?"

She took a deep drag of her cigarette and said nothing.

"Scientists," he said, his mocking smile making her want to punch him. "You're all the same. You never get that some things don't want to be discovered. Some things should be left alone."

"You've got a funny way of leaving things alone. Did you even care if there was anybody down there before you dropped a fucking bomb?"

"I don't make the decisions. I was following orders. But no, I didn't care."

"Now who's all the same?"

They both stood at the edge of the deck, smoking.

"It doesn't matter much anyway," he finally said. "Because whatever's down there didn't seem to sustain any damage. And since we haven't been bombed to hell in retaliation, I'm thinking that ship died a long time ago. So who knows, maybe someday someone will get down there and take a look inside and discover the meaning of life."

She tamped her cigarette out on the steel of the rail and let it fall into the sea. "So we're calling it a ship now?"

15

Cyler stood in the dark as the *Kalelah* took stock of itself. A machine voice filled the air, offering a status report of the situation but no explanation. The lights would be coming on shortly, it said, all other ship systems remain in operation. Despite those words of encouragement, the panic of the previous few moments still lingered. Her heart raced. The darkness was total. She could see nothing in any direction. Even lights run by the back-up systems were out. She felt a chill as her sweat-soaked suit and hair cooled in the stem's air conditioning.

Someone called out to anyone in hearing range if there were injuries to report, if people were okay. Answers trickled out slowly, in single words and short, quivering phrases. It didn't seem like anyone was truly hurt, but people were unmistakably shaken. Even with the warning of the alarm and the captain's words of preparation, the force and duration of the event were beyond anything she had expected. What natural event could rock a ship so massive, so usually sure and dependable, a mother and father, a home for their entire remaining lives? What dangers, she wondered, lived here on this planet they hardly knew but must win over?

The emergency lights were the first to come on. They dotted the giant concourse and a few people shouted their relief. When the rest of the lights switched on, throwing the stem into the bright, familiar glow of normal, everyone cheered. The all-clear tone sounded, and Cyler's straps went slack and she was able to push away from the wall free from constraint. It was like the Waking began all over again. Only this was a dimmer version, clouded by the new and sudden awareness that the *Kalelah* was somehow vulnerable and all the distance she and everyone else had traveled and all the years that had slipped away seemed like impossibilities. Regret flooded in, a sorrowful wave, unexpected and unwanted. It scared her.

Daddy, maybe you were wrong. Maybe we were both wrong.

"I joined today," she said to him, standing at the threshold of his office at the back of the house.

He acted like she was saying she'd eaten lunch today, or seen a bird. He kept to his work. "You joined what, honey, a study group?"

"No, Daddy, I *joined* today. I signed."

He swiped away the case file that filled the room and turned to her. "What do you mean? What did you sign?"

"I signed the service pledge." A smile too big to contain bloomed.

"No."

"Yes!" And now laughter.

"Yes? Really?"

"Really! I start training in three days." She held her palm out to him so he could see the academy pin, silver toned and bright.

"Three days! God must be dancing." He spread his arms to embrace her, but then he stopped, as if catching himself. Instead of putting his arms around her, he grabbed hers just above the elbows and held her straight. He bent down to face her eye to eye and looked at her with all the seriousness she'd ever seen. The face he used in court. The face that couldn't be tricked. "And you're sure about this? You're absolutely sure?"

"Yes, completely." Her smile left her. "Aren't you?"

"Of course. But—"

"But what? You thought it would be Sahn, not me."

"The way he worries? No. There's no peace in that boy. Strength, plenty. But no certainty. He's prayerful and dutiful." Her father paused and looked away. "But he doubts."

He looked back at her again, his smile returning, all teeth.

"So it had to be you. I prayed and prayed. And now you've done it. God is dancing, you've done it." He took her face in his hands and kissed her on the head.

"Did you? Worry? I mean, when you were Sahn's age—service age?"

"No."

"Then why didn't you join?"

"I grew up in a different house than what your mother and I created for you. We prayed, we followed. But your grandparents wanted more than prayer. They wanted you. And Sahn. And so, for me, they wanted marriage." He said those last few words looking at the floor again, a sudden tiredness in his voice.

"You're ashamed."

"No, of course not. Look at you. What kind of father could be ashamed of having made you? But before you were born, I made a promise to God."

"What did you promise?"

"That somehow we would do our part. And now you are keeping that promise for all of us."

She smiled.

"There is no greater work you could do," he said, his voice thick, his eyes misting.

"I know that," she said, and kissed him on his salty cheek.

But this was something that happened thousands of years ago. And now, looking back on that moment, remembering his pride and his surprising gratitude, she found that this memory, one she had played back a thousand times before, a happy memory, had a new edge to it. It was grayer on this particular playback. There was static in the images. More shame in the way he spoke of his destiny to make mere children instead of a new world for God. Now she wondered if she hadn't confused the memory all along. Maybe the choice she made that day and her father's ecstatic response to it were wrong from the start. Maybe living a life her father could only imagine and never share wasn't the greatest work she could do. She'd be a mother of sorts now.

But never in the way hers was. The love she felt for her father when she told him her news wouldn't be returned to her by the population on the surface. They would never know her. Yet she would watch over them, teach them, guide them—and never know them.

For her entire life, there were never questions without answers. The Plan provided almost every bit of knowledge that needed knowing. Whatever she couldn't glean from the ancient texts, her father could provide. Certainty. He was always so sure. And so was she. The moment she joined the service felt like she was reading off a set of instructions somewhere in her soul. Step 1: read pledge. Step 2: sign. Step 3: leave your loved ones, your home, your world, your everything. Step 4: never come back.

Was there some important detail, something she'd missed along the way to Step 4, that she should have noticed? Was there a truth about herself that would have made so big a step, so irrevocable a path, so obviously wrong?

No. Shooting through space and time to a faraway planet, a violent unknown place, to work and sleep for eons, didn't seem like madness. It seemed like righteousness. Living her life millennia from everything she'd ever known, had, and loved seemed like nothing less than a powerful glory. Any question that her decision was a choice God had made for her was banished from her thoughts. Her path had to be the work of God. There was nothing, nothing else it could be, and her new and remarkable life on the ship made it truer every moment. Until Trin. His presence in her life changed things. Having gained something put the prospect of losing something on the table again. It crept in slowly. Just a few thin, worrisome notes playing in the background when she closed her eyes at night, or when she'd look at the ship's great windows expecting to see the marvels of her new world but saw instead just the thick, impenetrable alloy shields and feeling for the briefest instant that the life she was living, the life she chose, was disconnected not only from her home but from everything. She was suspended, floating in a shell of a world that was no real world at all. The disturbance, or whatever it was, had suddenly turned up the volume of the troubling music playing in her head. The notes of doubt became clearer, almost coherent. And, worse, still no reply from Trin.

She started walking with the crowd toward the labs but looking for Trin as she went, rising onto tiptoes, wiping her eyes. She moved with the flow of traffic out of Stem Three and into the even more cavernous main stem. The lab would be getting back to the work they'd put on hold since the last Skip began. A hovering gurney made heavy with yet another victim of the strange Waking glided across her path.

As she walked, a long-bearded man came up beside her, moving at her pace. He stayed even with her for quite a way before he spoke. "You've been given an invitation," he said.

"I can't accept it. Not now." She wiped her eyes again, annoyed by the disturbance to her worry.

"It's not yours to choose, child, God has called."

"I'm not a good candidate anymore."

"God disagrees."

She looked at him briefly but kept her pace. "I need some more time, okay?"

"But you're needed now."

"I have things. Things I need to sort out."

"The Plan has the answers. You know that. And once a part of the perfect circle, you'll also *believe* it. There's a difference—"

"Between knowing and believing," she cut in. "Every five-year-old learns that poem."

"Good, then you understand the comfort that awaits you. The peace you've longed for is very close."

Peace. She stopped and finally faced the man with the beard. His eyes had that ferocious, unblinking conviction she'd seen the first time they met. But there was something that almost looked like kindness too. "What if I can't believe ... like she does? What if I'm different?" she confessed.

His brow furrowed for a moment and she could see a sudden darkness come over his eyes. And just as quickly, it was gone. He flashed a smile. "We're meeting tonight."

"Where?"

"You'll know."

And with that he moved away and blended back with the rest of the traffic heading to their posts.

• • • •

Two hours later, the activity of running the ship and managing a check was back in motion, though nothing was at all normal. In Command, Argen was huddled with Smenth Ganet as engineers from all around the ship reported their status. The device's nuclear signature had been tracked from the moment it came within two hundred miles of the ship, its potency calculated within seconds. There was never an immediate worry for the vessel itself. Not as the device drew nearer to the ship, and not as it sank through the unsuspecting waters and unleashed its fury just half a mile above. But in its aftermath, in the pale and bewildered faces he now saw around him, and in his heart, which had broken with the blast, Argen knew there was no denying what had happened. This mission, his first deliverance, was badly damaged. He looked about the room. He saw no cracks in the walls. He saw people at their posts, busy at work. There were no bandages, no splints, no bruises to be seen. It was a scene that could easily pass for routine.

Except he knew that no matter how quickly a body could be made to recover, a soul will take its own time. He knew the calm orderly game faces being worn all around him belied the real storms inside his crew. He knew parts of them were still reeling, still feeling the wall straps bite into their shoulders, still wide-eyed in the dark, listening and praying. Screaming. There was no pretending otherwise, the *Kalelah* had been hurt.

The Keeper Phetra and XO Laird entered Command from a side hallway that connected the more private Leadership meeting spaces to the big, brightly lit and float-filled open space of the workstations. They made their way directly to Argen and Ganet. The Keeper offered reassuring smiles to the timorous glances of those who turned her way as she walked. Laird met no one's eyes but Argen's. And when they were close enough to speak, she didn't bother asking how he or Ganet had weathered the explosion.

"Are you ignoring protocol *again*, Captain?" she said.

Argen turned to the Keeper first. "Glad to see you in one piece, Phetra." She nodded a silent thank-you. "And, XO, I'm guessing you have something on your mind."

"You know exactly what's on my mind. Every person in this Command Center knows what's on my mind because it's on theirs. We have a failed Delivery, Captain. We've slept through our checks. The population is beyond God's reach. You know what has to be done. So what are you waiting for, Captain? Where are your orders?"

"I'm afraid she's right," the Keeper said, her face quickly solemn, tired, looking almost its age. "The Plan is quite clear on this, Jan, there's really no debate here. The creatures above ..." She paused, searching. "The situation must be righted."

"I know what the Plan says, Keeper, I go to chapel and I pray. The Plan also speaks to the blessings of knowledge and understanding. *I do not fear the dark for study is my light.* This is a ship of science. We have a responsibility to learn before we act."

"This is a ship of God's command," said Laird. "Science is our means. Deliverance our ends." She took a step closer. "Captain, are you wavering in your duty to God?"

Ganet moved forward, putting himself almost between them. "We have work to do, XO. And I'm sure you do too, sir. Why don't we all get to it," he said.

Laird let pass the chief's unrequested address to a senior officer and kept her eyes on Argen's.

"It's all right, Chief," Argen said. "We'll finish this first. My duty, Hanta, includes the people here in this room and throughout this ship. And—"

He paused and looked to Phetra, her eyes offering no help, only a plea to hold whatever it was he was about to say.

He looked back to Laird. "And the *people* up top."

Phetra turned her gaze to the ground.

He squared his shoulders. "I'm not ready to deem them unworthy."

Laird smiled. "Well, Captain, I consider it a blessing then that we are not required to wait for your readiness. That, too, if you've forgotten, is protocol."

She turned and walked toward the large main door leading out of the CC. She stopped at the threshold and turned to the captain. "The *people* up top," she said, loud enough for the room to hear. "A lovely sentiment, Captain. Lovely." She turned again and continued out. A dozen sets of eyes followed her. A few others stayed on Argen and Keeper Phetra.

"The population on the surface, Jan," the Keeper said softly. "You should not have called them what you did. It's a blasphemy she won't forget."

"I know. But are you so sure they aren't … *people?*"

"It doesn't matter. And you know that, too."

16

God is not your conscience. God sees. God decides.

And God, in His strength, tells.

His words are His soul. His gift is the Plan.

Your obedience, though, is your choice. But choose it you must. Your brother, too, must choose.

And your task is to guarantee, at any cost, your brother's heart.

God asks not what you cannot give. He asks only for perfection.

Let none forget. Let none dispute.

—Origin 3, Scroll 14

Without sin, what would salvation do with its days?

Even in a universe ordered by a single belief, even when humanity in all the known far corners of existence was in agreement, an argument began. A schism.

One side was satisfied with a universal spread of the Plan. It was content to know that the principles of the Plan were what united humanity. The fact that some people were more devoted than others, that varying levels of orthodoxy existed and were even common, didn't raise any cause for alarm. A single belief, an end to generations of bloody war, was enough. More than enough. It was a victory.

But another side felt differently. Mere agreement with the Plan was not enough. Devotion was not enough. True faith, they elected to say, required more. It demanded nothing less than a practice of perfection. They drew a line in the sand of civilization and with the force of their strident conviction bent it round to life's perfect shape and called themselves the Circle. A ring of truth, the purest form, a congregation without a Keeper or a chapel, without sanction or review, the Circle watched over the executers of the Plan as judge and jury from behind a veil of anonymity, ordinary clothes, and whispers on the air.

No one sought membership in the Circle. There were no auditions. No applications, no tests. The Circle selected. And in that quiet, soft-shoed way, an army of the fiercest chosen was built.

In the course of its thousands of years in existence, few have publically acknowledged their membership in the Circle. Which was as planned. It didn't crave notoriety. It didn't record its history or deeds. It was happy to be more rumor than real. The Circle's members were all around, everywhere. And nowhere.

• • • •

Cyler stood at the shore of the big lake in a far corner of Stem One, still wondering if she'd done the right thing by answering the invitation. She followed the directions the anonymous message contained. It was far from the lab, and it took her nearly an hour to walk the lengths of several stems and navigate her way.

She had only seen the big lake once before, in training. Its ceiling soared double the height of most places on the *Kalelah*. Blackened like a night sky and dotted with projections of the star field and planetary system of the First Place, it had all the appearance of infinity. When the ship was buried between checks and the shields were up, a facsimile of day and night was synched with the planet's orbit around its sun and simulated throughout several of the ship's large spaces. It helped with sleep cycles. And sanity. Sim skies were no novelty to her. But never had she seen a sim night so beautiful. The reflections of several small moons could be seen in the still water of the lake. Every now and then a fish would break the surface of the water and bite the air, hoping for insects it never found.

The lake was surrounded by low grasses, and she did not want to leave the shoreline or the calm she felt there. But after a few minutes, she turned from the water and walked toward a doorway just beyond the blue-leaf trees on the near side of the lake. Her chest pounding, she pushed open the panel and walked in. For a society that had managed to stay shrouded in secrecy for millennia, it wasn't very hard to get into one of its meetings. But that, too, could be an illusion. The space was dimly lit. She breathed in a sweet and heavy scent of incense and found a back wall to lean against.

She could see faces; some she knew, most she did not. If the room was a chapel, it was a strange one. There were no halo glasses, no rows for kneeling and no prayer rings suspended from the ceiling. If this was a place of worship, the prayers weren't going anywhere, not without rings to transmit them to the celestial winds.

Despite the insistence of the invitation she'd been given, this did not look like a place she belonged. Perhaps she should not have come. XO Laird was farthest from the door, and next to her stood the man with the long beard. He saw Cyler and sent his strange smile her way for an instant but made no other effort in her direction. People milled about, making small talk. Someone handed her a glass of wine and melted away into the small crowd before she could say thank you.

She tried the wine. A smoky taste she couldn't place, but not unpleasant. She took a bigger swallow, and a warmth radiated as it went down. Someone nearby, an older woman of high rank, met her eyes and gently tapped the edge of her glass to Cyler's. Cyler bowed slightly in return. With the gesture, the warmth in her chest seemed to heat up even more. She took another sip. She didn't know if it was the wine or simply the acknowledgment of the old woman, but she began to feel less conspicuously out of place. She could literally feel her nervousness and apprehension begin to dissolve. She finished off her glass.

A tall woman wearing the same rank of jumpsuit as Cyler walked through the crowd with a small chime orb. It pulsated in her hand, playing an ancient melody audible only within a few feet of it. As the orb woman moved throughout the space, those in hearing range quickly quieted, and once the whole room had stopped talking, the XO began to speak.

"Circle, a moment we cannot let pass has come. We are in crisis, and God has asked us to look deeply into our hearts and summon the most of our courage. Our world here is lost. Worse, it's we who have lost it. We failed our ship and we failed God. There will be no Delivery. And without Delivery, without the worship from a people fully accepted by this place, God's claim on this planet will not hold. You heard the explosion. You felt the anger push its way through the *Kalelah*'s skin, and you felt your own skin tingle from the electromagnetic pulse of a Halfborn population gone unchecked. Gone rogue. They should not have the weapons they possess. They should not be writers in an unholy language or readers of an unholy word. They should not yet be able to navigate the seas or the skies. They should not have the ability to destroy. They should not because they don't yet have God to guide them. And so now it's too late. Like it was too late when God defeated His enemies for command of the universe. The Plan makes clear that God's own history must not be repeated. Do you remember? Do you remember how He offered His kindness to the traitorous powers He conquered? He offered them all a second chance to follow Him and serve. Tuninah, who was first to betray God's trust, was given a second chance. Pentar, who killed God's own son and burned His own planet, was given a second chance. And we all know how those gracious chances were repaid. With treachery and betrayal! And so God was forced to wage his horrible wars again. And when He had won for the second time, He vowed to remember the futility of the second chance. God learned the truth that once a spirit has gone its own way, once it walks in paths that don't lead to God, it's too late."

Several people nodded their agreement. Others spoke theirs out loud.

"The captain knows this too. He's not ignorant. He loves this ship and he'd die for any one of us. But he's choosing a path of his own and believing it's right. Luckily, we know it's wrong. Like so many, like too many, the captain has allowed the distance we've come to weaken his hold. He's let go of the thread and become like the worst kind of men. He's become a man of his times. With every generation, with every new leap through space, we find ourselves further from the First Place, further from our true home. Jan Argen has never been there. He has never breathed its air or tasted its rivers. He is a man of other worlds. We are all men of other worlds. New worlds. But when we bring God to those worlds, we complete the circle and we come home. We join the old worlds and the stream of things that are forever. When we follow as we're taught, as is true, we are not mere men of our times. We are men of all times. Of all *time*. As God is. The Plan is our link. It is the golden thread that connects us, binds us, and tethers us to our purpose. If we don't hold on tightly to that thread, if we don't keep it wrapped around our hearts and keep true to it, then we're just travelers, nomads roaming the galaxies and wasting the spark of soul God gave us on nothing more than ... sightseeing. But we in this room, we're not afraid, are we? When others fail, the Circle is the last grasp on that golden thread. We are the clenched fist fail-safe!"

The room was rapt, and Cyler found herself dizzy with emotion. Laird's words were carrying her up like a mother lifts a child. She felt herself surrender. Her earlier thoughts and doubts she suddenly knew were all part of this plan, a kind of foreplay to belief. Now that she was here, she knew she had made the right decision. She knew it was His decision. And more than that, she *believed* it. Somehow her glass had been filled again. How could she have missed that? She took a swallow as she swooned in rhythm with the room. And when she felt a hand slip around her waist, she clasped it and held it there. And she and the man with the long beard swayed with the crowd.

"Are we going to waste His gift?" Laird said. "Are we going to be the disconnected and wayward men of our times? Or are we going to hold on tightly and pull the thread of God forward? With purity? With might?"

The group shouted *Yes!*

"Captain Argen has let go of the thread and has set the *Kalelah* adrift," Laird was shouting now. "He and this ship are tumbling in the void. You can feel it. Can you feel it?"

Again, the group shouted *Yes!*

"And so, it's the Circle's blessed work to save him and this ship. We will bring them both back, wrap the thread around them tightly and do the will of God as we've been instructed. *Exactly* as we've been instructed."

Glasses of wine were hoisted in the air and the group shouted *Yes!* again, louder than before.

"Tomorrow we are going to take control of the *Kalelah* and bring this ship back to God. Will you embrace that work? *Will the Circle hold?*"

This time, Cyler was almost the first to shout, "Yes! Yes!"

17

Private Com Link: 43 - STEM 12 - 9074

- how quickly can you modify the language swarm …
- i can't do that …
- we're going above … we'll need communication …
- who …
- you … chief … me … how long would a swarm take …
- this is strictly prohibited …
- aware … it's on my orders … how long …
- six hours … but which …
- choose the most common language to the vessel above …
- yes sir …
- be ready at 075432.09 … tell no one … out …
- yes sir … out …

T he float winked dark. Trin lay in his pod, thinking through what the captain's order would mean.

"Shit," he said out loud.

He rolled off the bed and went to work. Six hours would go by quickly.

• • • •

A drillbot ground its way through the silt and sand that lay atop the far rear leaf of the *Kalelah*. It took the autonomous machine a good hour to clear the necessary path. When it reached clean water, it spun on its central axis, traveled backward through the tunnel, and parked itself into its bay. A few seconds later, a small, round transport ship shot through the newly made tunnel and began its long ascent.

Trin's stomach was in knots as he, Ganet, and the captain streamed upward. This was a secret mission. Thanks to the captain's credentials, Trin was able to order the *Kalelah* to scrub any records of the transport's movements the instant they were inscribed, effectively erasing their footprints as they made them. To the code, they were invisible. In fact, without radar, they were actually invisible. The little ship was coated in a reactive nanowool cloak studded with mirrors, each smaller than a grain of sand. It gave the transport more camouflaging skills than the most talented chameleons. Even as the ship rose into the light, there was nothing the human eye, or otherwise, could see. This and technologies like it were part of the Guide Service's critical bag of tricks. Guides were never to be seen by a Halfborn population before it was ready. They did their work in the shadows, or behind a billion microscopic mirrors. And yet they were about to pop out of the water, out of the blue, and say hello. Fuck.

The little ship streamed upward toward the source of the bombing, changing to match the water through which it pushed. Black to black-green.

"If they can scan, they can detect us. They'll have plenty of warning time to prepare," Ganet said.

"I know," said Argen.

"What makes you think this isn't suicide?"

"They're smart enough to find us," the captain answered. "They're smart enough to build a nuke. And soon they'll learn we're still alive. Which means they're smart enough to know the game has changed. We're not so easily killed."

The captain's face was hard, expressionless. But Trin saw him swallow hard.

"I'm betting on their curiosity," the captain continued.

"It's a big bet."

The ship hit the watery strata of the sun's deepest reach, and the mirrors of its skin flipped and turned to blend its foreign silhouette away again.

They each injected the swarm. A few minutes later, Trin could feel his arm grow cool. Then his shoulder, then his face. He sat and waited while the liquid, with its army of robot cells that would give his mind a lifetime of language learning, made its way to its destination.

He was now in over his head in a way he had never felt before. Messing with the language swarm was a crime punishable by death. The scrolls made clear the reason why. There was a time when peoples of different places developed different tongues. It always led to conflicting interpretations of the Plan, which inevitably led to conflict of the bloody kind. The specifics of those languages, their forms, their sounds, their beauties, their vulgarities, had been swept from human and machine memory millions of years ago. As humanity spread from planet to planet, a common vernacular and connection spread with it—a bond of sound, meaning, and logic that created a consensus of the tongue, the ear, and, ultimately, the heart. Except here. Trin's last count told of a planet filled with thousands of written languages. No wonder its first reaction to finding the *Kalelah* was to try to kill it.

Still, he blushed with shame at what he'd done. He pictured the looks on the faces of his parents if he were caught, prosecuted, and sentenced to die for a crime that violated such a core element of the contract governing their lives. It actually hurt his stomach to imagine his father's embarrassment, his mother's disbelief and tears. How could their amazing child, their genius, be so reckless? How could he kill the source of all their pride? It helped a little to remember they were dead. He was light-years away. They were thousands of years gone. They'd never know if the worst were to happen. Nor would Lamir.

He looked at the captain and Ganet as the swarm did its work on them. In his orphan gloom, he forced himself to see them as the good guys. He twisted his feelings to tell himself he was a part of something important and noble. This mission was why he had the brain he'd been given. It was why the captain had picked him out of every other soul on that giant ship to be the first to wake.

By the time the ship hit the three-mile mark of its journey to the surface, the cooling sensation in Trin's face had calmed and he felt warm again. He looked about the ship and warily tested the potion he'd concocted.

"I know. I know … two things … about everything," he said aloud in new words that seemed like memories from another life. He smiled. "Ev-er-y-thing."

"I was unsure about this," said Ganet. "But now I do not know why. It feels perfectly normal. Just like me." He laughed. "My mind is moving very quickly. Racing. Racing is the word for it. Racing. This language is fast. Do you feel it? Tight, and economical."

"Illegal as well," said Argen stiffly. "Be careful with this. We have taken a great risk."

"We must practice. Let us talk more."

"The virus does the work," said Trin. "By the time we get to the surface, this will be as automatic as breathing."

"Let's talk anyway. I love this. This … *English*."

"See that?"

"See what?"

"You shortened 'let us' to 'let's.' That's the virus uploading and integrating."

"Incredible. It's incredible! Can you swear yet?"

Trin looked to Argen. "Sir?"

"How could swearing in English make a difference when any word not spoken in Origen is already a blasphemy? To the Keepers, we're doomed anyway. I think you're free to explore."

"Fuck."

"Fuck," Ganet repeated.

Argen smiled at Ganet. "Senior officers excluded."

The console of the little ship sounded an alarm signaling they had come nearly to the surface. Ganet checked the screen and took over control of the ship.

"Are we ready?" said Argen.

"I am definitely not ready," Trin said.

"Good. Confidence is a killer. Stay alert, but stay calm. Anything could be waiting for us."

The ship broke the surface. The transport's scanners showed the *Lewis* floating not more than one hundred yards away. But Argen gave no orders. They waited, knowing the nanowool was confusing things for the Halfborn, their instruments saying one thing, their eyes something else.

"Okay," said Argen. "Let's open the glass and say hello."

The captain and Trin both turned their chairs to the cockpit's only windows and Ganet retracted the nano that blocked and protected the glass. To anyone on the *Lewis* looking through binoculars, the shields receding would look like an impossible hole opening in the seascape to reveal a hidden world, populated by three faces staring back in apprehension.

The *Lewis* was a grotesquery of a thing to see: completely expected and totally surprising. They'd been shamelessly scanning since they floated the orb and detected the aircraft. They'd vacuumed data from billions of sources. They felt the quake and terror of the bomb. They all *knew* the Halfborn were thousands of millennia of development from the primitives Forent promised. Yet up to this point, the rogue Halfborn population had been a digital abstraction. Numbers, pictures, motion pictures, music, conversations in thousands of languages no one could be allowed to understand. But now, seeing one of their vessels in the metal suddenly made real the scale of what had gone so horribly wrong.

For Argen, there was no more last hope of an error in the code. Every glitch theory he'd kept stashed away in the back of his head instantly crashed. They were what he feared. His mistake was what he feared. And Laird may be right—the population might be forever lost to God. Nevertheless, he kept to his own plan.

"Take it all back," he ordered.

Ganet let the whole ship be seen and they waited there from one hundred yards out. At that distance, their weaponless craft might still be able to escape an attack. When nothing happened for several minutes, he told Ganet to move in closer.

Ganet let the ship move forward, but slowly, almost at a crawl. It was only a few seconds before the little transport's scanners began to pick up radio bursts from the *Lewis*.

"They're trying to hail us, Chief," said Trin.

"Are they threatening?" asked Ganet.

"They're demanding we stop and identify ourselves."

"Then we'll stop. Let them know we have no weapons, Trin. Tell them they're welcome to scan us to verify."

"They want to know who we are, Chief."

Ganet turned to Argen. "Captain?"

"It's amazing, isn't?" he said, looking out the thick glass of the front screen. "We just left them. Like infants. And now look."

"The hails are coming faster," Trin said.

"Jan, what do we tell them?"

The captain said nothing. He just looked ahead, frozen by the image.

Ganet leaned in closer to the captain. "If they fire, we have nothing to fire back."

"They won't fire."

"You don't know that," Ganet said.

The captain leaned forward in his chair as if the extra few inches closer he got to the screen would give him the inspiration he needed. "If you saw us, in this ship, what would you think of us?"

"I'd think we were killers."

Argen looked at the chief with admonishment.

"It's the language," Ganet said. "It makes me paranoid."

"Nonsense."

"You don't feel it? Now that we understand their words, now that we understand *them*, it changes everything. Back on the *Kalelah*, I agreed we had to give them a chance. We had to at least try. But we knew nothing then."

"We still know nothing."

"No. We know too much. Like they do. Listen to what's in your head, Jan. Now that you know their words, the lies they believe, the truths they shouldn't possess, can you still say Laird is wrong?"

"This isn't just a seed population anymore, Chief. This is a world of seven billion."

"Doesn't that make the chances of fixing this even more impossible? You think you can convert seven billion? Listen to the words in your head, Jan."

"I won't force you to do this, Chief. Once I'm aboard that ship, you have permission to go back to the *Kalelah*."

"Where you go, I go. And I'm asking you to go back," Ganet said in Origen. "Now."

The captain ignored the appeal and continued to speak in the outlaw language. "This isn't their crime, Smenth."

"It's not ours either. Deliveries are full of risks. Success is never guaranteed. That's the first lesson we learn in Academy. That's why the protocol is there. The Plan anticipated this."

"Not this. We brought them here, and then we went to sleep and didn't wake up until it was too late. We owe them ... something."

"We owe the *Kalelah*, too. If we turn around now, we can still do the right thing."

The captain looked at Ganet again, this time with disappointment. "We are doing the right thing."

Trin took his earpiece out and swung his chair toward the two older men. "Chief," he interrupted. "Listen!"

Trin put the hail from the *Lewis* in the air where all three could hear it.

"This is the survey ship *Lewis*, operated by Allied Oil of Houston, Texas, USA. Please identify yourselves. I repeat, *please* ... identify yourselves."

The right corner of Trin's mouth turned up just a bit. He looked at Ganet and Argen to see if either had heard what he'd heard. And he could tell from the captain's eyes, the way they steeled, that he had.

It was in that last *please*. A hitch in the speaker's voice. Almost imperceptible, but it was there. They all heard it. And when they did, they could imagine the speaker's heart beating just a little too fast, his palms just a little too wet. In that barely audible hitch was something that shot like a comet across worlds and across time and across mistakes.

In that hitch was a sound that only a human could make.

"Analyst, tell them who we are," said Argen. "Tell them we are their last chance to hold on to this world."

18

With the *Pueblo* gone, the small fighting group escorting the deputy secretary of defense was without the big ship's heavy weaponry, though it wasn't entirely benign. An array of small automatic weapons was at the ready to greet the strange little craft as it rose from the water and hovered just above the top deck of the *Lewis*.

Riley seemed to be in charge at this moment, which only served to amplify Sarah's feelings of apprehension. Scott and Henderson were allowed to join the deputy's contingent. And Henderson surprised her by insisting she join as well. Riley said nothing, he just shrugged a shoulder. She took it for a yes. The rest of the crew, the people who did the work of keeping the *Lewis* running, were ordered below deck in case things went wrong. What kind of wrong he didn't say. But everyone knew that whomever or whatever was about to get out of the little ship just came from a much bigger ship. And it took a nuclear explosion with hardly a scratch.

A round hatch opened in the underbelly of the hovering ship's hull, a ladder lowered, and three ordinary-looking men climbed down. After all the expectations and wonder about what was down below, after all the worst imaginings, what emerged were just, apparently, seemingly, *men*. Two looked to be in their thirties, one dark skinned and one pale. The third wasn't much older than a teenager. It was almost disappointing. Instead of bringing about a sense of relief, the image of the three profoundly familiar beings only created more confusion. Rather than monsters from another world, were they facing enemies from closer places? From Russia, or from Iran, as Riley had been saying all along? Could that asshole be right after all? Sarah had to admit, in a weird way, monsters who could build a ship four miles long seemed less worrisome than Russians who could.

Riley unsnapped his holster and drew his sidearm, but he kept it low, below his waist.

The biggest of the three men from the little ship regarded the gun with what looked like honest curiosity. Something about his face, his look at the gun, like it was a totally alien thing, let Sarah relax just a bit.

"We told you we had no weapons," he said, his accent awkward and difficult to place.

"Safety first," answered Riley. "You aren't what we expected."

"Neither are you," the strange man said.

"Your ship is unmarked. Your uniforms have no flag. Who are you?"

"I am Captain Jan Argen of the Guide Ship *Kalelah*. This is the ship's chief, Commander Smenth Ganet, and next to him is Analyst Trin."

Riley seemed to recognize that answer. He offered a knowing smirk. "I'll ask again," he pushed back, "who are you?"

"And I've told you," the one who called himself captain replied. He was so oddly calm. Sarah could feel everyone else on the edge of freaking out. Bronner was almost trying to hide behind Henderson, whose face was the reddest she'd ever seen it. Wilson tried to look in command, but she could see his left knee shaking. And Riley's eyes were ablaze with nervous energy. Even the two others who'd gotten off the little flying submarine thing, whatever it was, seemed a bit on edge, the older one more than the young one, Trin.

But this Argen, he seemed completely unfazed.

He gave everyone a good, slow look. His eyes moved from Wilson to Sarah, and then to the soldiers behind Riley. He turned his gaze to Riley again. "You really don't need these weapons," he said.

Riley just laughed. But he quickly got serious again. "Okay, Captain Argen, if that's who you really are. I'll put my weapon down when you start making sense. I'll give you five seconds."

"It won't be an easy thing to do in five seconds." Again, so calm.

Riley narrowed his eyes. "Try. Really. Hard."

Wilson stepped around Riley and approached Argen.

The tallest one, Ganet, stepped in front of Argen, a little too quickly for Riley's men, who cocked their weapons and took more aggressive stances.

"Nobody shoot," Wilson said as calmly as he could while still making himself heard. "Nobody shoot." He took a small step back. "Len Wilson, United States Deputy Defense Secretary."

"Deputy Defense Secretary. You're a military man," Ganet asked.

"Civilian. I report directly to the secretary and she reports directly to the president. Is there a message you want relayed? Is that why you've come to the surface?"

"We're here to help you, if it's possible."

"And why would we be in need of help?" said Riley, asserting himself again.

"Because you're in grave danger."

Riley moved in closer. "From whom?"

Ganet's eyes went to his captain for a flash and then back to Wilson. "The explosion. It's made things ... complicated."

"These are our waters," Len Wilson said evenly, giving the words a confidence that made them sound beyond contest. "You must have known we scanned you. But you gave no response. Either your ship was already long dead or it was playing dead. We had no way of knowing which was true. The bomb was an insurance policy. Also our right by international law." That last statement was clearly another fact Wilson wasn't willing to debate. His leg was still shaking, though. Sarah had a sudden gush of admiration for Wilson.

"The bomb has become an argument against you, among other things," Argen said. "I don't expect you to understand why, but powerful forces are now in motion, and we have very little time."

"Whose forces?" Riley said, his voice still packing plenty of suspicion.

"Mine, unless we can persuade them to see things differently, to have some patience."

Riley's head cocked like he hadn't heard right. He shifted his stance and raised the aim of his gun just a bit. "You introduced yourself as captain. Don't you have command of that ship?"

"Of the ship, yes. But as it concerns the beliefs of its people, well, that's a different command."

The two groups stood silent, each taking the other's measure. Trin, though, seemed to keep his eyes just on her. She had no idea if Riley was right, and whether this was some kind of elaborate scheme by one of America's many enemies or if the crazy ship really was what Argen claimed it to be. But something about Trin, and the way he looked at her, made her want to trust him. Though that did nothing to make her feel any more comfortable. Riley in particular looked increasingly agitated.

"Your accent. It's unusual, like nothing I've heard before," said Wilson. "Where are you from?"

"The where depends on the when. We've been here a long time. Longer than you can imagine."

"I have a pretty good imagination, Captain," Wilson said, an unmistakable tinge of annoyance in his voice.

"As I said earlier, it's not a simple story. I don't know what you'll believe—"

"Not likely much," interrupted Riley.

"Let him talk, Major," said Wilson.

"Whatever you might think of what we'll tell you," Argen continued, "what's important to know is the three of us are here to change the course of events. We want to help you. But we need something from you first."

"If it's a negotiation you want, I'm authorized to speak on behalf of the United States."

"This isn't a negotiation. We're here for something quite specific."

Sarah felt Wilson tense.

"Are you looking for asylum, Captain Argen?" Wilson replied.

"Asylum?"

"Are you defecting? Do you seek the protection of the United States?"

"No. We need no protection."

"Then what is it you want from us?"

"Proof," Argen said flatly.

"Proof? Of what?"

"God."

19

The small group moved below deck to the mess and sat around two steel tables that had been pushed together. Wilson sat across from Argen, who in this setting looked twice Wilson's size. Riley sat across from Ganet, the chief. Bronner and Henderson sat to Sarah's right. And she sat across from Trin the *analyst*, whatever that meant.

The soldiers didn't sit and instead remained at attention, their weapons ready. They made Sarah uncomfortable. It was a lot of hardware for a small room. She didn't like guns much in any case. And here, in this place at this time and with these people, the guns felt all wrong. She could only imagine how they were making their three strange guests feel. But, again, Riley seemed to be determining the posture of things.

There was pasta, bread, and salad on the table with water and iced tea. Trin was first on their side to fill a plate. He messily managed some pasta, wrestling with the utensils, getting only about half of what he grabbed on his plate. Sarah watched him with a mix of amusement and doubt. *What's up, dude? First time eating?*

"I'll be honest with you, Captain," said Wilson. "You're not making much sense. It's got a lot of us nervous, and I'm not sure that's what you want. So let's start with that big ship down below. What's its purpose?"

"The ship's primary purpose is transport," said Argen. "But it's also our laboratory, and our home. And at one time, a long time ago, it was your home, too."

Sarah put her fork down. Everyone from the *Lewis* stopped eating. Out of the corner of her eye, she saw Riley shift a bit in his chair.

"Our home?" said Wilson.

"The *Kalelah's* mission is Delivery and Guidance," Argen added. He stopped and looked around the table, waiting for it to sink in, but no one looked any less confused.

"Delivery? Delivery of what?" asked Wilson.

"The seed population."

"Seed of what?"

"The seed that would eventually lead to … to you."

Henderson coughed. "Pardon me?"

"Are you saying you brought us—I mean *people*—you brought the people to Earth?" said Wilson.

"That's right."

Henderson's neck turned a new color of red. "For fuck's sake, son, this is a bad time to be joking around."

"Brought from where?" Wilson jumped in.

"Sir!" Riley turned to Wilson. "Really?"

Wilson thought for a brief minute, as if Riley might have a point. He turned back to Argen. "Brought from where?" he repeated, a little louder, a little more assertively.

"From the place of the beginning. The First Place. From God's world," Argen answered, a calm, earnest look on his face.

"God's world?" Henderson frowned. "That's the cover they gave you? You're on a mission from God? Don't y'all watch the movies?"

"Enough bullshit," said Riley. "Let's put these people in cuffs and get the State Department on the line."

"Amen to that," Henderson said, his cheeks beginning to bloom. "These boys don't look Russian to me, but they're playin' with us like they are."

Wilson twirled a fork around some noodles. He looked calm, but Sarah could see his jaw clenching. She got the feeling Wilson wasn't ready to shut this down yet. At least she was hoping he wasn't. There was something about these strange men that didn't seem like a scam. It seemed too crazy, too dangerous, to be a scam. But still, she had to admit, what else could it be?

"Is that what's happening here, Captain Argen?" Wilson asked after he chewed down his forkful of pasta. "Are you playing with us? I ask because there's another explanation for your presence here, one I'll have no trouble selling to my bosses in Washington. It goes like this." He put his fork down and trained his focus on Argen. "A foreign entity is conducting a test of experimental military vessels in American protected waters. When I send that message, it won't take long before such an action is deemed an act of war."

Argen said nothing. Sarah looked at Trin. She did not see the face of someone who had concocted some elaborate lie. If anything, she saw confusion, even a hint of worry.

"Now, if that were the case," Wilson went on, "the United States would not restrict the next assault to a few kilotons. You'd feel the full force of American power, Captain. Is this making sense to you?"

Argen pointed to a breast pocket of his jumpsuit and looked to Riley. "May I?"

He pulled a small square of blue glass from the pocket and placed it on the table. He tapped a corner of the glass, and a large projection floated above the table surface. It showed an image of a blue planet spinning slowly on its axis. Were it not for the shapes of the landmasses and its three moons, it could be Earth.

"Our home," said Argen softly.

"And where is this *home*?" said Wilson.

Trin stood and tapped the glass twice, and the image expanded and the room was filled with stars, the spiraling swirls of galaxies and the billowing, beautiful clouds of nebulae blown from a nonexistent wind. It appeared a miniature expanse of the universe entire. He placed his fingers in the projection and the scene began to move, and to Sarah the room felt as though it were rushing through space, faster and faster, until the air all around smeared with light.

Despite her nervousness, or maybe because of it— or maybe because it was Trin who had touched the screen—Sarah outstretched her arms slightly as if to feel the rush. And even though she knew it was just a projection, just light, she actually felt the force of movement around her. She checked the sleeves of her shirt for any signs that might confirm the rippling, whirring space she was feeling. It could have been a trick of the eye, or the play of light, or simply the influence of awe, but she was convinced a real current was in the air, an energy she could feel. She felt it pull at her clothes, push its way through her hair. And just as quickly as it appeared the strange energy was gone. The scene suddenly stopped to rest with a small cluster of stars directly above the table.

"Here," said Trin. He raised his hand within the cluster and the image zoomed in to reveal the same Earthlike planet Argen had conjured orbiting a small sun.

"You traveled to Earth all the way from there, huh?" Riley said with more than a hint of condescension.

Argen looked to the group. "We all did." He touched the glass and the stars disappeared.

Riley began to clap his hands slowly. "Nice show. I mean, that was some Industrial Light and Magic-level stuff. And the IMAX bit—impressive." His mock appreciation stopped and the insincere smile left his face. "But do we really seem that stupid?" He turned to Wilson. "If the PowerPoint portion of the seminar is over, can we get on with arresting these people?"

Argen picked up the glass, flipped it over, and placed it back on the table. "I'm sorry to say that stupid is not our impression of you. I wish it were." His voice lost it softness. "It's why we have to get to some kind of understanding quickly. Again, forces are in motion." He touched the glass once more and this time the room filled with images of the Earth in space.

Argen stood within the image, inside the slowly spinning Earth. With his dark skin bathed in the soft blue light of the projection, he looked like an apparition.

"Many years before the *Kalelah* made its home on the canyon's floor below us, we transported small populations to seven locations." He pivoted a half circle, reached out with an index finger, and tapped on the seven places as he spoke, leaving a trail of glowing blue spots hovering over the projected planet and himself. The spots formed a series of lights along the eastern quarter of the African continent.

He touched a spot in what today would be modern Nigeria and the image changed to a view rising slowly upward from a seething crowd of maybe two hundred. Those in the crowd were naked and panicked and getting smaller and smaller as the view gained altitude. The ground on which the subjects of the film ran and tumbled and kneeled and screamed or stood pulling at their hair was wet and muddy. A light rain was falling. As the image climbed higher still, Sarah saw mountains in the distance, a small jungle, and, through the jungle, a flowing mud-bottom river.

"What are we looking at?" asked Wilson.

"It's called Delivery," said Argen.

"Delivery? Delivery of what?"

"This is a Halfborn population. Seeds of a new life. Should they survive."

"Why are they naked? That can't help their chances for survival."

"God demands it. We must come without affectation, without remnant, to be made new by the soil of a new world."

"Made by the soil of … oh my God," said Bronner. "Does no one else see the similarity?"

"With what? You going Bat Boy on me again?" said Henderson.

"And the Lord God formed man of the dust of the ground," Bronner said barely above the level of a whisper. "Adam … Adam came to the garden naked."

"Shut up, asshole," Henderson said. "This ain't goddamned church."

But Sarah didn't want him to shut up. For the first time, she was seeing Bronner in something like a positive light. He could be useful in this crazy situation. At least he was trying to be constructive. Of everyone, he seemed to offer the most benefit of the doubt to the strangers, the most … unfettered wonder. And if there were some common ground, some similarities, wouldn't that be a good thing?

"There's more you need to know," said Argen, apparently unmoved by Bronner's attempt to connect some dots.

He began to wave his hand in small beats, and with every motion the image changed to another location but the same scene. A people in confused terror being left alone, stripped, and strange. Some lands were wet, some dry. Some cold, some warm. Each abandonment was like the violent slap given a newborn.

"Most of these creatures we knew would die shortly after," Argen continued. "By starvation, by predatory animals, or by genocide. Those that somehow managed to survive would be the start of godly life on this planet. Planet 07-347-28." He touched the glass and once again the image collapsed into the tiny blue square.

"That start was the beginning that led to you. Your ancestors on this planet were the *Kalelah*'s children. They were put here because they would someday represent the continuation of God's Plan. This, of course, is now the problem."

Wilson swallowed hard and turned to Argen. "If this is true—"

"But it isn't," interrupted Riley.

Wilson lifted his hand off the table to stop Riley's next objection. "Why is it a *problem*?" he said to Argen.

"The Plan—God's Plan—is quite specific, I'm afraid. Exacting, actually. *God speaks, the Plan records, and Humankind follows.* And this ..." He looked about the mess hall, stretching out his arms as if to make the room and everything in it an example. "None of this should be here."

"I don't understand. *We* don't understand," said Sarah desperately. She turned to Trin. "If this shouldn't be here, why bring us here in the first place? It makes no sense."

"We didn't have a choice," he answered softly.

"The universe is a crowded place," Argen continued. "But a planet like 07-347-28 is a one-in-a-million discovery. It can't be left godless."

"Life," said Bronner. "Is that why?"

"Not just life," said Argen. "Life is almost every-where. Life is the easiest thing to find. But when we look for God's next world, we look for his first. This planet isn't just capable of supporting human life. This planet is capable of supporting human life as human life is meant to be lived. As it was on the First Place, it could be on this place. The size of this planet, the land-to-water ratio, the volcanic activity, the chemical composition of its atmosphere, all of it. It's nearly identical to the First Place. It's nearly home. It is, as the Plan says, 'a holy place in waiting.' And that's why the *Kalelah* was sent. We came here to finish the work. To end the wait. We came here to add the sacred ingredient that would bring this planet into God's orbit. You, us. But something went wrong. And *that* is the problem."

"What was the something? What went wrong?" said Sarah warily, afraid of what would come next.

"The population."

"Us? What's wrong with us?" she said defiantly.

Argen blushed now. "I'm being coy. I shouldn't."

"If you ask me, sailor, coy ain't quite the word for it," said Henderson.

"It doesn't matter," Riley flared. "He's said enough."

"Hold on, Riley," Wilson said. "We have to understand this."

"I understand plenty. We're moving on. Sergeant—"

"Nobody's doing anything," said Wilson, his professional cool slipping for the first time. "Check your field manual, Major. This is my operation."

"Technically," Riley said, mocking the legal nuance.

"Technically is all I need. Now, we're going to let the man finish. Think of it as an interrogation if it'll make you feel better."

So much for that tight little twosome, Sarah thought. She felt herself grasping the edge of the table. She glanced at the three visitors; they looked only slightly less uncomfortable than she felt. Riley was getting to them. He was getting to her too.

Wilson took a breath. He clasped his hands in front of him and put them on the table, as if he was resetting the clock, giving the table a chance for a do-over. "Go ahead, Captain. We want to know everything."

Argen nodded slightly. "Very well. Deliveries are fragile things. Bringing a population is the easy part. Finishing the task, managing a successful Delivery, that's the hard part. Living planets are wild things. They're full of secrets they don't reveal easily or quickly, especially to visitors. This planet looks like the First Place. It's warm and has flowing water like home. It smells like home. But 07-347-28, the place you think has always been yours, is still an alien and dangerous world. We lost dozens of planets at the start of God's travels. It took us millions of years and the help of God's gift, *the Plan*, to learn the essential lesson in creating new home worlds in waiting."

He paused for a minute. Sarah thought he was trying to read the room, but she wasn't sure what he might make of it—or what Riley or Henderson might do with the breathing space—so she jumped in before too much time ticked away.

"What was the essential lesson?"

"Integrate," he answered. "Blend in."

"I don't get it."

"There's no invading an alien world with hopes of conquest. No technology can stand up to the natural immunity every planet possesses. A planet can sense a foreign element and does everything it can to reject it. So, instead of shelters and machinery and the import of our familiar ways, the only strategy that has proven to work is to come naked, with no language and no culture, and do what every other successful organism in the universe has done."

"Adapt," said Bronner.

"Exactly. In order to succeed, an organism must become no less an elemental part of its world as water to a river. And that's the process we set in motion a hundred and twenty thousand years ago."

"One hundred and twenty thousand years ago," said Bronner. He looked to Henderson, "Sapiens. In the fossil record, that's pretty much where modern humans show up."

"Dial it down, Bronner," Henderson said coolly. "You're in over your egghead here."

But he did not dial it down. "But there were others, I mean, other kinds of humans, already here," Bronner said in a way Sarah interpreted as tossing Argen a softball. "Maybe as many as six different branches."

"Yes, there were others. But not human others."

"Our scientists say they were. They were intelligent. And upright, and social. But eventually, our branch dominated the others, and, well, we killed them off."

"Your scientists have learned without the help they needed to truly understand the universe and our place in it. The biology of small, living, rocky worlds is universal. Stir the right chemical cocktail and eventually you'll get creatures that look like us, walk like us, and hunt like us. But they are not us. We are different."

"Okay, what's he talking about, Bronner?" Henderson said sheepishly.

"God," said Bronner, looking happy to actually be of help.

"Yes, God," said Argen softly. "Only we are given His touch and His charge. And this is why the stars are ours."

"We killed the others," said Sarah. "That doesn't seem like something God would want."

"It's precisely what God would want. If His people don't survive, He won't survive. He can't grow without us. We're how He moves throughout the cosmos. What would happen to the worshipped without His worshippers?" said Argen.

"This Delivery thing—you've done it before?" asked Sarah.

"Not me, not the *Kalelah*, but yes, there have been many Deliveries."

"Many," Wilson gasped. "How many?"

"One thousand and twelve."

"My God."

Wilson seemed stunned. He wasn't alone. Except for the three visitors, everyone else lost a little color in their faces.

"But we've … we've been searching," Wilson said, stumbling over his words. "For others. For proof that we're not alone. And we've never found even the smallest evidence of their existence. How can it be?"

"The universe is a bigger place than you know. You just found us. And we've been right under your noses."

Henderson exhaled. "Oh, hell. This is nuttier than a fuckin' Payday bar."

"And it always goes the same way, like you showed us?" said Sarah. "You just leave the people with nothing?"

"Not with nothing. We wipe away their memories of any time before Delivery. They have no technology. No language. No culture. And, at the start, no God. That's why they're merely *Halfborn*. They must be clean slates awaiting the natural scribbling of their adopted homes. But they have cognitive advantages to help them. And, of course, they have us. The Guides."

"You teach them? That's what you do?" Sarah asked.

"Not directly. We influence them. We implant ideas to manage a population's pace of discovery, as well as what it discovers."

"Some kind of mind control?" Bronner asked.

"Viruses, mostly," Argen answered. "We infect the water of a river, a fresh kill meant for dinner, or even the rain. The microbes enter the bloodstream and make their way to the brain, and suddenly another step toward language is taken. Or the notion of a particularly useful tool is imagined. Eventually, when the time is right, we ensure the population finds God, as the Plan says it should."

Riley stood. "Wilson, how much more of this crap are you going to take? These people are lunatics or an enemy trying to distract us. Or both."

Ganet stood up and faced the major.

"I think you're confused about where the lunacy is here, Major. Tell me, what did you think would happen when you sent a nuclear device down to my ship? Were you crazy enough to think it would surprise us, that we couldn't sense its signature from a hundred miles away? Were you sane enough to imagine the ship would survive? That I would survive? The captain and Trin—did you have enough mental clarity to expect them here today? And what about the twenty-two thousand others on the *Kalelah*? Did you predict their survival too?" Ganet put his hands on the table and leaned forward. "Your bomb was a moment of bad weather. A storm that passed in the night. But mostly, it was a mistake. A bad calculation. Things don't always happen as we think they must. And things are often not what we believe them to be." He turned to Argen. "Captain, we're wasting our time here."

The captain kept his eyes on Wilson and Riley, but not with the same indignation as Ganet. His expression remained warm. Calm. "There are plenty of mistakes to go around, Smenth."

"If we go back now," Ganet said, "we can still erase our tracks. The longer we stay, the fewer options we have. Laird will have more than she needs to take the pin."

"This is bigger than who has the pin."

"Not if you're wrong."

"Then I have to be right." He smiled. "No, we stay the course here and tell them as much as they need to hear to believe us. We tell them as much as they need to hear to *trust* us," Argen said, turning to the chief. "Otherwise, we won't just have wasted our time. We'll have wasted everything."

Ganet sat down reluctantly, eyes smoldering. Everyone else looked to the captain.

"Riley," Wilson nudged.

Riley sat, but he didn't look happy about it. Argen touched the glass one last time.

"The *Kalelah*'s skin is very protective. Your scan could detail the exterior of the ship, but not the interior. If it had, perhaps you wouldn't have dropped that bomb. Or perhaps you would have used a much larger one." He spun the glass and an image of the ship appeared, hovering, no longer buried by sand and lit by a thousand lights.

The image of the ship, so different from the specter she'd discovered in the sediment scan, took her breath away. She'd never seen anything so marvelous in her life. "Like sparkling leaves," she gushed.

"It is a wonder," admitted Argen with a glint of pride in his eyes. "And for every planet like home we find, there's a ship just like it, whose one job is to guide human life as the Plan guides us."

"Okay, Captain." Wilson's mood had shifted. He sounded impatient. "Let's finish the story already. You've guided more than a thousand planets. And you've been guiding this one for a hundred and twenty thousand years, you say. Which, frankly, seems pretty damn impossible. But just because we've already come this far, tell us—what the hell went wrong?"

Trin stood up now. But slowly and carefully, like he didn't want to ramp up the tension again.

"Actually, we didn't guide you," he said apologetically. "There was some kind of malfunction of the time clock." He took control of the glass from Argen and filled the room with digits and symbols. He pointed to two strings of symbols no one off the *Kalelah* would even recognize. "See, the timing's all off."

"Hell yes, son, anyone can see that," Henderson teased.

"Sorry." Trin blushed. "What this shows is the guide model for this planet. Each one of these graphlets along this line signifies an epoch of time," he said, pointing to a series of round, knot-like marks. "And these marks indicate the guide checks, or E-checks, the moments when we monitor the population and guide, or administer the influence needed. And since adaptation only works if it works slowly, you can see that this model called for forty-one E-checks, and a total span of 156,000 years."

"How can you possibly span that time?" asked Wilson.

"We sleep. A sleep so deep it lets us perceptually fold time. It's called a Skip. And usually, we don't Skip for more than ten-thousand years. At least not on purpose. Most Skips are planned to be much shorter. When we woke it was supposed to be E Two, just six thousand years from the first E-check. And just nine thousand years in total since Delivery. Except that isn't what happened. Somehow, we overslept. To E Thirty-Seven. To now."

Bronner gasped. "Holy—"

"Shit."

"That's right," said Ganet. "Which means you've been on your own for a long time. For too long a time."

"You got a ship that can take a nuke better'n my face makes it past my mornin' shave and you forget to set your damn alarm clock?" said Henderson.

"We don't know what went wrong," said Argen. "But here we are. And here you are."

"At the place where we lose our hold on this world?" said Wilson. "Is that what you want us to believe?"

"The things you know, the things you think you know, the things you possess—all of it was acquired without the benefit of the Plan."

"If you ask me, we did pretty good without you, bub," said Henderson.

"Our people see it differently. The things you have and believe—they're forbidden."

"Well, I got news, cousin, no one here is gonna go along with that."

"They'll have to. But first you have to trust in what I'm telling you. Because as things currently stand, the *Kalelah* has an obligation and my crew won't abandon it."

"An obligation to whom? Or what?" asked Wilson.

"To God. To the Plan. One and the same. The people on the *Kalelah* don't need my orders to know what to do. I've been buying time for the last few days, but with the chief and I off the ship, I wouldn't be surprised if a Correction is already in motion."

"Correction?" It was Wilson's turn to freak. "You're going to try and reeducate us? Seven billion of us? Half the world doesn't even believe in evolution. You expect it to believe in *you*? In this?"

Argen's face was of a man already in mourning. He looked at Wilson for a long time. "No."

"No?"

"There's no reeducation. It's not *you* a Correction rights."

"What the fuck is that supposed to mean?" growled Henderson. "You're speakin' English but the words don't make any sense. What in the living fuck is a Correction?"

"A fire."

"A fire?" asked Wilson.

Argen put his two index fingers together and then made the shape of a circle. "An enveloping fire."

"What?"

"The *Kalelah* will burn the planet clean like lightning scrubs a forest. When it's over, life will begin anew. And, in time, this planet will be ready for God's children again."

Riley slowly pushed his chair back from the table. No one else moved. No one else seemed to notice. Argen's words had taken most of the oxygen out of the room, like the flames they promised would do again. Sarah was dizzy.

"Earlier," said Wilson, "you said deviation was no longer allowed. But it was once? Allowed?"

Argen shrugged. "There's an ancient song we learn in school. It speaks of a time of wars. Brutal wars. Some say they were fought over what the Plan means and how it should be followed. But those arguments ended millions of years ago. Now there is no debate. There is only one story. There is only one truth."

"You say you're a religious people. Is there no forgiveness in this plan of yours?"

"Don't beg this thing, Wilson," said Riley with a coldness Sarah would later wish she'd noted with more alarm.

Argen took a deep breath and let it out slowly. "We are also an observant people. Dutiful. Perhaps to a fault. Many aboard the *Kalelah* take the Plan literally. That's what makes this situation so dangerous." He looked around the room again, trying to make eye contact with as many people as possible. "I know what we've been telling you these last few minutes seems too much to believe. I can see it in your faces. But I'm asking you in every way I know how: trust us."

That cool veneer Sarah had seen and admired on this strange man throughout this entire encounter—and what else could it be called but an *encounter*—was starting to peel away. Maybe he was crazy, but he looked like he believed every word. Believed it like his life, and hers, depended on it.

"You've seen the *Kalelah* with your scanning technology. You've seen one of her transport ships with your own eyes. We risked more than you know to come to the surface, and I'm honestly not sure we can change the course of events. I'm not sure there's time enough to stop what's coming. But we want to try. We want to help. So please, while there might still be a sliver of time, trust us."

"By proving we believe in ... God?" asked Wilson.

"It's the only chance there is. The only one there ever is. If we can show the people of the *Kalelah* that God is already here, already with you, maybe in a way humanity wouldn't immediately recognize, but *here* nonetheless ... if we can find Him, then we can make the case that you are not merely a population lost, not just a failed Delivery. We can make the case that you are ... human."

"Fuck this."

Riley swung his hand up, and before Sarah could register what was in it there was the sharp concussion of a firing pin hitting its target and the shrill ping of a bullet mushrooming into a metal wall. She awoke like from a spell. Argen's mouth was open and a small red hole glistened in his forehead. His eyes went blank, his shoulders slumped, and his head sank gently down upon the table, almost as if he were just tired and had decided to rest. His blood pooled black on the dark wood. Bronner was mumbling something incoherent; she noticed a faint smell of urine coming from his direction.

Riley sat calmly, veiled by the smoke from his service pistol.

"Now I trust you," he said.

FALLEN ARROW

BOOK II OF THE KALELAH SERIES

As seed we are Delivered unto new worlds.

Halfborn, naked, without language or tools, we wait the epochs until our alien scent is carried away by native winds.

We wait the generations while our Deliverers, our Guides, mold our ways and minds to the work of God, the Plan, and so holy becomes our world and so bound to Him become our souls.

Bless the ageless servants of the eons. Only through the Plan can we be Human and God travel the cosmos. Only through the Plan can all become One.

Only through the Plan can the universe wait no more.

Let none forget. Let none dispute.

—Origin 7, Scroll 18

1

G anet cradled Argen's body in his arms and made a noise, something just shy of a howl. It was a child's grief, shameless and complete. Sarah had seen a look of devastation like the one Ganet wore before, but never on a grown man. It made the situation seem all the more desperate.

Riley's men had moved in behind the army major's chair with their weapons pointed at the swaying, grieving Ganet and the young one Argen had introduced as Trin. Sarah got up from her seat and ran to the strangers' side of the table. She stood next to Trin facing Riley and the guns.

"Are you going to shoot me, too?" she said.

"These people are enemy spies," said Riley coolly, not even looking at her. He kept his eyes trained on Ganet. "Tell me you're a spy, blondie, and—yes—I'll shoot you, too."

She ignored the blondie crack, though it stung in its usual way, a hurt she hadn't felt in a long time. "They're not spies," Sarah pushed back. She took Trin's arm in her right hand. "Did you watch him eat? It was like he was seeing a knife and fork for the first time."

She looked at Ganet, who was still stricken and unwilling to let go of the captain. His face and clothes were streaked in the dead man's blood. The bullet hole in Argen's forehead was surprisingly small and as perfectly round as a bindi dot between the eyes of a Hindu man—which the captain's deep olive skin made even more convincing. But the bullet's exit left the back of Argen's head a gruesome mess. The table was covered in gore. She had never seen a man shot before. Or die before. But at this moment, her immediate concern was stopping another from suffering the same fate. These three men said they were from the ship. The ship she had found. The ship she'd lost to the government when they helicoptered in and took over the *Lewis*. And she was done with losing.

Wilson stood and turned to Riley, calm as usual. "Major Riley. Hand me your sidearm."

Riley sat in his chair, his eyes still focused on Ganet.

"Hand me your sidearm, Major. Now."

Riley leveled the gun once more and turned it toward Wilson. He stood slowly, the gun's dangerous end tracking along Wilson's body as he rose. When he was finished, the eight inches of height he had on Wilson stopped the still-warm barrel even with the deputy secretary's chest.

"You really think they're telling the truth?" Riley said. "You believe this fucking comic book story about a ship from some star field who the fuck knows where that came here to bring the first humans? And these jokers here—you think they watch over us like gods? Some gods." He nodded his head toward Argen. "This one only needed a single bullet." He laughed.

Wilson didn't blink, didn't look at the gun. "I know the ship down there is like nothing any of us have ever encountered before. Did it come from the far end of the universe like Argen said? I don't know. But it's bigger than the town I grew up in. It's seven miles down, at the bottom of the deepest ocean trench on Earth. And somehow it has living, breathing people on it. And I know we didn't put it there. And if it's not Chinese or Russian, and nothing about it or the intelligence we've gathered so far says it is, then I have to consider every possibility. Including the comic book possibility. The impossible scenario that says the guy you shot in the head leads a crew of people who were supposed to guide early humans over thousands of years so they'd believe in certain things and behave in certain ways. Except something went wrong, and we happened instead. I have to consider that crazy, cartoon possibility. Because what I *believe*, Riley, is irrelevant. I was raised in the Protestant Church. And according to everything I was taught there on those hard-as-rock pews, the last few days we all experienced are supposed to be impossible. But here we are. So, the only things I'm absolutely certain of right now are these: You just killed an unarmed man, Major Riley. And killing the two people he brought with him won't make anything he said before you blew his brains out any more untrue than you think it already is. Which means at least as far as the short term is concerned, I know what has to happen next. Now give me the goddamn gun."

Riley moved closer and brought the muzzle of the 9mm pistol up to Wilson's neck, the blast residue from the shot that killed Argen leaving a dark circle on Wilson's pale skin.

He spoke slowly, a small crooked smile on one side of his face. "You're right. I killed that ... whatever he is. But Wilson, if you and the other assfucks in Washington follow this crap down the rabbit hole ... you're going to kill us all."

Trin started toward Riley, but Sarah pulled him back. And she did not let go.

Riley looked over to Trin and his smug smile turned sad. Was it because he'd just killed this young man's captain and shown the worst of himself, the worst of us, to a stranger? Did he lose his smirk because he saw Trin as an enemy with the face of an innocent? Or could it be that Wilson's words had finally sunk in and Riley's run at protecting what he believed in was over? Sarah would never know. Riley reached over with his other hand and changed his grip on the pistol so he was holding the gun by the barrel. He lowered it into Wilson's hand. Wilson grabbed the gun and moved back just a step. He looked to the men behind Riley.

"Sergeant, you and your men are to put Major Riley under arrest. Cuff him to the bunk in his quarters until we're back in Hawaii."

The sergeant hesitated just a moment, not quite sure if those were orders he actually had to follow, but Riley offered a curt nod of his head to concur with Wilson. The soldiers took him away. And that left just a small group of them alone with Argen's blood still warm on the table, along with the now-shared question of trust hanging in the air.

"I'm sorry," said Wilson to no one in particular.

Ganet gently let go of Argen, set the still-bleeding head back on the table, and closed the dead man's eyes. "We should return the captain to the *Kalelah*," Ganet said to Trin, more collected than before. "We can't leave him here like this."

Trin looked at Sarah. "We can't leave them either, sir."

"They just killed the captain, Trin. They killed my friend."

"Not they."

Ganet stood and rubbed his hands on his jumpsuit to wipe off the blood. He looked at Wilson, Sarah, and the others.

"Argen was right, you know. Laird is likely already on the move. She and the others. The *Kalelah* is probably being prepped for Correction as we speak."

"Then we have to move faster," Trin said. "The captain had a plan. I say we stick to it. Laird can go fuck herself, sir."

Ganet smiled at Trin's comment. Whoever this Laird person was, these two were not fans. But the chief didn't embrace Trin's conviction just yet. "The captain's plan included the captain. We're a big man short."

"We can do it. You take his place here. I'll handle the *Kalelah*."

"There's no taking his place. And you'll handle the *Kalelah*?" Ganet said incredulously. "The XO will eat you for a midday snack. Do you even shave yet?"

"I'm the youngest junior officer in the history of the service, sir. I jumped six grades in school. Which means I've been the youngest person in the fucking room for as long as I can remember. Which means I've had to kick bigger guys in the balls my whole life. And I can tell you this, they never see it coming. I'm smarter than Laird. With all due respect, I'm smarter than you. Our captain is dead. We owe him this. Your friend is dead. So I couldn't care the fuck less what you believe about our chances or whether or not you consider the population worthy. You owe him this. And yes, sir, I shave."

Ganet sighed. "Well, it better be twice a day, Analyst, because this will take a whole lot more than smarts. We'll be up against some very powerful forces." He stood now and squared his shoulders. "All right, boy genius. Who, then?"

Trin leaned his head toward Sarah. "This one."

"Wait, what?" Sarah said, startled.

Ganet gave a long look her way and sighed again. "You sure?"

"Yes sir. She can do it."

"Because you know her so well."

"It's a feeling, sir."

"What can I do?" Sarah said. Even she could hear the dread in her voice.

"Hold on a minute," Wilson interrupted. "No one's doing anything. We have protocols for first contact. This isn't one of them."

"We have protocols for this?" said Henderson, looking more stunned about that revelation than he had been about anything else so far, including Argen's original tale of a planet seeding gone bad. "This shit gets crazier by the second," he went on. "But I'm with Wilson here. Sarah ain't doing anything. For Christ's sake, she's not even a VP."

"Your choice," said Ganet. He looked neither disappointed nor pleased. "But if I were you," he continued. "I'd take any chance I could. Even if it meant losing one of your own right now."

Time fucking out.

"Hey assholes," she said loud enough to get the room's attention. "I don't know what everybody's even talking about, but I'm pretty sure I get a vote." She looked at Trin. "You said I could do it. So, tell me. *What* can I do?"

But it was Ganet who answered her.

"Trin thinks you can save the world."

2

Hanta Laird knelt in front of her prayer glass. She whispered along with the tiny halo Keeper, softly chanting the day's First Commitment. But she found no comfort in the words, nor any way to change course. It was only days since the scan alarm let the ship's Leadership know a profound failure had occurred.

The wind flies cold and wet against me, the way long.
With hair of ice and skin of blue naked I do trudge.
Yet still my heart it sings with joy.
For the path is Yours and given unto me.

At first, she was heartened by the news. Her plan had worked. The Halfborn had managed to survive without guidance. Better yet, they had advanced beyond her wildest imaginings. If she hadn't gone to all this trouble for a completely different reason, they'd make a fascinating study in feral development. That fat

Forent and his lab rats would have a field day up there. The population possessed language and art and technology, and most important of all, it exhibited exactly the violent and blasphemous qualities that ought to guarantee the kind of moral clarity God had been waiting for so desperately. All this was good.

But Argen's decision to delay Correction, to argue that it might actually be an *optional* course, tore at her. For him, of all people, to put himself so dramatically at odds with God was not part of her plan. She expected others, plenty of them, to argue the easy path—to let the sin of sentience without God go unanswered. Since the Great Flights began, eons ago, humankind had been steadily slipping, the distance making itself felt more deeply with every generation. A crack here, a crack there. Each on its own can seem benign, just a hairline. But put them together and the weakness compounds and before you know it, before any real salvation can happen, the whole house comes down.

Salvation. She whispered the word when the Keeper paused for a breath. That was the whole point of setting into motion the disaster the *Kalelah* now faced. But Argen's break was a disappointing curve. She had expected so much more of him. If not for the sake of his own soul, then for hers. He was her lover, after all; didn't he know anything about her? It was like he didn't know how much his weakness would cut at her. Or maybe he just didn't care. Like the rest of them.

She put a bent finger to her eye to catch a tear. She looked at the drop and was surprised to discover it was real. She was really crying over Argen—over a man? Over a lover? It didn't seem possible. She had fought against just this sort of foolishness her whole life. However real and consuming they felt, however dizzy, breathless, or wet they made her, she knew the loves of this life were just practice. God's love, and hers for Him, were the real targets, the real reasons for everything. She had told herself a thousand times that what had been happening between her and Argen was mere biology, nothing more. That's what it needed to be. Clearly it had been for him.

Stop this inane leaking, she scolded herself. These tears were not about a man or even her feelings. These tears, she lectured her heart, were about a moral disappointment at the highest level. The highest level. If a captain, an authority in charge of God's most sacred mission, could lose his grip so easily, then what hope was there for the rest of them? What hope was there for God? Who wouldn't find a tear for such a state?

She got to her feet as the digital Keeper in the glass continued his chanting.

The way is stone, jagged, broken, and without mercy.
With feet bare, blistered, and shrieking I do plod.
Yet still my heart it sings with joy.
For the path is Yours and given unto me.

She walked to her closet, took out a gold hanging bag, and laid it on her bed. She went to her mirror and looked at her reflection. Another tear streamed down her face and into the corner of her mouth. The bitter taste of salt somehow woke her to what was really going on inside her. These weren't the tears of an injured lover or her purist soul crying for the cause. She was scared. The absolute control she thought she had over events simply wasn't real. Argen slipping so completely and without debate was a horrible miss. Whether he truly understood her was irrelevant. It was she who didn't know *him* well enough. And as she looked in the mirror at the sad spectacle of her red-rimmed eyes and her wet face, it became all too clear she didn't know herself either. She rubbed her eyes with the heels of her hands. She pushed the tears away but they came right back.

God, please. I can bear the knife in my gut. But must you twist it, too?

She decided not to let this turn into a childlike monsoon. She sat for a moment and did not think about Argen, whether she loved him or not, or the code she loaded into the *Kalelah*'s clock. She did not think of the heathen Tanter and the ugly gurgling sound his met-tube made when she pulled it from his mouth and ensured he'd never wake again. She listened to the Keeper chanting and moved her lips with his song. And after a little while, she could rub her face and her hands would not be wet. She went to the mirror again and tidied up her hair. Then she turned to the bed and stood looking at the gold bag.

She tapped her identification code on the glass that covered the clasps along the bag's closure. At the prompt, she bent and directed a soft breath onto the glass's flora sensor. The clasp released and she opened the bag. She took out the jumpsuit bearing a captain's rank and stepped into it. As she laced up her shoes, the

149

Keeper sang on, and the *Kalelah*'s new leader continued to whisper along.

> *The sky is black and starless and guides me not.*
> *Twisted, weak, and blind, on knees of blood I crawl.*
> *Yet still my heart it sings with joy.*
> *For the path is Yours and given unto me.*

She pulled open her drawer and retrieved a metal case she hadn't looked at since her days in training. Lifetimes ago. She opened the lid, took out the weapon, checked its works, strapped the braided metal belt around her hip, and holstered the heavy piece.

She knelt a final moment in front of the glass. In its dark and polished surface, she could see the reflection of her eyes, no longer red and welling but clear and steady. With the Keeper's last word, she got up again and walked toward her door and the day she would grimly rewrite the *Kalelah*'s mission and make His stand.

As she pushed her way to the concourse of Leaf One, she whispered softly. *For the path is Yours and given unto me.*

3

Rome's summer had been especially hot and humid. Even so, Father Balsconi suggested he meet the visitors near the river and escort them on foot. Black cars and the entourages these people normally traveled with would be sure to attract unwanted attention. Best to be just six simple priests, looking the parts of uncelebrated cogs in the working machinery of Vatican bureaucracy. Men who did not even rank a parking space for their Fiats inside the walls let alone drivers. He had them dress in priestly black, take the train from the airport to Lepanto station, and walk the two blocks to Via Pompeo Magno, where he was waiting. Those who would shook hands, others just bowed their heads slightly, and they were on their way.

They took an indirect route, keeping to the narrowest streets with the most shade. He had planned on giving them two hours to walk what would have been less than two kilometers if they had kept to a straight line. These were old men and the heat was merciless. He kept the pace easy. He tried to get the men talking, but they didn't engage beyond a one- or two-word reply. Before long he stopped trying, and they just walked.

Near the Piazza del Catalone, there was a small fountain built into a wall and old cement benches placed among the cobblestones nearby. A bakery was just across the tiny square on a narrow street, and he went to the shop while his charges took seats at the benches under the canopy of a large and ancient ash tree. Moments later he came out with two loaves of salty bread, sat down at the end of a bench, and tore the loaves in pieces. Then the men fed the birds like men in no rush to get back to business that required no urgency. An ice vendor rang his bell as he peddled by on his dented and pockmarked cart, decorated with the fading images of lemons, crushed ice, and happy colored cups. The ice vendor spared the solemn men his usual singsong pitch, knowing they would refuse. He simply touched the brim of his sweat-stained American baseball cap as he went by and readied his salesmanship for the bench ahead where a small boy was already tugging at the sleeve of his exhausted mother. The odd group sat in silence, the fountain spray misting every so often in their direction with the luck of an occasional breeze. When the bread was gone and the birds with it, the old men and the priest got up and continued their slow walk.

They kept to the smaller streets until they entered Via dei Corridori, which would take them to the colonnade that ringed the north edge of the great piazza bustling with tourists and pilgrims. They stayed among the towering columns, enjoying their shade and cover.

Via dei Corridori ends at an old iron fence and gate that separates the road's walking traffic from the palace and the papal apartments just beyond. There was a stone-faced gendarme behind the gate who said and did nothing as the priest retrieved a large brass key from his pocket and twisted open the old lock. The key had not been easy to obtain and would not be his for long. Getting the key had been a project all its own. Names were dropped, privileges traded. But if something needed getting, Father Balsconi knew how to get it.

The key opened two additional doors that brought Balsconi and his odd flock to a dark circular stair hall just a few levels below the pope's apartments. These winding metal stairs he knew would stop short of the top floor, but they'd take him to parts of this palace he'd never been. Inside the tight space, there was little change in the temperature. The humidity, though, was far worse. As he and the others slowly climbed the clanging spiral of the narrow and windowless stairway, he could feel the sweat roll down his back and collect along the waist of his trousers. He stopped and turned to the old men, worried of leaving them too far behind.

"My apologies for these ancient, twisting stairs. And the air conditioning is not so good here, I'm afraid. We are having a bad summer."

"Most of us are from the Middle East," the youngest of the old men said, his thickly accented Italian making his geographic reference unnecessary. "We always have a bad summer."

Finally, an answer in the form of a full sentence. He decided to push his luck.

"Of course, how stupid of me. Still, I cannot help but feel badly about the weather. Discomfort can be a distraction. And the topic of conversation with His Holiness is so important. I pray much progress is made today."

"If you don't mind my asking, Father, what is your age?" said the Israeli a few steps behind him.

"I seem young. I hear this often."

"Yes. And are you also in disguise?" He laughed. "Is there a red galero hidden away in your pocket, maybe? Are we being escorted through the back stairways of Vatican City by a secret cardinal?"

"No, Rabbi," he answered flatly. "I am a humble priest. A servant like the rest."

A pause.

"I was just joking, Father," the Israeli said humorlessly. "Please don't be offended. We're grateful for your efforts and your cunning." And the Israeli's attention shifted back to his climbing, the sudden interest he showed in Balsconi gone.

"My pleasure," Balsconi offered.

He turned to offer the sincerest smile he could muster, one he knew would convince but also acknowledge the truth: His attempt to get anything more out of these men would fail. He'd have to be patient. Which, when the situation required, he could be.

When they had finished their spinning climb, he kept the group to interior hallways, away from windows and the risk of cameras. The temperature brought out the odor of age in the wood behind the plaster walls and the still, moist air was filled with the scent. It was a pleasant aroma. It smelled like history and it made him feel at home.

At last he reached the door to the private library. He pushed it open to reveal a small antechamber with yet another door, this one tall and polished brass and flanked by two Swiss guards. The priest showed them his ID. One guard checked an iPad, looked over the group one by one without expression, and then opened the door leading into the next room. But before Balsconi could enter, the other guard took hold of his elbow and pulled him aside while motioning for the others to proceed. When the darkly dressed men had walked through the threshold, the guards closed the door, leaving Balsconi in the antechamber.

"I was told to bring them," he said to the guard on his right.

"You brought them."

"There must be a mistake. Check your list again."

"There's no mistake. *Father.*"

"His Holiness himself made the request."

"I'll bet you're proud. Now fuck off."

"Why would Papa specifically ask for me and then keep me from the room? It makes no sense."

"If you were supposed to know, you wouldn't need to ask."

"Come on now, move along," said the second guard.

He turned and made his way back toward the hot, humid stairs. He wasn't insulted by his treatment from the guards. They were just doing their jobs, and he'd experienced worse. He decided, too, that he had gotten plenty from his strange guests' silence. A little mystery, a stubborn knot to undo, was even to be welcomed. He was bored as a second assistant to a middling bishop who'd never make the college. He needed a side project, and this was looking like exactly the right kind. If there was one thing he'd learned in his six years at the Vatican, it was this: The less people talk about something, the more valuable that something is. Never had he been so close to the central players and still been so completely in the dark. This had all the markings of a six-figure leak. All he had to do was find the right pressure point.

He put his hand in his pocket as he wound his way back down the dark stairway and took out the big, heavy key he'd used to open the old gate. He spun it around his fingers and then tossed it high into the air along the outside edge of the spiral staircase. The key flipped over and over upward into the dark until it lost momentum, and the tarnished piece of ancient brass began to fall again. The priest kept moving downward through the dimly lit stairway. After two more circles around the stairs, he stretched out his arm, opened his hand, grabbed the key from its fall, and put it back in his pocket. The key, he knew, was just the beginning of what would soon fall into his hands.

4

Trin piloted the little transport back to the hole it bore earlier in the sediment that covered the *Kalelah*. With the giant ship still buried and the guide crew idled by the discovery that the time for guiding the population on the surface had long since passed, their work over before it ever really began, there'd been no need for dock control. Trin was able to initiate the parking sequence without communications with Command. On a human level, he was flying below the radar. No person, at least, knew the transport had ever left the ship.

The *Kalelah*, though, was a different matter. She and the little transport were inseparable, leashed together by a digital frequency that kept mother in constant touch with her child. A careful record of where the transport had gone these last three hours, and with whom, was already in the *Kalelah*'s database. A security team could find it in minutes. Trin was betting on his ability to find it even faster.

He guided the little craft through the *Kalelah's* mostly dark airlock. He hovered while the outer doors shut, the lock drained, and the doors to the ports proper opened. The rows of berths and bays were even darker and seemed completely deserted. Not even a maintenance person in sight. *You're a lucky fuck.*

But he knew this was the easiest part of what lay before them. While he was pretty confident his own empty post might not have been too keenly felt for so short a period of time, he knew Captain Argen's and Chief Ganet's absences were sure to be noticed. They'd have pushed a nervous question throughout the CC. And then there was Sarah, for whom no good explanation existed.

She was quiet the entire way down from the surface to the ship, her movements small, tight, like a bird on the wrong tree. When Trin put the transport into its bay, she let out a breath.

"It's okay. We made it," he said.

"So far." She straightened her shoulders a touch. "But it's not going to work, you know."

"It has to work. If Laird starts the Correction, there won't be any stopping it."

"You don't know us. What Wilson and Ganet are trying to do ... people have tried forever. It's never worked."

"It's probably hard for you to grasp what a Correction is all about. We fail and there'll be no safe place, nowhere to hide. Everyone dies. Everyone and everything."

"Everyone's died before. Lots of times."

There was a gloomy confidence in her voice that told him not to interrupt her with the obvious: her own existence was a pretty convincing argument against whatever point she was trying to make.

"In grad school, I saw pictures of dig sites where the only way to explain all the human bones being found in the same layer of sediment was war. Babies, boys, girls, men, and women, all dead at once. There were thin, sharpened blades of rock next to neck bones. There were round rocks next to skulls. Those people didn't know a world any bigger than what they could walk in a day's time. Two thousand dead would have been the entire universe to them. It would have been everyone. And massacres like that happened over and over. They still happen. There's a lot of people like Riley in the world."

"You're not like Riley."

"We're all a little like Riley."

He looked at her and said nothing. This wasn't the first time since he'd met her that Trin had found himself just looking at her, nearly stunned by her beauty, saying nothing. His fascination shamed him. The direness of the situation should have made noticing her in this way entirely irresponsible, or even impossible, but he couldn't help it. And why? He could name a dozen women with blonde hair like hers—Cyler, for one. And the ship was full of women with her long legs, her seemingly perfect breasts, and her full lips. But this woman had a presence he'd never seen before. A force both familiar and foreign. It hit him the instant he saw her on the deck of the *Lewis*. She'd been watching the three of them walk down the transport's ladder, he'd been last behind Ganet with Argen in the lead. The only thing that should have been on his mind was first contact. After all, it had never happened before, at least not that he'd ever been told. Contact was strictly forbidden on E-check. Or ever, actually.

Guiding never happened directly; it was always from a distance, invisible, untraceable. But all he could see as he made his way down the ladder to the most historic moment in Service history was her. He'd been nervous. Argen was nervous. Ganet was beyond nervous. But she'd seemed more interested than nervous. He could sense it from up on the ladder. Her hair was blowing wildly in the stiff breeze, but she hadn't seemed to care. She never once reached up to smooth it or contain it. And of all the faces he saw looking up at him those few hours ago, hers was the only welcoming face. She was the only one to look at them without even a hint of judgment or panic. Even when Riley first challenged the captain, she stayed open. That was why he picked her. Wasn't it?

Now, getting ready to bring her into his world, he wondered what she'd be like if the glitch that had forced the *Kalelah* to stay in Skip sleep too long hadn't happened. What if the 120,000 years the population had developed on their own had been guided as they were designed to be? Would she still be as strangely compelling? Would he still be fighting the urge to touch her, to move in slowly and kiss her neck? Or would she be just another beautiful woman?

He turned and reached back behind the second seat and twisted the handle of a small panel on the side of the transport's cabin.

She looked out the ship's big front glass to the docking bay surrounding the transport. "Can I smoke here?"

"Smoke?"

"Yeah, is it okay to smoke here? Or is that not cool?"

"Of course it's not cool. Smoke would be hot. Warm at least. A vapor, though, that can be cold. What are you talking about?" he said, still fiddling with the handle.

"Never mind. Forget it."

Trin offered a small shrug as an apology and returned his attention to the cabin wall. He had the little panel off now, revealing a small storage compartment. He reached in and pulled out a jumpsuit of low rank.

"You need to put this on."

"Here?"

"You can't leave this transport in those clothes. You'll draw attention to yourself too soon."

She took the jumpsuit. "Beige? This is a bad color for me. It's a bad color for everybody. And it looks big."

"It'll get you to our first stop. The jumpsuit is the least of our problems."

"What's the most?" she asked, smelling the jumpsuit and crinkling her nose.

"Your cloud."

"My cloud?"

"Yours is fucked."

"What, exactly, is my cloud? And why is it fucked?"

"Every complex being is surrounded by a veil of viruses and bacteria. A microbe cloud. And each is more unique than a fingerprint or even a pupil. Yours won't be recognized, it won't scan. That'll be a problem."

"When will it be a problem?" She held a hand up in the light to examine it.

"Sooner than we want."

"Great. Okay, turn around."

"Why?"

"I'm not changing my clothes in front of you."

"Why not?"

"Because people don't do that."

"Of course they do."

"Not women in front of men. Turn around. Please."

He did as she asked. But with the protective-alloy wool on the outside of the transport's windows back in place, the inside of the glass was nearly as reflective as a mirror. He could see her almost as clearly as if he hadn't turned at all. God, she was beautiful. But she was serious about him giving her some kind of privacy. Reluctantly, he turned his head just enough to respect her wishes and waited for the all clear. Could another woman have made him do that? He didn't think so.

When she was ready, they opened the lower hatch and walked down the laddered stairs to the dock's main concourse. Sarah looked up at the metal ceiling with its graceful arches and its soft lighting and its impossible height.

"Jesus Christ."

"Don't talk out here. You need a language dose first. And don't gawk at everything like it's the first time you're seeing it."

"Well, it's my first time on an alien spaceship, so, you know, manage your expectations, okay?"

"Don't think of it that way. As alien."

"Oh, right. It's my great-great-great-great-great-great-grandma's house. I just didn't recognize the curtains."

"And this is just the dock. When we leave this area, things will look stranger still. Can you stay calm?"

She took a deep breath and let it out. "I'll be cool."

He raised an eyebrow. "I have nothing else for you to wear right now. Can you stay calm?"

She managed a small smile. "Yes."

The two walked another fifty yards to the large door that would take them to the lower level of Stem Six. He waved his hand across the glass in the door, leaving small, glowing, white dots where flora sensors did their work. The dots quickly turned green, and the door slid left and the lower stem of Leaf Six opened up before them. Trin walked quickly ahead.

But Sarah moved slowly, taking just two steps past the threshold before stopping. The stem was not particularly crowded, but like every thoroughfare in the *Kalelah*, it was a city unto itself. Its scale dwarfed that of the dock and its own massive concourse. As Sarah looked around, her eyes fluttered, and she dropped to her knees and then gently fell to her side.

Trin ran back, bent down, put one arm under her head, and lightly slapped her cheek. Her eyes opened slowly, reluctantly, and as she was about to speak, a voice called out.

"Is she hurt?"

"She's fine," Trin quickly called over his shoulder. "Just hungry I think. Sir."

A gray-haired woman in a lieutenant's jumpsuit kneeled down next to Trin to get a closer look. She put her hand on Sarah's forehead. "She's cold."

"Like I said. Probably hungry."

"How are you feeling, Initiate?" the woman asked. "Can you stand?"

Sarah looked at the woman with groggy eyes and brushed her fingers across the woman's collar. "Such a pretty color."

The lieutenant looked at Trin, confused, and then back to Sarah. "What did you say, dear?"

"Maybe she shouldn't talk right now," said Trin. "I'll get us a table over there and some food."

"Are you sure? That was strange. I've never heard sounds like that. She's probably delirious."

"She's done this before. She gets some food and she's better. Thank you, Lieutenant, very kind of you to stop. I promise to watch her."

"All right, Analyst," the woman said as she got back on her feet. "You do that. As I'm sure you know, this Waking was unusually deadly. If she doesn't snap back quickly, you get her to a hospital."

"Yes, sir. And thank you."

Trin got her on her feet and walked them both slowly to a nearby café. "I'm going to get you something to drink. Can you sit straight?"

"I think so."

"Shit, that was bad. Don't make eye contact with anyone and, please, don't speak. That lieutenant could have fucked this whole thing."

"What thing? What is this plan of yours? I can't possibly blend into ..." She looked around her. "This."

"That's the plan. Temporarily, anyway."

"I don't get it."

"When the time is right, your job is to be yourself."

"That sounds like a stupid plan."

"It's the one we've got."

"Jesus."

"You're going to have to stop saying that."

"I thought you said be yourself."

Trin tapped a triangular piece of glass embedded in the left sleeve of his suit and a small array of numbers and graphics floated between them. He touched several of the digits and the float collapsed and disappeared.

"What did you just do?"

"I reached out to a friend. She can help us for a bit while you dose."

"How do you know she'll be on our side?"

"She'll be on my side."

"Oh."

Their eyes met just briefly.

5

Sitting safely if not exactly comfortably on a small metal chair, Sarah was able to look around the enormous concourse and not worry about her knees going wobbly again. If someone had asked her to imagine what might be inside the object she'd discovered just days ago at the bottom of an abyssal sea, the impossible thing that looked like a giant arrowhead, she'd never have come close to the reality of it. *Is this real?*

She remembered the stupefying fascination she'd felt on her first trip to New York. This was before her mother had even met her stepfather. It was just the three of them then, two little girls and a young mother probably just a year or two older than Sarah was now. They spent nearly two days on a bus from Ohio and the first thing her mother wanted to do was go to the train station. "Why do we have to go *there*?" Sarah complained. "You'll see," her mother said, "you'll see." They walked for blocks, Sarah between her mother and her sister, each lugging a small, cheap suitcase on wobbly plastic wheels.

It seemed like an eternity until they reached their destination and pushed their way through enormous brass doors and into a tall passageway. There were no tracks or trains like she'd expected. Instead, there was a beautiful marketplace. Flowers and pastries and food of every conceivable kind lined the sides of the passage. Every other inch of the place seemed filled with people. Delicious aromas and the sounds of a dozen languages filled the air. She wanted to stop at every stand but her mother insisted they keep moving.

When at last they reached the end of the market, she understood why her mother had walked them across half of Manhattan. Just beyond the mouth of the passage, the throngs of people thinned out and the world seemed to open up to the sky itself. The sun streamed down in square shafts of white light onto a polished stone floor shiny as a mirror. It was like a scene from her *Golden Children's Bible*. She half expected to see Christ himself appear at the top of one of the ornate stairways to preach. This was the main concourse of the Grand Central Terminal, her mother declared with a kind of pride that suggested she might have designed the spectacle herself. Sarah was so taken she couldn't utter a word. She just stood looking up, her mouth agape and her free hand limp at her side. It was the biggest and most imposing thing she had ever seen in her life. And the most beautiful. She remembered feeling dizzy in those first moments. With its soaring windows and its ceiling painted with stars and constellations, it truly seemed the universe complete.

When she caught her breath and looked around, most people weren't gazing at the roof in amazement or even much aware of their surroundings. They were just going somewhere and in a rush about it. That's what struck her the most—that people could just walk through a place like the main concourse of Grand Central and seemingly feel no awe at all. It was just normal to them, routine, home. She never understood why, but their nonchalance made her feel different and foreign and it stole the joy from her own wonderment. She looked at her sister and mother. Entirely happy being tourists, looking and pointing, they showed no signs of sharing even a shred of her inner conflict. There would be many such moments to come in her life, but that was her first taste of loneliness, right there in the heart of Grand Central Terminal, amid thousands of people and even the two who loved her most in all the world.

Yet the place Trin had taken her dwarfed the Grand Central Terminal. New York itself was a primitive backwater compared to where she suddenly found herself. And once again she seemed to be the one marveling at the ceiling while everyone else went about their daily routines, oblivious or simply desensitized to the wonder of it. And worse, this time her jaw had dropped so hard she had fainted and actually hit the ground. *Nice move, Sarah. Slick.*

She watched the crew as they went about their business in their different-colored jumpsuits. A few were soft lavender or sky blue and warm green. Most, though, were the horrible beige she wore. She had no clue what any of the colors signified, though she guessed just by the number of jumpsuits that beige was the universal color of ordinary. Then she looked past the uniforms to the people. Their hair, their eyes, their faces. She looked for horns, for monstrosities, for anything that might make what Argen had told them easier to disbelieve. But all she saw were people, extraordinary only by the story she'd been told about them. And about her. If everything she'd heard was true, these were her people too. And she theirs. Yet never in her entire life had she felt so strange.

No, Trin, "alien" is the perfect word.

She closed her eyes and pictured herself back on the mid-deck of the *Lewis*, with the starboard view of the ocean spread out to infinity before her. In her mind, she saw an endless gray-blue beneath a soft pink and orange glow of the day's last light falling behind the edge of the world. She imagined the sounds of the ship's engines, the water's frothy wake along the hull, and a bird's call, thin and high and moving away from the ship to who knows where. She conjured a cigarette between her fingers with such potent realism she could actually feel it there, smooth, tightly packed, and promising. She lit it and took in the warm chimera of smoke as far as she could.

It was a long time before she exhaled.

6

Behind the large metal doors somewhere in the Vatican, in the room Balsconi was not allowed to enter, gathered what looked like a joke that starts like this: "A priest, a rabbi, a preacher, and an imam walk into a bar."

The pope had called a secret meeting among several of the world's leading religious figures. Not a woman among them, a tradition not even this peculiar moment could change. Getting them to agree to come at all had not been easy. But once one agreed, they all agreed. Rivalry, it seems, never loses its magic touch.

Together, these wary men represented more than half the world's faithful. They took their teacups in hand and shared pleasantries for a few moments, but even for these jaundiced and practiced politicians, the small talk seemed particularly shallow. They all knew what needed to happen here, so why not just get on with it already? And so, the pope, a beardless rabbi, a stern Saudi, a slick-haired American preacher, and an old and fragile imam began the unwelcome task of discussing the surreal situation in which the world had been plunged. The alien equivalent of Moses's tablets had suddenly been thrust upon them by strange and powerful new prophets. A man who called himself captain of an impossible ship and a man named Smenth Ganet had risen from the ocean to challenge their notions of God and speak of the end of the world.

A response was required. What kind of response? Well, that was the question of all questions. And they all knew it.

"God is testing us," said the pope once everyone had taken seats around the lavishly appointed room.

"God is always testing us," the Saudi scoffed, looking down at the glowing phone in his right hand.

"Yes, but this is a test we have to pass together."

The sheikh, looking uncomfortable in his borrowed disguise of collar and cassock, kept his eyes on the screen. He spoke softly, but there was a hard bite to his tone. "The world holding hands. United in its show of consensus. It's a pleasant fantasy. But a fantasy."

"Nothing is impossible. I think we know that now to be true."

"And yet I see no Greek beard here, no Tibetan monk. No Hindi. Some of us are not even the most senior representatives of our faiths. Not quite a *minion*, right?" he said to his phone.

The rabbi didn't take the bait, so the sheikh continued in his work of discrediting what hadn't yet even truly begun.

"They say you are a brave man, most Holy Father. A different thinker from your predecessors. And yet here you are, hoping for a miracle."

"I don't hope for a miracle. I intend to produce one."

The Saudi looked up for just a brief moment, enough to convey the futility he saw in the pope's determination. But it was just a flash. He returned his gaze to his phone.

"Are you preoccupied, sheikh?" said the pope. "Has the end of the world come at a bad time for you?"

The Saudi met the pope's eyes and smiled. "Apologies. A man of my times, I'm afraid." He let his smile recede. "The American president, Lee, you met with him personally?"

"I did."

"And how did you respond to him, the president?" He said the last word with a touch of a sneer.

"Are you asking if I believe him?"

"You should not believe him, not one little bit," interrupted the man with the Mississippi accent and light-colored hair oiled back from his forehead. "This is not a president to trust. Why, if Lee told me it was gonna be sunny and warm tomorra, I'd pack a coat and carry an umbrella." He chuckled alone. He plowed on, oblivious to the audience's indifference or perhaps inspired by it.

"See, I'm not here because of anythin' those people in Washington are tellin' us. I didn't need to see the scanner evidence. I didn't need a meetin' with the Defense and State Departments. Oh, I listened to their engineers and their astrophysicists and their biologists. I sat through it all, but I needed none of it. Not one shred of it. And do you know why?" No one answered. "Because this isn't science. And this isn't politics." The man from Mississippi, his face flush now, his eyes piercing, put his teacup on a low table in front of the huge sofa at which he sat and slowly unfolded his nearly seven-foot-tall body to stand for his next point. "This is Providence, pure and simple. This is Scripture in action." He paused as if to give the room a chance to soak it in, exactly how he did every Sunday morning standing in the center of the pulpit-in-the-round of his enormous church packed to the I-beam rafters with more than fifteen thousand rapt congregants. After a few dramatic seconds had ticked away, he sucked in a breath and resumed his oration with a closing argument that finally produced a response from the unusual audience. Though perhaps not the response he wanted.

"A red heifer has been seen," he said, eyes closed, his head tilted slightly upward.

The pope sighed heavily.

"Red like hellfire! Red like blood! Red like the sun setting on the end of days!"

"He is very good," said the Saudi, checking his phone once again. "Really, I am quite entertained."

"You don't have to believe *me*, sheikh," the oily preacher said with a practiced thousand-watt smile, seemingly unfazed by the sarcasm. "Because I have, in my hand, the word of the Lord." And he did. A well-used, leather-bound Bible was clasped between the gigantic fingers of his left hand; a large gold pinky ring sparkled brightly against the pebbled, black skin of the book. "There are no fairy tales or fables in Scripture. The testaments are not metaphors, and what's about to happen to the world is no drill. It is real. The signs are all lit. Gentlemen, we must accept the fact—nay, we must *celebrate* the fact—that His time is at hand." Perhaps by force of habit, the preacher stayed standing after his climactic finish, as if waiting for the thunderous roar he usually receives. But this was not his mega church surrounded by a four-thousand-car parking lot. So he simply closed his eyes once more, made the long crouch back down to a sitting position, and, with as much studied dignity as possible, said, "Amen."

"I wish and pray that it were so," said the pope softly, already looking exhausted, though the meeting had begun just minutes ago. "But the cardinals have been working day and night on this subject since our meeting with the president. We do not see God's moment here. We see something else. We see his work in grave danger. We see a task here for us in this room. Our job is to save God's creation. That is the test at hand. And peace among us is how we survive this test."

The old, gray imam whose thick eyebrows ignored his age by clinging stubbornly to the black color of his youth sat in the corner some distance from the rest and gently cleared his throat. But for the dark line above his narrow eyes, he was ancient and frail, practically swallowed whole by his ill-fitting Catholic vestments.

"Here in this room, where no blood has spilled, we have the luxury to talk of peace," he said in a voice so low and soft and aged it forced the others into silence and complete attention. He made no eye contact. He only looked into his cup of tea as if divining his next thought from the surface of the liquid. "But away from this room, away from this palace, our people are centuries at war. A time long enough to count as forever. Oppressed and oppressors all. How can these things be forgotten?"

"They can't," said the pope. "But peace doesn't demand amnesia. Just forgiveness. And a willingness to focus on the things we share."

"*Adonai echad,*" the beardless rabbi said to no one in particular.

"The Lord is One," said the Saudi, translating the Hebrew, his eyes flickering up from his screen seemingly awakened by the Israeli. "The last words of the Shema. What's your point?"

"Ah, I think you know my point." The clean-shaven rabbi looked around the room. "All the great faiths believe this, the concept of Oneness. In the Qur'an, it says that everywhere you turn is the face of Allah." He looked toward the preacher now. "In John we read 'He who has seen Me has seen the Father.' And my people say '*Adonai echad*—God is One. And God is everywhere. So, he must, by default, be there, too." He pointed upward. "Among the distant stars?"

"You mean what if the god these people from the ship describe is … God?" said the pope.

"Yes. What if the God who revealed himself to Abraham, deafened the throngs at Mount Sinai, and spoke to the Prophets is also *their* god? In fact, if we believe what we believe about God, how could that *not* be the case?"

"This is blasphemy," croaked the imam.

"No," said the rabbi. "It's logic. Simple logic. Either God is One or He's not. But, of course, He is. We all say it. Every day we all say it. And we all believe it."

"Belief is one thing," said the preacher, who even when sitting was still the most physically imposing presence in the room. "And salvation is another. This is the apocalypse, make no mistake. Which means this is the time to choose sides. That's why I'm here today, gentlemen. To help you choose right. To help the world choose right. So we can all find salvation."

The rabbi smiled. "You make my argument for me, reverend. I'm saying that belief must now matter more than the differing *ways* we believe."

"Are you about to suggest we convert?" asked the sheikh incredulously.

"The entrance to heaven depends not on affiliation but on doing righteous deeds, yes?" the rabbi answered with another nod to the Qur'an.

"And the righteous deed you are proposing now is to abandon Allah?"

"Not at all. We just change the *way* we worship God."

"You've got it all wrong, sir," said the American. "Why, now is the time to fight. My friends, this is the war we've been waitin' for! The Antichrist is here, and together we are gonna bring down from heaven the Army of Jesus. I have ministries all over the world prayin' on this. Make no mistake. Our Savior is coming home. And when I say our Savior, I mean the redeemer of us all. When the Prophet conquered Mecca, he sent his followers into the Kaaba to destroy the idols. But two objects were spared, and do you know what they were? I'll tell you what they were. The icons of Mary and Jesus. Everything else was smashed, broken to bits, but the Prophet saved the Virgin and the Son of God. Because the Prophet also knew this day would come."

The Saudi sheikh clicked off his phone angrily and pushed it into the big sleeve of his borrowed cassock. "I'm afraid the time for superficial politeness is over. You think in those stone carvings and chiseled blocks of marble the Prophet saw something of the divine? Something truly sacred? No. He spared those objects simply to teach his followers the ideas of restraint and respect. Lessons I am having a more difficult time heeding with every minute of this discussion."

"Let me remind you all, please," the rabbi interrupted. "We are about to be outlawed, forbidden. Eliminated. Unless we finally stand together."

This seemed to wake the old imam, who had again gone quiet in the corner, his eyes closed. "Ah, yes, we are back to the beginning. To the idea of together. A grand bargain. Shia and Sunni, Jew, Christian, and Hindi, an instant collective. You sound like the American president, though this is to be expected. Stand together, he says while he tears the world apart. So tell us, for what shall we stand? Apostasy?"

"A game."

"What game?"

"The oldest. The game of survival. It's one my people have had to play for nearly all of our existence. We're quite good at it."

"So far," said the Iranian into his tea.

The pope again sighed loudly. "Go on, Rabbi, please."

"In fifteenth-century Spain, it was illegal to be a Jew. Or a Muslim, for that matter."

"We all know the history," said the imam, waving his hand for the rabbi to get on with it.

"Then you know there remained those Spaniards who observed the Sabbath and those who rolled their prayer mats out in the direction of Mecca five times a day."

"And many were caught and killed, I'm ashamed to say," said the pope.

"Because they were betrayed. By their neighbors, their customers, their friends—"

"By *Christians*," said the imam.

"Yes. By Christians," said the rabbi. "But soon, being a Christian won't mean anything. Being a Christian won't save you. Being a Muslim won't save you. Soon, we'll all be … *others*. Every earthly faith will be suspect. We'll all be Jews."

The sheikh howled a cynical laugh.

"This doesn't have to be an apocalypse," the rabbi continued. "What we need is time. Unity and a bit of deception buy it for us. The mouth is not the heart. We tell them what they want. Outwardly, we buy in. After all, *Adonai echad*. Oneness. We all look out for each other. But in our basements, in our basements we remember."

"I won't be a modern-day converso," said the reverend from Mississippi. "But more important, you're still missin' the big point. This *does* have to be an apocalypse. Jerusalem's time has come. Your time, Rabbi. God is telling you this is your real fight. And your last time to enlist. When His Army comes, you need Jesus in your heart. You need Christ as your Savior. Let me help you. Let me help you all."

178

"I don't need saving," snapped the sheikh. "And Rabbi, you think we have this power? That God would even allow what you're suggesting?"

Now the pope stood. "God gave us the Earth to protect. All of its creatures, we among them, are our responsibility. Our sacred responsibility."

"You think we can ask billions to worship falsely? You will ask Catholics to surrender canon law? You are not this brave."

"Constantine persuaded millions to change how they worship. He took ritual elements of pagan beliefs and mixed them with the teachings of Christianity, and he saved countless lives. We, together, could do the same."

"Constantine was an emperor, and of only a tiny swath of the world. A much bigger part of it didn't even know his name. And for his trouble he is broiling in hell. What you propose is an unholy compromise."

The pope sat again and drank from his cup of tea. "This would hardly be the first time the House of Saud has made a deal of convenience."

"Not, I think, with the frequency and facility of the Holy See. Your predecessors are quite expert at facing the malignant by looking the other way. But in this, Islam cannot. The invaders will pay in blood for their lies."

"It can't always come back to blood," said the pope.

"While the devils are here in this world, we have no choice," croaked the old imam. "And this, too, is a devil's game. But which devil is the trickster this time? The Zionist devil, the American devil, the Christian devil, or the jinn in their bottle from space?"

The pope thumped the desktop with his hand. "These old battles must end! They can't matter anymore. We actually have a common cause now, for the first time in human history." He was nearly shouting.

"A common cause?" the ancient man scoffed. But he did not raise his voice or shake his fist. For the first time, he actually picked his head up to look at the others in the room. He spoke even more softly than before. "Yes. It is common only because we have seen it so many times before. In every century, your cause is the same. The end of Islam."

The pope leaned forward in his chair and looked the gray cleric hard in the eyes. "Or the end of *man*, imam. Which now would you choose?"

The imam stood and walked slowly toward the door. The sheikh rose with him and took his arm to steady the old man's travels across the carpets. As the sheikh grabbed the handle to open the door, the stooped Iranian turned back to the small group of men, and now his eyebrows drew an even darker line across his long, crinkled face.

"Allah will decide."

And then the two bitter enemies walked out of the room, arm in arm.

The pope slumped back in his large chair. He didn't look surprised, nor he did look the least bit hopeful. He just looked tired. More tired than even the most inopportune photograph of His Holy Father, the pope, ever captured. It was a face that could never be shown outside the secret library with the imposter priests, because it was a face that would bring millions to their knees, shaking with fear.

Whether the pope knew it or not, that day was soon coming in any event.

> *"Therefore wait for Me," declares the Lord,*
> *"For the day when I rise up as a witness.*
> *Indeed, My decision is to gather nations,*
> *To assemble kingdoms,*
> *To pour out on them My indignation,*
> *All My burning anger;*
> *For all the earth will be devoured*
> *By the fire of My zeal."*
>
> *—Zephaniah 3:8*

7

"God help us," she whispered to herself.

The Keeper studied the space where she had aired the video view of Stem One, her piercing green eyes scanning the image rapidly, double-checking areas of the blue-gray float to confirm the grim details.

Given the bitter split within the Leadership over the status of the Delivery, she couldn't say she was entirely surprised by what she was seeing, but it frightened her nonetheless. Things had somehow deteriorated badly. There was no other explanation for the scene playing out in front of her: Moving confidently through the crush of midday traffic crowding the concourse that connected Leaf One to the main stem of the ship strode the ship's captain.

There was no denying it. The jumpsuit, white with gold shoulders, could only be worn by one person. She tapped the image larger and just above the chest was the captain's Oath Pin, two gold hands with palms up and fingers interlaced to cradle a small, naked, sleeping infant. The hands of benevolence and stewardship, protection and deliverance. How that jumpsuit and pin came to be Hanta Laird's, she didn't know—which was just the second-scariest thing about what she was watching. Somehow, the XO of the ship had been promoted to captain but the ship's Keeper didn't know about it in advance. In anything like a peaceful transfer of power, that wasn't how it worked.

She'd pushed a private hail to Argen several hours ago, in the CC and in his quarters, but had heard nothing back. Ganet, too, had gone dark. For the captain and chief of a guide ship to be unreachable for so long was unthinkable. It was as if they had simply vanished. Which is why she had secreted herself in a small room behind the pulpit of the central chapel: to browse the ship's cameras, hoping to catch him somewhere. Argen's personal quarters were blind to visual search, as was the briefing room, but her hails would have reached him in those places even if the cameras could not.

And now here was Laird, making everyone she passed do a double take.

The Keeper pulled down a directory and set aglow Dent Forent's six-graphic hail. Seconds later, the image of the well-fed Guide Lead hovered next to the one of Laird making her way toward the CC.

"Are you seeing this?"

"I am now. Impossible."

"I didn't bless this."

"No one talked to me about it either."

"No. I mean I *literally* didn't bless this. And as Keeper, I'm supposed to bless this. A new command requires God's acceptance, and for that to happen, three priestly prayers have to be said. I'm the ship's only priest and I did not say them."

Forent rubbed his padded chin and scowled at the image of Laird navigating the concourse. "Maybe we're all still sleeping, Phetra. This whole week is like some crazy dream we can't wake up from. I'll pinch you if you pinch me."

Dent Forent was typically the one to try and lighten things up. His jokes were always terrible and always ignored. But she could tell by his face that this wasn't just Forent being Forent. He was as worried by what he was seeing as she. "Dent, have you spoken with Argen in the last few hours? Have you seen him?"

"No, but there's nothing new about that. He and I have a deal. He stays away from the science and—"

"I can't reach him."

"What do you mean you can't reach him?"

"He's not responding to hails, and I can't get a visual on him anywhere. He's just ... gone."

"Impossible. Where would he go? And besides, a captain can't just turn off a comm implant. The only way it goes off is if, well, I don't even want to say it."

"But that's what I'm afraid of. He started something I don't think he knew how to finish. Now Laird's in gold top and pinned and he's nowhere."

"He's not nowhere. Let's take a breath here before we start something too. I'll check the transport files and see what that tells us. I think we both need to get to the CC."

"There's one more thing. Ganet's missing as well."

"Impossible."

8

For the second time in just a week, Hanta Laird walked through a stem toward a perilous mission. The first time, she'd had to skulk along the dark edges of an empty concourse lit only by emergency lights on her way to cut the last remaining link to the truth of how the *Kalelah* came to oversleep an Epochal Check by 120,000 years. But this time the big lights were on, the concourse was buzzing with activity, and she was walking straight down the center of it, purposefully drawing the surprised and confused eyes of all those around her.

The captain's jumpsuit was unmistakable—white with gold shoulders—and just above her bustline shone the Oath Pin, gold and illegal to wear except by one person. The sooner people saw it on her the better.

The few walking the opposite way and unlucky enough to accidentally lock eyes with her coughed out a hesitant "Good morning, Captain." But most said nothing. She was fine with that. What mattered most was what they'd say to others: that Argen had lost his chair. She had no hopes for instant loyalty outside the Circle. Argen was a popular leader. And if her command was going to stick, she'd have to make it clear as quickly as possible that Argen would never wear the rank of captain again. But first she had to get Argen out of the picture, preferably without making a martyr of him.

She walked close to the flora scanner that operated the Command Center doors. After they slid silently open, she paused at the threshold before moving forward. She stood quietly and looked about the room. Gradually, without any words, the Command Center's crew became aware of her presence. A few older crew members, diehards who'd seen plenty, were expressionless, but most were not. Faces blanched, eyes widened, eyebrows arched. A young female officer put her hand to her mouth, her eyes welling.

For her part, she let nothing of the second thoughts or the sudden disappointment at her crew's reaction show. *Her crew.* What was she thinking? This was Argen's crew. She could see it everywhere. The nuclear device that exploded a few days back, or this? She wondered which of the two would be the bigger bomb, and which would cause more damage.

Can't worry about that now, she scolded herself. *This is the way it has to be.*

When she was sure she had everyone's attention, she stepped forward and let the big doors to the CC close.

"As it is my sworn duty to protect the laws and customs of the Origin and God, I have exercised succession clause number 478-624 within the Guide

Service Code of Conduct," she said with calm authority.

Silence.

She continued. "The clause demands that should the captain reject his own oath in such a manner as to endanger the mission of the ship or the souls aboard it, the XO is to take command. By refusing to initiate a Correction order to remedy a failed Delivery, former Captain Argen has not only endangered this ship, he has acted in discordance with the Plan and God and put humanity's entire way of life at risk. It is my responsibility to act, and so I have. I would like two security officers to report to the captain's conference room immediately. And, communications, please have former Captain Argen and Chief Ganet report there as well." She paused for a moment before giving her last order. "If anyone wishes to raise a formal objection to my actions, raise it now and it will be noted in the log."

No one spoke. And then Dent Forent and the Keeper took a few steps from the back wall. Two security guards moved with them just a step behind.

"XO, I don't believe the succession can be complete without my assistance," said Keeper Phetra, a slight hitch in her voice.

Laird knew the toughest to win over would be the Leadership team. Unlike her, they were Argen's hand-picks. Laird stood still, her face expressionless, though the crew closest to her could likely see her ears and cheeks redden. She willed herself not to sweat.

Phetra didn't wait for her to respond. She jumped right back on it.

"I suggest Guide Lead Forent join us in the captain's con as witness while we wait for Captain Argen and Chief Ganet."

"Of course, Keeper. I'm grateful for your dutiful reminder."

By the looks on their faces, she doubted anyone in the room believed her. She didn't believe her.

• • • •

Minutes later, Argen's leadership team was once again in the small conference room adjacent to the Command Center. This time, though, things were quite different. Forent wasn't cracking any ridiculous jokes. The Keeper looked tired and worried, suddenly older, her tenacious beauty not quite as lustrous as usual. Laird, though, having made her command public, finally felt at ease.

"I assume there are no objections from you two. Am I right?"

"Well, sir, this is unusual. The captain should have called a Leadership meeting to discuss so profound a ... change," said Forent.

"I have called one. All we need are Chief Ganet and former Captain Argen to join us," Laird said, with a little extra push on the word *former*. "You heard me order communications to hail them here."

"So the captain hasn't conceded—" Forent took a breath and attempted to correct himself. "You haven't *told* the captain yet."

She didn't need his *permission*, she wanted to scream. She had all the permission she needed. But she stayed even. She knew these first hours were treacherous. Impressions were being made that would not fade easily. She had to be more than just right; she had to be captain.

"No. And I'm not required to by law. He was in flagrant dereliction of his duties. The Plan is unequivocal on the matter. And, Keeper, just yesterday in the CC, before the former captain made his unfortunate and blasphemous statement by referring to the population up top as *people*, you yourself confirmed the specific point of Plan Law. I'm completely within my rights. God's command can't be ignored any longer. I'm doing what's right for all of us. The crew, the ship, and God are all that matters."

"Just what do you plan to do?" asked the Keeper.

"I plan to get this ship ready for Correction."

"I mean with Argen."

"That's up to him. If he cooperates, I'll find a spot that can take advantage of his experience. He may be an apostate, but he knows this ship." She paused for a moment. "And he has the crew behind him."

"And if he doesn't," said Forent, "cooperate?"

Laird paused again and looked them both straight on. "He'll be arrested and jailed."

"Even for you, XO, that seems harsh punishment," said Forent.

"Even for me? Mr. Forent, you're forgetting who wrote the Plan. God's Words, remember? We are but humble servants. You, me, all of us. And while we're on the subject of all of us, a Correction can be hard on the crew. Which means we wouldn't want any confusion among us to add to their struggles. So call me XO again

189

in public, or anywhere for that matter, and you'll be in the cell next to Argen's."

Forent's lips tightened into a thin line, practically disappearing in the soft mass of his jowls. He was mad. But he got the message.

"Captain, the blessings?" the Keeper interrupted.

"Yes, the blessings. I'm honored, Keeper," she said with a smile that was more than a little forced.

The Keeper met her eyes for just a moment, then looked off to the left and aired the first of her three prayers to bless the change of command. Forent stood as witness. But she doubted he would actually watch.

9

In a long, white room lined with weapons neatly arranged on racks, the tall man with the long beard stood waiting. His eyes were closed. His arms, which seemed to stretch nearly to his knees, hung loosely at his sides. He was perfectly still, except for his fingers, which appeared to be conducting a tiny, invisible, and silent orchestra somewhere. He'd been waiting in the white room for hours with nothing to do but stand and wait. He didn't like idle time. There was nothing to do for the weapons; they were well maintained. The posting that had put him in the weapons room to begin with was really just a precautionary measure. Just in case of trouble, he was told. But it left him with little to do but stand and wait, which he did not like.

He liked to be busy, his mind occupied and focused. Idle minds were ripe for takeover. He was testament to that. He knew control over his own thoughts was never a sure thing. In fact, only with a concerted effort on his part was he able to be someone he could tolerate. So, while he was standing guard over the weapons, he set to work protecting his mind.

The Sojourner's Prayer was his favorite. It was long and meandering, its trope unintuitive and tricky to master. It took extraordinary mental concentration to do it without the help of a scroll or a Keeper. Thirty-seven verses and meter changes that seemed whimsical rather than purposeful. His fingers helped, not just for keeping time but for the challenge of doing two things at once. The key thing about Sojourner's was that it always managed to keep him awake. Some prayers were like a hot bath. A few minutes in and he was nodding off. But not with Sojourner's. That bastard kept him up. And thank God, because the only thing he liked less than waiting with nothing to do was sleeping.

Sometimes he used a little reinforcement. He kept a two-inch piece of rope in his pocket. If he was really worried about who was in control of his mind, he'd take the rope out and rub it between the fingers of his left hand. Since his whole mission that evening was just in case, he decided to take the rope out just in case, too. It was always good to line things up that way, one "just in case" for another. It was like double protection— triple, actually, because he had his right hand keeping time. All this precaution made perfect sense to him. He needed all the help he could get that night, he could tell. He rubbed the rope between his nervous fingers while he waited and prayed and kept time. He fought the urge to lean against one of the weapon racks and close his eyes; he'd fallen asleep like that before, and the lock on the door to his consciousness was particularly fragile. He knew it wouldn't take much to break, just a little sleep. To nod off for even just a moment would have been enough to start him remembering.

And remembering was just something he could not afford. Especially when so much had happened and people were so on edge. The ship was different since the explosion. And Laird taking Argen's pin—it worried him. And that's always when things got bad: when he worried. Worse, worrying was tiring. Exhausting, actually. He had to stay awake. Asleep, the little scrap of rope that busied his fingers would have dropped to the ground. Asleep, the din of his constant prayer, the verse and rhyme that kept the lunatic truth from crashing in like a wave on a shore, would go quiet and his mind would be defenseless. And once that happened, there'd be no stopping the breathless, perfumed seduction of remembering. He'd dive in, hands outstretched, fingers probing, feeling, sensing, alive again. The hunter reborn. In that state, with electricity coursing through his veins, he always found her fast. *Her* could be anybody, really. A brunette. A redhead. Or maybe, if it was a particularly lucky chase, a blonde.

But once he went deeper, and the remembering started, the surge of power and elation never lasted. It turned to something that covered him in shame. And his remembering was always the same. The hair color might change, but never the face, the lips, or the sequence of events. They went like this, always precisely and horribly like this:

He slowly tightened his grip around her throat, gasping when he felt the blood pumping through the big artery in her neck. She fought. She always fought, panicked and wild. She fought for her life. But he

193

always knew she was fighting for more than that. She was clawing and scratching for everything she wanted her life to be. He saw that in her eyes. Her eyes told him everything about her, like movies. They always did. He hated to see those pictures, the bright, flickering candles he was snuffing out with every second.

Worse, for all her desperation, it was never a fair fight. Forget his strength, which he knew for a fact he had plenty of, too much, maybe. It was his remorseless betrayal that always wore her out. He had befriended her at some point, the details didn't matter, but he always knew they were friends. He to her and she to him. That's how it was. No specifics, just the sense that what he was doing was terrible in ways beyond the obvious. It was as if the breaking of her heart did more damage than the breaking of her neck. And that's when he usually had enough, too. He squeezed harder and harder until they both finally shuddered, she from the spasms of death, he from the spasms of ejaculation.

And then he woke, uncomforted by the realization that it was just a dream. Because for him, of course, it was never just a dream.

Years ago, before he learned to manage his memory when he wasn't sleeping, the pain of remembering who he was grew too much to bare. A kill was fast, over almost as soon as it began. But unlike the young women who never really had a chance against the frothy boil of his mania, his sorrow knew how to fight for its life. It descended like an acid rain from a cloud of inexhaustible supply and never left. Only the few delirious minutes of a kill gave any relief. So, after years of the vicious cycle, he wrapped a rope around his neck, threw the loose end over the branch of a large tree, climbed up the four steps of a short ladder, tied off the loose end of the rope, and kicked the ladder out from under him. He dropped the two feet of play he'd tied into the rope and twisted there under the thick branch. He twisted for minutes and minutes. He felt the iron force of the rope closing off his windpipe. Hanging there, dying but not yet dead, he knew the terror and pain he had taught so many. Then, finally, all was black.

But the relief he sought never came. Instead of passing on to whatever hellish world might await a man who took the lives of the innocent just to satisfy his own madness, he awoke days later in a hospital. The doctors called his survival a miracle. The hospital's old, half-blind Keeper called it a gift from God. The branch, more than four inches thick, had cracked and broken, sending him to the ground just seconds before his heart gave out.

His recovery was largely spent in the hospital's chapel, where he received enthusiastic instruction from the tottering Keeper. It was just what both of them needed.

The Keeper said he couldn't believe his luck, to suddenly at his age have the job of real ministry again. So many people who come to chapel are just passing through. But you, he said over and over, in your need of the gift, have become one. He doted over the bearded man and even gave him a kind of a nickname. My gift.

Yes, my gift. Very good, my gift.

The old cleric's eyes were in such ruins he couldn't see how wildly his gift's eyes darted around the text, how often his gift had to sit on his hands to keep them from grabbing the old man's neck and snapping it. Over time, though, the old man's work paid off. The more his pupil learned, the quieter his student's eyes became. Not that the old Keeper could ever see the transformation, but something like kindness came over them, and the man with the beard would genuinely weep with gratitude.

When the tall man was physically healed, he returned to his work as a security officer in a government building, a job that offered him the opportunity to befriend the young, ambitious women who worked late into the night to further their careers. But having been inoculated by his twice-daily chapel visits and his little scrap of rope, he proudly patrolled the hallways and workstations not as wolf, but as guardian. With God at his side, the maniac was quiet, sleeping, and the tall man could do his job without distraction. Which let him actually think about his job as an end in and of itself, rather than just a means to fulfilling his own evil desires. Suddenly, he wasn't in a hunting ground anymore. He had a calling, and it wasn't long before genuine ambitions began to bubble up in his consciousness. He realized he wanted to do more than protect a government building. He wanted to protect the Plan.

Six months after trying to take his own life, he joined the Guide Service, his devotion to the Plan impressing enough to overcome the strangeness of the route he took to enlistment.

And so, his remarkable journey behind him, the tall, bearded man was standing, almost still, guarding weapons, praying for the captain and trying especially hard not to sleep. Because beyond the remarkable politics of the moment, something else had recently made the ceaseless work of his distraction more strenuous than usual. Something else had stirred—ever so slightly—his singed and demented soul. A woman with scented blonde hair called Cyler. Every time even the faintest image of her squeezed through one of the many hairline cracks in his protective wall of prayer, his fingers were forced to work just a little harder on his scrap of rope. The verses were tasked to come a little faster. And he tried as hard as he could not to sleep.

10

Father Balsconi entered the kitchen of the Apostolic Palace from the loading door farthest from any of the halls the kitchen served. It was an ancient space with tall, barrel-vaulted ceilings built of brick and blackened by centuries of smoke and burnt oil. The pontiff was hosting a congress of bishops from Africa and more than a dozen cook stations were busy at work. Despite the Vatican's new embrace of frugality, the dinner appeared to be an elaborate affair in the making.

He passed by rows of pots four feet tall, held at an angle by stout steel legs above gas burners in the floor and manned by cooks wielding spatulas and spoons big enough to look more like garden equipment than cooking utensils. Trays of whole baked fish were coming out of ovens. Bowls of soup were being filled from huge, steaming aluminum pots.

Perfect timing, he thought. The waiters would all be here readying their trays. Silent unless spoken to, able to glide in and out of lives without so much as brushing a shoulder, a well-trained waiter who serves the dining halls of power can learn many things. And the one he wanted to find was now standing just a few feet ahead of him.

"Antonio," he called to a straight-shouldered layman in a red jacket with epaulets and gold trim. The man in the jacket had salt-and-pepper hair, a thin moustache, and a busy look on his face.

"Ah, Balsconi," the man sighed, giving the priest only half a glance. "What are you doing back here? If you want a job, forget it. You'll eat and steal more than you'll serve."

Balsconi made a theatrical show of pain when he got closer. "The things you say to me, Antonio, like arrows in the back. I'm a giver, not a taker." He wrapped his arms around the taller man's bright red jacket and gave him a showy, unpriestly kiss on each side of the harried waiter's face. "How else would an alcoholic, adulterous cunt such as yourself be a captain in a place such as this?"

"Forgive me, *Father*. If I forget your generosity, it's only because you're such a total asshole."

"We all have our strengths."

"Enough bullshit," said the head waiter as he broke loose from the priest's grip. "The soup is being ladled, so if you want something, ask now."

"There was an interesting meeting yesterday in the library of His Holiness."

"Forget it."

"Forget what? You don't even know what I'm asking."

"What's the difference? One request from you is the same as any other. Besides, I can't tell you who was there. I don't even know."

"Ah, see, Antonio, you always underestimate me. I know the guest list. Because I brought them there."

"Good. Then you can leave me alone now."

"I just need one piece of information. A little piece. A trifling."

"You already know more than I do."

"The waiter. I just need his name."

"There was no waiter."

"When the door opened, I saw a tea service on the table. Are you telling me the Holy Father kept his guests' cups full by his own hand? Where there's tea, there's a waiter."

"Even if there was, it wouldn't matter. We are not allowed to stay in such meetings. We serve, we leave."

"But you don't go very far, right? Because at some point a cup goes dry, yes?"

"When I'm close enough to hear, people don't say important things. Not important people, anyway."

"I thought you didn't know the guest list, Antonio. What's become of our relationship, my brothel brother? We used to have such fun."

"That was a long time ago, Freddy. I have a job now. A wife. And I paid my debt. I don't owe you anything anymore."

"All, true. And your wife. You are a lucky man indeed. But these were not the normal sorts of important people I am usually asked to escort. Something very serious was the subject of that meeting. Those men don't travel like that unless they have to.

One could barely walk. And an Arab in priestly black? His Holiness doesn't host a meeting of such men to talk football."

Balsconi stuck his finger in a soup bowl and put it in his mouth.

"Needs salt. The names of some in that meeting, His Holiness would not want public."

"Well, like you said, you have their names. You can do what you want with them. Leave me be."

"I need more than the names, Antonio. I need *why*. I need why the pope would meet with such people. Then we have something big, Antonio. Maybe the biggest thing we've ever touched."

"Maybe too big a thing, eh, Freddy?"

"Maybe. But if I'm right, the *last* thing, Antonio. The last thing."

"I've heard that before. But there's always more with you. It's never enough. I thought God was all you were supposed to need."

"I'm a man of the cloth. Is it my fault I like silk? Listen to me, we do this and we won't need a next thing. Ever again."

"Swear on your mother."

"I swear."

"Easy for you to say, no mother would have you— you son of a wolf."

For the first time, they laughed as old friends. Balsconi threw his arm around Antonio's shoulders and grabbed hold of an epaulet as he pulled the taller man close again.

"Trust me, it will be enough for you to take this ridiculous captain's coat off and burn it."

"My wife likes this uniform."

"You should see what this collar does to her."

Antonio pushed Balsconi away with a crooked smile. "You little shit. I'll get you the waiter. Now get the fuck out of here before the soup cools and I get fired. You're a prick, you know that?"

Balsconi made his way back toward the door. "Asshole, shit, prick," he called back as he walked. "Such language. I'll expect you in confession!"

11

"Lee is a coward," the Russian president said as he paced behind his enormous desk.

Chantankov threw back a swallow of vodka and looked past the sallow-faced politician to the ornately dressed windows behind the large desk. "Every American president since Reagan has been a coward. Or a fool. Why do you even worry yourself about it?"

"He capitulated and now he's left us no choice."

"Mr. President, I understand your need to think this through. But truly, this is a waste of your time. Sit, please. Where is this second-guessing coming from? It's not like you. Lee is just another rental. Gone in two years. A blink of the eye. He has no sense of history, Vladimir. And no place in it. The American election machine is already in motion. They are all distracted. You, on the other hand, you have a different course. You will change the world. And then you will own it."

"What is left of it."

"Remember what you said to me, Vladimir? Last week?"

The president said nothing.

"Only a man without God could ask another to give up his."

"I only spoke the truth. Lee is a godless fuck."

"That's the point, Vladimir. He is a lost man. And so, exactly, what choice do you have? It must come down to you."

"China agrees to this plan?" He spat the last word like it had a putrid taste. "You're sure of this? Because *me*, I can never tell what that son of a whore thinks. There is nothing on his face. Nothing."

"I spoke with Wu today. They are with us. One hundred percent."

"Or are they just against the Americans?"

"Does it matter?"

"Not at first. But it may. After."

"After is after. We don't know what after looks like."

"Tollavich, from the ministry of science, you read his report? He does not agree with this idea. And some in the politburo are worried. I'm spending half my time on the phone."

"Scientists." Now it was his turn to spit. "What do they know about politics or destiny? Forget it. If he keeps it up, I'll send him to Stark. Then we'll see what a good raping and a little frostbite do to his scientific point of view. Have a drink, Vladimir." Chantankov placed a glass at the center of the giant desk and filled it nearly to the brim.

"These *guides*," Chantankov continued, "or whatever the fuck they are, have one ship. One ship? How can it survive a full-scale Russian and Chinese attack?"

The president gave the vodka a look, sighed, and pushed his hands into the pockets of his pants and kept on pacing. "Tollavich said a craft that large would require a propulsion system we could not yet even imagine. What does that say about their weapons? And it already survived a nuclear attack."

Chantankov got more comfortable in his chair. He placed his arms on the rests and crossed his legs. "North Korean garbage, what did you expect?"

"It wasn't North Korean."

"You have your theories, I have mine. The signature was pure PRNK. Either way, it serves us to play along. Let that lunatic heathen be a hero to his starving idiots."

"I don't care about that freak," the president said, his voice rising. "I'm talking about the fucking ship. Not even a scratch, Tollavich says."

"It was a half measure. One kiloton—it tells us nothing. A very weak showing, if you ask me."

"I didn't."

Chantankov stayed on point. He knew when his boss was blowing off steam and when there was real anger to work around. "What choice do we have? With oil at forty dollars? There are already riots in certain quarters."

The president stopped his pacing and looked at Chantankov.

"Oil. I told you ten years ago this would come back to haunt us."

"Yes," Chantankov said with as pointed a smile as he could muster. "But your extraordinary predictive skills didn't stop you from buying mansions and beautiful women, did they? You are the richest man in the world."

"You are not so far behind."

Chantankov picked up his glass in the gesture of a toast. That was an improvement, the president acknowledging their special connection.

"We all make our choices," he continued. "You made yours then. Now you have another to make. One that will restore the proper order in the world."

Chantankov continued to drink alone, despite his entreaties to his old friend. No reason for the two of them to stay sober during this particular therapy session. It was a burden to deal with the president's moods. But he was glad it was his burden. Things got done this way. And the vodka, of course, made it reasonable enough work.

"The Chinese, those cocksucking scum, they can't be trusted," Putin said again.

"I told you, I've made arrangements. *Persuasions.* Things you must not know."

"Tell me anyway."

Chantankov raised an eyebrow. "Vladi, since we were children and those bastards from the blocks would try to steal the bread your mother sent you to buy, haven't I always protected you? Let me continue."

"These are not boys you can just hit with your uncle's pipe wrench and bury in the woods. They don't think like us. What did you give them?"

"The Arctic."

His friend stopped in his tracks. "You bargained away the biggest oil reserve on the planet? You got us neck-deep into that business and then you give it away?"

"Give it away! You're always so dramatic. I gave them a slice, that's all. And one we are not even biting."

"That was the future you just gave away."

"Let me describe for you another future. Without the US, we can forget about NATO. There'll be nothing stopping us from retaking Eastern Europe. Better still, remove the US and the Saudis will have nowhere to turn for protection but to you, Vladi. Toss in Iran, which is already ours, and soon enough the entire Middle East is ours. A planet split in two. Half for China, half for us. A fair trade, I think."

"We will see. And this attack strategy of yours. I want the details."

"Again, I beg you to let me worry about such things. Your response must be sincere."

"My response will be what I think it must be at the time."

"We will jointly attack the ship if it rises from the ocean."

"And?"

"And in preparation for such a circumstance, we will notify the Americans of our plans."

"They'll try to stop us. But mostly, they won't believe us."

"Yes, of course. So we will give them an unprecedented level of access to our battle planning. No secrets. Everything will be shared: timing, weapons, personnel. Everything. We will treat them like full partners."

"Except?"

"An accident will occur. An unfortunate unforesee-able event."

"What kind of unforeseeable event?"

"During the actual attack, three missiles will malfunction and find new targets. Trajectory miscalculations combined with enemy interference, da, da, da. A tragic accident."

"Shit." The president sat down. He put his head in his hands and sat quietly for several minutes. Chantankov let him have the time. He'd seen this a dozen times.

Finally, the president looked up, but this time he did not look as calm and resolute as Chantankov expected. A distinct worry remained in his friend's eyes, a look he'd known for nearly all his life.

"It won't work, Tata. He'll launch on warning."

"No, Vladi. *You* would launch on warning. You would not hesitate. But he will. He will pause just long enough. And why? Well, you said it yourself a dozen times. He's a pussy."

"We are making a big bet here. What's the window of advantage?"

"Unless he jumps to DEFCON 1, which he won't due to the aforementioned affliction, they'll be an hour away from a retaliatory response large enough for a decisive win. And since we're already taking on the alien ship, we'll be at full combat readiness. We'll have a forty-five-minute jump on them. More if the satellites do their job and take away their early warning capabilities."

"That's just first-level defense. They have others."

"I have taken the liberty of initiating Status-6."

"That was brave of you. And stupid. The mothership must be close enough for accuracy. We have discussed this point a hundred times. Status-6 is a theory, a PR stunt to make Washington sweat and Iran spend more on weapons. I have said I do not want a fucking nuclear-tipped drone flying half way across the world on its own. It could land on one of my goddamned dachas."

"Vladi, I am insulted. The drone will be escorted to a position just a very short flight from its target. It is practically guaranteed. In fact, the submarine *Khabarovsk* has already slipped past the Greenland-Iceland-Denmark Gap. It is nearly in position now with Status-6 safely in its silo. A momma and her bad little baby. It will launch through the shallows of Baffin Bay and then … check. We will take out the radars at Thule at the same time we launch the attack on the alien ship. The confusion will be too much for them. And they will be blind as bats. Our big missiles will fly through their defenses like bullets through tissue."

"The minute they lose signals he'll launch."

"Again, do not equate him to you. He does not have your conviction. He won't act on electronic data alone. He'll want confirmation of the actual detonation at Thule. But by then it will be too late. They'll know exactly where our subs are. They'll do the math. It will be game over. He's a pussy, but he's not stupid. He'll cut his losses."

"My God."

"This is your time. This is Russia's time. We've been waiting for this our entire lives."

Chantankov watched his friend turn his chair toward the window. "How many?" he said softly.

"I told you, three missiles."

"No. How many will die?"

"In the first hour, four million."

"And over the next six months?"

"Fifteen. Eighteen at most."

"How many, Tata? I want the real fucking number!"

"Thirty million. Tops."

Again, Chantankov knew when to stop talking. He let his friend and co-dreamer think. The president got up from the oversized chair and walked to a window and stood peering out into the night. He stood there a long time. Whether he was picturing the hell he might unleash with a word or simply counting the cars, Chantankov couldn't say. After several minutes, still facing the glass, the President of the Russian Federation, a man Chantankov considered to be his own greatest achievement, spoke. This time, it was without the agitation and anger that had pushed this particular therapy session well into the night.

"Approved."

"Thank you," Chantankov said as he grabbed the president's still-full glass and emptied it with one swallow.

12

The woman Trin called Cyler threw her arms around him. He gave her a quick kiss, quicker it seemed than the woman wanted.

"This is the … this is Sarah," said Trin with less than his usual bravado.

Cyler turned her attention fully now to Sarah, with a kind of curiosity Sarah had seen from overworked doctors in the ER. You're more a sore throat, or a broken arm, or a stomachache than you are a whole person. There's concern, but mostly there's a focused curiosity. What's wrong, how can I fix it, and how quickly can I get to the next problem. Or in this case, Sarah felt, how quickly can I get back to my happy, wet, and sloppy reunion with Trin, without this thing he calls Sarah hanging around.

"It's pretty," she said flatly. "You didn't mention that."

It appreciates the compliment, bitch.

Cyler took a step back and looked about the concourse. "What do you want me to do?"

"Can she—can Sarah stay with you? Just a few days, just long enough for me to create a scanner identity for her."

"A scanner identity? Trin, do you know how dangerous this is for you?" She looked back at Sarah again. "For us?"

"I'm sorry," Trin pleaded. "If there was any other way, anyone else."

Cyler moved in closer, making Sarah feel like a bug under a magnifying glass. Cyler reached out her hand to touch Sarah's hair but stopped just short. *No cooties, lady, I promise.*

"Is it true, then, what they say about the population?" she asked him.

"What do they say?"

"That it's damned."

"That's partly up to you now."

She glared at him. "Can it speak?"

"I can speak," Sarah said softly, uncomfortable with the strange language her mind was still absorbing, the swarm having been administered just hours ago.

Cyler, startled, turned to Trin. "How?"

"I dosed her."

"My God, Trin." She sat down on the bench built into the wall along the concourse. "Why?"

"She has to be able to communicate here, to navigate."

"No," she said, her eyes beginning to fill. "Trin, why did you do this?"

"I told you, it's just for a few days."

"No," she said, closing her eyes and shaking her head. "Why did you go with Argen?"

"He's the captain. If the captain says go, you go."

"He broke the law! You had a legal right to challenge him."

"I didn't see it that way." He sat down next to her. "Shit, Cyler, you weren't there. You didn't see them."

"Yes, I did. I saw them at E One. I saw them naked still, without fire, digging in the ground for larvae, licking water from leaves, eating ants from sticks. I saw them as I was supposed to see them."

"E One was a long time ago. That's not who they are now."

"Laird says the Delivery failed." She looked at Sarah again, coolly. "We're going to prepare for Correction."

Sarah felt dizzy again. Hearing this word from this woman was more frightening than hearing it from Argen for the first time. A part of her always assumed Argen was crazy, or exaggerating, or it was all just something she conjured in a fever dream. She had bad dreams.

"No, Cyler," Trin countered. "Laird doesn't understand. The Delivery didn't fail. It went in a different direction, that's all, one we didn't control, but it did not fail. We can't just kill these—" He paused. "These people."

Cyler slapped him. "Don't ever say that to anyone else, Trin. The captain violated the Plan. Everyone's talking about it. And this." She pointed to Sarah. "This is worse. Bringing it here."

"The chief and I, we have a plan."

"A plan? A plan for what? They'll lock you up for this. They'll remove the captain from his post."

"He's dead, Cyler."

"Who's dead?"

"The captain—Argen."

"What?"

"He told them everything. Why we're here, who we are, who they are. What's likely to happen. And something else. He told them about God. He told them about the Plan. And he was killed for it."

Cyler looked at Sarah and took another step away. Now they were both scared.

"Don't you see?" Trin continued. "The captain wasn't lost like they say, Cyler. He didn't forget about his obligation. And he sure as shit wasn't a criminal. Maybe he didn't follow the Plan exactly to the letter. But he died for it, Cyler. He died for God."

Cyler looked at Sarah. "Did this ... *thing* do it?"

"No. But the man who did was fighting for what he believed, too. I'm convinced of it."

"And what can they possibly *believe*?" she nearly spat.

"That God is everywhere," blurted Sarah. It just came out. Sarah had never said those words aloud before. But it occurred to her in that moment of insult that she'd always believed it. And this Cyler girl needed to know she wasn't the only one who'd ever been to church.

Cyler waited a long time to reply. "Did he teach you to say that?" she finally asked, tilting her head toward Trin.

This lady was not going to be easy to like, thought Sarah.

"No. My mother taught me that."

"Your mother," Cyler whispered, as if she couldn't imagine the possibility.

Trin stood and took Cyler gently by the arm and urged her closer again to Sarah. When he let go of her, the two women were just inches apart. Sarah instantly understood why he'd done it. The physical similarities between them were astounding. They were almost the same height and had nearly the same figures and precisely the same color blue in their eyes. They could have passed for sisters.

"Look at her, Cyler," he said. "Are you so sure she's not what she thinks she is?"

Cyler looked into Sarah's eyes. She put a finger to Sarah's cheek and then pulled it away, but slowly, not like she was grossed out.

"I don't like bugs," Sarah said, keeping her gaze locked on Cyler's.

Cyler spent what seemed like a long time processing those four simple words. Maybe it was her accent. This language twisted her tongue in crazy ways. She was shocked she could even do it. But Sarah kept Cyler's stare, working hard not to blink too much or show any fear. Somehow, she thought that was important: to appear fearless, despite the shaking in her knees.

"What?" Cyler finally managed.

"Insects. Ants. I wouldn't eat them from a stick. Or from anything. I wouldn't eat them. Not on purpose, anyway. I'm more of a pizza gal." The last words clanged in her head; with no translation in the crazy language she was mumbling through, she had to say them in English, which only made a stupid thing to say sound even dumber. *Slick Move Two, Sarah.*

"Pizza gal," Cyler repeated in that same astonished whisper. "What does that mean? To be a pizza gal?"

"It's a saying. Like if you really liked music, you might say, 'I'm a big music guy.' Or if you were a super sports fan, you'd say, 'I'm a sports gal.'"

She paused a minute, seeing her words were doing nothing to ease the confusion on Cyler's face.

"I'm sorry, I can see none of this makes any sense to you. I'm just saying, I don't eat bugs. No one I know eats bugs, at least not on purpose. Sometimes they can fly into your mouth and you just can't help it. But pizza, everyone *loves* pizza."

A wave of nostalgia warmed her face. That seemingly meaningless fact—everyone loves pizza—wasn't meaningless at all. It suddenly seemed like the most important thing in the world to her. It was part of who she was: a lifelong member of the world that loves pizza. And she imagined herself swooning, like she does, like everyone does, when a pizza still hot and bubbly gets put on the table and the air around you fills with the aromas of just-baked crust, tomatoes and oregano and garlic and melted mozzarella, and even before you pick up that first slice and bring it to your mouth you're already tasting it, already feeling the cheese stretch and pull away from the slice, it's so real, so vivid, even before your first bite, and so she couldn't stop herself from holding this thought and reveling in it and being strangely proud of her own little slice of the world she shared with so many billions in it, because for the first time in more than three days there was something in her head she understood completely, an image that didn't make her feel like crying, something over which she had total command.

And so, to make a connection with this woman who still couldn't believe she could talk—to take her first step toward saving Earth—fuck it, she was going with pizza.

"It's just kind of the perfect food. You can eat a small one by yourself. But most of the time, people share pizza. That's part of what makes it special. Every major city on Earth has a pizza restaurant. Some have hundreds. I can't summon the words yet to describe it to you, the way it smells or the way it tastes. Except that of all the things there are in the world to eat, pizza is the thing I crave most. Almost nothing can make me happy. But for the few minutes I'm eating pizza, I'm happy. Or at least I think I am. Which is good enough."

Cyler was silent but her face had softened.

"Do you have a favorite food?" Sarah pressed on, but softer as well. "Something that makes you happy when you eat it?"

Cyler thought a long time. And then, tentatively, as if she'd never had to make such a declaration before, she said, "*Tunlot.*"

"Tun-lot," Sarah repeated, trying to match the pronunciation. "What is that?"

Cyler smiled just a little. "It's a kind of bread."

"It's your favorite?"

"Yes, I guess it is."

"Well, someday, if there is a someday, I'll take you for a pizza. In the meantime, maybe we could get some … *tunlot*? This place has me totally freaked, and I can't smoke, which is not helping at all, but I'm finally a little hungry. And who knows, maybe *tunlot* bread is a little like pizza."

Cyler took some time again before answering. "There's a shop not far from here."

Sarah's face lit up for the first time in days, and her smile was big and easy. Cyler took her hand and led the way. Trin hung back a few paces behind. And as they walked, Trin behind them cautiously smiling, Sarah wondered if this was what he had meant by "just be yourself," if this had been Argen's plan: helping people in the ship see the population as something more than the nameless beings they'd been at the moment of Delivery. Putting a face to the numbers, revealing a soul where none was thought to exist.

Cyler looked at Sarah and then back at Trin. And for just a moment, Sarah thought she detected a flicker of sadness in her eyes.

13

Gripping the steel ring as the subway car raced under Manhattan toward his office in Battery Park, Stanley wondered if it was time to retire. Maybe it's just another bad week, he told himself, a rough patch. And why not? Stanley Posner had been having a lot of bad weeks lately.

Three bad weeks ago, his publisher cut short his book signing tour. It was just as well, since hardly anyone had showed up to the first three dates. And before the book tour that wasn't, there was the cable show that shouldn't have been. What was he thinking? He wasn't that kind of guy, a face man. In front of a keyboard, he was glib. In front of a camera, he was stiff. A stiff. And once that show was officially pronounced dead after just four weeks, it was like everything about him died. Except he kept on living, and writing about world affairs for the *Wall Street Journal*, and riding this damn train to the office every day.

But there was no doubting it, he was now a ghost of his former, less-see-through self. And things had just gotten progressively worse. In this particular bad week, he learned his last real grip on relevance was slipping, or at least his click-through numbers were. The moment kept playing over and over in his head, like a squeaky tune stuck in the back of his consciousness that wouldn't shut up.

The Outlook invite from his editor came at 9:00 for a 10:00 meeting. Never a good sign. He showed up to the meeting three minutes early and all but one of the chairs were already occupied. Also never a good sign.

"Have a seat, Stan," said his editor, who was twelve years younger than Posner.

"What's up, Bill? Got the whole office here?" He gave a chuckle, but no one else followed his lead, so he just sat down in the last empty chair. The last man sitting.

"You know, Sean, right?" His editor gestured toward the head of the table. "Sean runs the dot-com. And Jennifer, she's in performance metrics. Analytics."

Posner offered them both a smile. "Sure. I think we met at the breakfast thing last month."

"Oh, yeah, we probably did," said Sean, age thirty, no socks, cuffed skinny jeans.

Jennifer just half smiled, said nothing.

"So, what's up?" he said to Bill again. "The world is on fire and you're gonna be screaming for a column in about four hours."

"That's what we're going to talk about, Stan." Bill then gave a small, quick nod to Sockless.

"Right," said Sockless, taking the cue. "We've been doing a progression analysis of your numbers, Stan. And there's a problem."

"What kind of problem?"

"All your KPIs are down."

"I didn't know I had, um, K-P—"

"Key performance indicators. KPIs. We don't like how your content is trending."

"It's the news, Sean. I don't make it up. You know I report on world affairs? You can't rate it like a TV show or a cat video. It's more of a public service. The newsroom isn't like other sections of the paper."

"We're competing on every pixel, Stan. I don't have to tell you that," said Sockless. "So when it comes to the analytics, I'm sure we'll be on the same page here."

"I have no idea what page you're on."

"The big numbers, what got read what didn't, really don't tell us much anymore, right?" he said with an up-speak on his last word. "You want to know exactly what people engage with and how deeply they engage, right?"

"I'm not sure I do. I see it as my job to inform people of important things they need to know about. I'm not an entertainer."

"The data we're getting now is very exciting. You'd love it. We'll get you the raw numbers. A guy like you will eat it up. We're at the point where we know exactly what people are going to like and what they won't."

"Nobody likes it when a group of crazies kidnaps two hundred schoolgirls and turns them into sex slaves.

No one needs your data to know that. The world's a messy place. It's not always easy to like."

"Let me just top-line this for you. Your searches are down, your traffic growth has stalled, your bounce rate is up, your time-spent-per-page-view is, eh, not so bad, and while you're holding fairly steady with prior reads, your total number of uniques is low."

"Very low," concurred Jennifer.

"My uniques?"

"Your non-duplicated reads."

"Oh, right, of course. What are they talking about, Bill?"

"But really, it's your social sentiment that's got us more worried," said Jennifer smugly.

"I didn't know I had a social sentiment."

"We use a listening tool to understand what people are saying about your stories, or you, on social media."

"You mean you're worried about what people are saying about me on Twitter and Facebook?"

"Right on," said Sockless with the bright look of a satisfied teacher. "You get it. You understand why we're here, then."

"You want me to change my social sentiment numbers."

"Exactly. And we have a ton of super-cool ideas for you."

"Ideas about how to get people to like the news more?"

"Exactly. That's how you bump your uniques, and that's how we sell ads."

"Go fuck yourself."

"Pardon me?"

"If a guy blows up a bus in a market in Tel Aviv, it's not a thing one is supposed to like. You're not supposed to put a *thumbs-up* on that. And we're not supposed to celebrate how fucking engaged people are with the latest ethnic cleansing in Africa. Whatever it is, it's a horrible thing to happen, to write about and to read about, because it rubs our nose in the fact that all the rules we live by every day, everything we've been taught about right and wrong and honor, about the soul of humanity, is total bullshit. It means every time you look at your kids you worry. But it happened, that horrible thing, whatever it is. And if we don't want it to happen more often, then we have to know about it. And that makes it our job to report it. My job, anyway. Are you telling me I need to worry about your little popularity contest before I report the fucking news?"

"That's not what we're saying, Stan," said Bill, but not in a particularly convincing way.

"But some things are just boring, right?" said Jennifer, jumping in: same up-speak, just at a different, slightly less effeminate pitch than Sockless's. She was the younger of the two Brooklynites, tall, lanky, and awkward. Yet despite all those virtues, there was an air of superiority around her. "We know you can't change the news, but you can change the angle of approach. You can find the thing in the story that bends it differently, makes it more interesting, more salient." She said that word with an odd kind of reverence. "All our research shows that salience is how you engage people, and engagement is the key to changing your numbers. We only get a few seconds for people to embrace our content. And boring is death, Stan."

"Actually, it's not. Bombs are death. And water shortages, and cholera, and poison gas, and politicians who kill people just to satisfy their egos. Boredom just puts you to sleep. But fall asleep on the train next to a guy in a suicide vest and, boom, you don't wake up."

"I don't think you're taking this the right way."

He had no recollection later if it was Jennifer or Sockless who said it, but it was the thing that pushed him over the edge.

"How should I take it? I'm getting coached by two idiot children from marketing. I put two Pulitzer Prizes on the board for this paper. And getting one of them got me a fucking bullet hole in my left calf courtesy of the first Iraq war."

"Most of our readers don't even know what the Pulitzer Prize is," said Sockless proudly.

"And whose fault is that?"

"Calm down, Stan," said Bill. And this time he meant it. "This is the way things are now. This is how publishing works, you know this. There's no surprise here for you. It's always been about the real estate. What's different now is we have the tools to know how well each quarter-inch of our real estate is doing. You need to look at this for what it is. It's just guidance, that's all. No one's telling you how to write. We're just asking that you look at the deck when you get a chance. They made a hard copy for you. And focus on the Facebook numbers. If you can move those, you'll rebuild your uniques. That's all we're saying."

"Make those market bombings more exciting, because, you know, the horror of senseless death is so, like, lame."

"Uniques, Stan. You need to rebuild your uniques. If you went to any other paper they'd have the same talk with you. You can do this. I know you can." Bill got up to signal the end of the meeting and that was it.

You can do this. I know you can. That's what had been replaying in his head, over and over. The way Bill had said those words, he'd made it sound like he was saying one thing but meaning the exact opposite. You're going to fail at this, old man. Your days are done. *They made a hard copy for you.* The book tour, the cable show debacle, the KPIs. Your personal, sun-blocking, dynasty-ending meteor has hit. And even if you could evolve, I don't want you to. That's what Stan heard in Bill's voice. That's what he saw in the smug girl's dismissive eyes. That's what he felt from Sockless's patronizing lesson in analytics.

And so, every day since that meeting, as the train rocked back and forth on his way into the office, he thought more and more seriously about getting out. His broker said he had enough money. His friends said he should quit. His wife said nothing, which was nothing new. But for some reason, he held on. To the keyboard, to the stories no one apparently wanted to read anymore, to the greasy steel ring hanging from the dirty ceiling of the crowded train. And it was in such a moment, a moment of inexplicable holding on, when his mobile buzzed.

"This is Stanley Posner."

"Mr. Posner," said a man with a thick Italian accent. "My name is Fredo, Fredo Balsconi. I work at the Vatican."

"What can I do for you, Mr. Balsconi?"

225

"Father Balsconi, actually. I think, Mr. Posner, I have a story for you."

"I don't really cover the Vatican, Father. But I can give you the name of our editor for religious affairs—"

"No, it's you I want to speak to. You're a very influential writer. You have much fame, Mr. Posner."

"Less so these days, it appears."

"Ah, you are too humble. This story, it needs your voice behind it."

"And why is that, Father?"

"Because it is a story not so easily believed."

"What makes you think I'd believe it?"

"Because I have the necessary proof. And given what a story such as this can do for, well, for a man such as yourself, you will want to believe it."

"I see where this is heading. And what will you want, Father?"

"Me? I am a simple priest, Mr. Posner. My wants will seem small to an organization as vast as yours."

"Well, Father, this is where I usually hang up. We don't pay for stories at the *Wall Street Journal*."

"You will for this one, Mr. Posner. I will give you half the story now. And when I pause, you will want to find the small token that I request, a trifle really, so that you may hear the remainder of the story. I guarantee it."

"And how is that, Father?"

"Because this is the story to end all stories."

14

The White House offered no resistance to Posner's inquiries. It was as if it welcomed the leak. Someone from the press office even furnished a file of the scan that showed the city-sized ship embedded in the sediment. The Vatican wasn't quite as generous. The pope offered no words of concurrence or comfort, but the Vatican didn't deny anything either. It pledged to watch the story closely and confirmed that the White House had indeed reached out to the Holy See.

Too easy, he thought, for a story like this. This was nuttier than Area-51 crazy. It was the kind of story a government or the church dismissed out of hand. Not even worthy of denial. And yet no one actually hung up on him. More like the opposite. They actually opened the doors and said, *Here you go, mousy, find the cheese.* Which, as any journalist worth a nineteen-cent Bic pen knows, never happens without there being an actual mousetrap somewhere on the other end. This was a setup. They wanted this story published, but they knew it was batshit crazy. So they needed a buffer.

They needed someone else to take the first shift as crackpot. They couldn't have the pope or the president of the United States announcing the discovery of aliens from another planet. For all he knew, Balsconi had been set up to be the leak. Posner and the *Journal* would be the cannon fodder. Then, once the initial rounds were fired and some of the energy released, the president and all the others could be the people with the plans of action. So long as the once-famous Stanley Posner played the role of Chicken Little, they could be safe to play the role of saviors.

That was fine with him. He had numbers to move. *Social sentiment,* those assholes in analytics called it. And Balsconi, whether he really knew what he was doing or not, was right. This would move them. Up or down, he couldn't say. But move they would.

The *Journal* broke the news online and in print simultaneously, but just barely. The debate over the headline was so furious and dragged on for so long the story nearly missed the print deadline.

The more conservative members of the editorial board pushed for credibility and fact in the big type: "White House Confirms: Alien Ship Discovered in Waters Off Hawaiian Coast." The idea of an alien ship would be more than enough shock value, they argued. It's not the *Journal*'s way to sensationalize, they said, and this story needs nothing to dress it up. But Bill, his editor, and the man who worried more about the paper's Facebook stats than the wishes of a Pulitzer-winning reporter wanted a more direct message. It's not the discovery that matters most, he said, it's what the discovery *means* that's important. He pushed for the words every editor has longed to print since man first learned that the stars weren't actually holes in the sky through which the glow of heaven shined:

"WE ARE NOT ALONE!"

Really? We're going with the line a dozen B movies gave us on spinning, white paper bundles that rushed toward the camera and stopped at just the angle required to render their shocking news readable to the throngs of distracted teenagers during the golden age of the drive-in theater. The boldfaced wonder and fear that only a squadron of wobbly flying saucers on fishing line could inspire. Somehow, he didn't think that was the salience Jennifer the lanky data jock and the tin-eared Sockless were looking for. Even if true for the first time in real life, it was still too ridiculously cliché. He could picture Jennifer the data jock putting aside her cynical smugness long enough to actually laugh. Or at least snort.

So he made the case for a headline that would not only contain the remarkable news of intelligent life elsewhere in the universe but would threaten humanity in a way even Hollywood had yet to conjure—and do it all with the concision required for the bold, graphic expression such an exclamation deserved. It nearly broke his heart to argue for such a shamelessly salacious approach. But with his career in a nose dive and his own stubborn refusal to just let go of the stick and enjoy the crash, at least not until he could hit the ground on his own terms, he pushed himself over his own line.

"Sudden emptiness," he said softly. He slowly got to his feet and straightened up for the pitch. "The prospect of an unexpected great loss is what sells papers.

A mass death is what goes viral fastest. So let's kill the biggest thing that's ever been killed before."

The fact that he loathed what he was saying made no dent in the passion he displayed for the cause. He'd already had a kid in the paper's PR department update his Facebook profile. He was logged into Twitter with a hashtag ready to go. He wanted to be shared by millions. But most of all, the next time he saw Jennifer, he wanted that look of mild contempt on her face to be replaced with something like respect. And from all those desperate and dangerous wants came the inspiration for the most resounding seven words the *Wall Street Journal* had published in decades:

"ALIENS TELL US GOD IS A LIE."

And so began the new crusades.

15

Chief Ganet's search for God on Earth began with an interrogation by the NSA. He underwent days of psychological testing, and by all measures accepted as reliable, he was pronounced sane. His prints were taken. His DNA was taken. He was photographed from dozens of angles. He was made to speak at length for recording devices. His facial features and the character of his voice were then run through every trustworthy recognition software in use.

When it was finished, a finding more persuasive than his sanity was his vexing anonymity. The world's most sophisticated intelligence apparatus was tasked with a background check and Ganet hadn't just come up clean, he hadn't come up at all. He existed in no database anywhere in the world. He was pronounced to be unknown—and this characteristic above all others was deemed the most impressive. Because outside of the very few remaining bush- and jungle-dwelling aboriginal societies, there are no unknowns left on this planet. Virtually everyone leaves a fingerprint somewhere. Yet here was a man with undeniable education and training, a man at ease in a modern world. So at ease, in fact, you could say he was a man wholly unimpressed with the present state of the art. Yet, somehow, he was traceless, recordless, a cypher. Deleted by a foreign government? Nothing or no one can be completely deleted. It was as if he'd fallen from the sky.

Oddly, this gave the authorities an encouraging comfort. His impossible anonymity lent a satisfying counterbalance to the impossibility of his claims. If he could've dropped from the sky like a meteor, why couldn't he have risen from the sea in a machine from a movie?

And so, instead of getting thrown in a prison or an institution for the mentally unfit, he got a meeting with the president of the United States. They talked for hours. They talked of history, of science, of other nations, of fears, and of joys. And of God. After all the conversations, Ganet began to believe that Argen may have been right. 120,000 years ago, he helped deliver a shivering, naked, ignorant population to a strange planet. Through an accident of error, a glitch, or a bug, the creatures had been denied the guidance every other creature like them throughout the universe had been given. Nevertheless, he continued to meet beings as human as any he'd ever met. Which side of this equation, he wondered, was more impossible?

He was given assurances that his story had not only been believed but had actually become a priority for this man called *president*. He was given what was called a research detail, a group of well-groomed men and women whose sole purpose seemed to be to help him in his mission to find the evidence he needed. He was given a plane and a pilot and armed men and the promise that no expense would be spared.

He was taken shopping to find clothes more suitable to his task. Somber suits, white shirts, crisp ties. He bought a briefcase for papers, a thing he had never needed in his life. He practiced writing with a pen. He struggled to use a computer with a keypad. He was given a crude device called a cell phone equipped with a speed dial to the president's office. He was learning to unlearn all he knew, to re-ask questions he'd long forgotten. What had been Argen's plan became his. He wept at night. For the multitude so at risk, for his family—the people of the *Kalelah* and the truths they still held. He wept, too, for the worry that he'd fail. He'd be too slow, and Laird would be too fast.

Meetings were set up with religious leaders across the world. Appointments were made with scientists and mathematicians.

Just two mornings from the day he and Argen had commandeered a transport to the surface, Ganet brushed his teeth by hand in a hotel room, dried his face and hands, put on his strange and uncomfortable clothes, took a frightening ride in an elevator, met his detail in the lobby, and walked out into the sun to a waiting vehicle.

The signature report of a Dragunov sniper rifle rang out in the morning light. Birds flew from nearby trees and the coping stones of buildings. Three of the six people around him hunched their shoulders, ducked their heads, and raised their hands to their ears.

Two turned in the direction of the sound. Ganet felt himself fall backwards and then stop. He looked upward into the sky, noticing the clouds that were exactly like all the clouds he had ever known, like the ones in the skies he'd watch float by as a boy lying on the purple grass of the hill behind his parents' house. The people rushed around him in slow motion, their faces coming in and out of frame, backlit by the same skies and clouds, their faces drawn in horror. One, a young man—a kid, practically, Ganet couldn't remember his name—knelt by his side, the sun and sky casting a halo around his red and brown hair. *What's his name?* Why couldn't he remember his name? All the names were so strange, so hard to keep straight.

The kid without a name looked so horribly worried. His face was stretched like a distorted picture, a signal losing its connection. The kid began to scream. Ganet heard the words, but for some reason he'd lost all understanding. He listened hard. He put every shred of focus he had on the kid's words, but he got nothing from them. Something had suddenly gone wrong, that much he could figure. But what? He had no clue. *Where's Trin? Trin can re-dose me. Then I'll understand again.* For the past two days, he was sure he had known the words. He could remember whole conversations. But maybe he'd been mistaken. Maybe it was all a dream. Argen, the girl, a man so angry and the flash of light and the acrid smell of the smoke. All just a dream. Or another life. A life gone fuzzy at the edges, like a word on the tip of his tongue, there but not, known and strange all at once.

He was suddenly thirsty, thirstier than he'd ever been in his life. His lips felt ready to split. The kid began to press on his chest. Pressing and pressing, over and over. With each heavy push, he felt himself flatten from the weight of it. The air got caught in his throat, blocked to his lungs by the weight on his chest. The kid started to cry. *Why can't I see what's wrong?* The kid wiped his face and his fingers left red streaks on his cheeks and around his eyes. The light behind the kid's red-brown hair dimmed. And then all Chief Ganet really wanted was something to get him warm. It had turned terribly cold. Too cold to breathe.

16

Pilot Donnalay took his chair and placed his hands in the gloves for the first time in 120,000 years. He sat there without moving, just listening. At least that's what he called it. There was nothing to actually hear. The pilot's room, a half globe of shielded glass at the very top level of the *Kalelah*, was silent but for the low, blue hum of the air handler. There was no radar chirping, no interface calling his attention to this system or that alert. There was nothing to make a sound at all. But through his fingers and the tiny, almost imperceptible pulses he could feel run through his body, he'd learned to eavesdrop on the ship's internal conversations around navigation and propulsion. After all, as a pilot, there wasn't much else for him to do.

The *Kalelah* did not need a pilot. The ship's sensors provided all the information its precise navigation required. And the code, emotionless and flawlessly accurate, was a far more capable pilot than a human could have ever hoped to be. But even if the

Kalelah itself had no need for a pilot, the crew of the *Kalelah* did.

The Guide Service sat on the crosshairs of two warring objectives. To live the Plan meant to spread humanity's reach, and God's with it, as far and as fast as possible. And for that there was no substitute for the piloting skill of machines. Yet scholars throughout millennia had proclaimed over and over that the Plan forbade self-piloting by ships.

> *So machine hath neither seed nor soul. So let only*
> *Human hands ensure humanity's true flight.*

—5-Scroll-12, Words of Journey

And so the pilot's room had a viewing glass only a human eye could need. In the center of the room, facing the glass, sat a reclining chair. On each side of the chair, attached by thick ropes of fiber-optic cable, was a transparent glove of woven strands glowing a thousand colors. Each glove was a circuit terminal in the communication between the ship's code and the ship's navigation and propulsion systems. If these two circuits had been connected by wire or radio band, the ship could pilot itself. But the circuits had no such wire or radio frequency. By design, the circuit was broken. To bridge the break, a pilot sat within the chair, placed a hand in each glove, and, with flesh and blood and the properties of conductivity they possessed, completed the circuit, his body acting as middleman and messenger.

The pilot did not steer, or even command. The pilot could have been sound asleep, in fact, with no danger to the course. He wore the gloves. His hands became the conduit that reconciled the machine's forbidden role. In this way, piety and necessity became one, and both Keeper and engineer got their ways. Humanity could prowl the stars to spread God's grace and do it at machine speed. Did God agree with the compromise—the clever legal jujitsu of Scripture? No one asked. And so far, God had not offered an opinion.

Pilot Donnalay didn't ask either. He was too busy listening to the ship worry itself about sand.

Sand and silt travel the ocean currents like leaves on the wind. And just like leaves, sand and its lighter cousin, silt, eventually work their way to the ground. Beneath the surface of the ocean, it's forever raining. Sparkling bits of silica, shell, dead plankton, and grains of rock come down in a perpetual drizzle.

When the *Kalelah* touched down on the canyon floor, it did little to camouflage itself. All that was required to disappear into the ink-black night of the abyss was to raise its shields against light leak. The constant mist of gently falling sand and silt would do whatever else was required. After a few thousand years, the great city of a ship would be just another slope along the topography of the abyssal seafloor.

Under normal circumstances, when the ship was sleeping for five or even ten thousand years at a time, the silt and sand would be no match for the *Kalelah*'s might. If the layer was especially thick, drillbots would perforate the sand layer around the ship with acre-wide holes. Dozens of them. The heat from the engines beneath the ship would rise up and through the holes, and when that hot water met the frigid abyssal waters, the billowing, twisting shafts of steam that formed from the collision would act like an army of turbines, churning the surrounding water to such a degree that much of the silt would be blown off the ship. Once the ship began to rise, the remaining sand cover would slide off quickly enough.

But after oversleeping for more than 120,000 years, the ship had become more than merely hidden. The sand layer was much thicker than anything the ship was expected to conquer.

Donnalay asked the ship to send a message to the Command Center. A man of few words, he kept it simple.

"We're stuck."

17

Wilson was in line at the CVS along with what seemed like half the city. His headache was on day four and he'd been popping so much Advil he'd finally run out. He looked at what people around him had in their baskets. Plenty of the usual stuff, like shampoo and soda. But there seemed to be a run on bottled water, bandages, hand sanitizer, rolls of gauze and white tape, brown bottles of hydrogen peroxide, ramen, and peanut butter. Crisis shopping.

He looked out the window at the street aglow with bright sunshine: a movie set lit for optimism, not phase one of the Big Panic. There were no toxic clouds floating overhead, no squadron of strange craft shooting up the cars and asphalt. But if people's shopping baskets were reliable indicators, the news stories were taking their toll. With the exception of the hard-right crank sites that claimed the ship to be a hoax, a conspiracy by the left to distract the world from the liberal plot to cede America to those who would impose Sharia law, the media had taken the Vatican leak and the subsequent tacit confirmation by the White House seriously. Then came Ganet's murder. His violent death—the alien's death, as the media called it—gave the stories just enough real drama to start the march toward chaos. And as far as Wilson knew, Ganet was their last hope of making any sort of case for their existence. *My existence,* he thought.

There was no denying it. As if the ground itself had moved underneath him, had moved under everyone, a destabilizing shift had taken place. No matter what happened next, nothing would ever quite be the same. This new knowledge, even if some refused to believe it, couldn't be unlearned. It was too juicy for the media, too perfect for the Armageddonists. And for Wilson, who had met Ganet and Argen and Trin in the flesh, it was simply too real.

He looked down at his own basket that contained two family-size bottles of Advil. For someone who lived alone, this would normally be several years' worth of the stuff. He knew the second bottle would likely expire before he'd get to it. We're stockpiling, he thought. Phase one of losing our collective shit. Next would be lines at the gas stations. Fights in the aisles of grocery stores. It wouldn't be long before the most heavily armed citizenry on earth started using its weapons against itself in ways the police couldn't begin to control. He was sorry he hadn't grabbed some peanut butter. But no going back now. He'd lose his place in line.

The cashier working the register was a full-chested black woman in dreads. She had a face that greeted the world teeth first. Her huge smile stood out like a string of pearls against the deep chocolate of her skin. Six people back in line and he could hear her say "Hello, sugar" to each new customer that stepped forward and then "Thank you, darling" with each receipt she handed over. *We're in phase one and she's still giving out the sugar and darling. Where does it come from?* he wondered. Was it just a habit, her usual contribution to the CVS customer experience? Or did she think she needed to be extra generous today, because of phase one?

A commotion at the back of the store broke his reverie. People were shouting. Someone fell to the ground. One voice was louder than the rest, a deep baritone. "There's no more time! There's no more time!" he bellowed.

The cashier lost her smile and looked in the direction of the noise. "Hold on a second, sugar," she said to an old man buying four jars of peanut butter and cheap gray socks.

She placed her name badge under the bar code wand, scanned it, and then walked out from behind the register.

"Everything okay back there?" she said as she walked toward the shouting.

She couldn't have been more than five feet two inches tall, but she had no trouble parting the crowd. A tall man in the back with tangled hair and greasy clothes and a twitchy, birdlike way about him turned her way. He was holding a makeshift sign that read The Ark Is Open!

"The choosing has begun!" he shouted to her, his voice the sonorous grunt of a bear, his breath reeking of beer and cigarettes, his eyes pointing in two different directions. His general demeanor, not to mention smell, had built a moat of dirty carpet around him. He was the person on the street the less obviously disturbed had long practiced avoiding. No eye contact. No slowing down. No engagement whatsoever. Like he wasn't there. But stuck in line at the CVS, preparing for God knows what, they couldn't just walk past him. Keeping their distance would have to do.

But Dreads wasn't the look-the-other-way type. She walked right up close, inside the moat, and flashed those pearly whites, and with the kindest voice she could muster, she did what no one does to a crazed man with hair like snakes and a mismatched gaze. She engaged. "I know, sweetie pie, and I thank you for reminding us. You've done your job, okay? I hear you. You understand what I'm saying? I hear you."

His brow furrowed in defiance. Apparently, Sweetie Pie was not quite finished. "On that night, two people will be in bed. One will be taken and the other left!"

With only a moment's pause, Dreads finished the tall man's inculcation. "I know, honey. And two women will be grinding grain together. One will be taken and the other left."

Now it was the tall man who created some distance. He stepped back a full two feet. He looked around at the people in line, he looked behind him, he looked at the ceiling, like someone expecting to spot a hidden camera. At last he met her eyes with the only one he had control of and said, "Amen," smiling enough to show his own yellow and broken teeth.

"Let's everyone say 'amen,' okay?" she announced, just like it was a perfectly normal thing to do on a Tuesday afternoon at a CVS packed with people on the verge of a mass emotional breakdown.

Thank the media for scaring the shit out of everyone. Thank Sweetie Pie for dropping a few notches down the crazy scale for a moment. Or give the nod to the way the sun shone through the windows to set the cashier's dreads aglow, because fifteen people had no way to resist the curious command of that five-foot, two-inch cashier. And in a perfectly synchronized response, strangers, each and every one of them, said "amen" in so reverent a harmony the filthy CVS—gripped by an alien urgency that all feared might never rest again—had a moment's transformation into something beautiful and connected, something holy. The man in the greasy clothes stopped twitching and stood slightly taller. And before he could open his mouth again, she took him by the arm and slowly walked him to the front of the store where the doors were. Surprised by her touch, or too bewitched by the halo of sun in her hair, he, too, could not refuse.

"We thank you for your time," she said sweetly. "Have a beautiful day, sugar." And with that, she led him out the big glass doors to the warmth of the sun outside. She waited as the glass closed between them and then turned and headed back to her register.

Before she was halfway there, everyone who had seen the tiny miracle was clapping.

When the store had quieted back down and the cashier was back ringing up the customers' baskets, Wilson thought of the proof Argen and Ganet had wanted. Had they lived, he thought, we might have taken them on a tour of our churches, synagogues, mosques, and temples. We might have performed every liturgy ever sung, danced, or burned. Yet all the evidence we needed was right here, working the register at the CVS.

And they'll never know it.

He walked out the store and turned left on New York Ave. He only had a three-block walk to his apartment near Franklin Square. His phone vibrated, and he pulled it from the left inside breast pocket of his well-tailored blue suit.

He tapped the home button and the screen lit with a notification:

Encrypted message, today, 1:36 p.m.

Shit. He quickly typed in his password to unlock his phone and then the additional password, more than twenty characters and numbers, to unlock the encryption.

US Armed Forces to proceed to DEFCON 3.

The ache in his head moved to his chest. It wasn't so much alarm; he'd expected this at some point. It was more the punch of sadness. The country hadn't seen DEFCON 5, the lowest level of readiness, essentially a peacetime posture, since 9/11. But the move from DEFCON 4 to 3 was significant. It meant the Air Force would be readied to mobilize in a fifteen-minute rush. And it meant the teams at NORAD and Missile Defense would be taking their coffees black. It wasn't the cocked pistol of DEFCON 1, but it was a big, neon Back Off sign to whomever had stirred the national security shit enough to force the president's hand in so dramatic a way.

Wilson knew all too well what would happen next. The security apparatuses of every country in the world would meet to put their plans together in case whatever it was that had motivated the jump to DEF 3 escalated into something worse. Not that there was anything anybody other than the Chinese, the Russians, or maybe the Israelis could do about it. And if the United States was moving to DEFCON 3, it meant one of those countries was the reason. But not anymore, he reminded himself. Now it could be something else entirely, something no one could have imagined just a month ago. And it could mean something for which the world was completely unprepared.

So much for taking the afternoon off to pop three Advil and close his eyes. He was going back to the Pentagon. As he texted his driver for a ride, he couldn't resist making a mental note:

We just entered phase two.

18

Sarah made her way through the cavernous concourse of Stem Five. With the help of the sim sky tricking the ceiling above her into the rose-colored light and clouds of early morning, it felt like the start of a new day. But at seven miles below the surface of the ocean and buried under thousands of years of sand and silt, there were no windows to confirm an actual daybreak was indeed in progress. For all she really knew, it could be as black as three in the morning up above. No matter; she was morning hungry, desperate for coffee, and even more desperate for a smoke.

She'd sneaked her last cigarette hours ago, and she'd been too afraid of setting off an alarm to take more than two drags. But that didn't stop her from imagining there'd be someone and some situation that would magically merge together and she could approach that person and say, as gracefully as the still-awkward words would allow, "Hey, could I bum a smoke?" And even though she knew full well that in this strange world of the ship, no one smoked, and no situation would ever arise that would quiet the throbbing spot in the back of her throat that wanted the rich, normalizing sensation of a deep draw—the thing that made everything okay—she held out hope. She kept her eyes peeled for the shimmering mirage of someone pulling out a cigarette or the oasis of a tobacco shop. It was idiotic, of course. But these were the tricks the addicted mind played. And knowing they were tricks didn't stop them from working.

She walked on as the morning got into full swing. Or at least what seemed like the morning. She was out to meet Trin. He wasn't far, just past the intersection of Stem Five and the main stem. Less than a half mile. She could see the busy main from here. As big as Stem Five was, the main looked twice its size. Not only were there throngs of people, there were vehicles as well. Sleek trams that moved like serpents through a giant river, gold and gleaming as they passed under the overhead lamps. She could see all of it even from her distance.

There was plenty of time before she had to meet Trin, so she decided to eat first. She couldn't remember her last meal. A small café up ahead to her left had just opened. She didn't know what it served, but she could smell the work of the kitchen and it was heavenly. Like warm bread and olives. She had no money but she wasn't sure she needed any. In the few days she'd been on the *Kalelah*, she'd never heard anyone speak of money and she never saw anyone use it. She took a seat closest to the stem traffic. A man in a yellow jumpsuit came out from the kitchen to her table.

"Good morning," Sarah said. "I'm starving. And I could smell whatever it is you're making back there for the last ten minutes."

The man in the yellow jumpsuit didn't return her pleasantries. He gestured with two fingers in the air and a menu appeared in the space between them. Then he walked off without a word. Strange, she thought, but what wasn't? With the exception of Trin, who seemed completely recognizable, like a much smarter version of the boys she knew back home, everything about this ship was foreign. A couple holding hands walked by the café and looked her way. Sarah gave them a small, hesitant smile, but the woman only scowled back and whispered something in the man's ear. His face went cold as they both walked past, staring.

She turned her attention back to the menu. She tried to read it but the characters all swirled together. None of it made any sense. She was certain whatever Trin had given her gave her the ability to read. She'd read as recently as just before her walk. And the sign on the café, she had read that with no problem. She knew, for instance, this café was open to all ranks. How could she know that if she couldn't read the sign? But the menu was just dots and shapes and swirls and lines. Meaningless. The man in the yellow jumpsuit returned, but she didn't know what to tell him. It was then that she noticed the scent. Faint, like the smoke from a distant fire, but undeniable. Impossible, she thought. The man in the yellow jumpsuit looked impatient so she gave the menu another look, but she still couldn't make any sense of it. And the scent of Old Spice was yanking at her thoughts, making it hard to concentrate.

"What do you recommend?" she asked.

"You don't get it, do you?" he said coldly.

"What?" But in an instant, she knew what. She knew that voice. And that scent—the recognition slammed her harder than if she'd been punched in the gut.

"You dumb little bitch. I knew you'd screw this up," he said smugly, a small, crooked smile forming. He walked behind her chair and bent over her, his hands on the small café table, his arms blocking her on each side. A cloud of Old Spice fell upon her, so thick and heavy she could taste it.

"What are you doing here? You shouldn't be here," she said, panicked.

"Shut up. You don't talk, remember?"

"This can't be happening," she said in a shaky voice.

"Of course it can. It's as plain as day, baby Blon-dee, plain as day."

"Don't call me that. I hate when you call me that. And it's not plain as day. Nothing is plain as day!"

"You were." He circled back around the chair, switched his grip on the table, and faced her. It was him. How could she not have noticed that before?

Could she run? She didn't think so. He was strong and fast. "I don't understand," she said, her eyes filling, distorting his face, making him even more the monster. "You shouldn't be here. You can't be here!"

"You think you got picked for no reason at all?"

She recoiled. "What?"

"How many times do I have to tell you, huh? There are no accidents, baby Blon-dee."

"What are you saying?"

"You asked for this."

"No. You're crazy. I'm just a little girl."

"Sure, sure you are, Blon-dee. But that doesn't change anything. And now you're in over your head, just like before. Quite the mess you've made for yourself."

"I didn't. I wouldn't! Don't say that." She was crying now and angry that she'd let him see her cry, which only pushed the tears out faster. "You're lying. You've always been a liar."

"A liar? I'm the only honest person you know. Your mother's the liar. Smiling, pretending. It's disgusting, isn't it? You hate her more than me, I think."

"Please, you shouldn't be here." She was practically sobbing now.

"What's with the drama? I have no control over this. This is your doing. You made your decision, remember? It's out of my hands."

"This isn't what I wanted!"

"Keep telling yourself that, maybe it'll help. But I doubt it. You screwed up."

"What's the matter with you? I'm just a little girl!"

He started to laugh. The couple was walking by again, in the same direction still. But they didn't stop. They just stared coldly and kept walking.

"I'm just a little girl!" she pleaded to them. But they never even slowed down. "Why can't anyone ever see that?"

She felt a shaking at her shoulder. She tried to knock his hand away, but he was gone. A voice she knew began to call her name.

"Sarah! Sarah, wake up!"

She opened her eyes and relief washed over her. Cyler was there looking down at her, one hand on Sarah's shoulder.

"You were dreaming," Cyler said softly. "But it's okay now. You're okay."

Sarah sat up in the small bed that took up half the space in Cyler's pod. She was shaking.

Cyler brushed the wet hair off Sarah's face and sat down next to her. "It must have been a bad one."

"Sorry, I get those every once in a while."

"You were crying."

"Yeah, that'll happen too. I'll be okay."

"My God."

She wiped the tears from under her eyes with the meaty parts of her palms. Then she took a deep breath and just sat looking at the wall. Cyler put her arm around her.

After she stopped shaking, Sarah finally spoke. "Argen said we were all the *Kalelah*'s children."

"He said that in your dream?"

"No, up top, on the *Lewis*—my ship. He told us that. You think we're children? Us, my people? You all see us that way?"

Cyler thought about that for a beat. "Some might."

"Yeah? Well, I'd really like to grow up already."

19

Wu Jianzhu, old and tremulous, picked up the secure line.

"Good day, Foreign Minister," he said, deploying his most elegant Queen's English.

"Good evening, State Councillor," the Russian said, also in English, though with an accent one would never describe as elegant. "I hope you enjoyed the bottle I sent. It's impossible to purchase outside Russia."

"Not yet. But I'm sure when I do, it will be a memorable occasion."

"Unless you enjoy too much, eh?" The Russian laughed at his own joke.

"I don't often overdo things, Foreign Minister," the old Chinese diplomat said flatly. "The secret to a long life."

"A pity." Chantankov cleared his throat, the usual signal that he was about to change gears without using the clutch. "But now, with the pleasantries out of the way, let's talk."

Wu saw no reason to be any more graceful in his own transition. "Yes, let's. The Americans' jump to DEFCON 3 is quite unsettling."

"Is it?"

"Of course. The Americans haven't been to DEFCON 3 since your country tried to put missiles on Cuba."

"I see your point, from a historical perspective. But history can only teach us so much. I am quite pleased with this development. In fact, I consider it a great success."

Wu wondered if the Russian had had vodka with his morning coffee.

"We hardly think the Americans increasing their readiness a 'success.' Unless my math is wrong, DEFCON 3 is just one panic away from DEFCON 2."

"You must see the whole situation, my friend. What matters most is not that they went to DEFCON 3, but *why* they went to 3. So, why did they?"

Wu made no attempt to answer. He was too familiar with Chantankov's smug rhetorical games.

"I'll tell you why," Chantankov continued. "It wasn't because of movements by our submarines or our destroyers or our ground troops. Our planes have not violated their air space, so you can cross those off your list. They advanced because with Ganet gone, they have more reason to fear the mystery ship than ever. After all—and I will share this bit of intelligence with you— the nuclear explosion recorded over the Mariana Trench was not from a North Korean warhead."

"We are aware of this."

"Then why are we debating this point?"

"Because we also know the ship had nothing to do with Ganet's death. It was a Russian arm that killed Chief Ganet."

The Russian laughed. "I expected nothing less from the vast skills of Chinese intelligence."

"I'm an old man with little time for games, Foreign Minister. You broke our agreement. You acted alone. And you were sloppy about it."

"People have accused me of many things, Mr. Wu, but sloppy, never. I like things nice and tidy. And that's exactly how they are right now. Nice and tidy."

Wu didn't consider any of this nice and tidy. This was now a risk too far. "We've lost tremendous advantage."

"Some, yes. It is true. But we still have a thirty-minute jump, more than we need."

"It's too small a window for us. The risk of the Americans countering is far too high."

"We discussed this weeks ago, Mr. State Councillor. Things are in motion now. This is not the time to get cold feet. Don't forget that the Americans' move to DEFCON 3 was always a possibility. An inevitability, in my mind. All we've done is to control that move, make it happen on our timetable and for the right reason. At D-3, we still have advantage to spare."

Wu's stomach sank. He'd been worried from the beginning about dealing with the Russians in this sort of game. They were blunt instruments, and even less precise when it came to the Americans. Too much history there, too much humiliation. He now doubted if the Russians could ever really be considered partners. It was true, what Chantankov was saying. Better the

Americans move to D-3 because they've lost Ganet, their connection to the ship, instead of in response to Chinese or Russian maneuvers. Wu understood the value of the misdirect, but it would have been much better if the Americans hadn't moved to D-3 at all. Chantankov was letting the rivalry between the two old Cold War enemies influence his thinking, making him take risks he shouldn't. Wu was angry. And he didn't like being angry.

"Don't let my wrinkles fool you, Mr. Chantankov. I'm not senile yet. And I fail to see how the murder of Ganet, a man the Americans harbored and trained, a man upon which they placed all their hopes, helps our cause."

"Tomorrow at eight o'clock a.m., Washington time, I will call the American secretary of state with Russia's sincere apologies for the unsanctioned actions of a deeply disturbed vigilante. I will also send her a video file containing the confession of the rogue sniper. Then, later in the day, I will have the man shot. This, of course, will also be captured on video and sent to the secretary."

He was floored. "So you intend to turn a murder into a gesture of goodwill?"

"The confession of it, yes. It is our long-standing policy to deny such things. Even when it is outrageous to do so. But in this case, we will take full responsibility. We'll 'come clean,' as the Americans would say."

"They'll never believe a word of it."

"Their belief is not required. Only their indignation. And it will be rewarded with Russia's contrition. It'll be a rare public relations coup for them. And more than that—as a bonus, they'll get read in to our battle plans against the ship."

"Exactly how much shit is your president willing to eat in public?"

"The president of Russia is a long-term thinker. He'll manage to work up the appetite."

"And what if they have their own battle plans, now that you've killed the world's last hope of salvation?"

"Then they'll be too busy to worry much about ours." The Russian paused for a moment before making his final point. "A day ago, the Americans pulled a bullet from Ganet's skull that will have all the signatures of a 7N1 load. They'll recognize it as the ammunition made solely for one weapon: a Dragunov sniper rifle, not so well known or sold as the iconic AK-47, but one of the Soviet era's greatest design achievements. Now, there are only two reasons such a weapon would be used in so high profile a killing. Either someone wanted to implicate Russia in this despicable crime, or Russia herself wanted to send some kind of message."

The Russian paused again, as if an old man needed the time to let the choices sink in. Wu did not. "Whichever it was is, of course, irrelevant," Chantankov continued. "Either way, an extremely agitated president of the United States should have been on the phone with the Kremlin. It's simple chess. And yet?"

"You've heard nothing."

"Quiet as a little mouse."

"You were testing him?"

"Let's just say I got the response I was betting on. The US president might have been willing to drop a small, tactical nuclear weapon in the deepest place on

Earth on what he likely thought was a dead ship. An act of security, a safety measure, something that would barely generate a wag of the finger from the UN Security Council. But open war with two nuclear powers? He doesn't have the spine for it. And so, quiet as a little mouse. Lee is no Kennedy. And Putin is no Khrushchev."

"You are the gambler I've been told you'd be, Mr. Chantankov. Let's hope you're as lucky as you are reckless."

"Eyes on the prize, State Councillor, eyes on the prize."

"This is what the gambler always says when he risks more than he can pay."

The old diplomat said his good-byes and disconnected the secure line. He lifted himself slowly from his chair and walked the length of his cavernous office to the desk of an assistant conveniently stationed just outside his large double doors of polished teak. The younger man instantly rose from his chair, but the old man waved his hand to put the assistant at ease. Then he let himself down in a straight-backed wooden chair at the end of the assistant's desk. He was winded from his walk and said nothing. He closed his eyes and breathed deeply, savoring each breath. He knew the assistant would not be rattled in the least by his informality. He had made his preference for face-to-face meetings, even with subordinates, well known. For this, and other things, Wu enjoyed warm relations with many under his employ and throughout the politburo.

When Wu had caught his breath again, his assistant asked if he could get the councillor anything. "Some water maybe?"

"No. I'm fine." He opened his eyes slowly, and eventually his gaze landed on a cluster of framed photographs perched at the back of the assistant's credenza. "How old is your daughter now, Yang?" the old man asked.

"She's twelve, sir."

"Twelve."

"Yes sir. Quite a handful."

"Yes, of course. But so were you. Am I right?"

The assistant gave a small laugh. "I imagine my parents would say you are."

"She's beautiful. Everything ahead of her."

"Yes, thank you. But what can I do for you, please?"

The old man sighed and tapped his fingers on his knee. He continued to study the collection of pictures. He was silent for a long time.

"Mr. Councillor?"

Wu needed to practically shake himself from his thoughts. And in a soft voice he finally gave his assistant a task. "Have the American ambassador in my office in one hour."

"Yes sir."

With a barely audible thank-you, the old man hoisted himself out of the little chair and began the long, treacherous journey back to his office.

20

Cyler scanned in to her pod after pulling a double shift in the lab. As quarters went, it was a small affair, just an L-shaped room barely big enough for one. The light was low and the room was mostly shadow. Pods for crew of Cyler's rank were just a notch above the purely necessary. Nothing fancy. A slightly arched ceiling to give the illusion of space. A single light band along the ceiling's edge. Muted colors of tans and warm grays and a dark floor of ceramic panels with specs of quartzite.

Small spaces got smaller when they're messy, so Cyler kept hers especially tidy. There wasn't much storage space, just shallow shelves and drawers hidden behind a few of the walls. But Cyler managed to find a space for everything she had in the world—which wasn't much. The service didn't encourage crew to bring aboard hordes of personal effects. Living so many millennia out of time, the less baggage, the less baggage. Cyler's room was as sparse as it was clean, the only decoration being a small glass vase her father had given her before she left, a cut crystal cylinder with a thick heavy base to keep it steady.

Before it was hers on the *Kalelah*, it was his on a large wooden office desk, throwing refracted colors across his walls as the suns moved along their arcs during the day. In her little pod with no windows, under the ocean with no light, the vase had lost its luminous magic. But whenever she saw it, she went home for just a second. Magic enough for her.

The multi-table was on the long arm of the L just to the left of the entry. It was a clever device that served as desk, dining table, or bed depending on the need. She could rotate the top to the desired mode with just the press of a button. It was in bed mode as she entered, unmade and recently slept in by Sarah. The two new pod mates traded shifts sleeping, Sarah using the bed while Cyler worked in the lab and Cyler getting the bed while Sarah went out exploring the ship. Trin had managed to hack into the flora-doc database and get Sarah's bios logged in. As far as the scanners knew, Sarah belonged. She could go wherever the rank on her jumpsuit allowed. It wasn't everywhere, but the ship was vast, and she could stay out of the tiny pod long enough for Cyler to get in just enough sleep. But the living arrangement was far from ideal, with the crazy-tight quarters being the least of the problems. Cyler could see that Sarah was bright, impressive, and surprising in many ways, but the foreignness of life on the *Kalelah* was undeniable. Even the simplest ways of the ship seemed to stump her.

Worse, Cyler had her own ways, and Sarah was still stumbling through figuring them out, managing to annoy more than please. The bed left unmade was another example. Cyler would have to run the table through its cycles to get clean sheets before she could get to bed. It wouldn't take more than a few minutes, but the double shift had worn her out. She was bone-tired. And now she was annoyed. She pressed the proper sequence on the controls, sighed heavily, and turned to wash up at the other arm of the L.

The washing wall was separated from the long arm of the pod by a thin partition that quickly rolled up into the ceiling with the tap of a finger on a small patch on the adjacent wall. She hit the patch, the separation shot up, and Cyler nearly walked smack into the chest of the tall man with the long beard.

She screamed and stumbled backward, but there wasn't much room to travel. The multi-table stopped her motion almost immediately, leaving not more than three feet between her and him.

"Shhh," the tall man said calmly. He put his index finger to his mouth and took a step forward.

"What are you doing here," she gasped.

"I prayed and prayed. I want you to know that."

"What?"

"I tried to be good."

"How did you get in here?" She pushed herself backwards harder, disbelieving the dimensions of the room.

"I can go anywhere. Anywhere I want. But I didn't want to come here tonight. I didn't want to come here ever. I prayed so very hard. You have to know that. I don't want to be here."

"Then leave. Just leave now. I won't tell anyone." Her words came out in bursts between desperate breaths. She tried to make her way sideways, toward the door that led back to the stem. But he pushed himself away from the washing wall so fast she nearly ran into him again.

"But you will tell. God would make you."

"No, no He won't. I swear. Just lea—"

But he was on her before her last word. He grabbed her hard with his right arm and covered her mouth with his left. The speed and shock of it made her knees go weak. And then everything slowed down.

She tried to wrench herself free but there was no chance, his grip was like iron. And just like that, with what seemed like no effort at all, he had her up off her feet and turning, the room around her swirling in slow motion. As she turned she saw the threads in the weave of the tan fabric covering the walls with such detail she could almost count them. She saw the soft glow of the light band smear in her vision as her gaze turned upward toward the arched ceiling. And then—*boom!*—she hit the table. She could feel the mechanism underneath her, doing its job, blind to the horror above.

He took his left hand from her mouth, but before she could scream again, his hands were at her throat.

So fast. He's so fast.

She looked into his eyes. He was crying. But before she could even register the strangeness of his tears, the pain in her throat took over. She hit him on the sides. She tried to kick, but she could feel herself losing.

She could feel herself drowning. She could feel herself giving in.

And then a blast of light entered the pod. He turned his head in the direction of the door and his grip loosened enough for her to take a breath.

She heard a woman's voice shout, "What the fuck!"

Sarah. Back early.

And then the table finished its cycle and began to rotate. It pushed the tall man away from her while she began to slide down the opposite side. He lost his leverage and was forced to extend his reach. His grip loosened even more. And then momentum took over. His hands slipped from her throat completely and she was off the table, gulping air, her own hands at her throat attempting to rub the pain away. The tall man stumbled. Cyler turned on her hands and knees. She had no strength to stand, but she could see Sarah's feet as they moved away from the door and into the room.

The tall man began to push himself off the floor. But Sarah kept coming. She had something in her hands now. Cyler looked up to see the wink of glass as it arced over Sarah's head. *The vase.*

No! she tried to scream. But nothing but a wounded whisper escaped.

It was too late anyway. Sarah had a look on her face that read no stopping. She brought the thick and heavy part of the vase down on the tall man's head. Cyler heard the crack of bone. And then all was quiet. The man slumped down, his eyes open, a fresh tear running down his face.

"What the fuck!" Sarah screamed again, this time wheezing like she'd just sprinted a mile. "This guy!" She pointed to him in disgust and disbelief. "Oh my God, I think I killed him!" And then she rushed to where Cyler was crouched on the floor and threw her arms around her. "Are you all right? He was choking you! Holy shit, Cyler, what the fuck just happened? Who is this guy?"

"The vase," Cyler croaked.

"What?"

"Is it broken?"

"I don't know."

Sarah looked across the small room where the tall man lay, with his head at a wrong angle and blood dripping down his lifeless face. She found the vase on the hard floor near the man's left hand. She reached across the floor and picked it up, keeping one hand on Cyler's shoulder.

"No, it's fine. All good."

"Thank you," Cyler said, and then her panic turned to tears and she finally began to sob.

"It's okay now," Sarah said in as soothing a voice as her still-heaving chest would allow. "He can't hurt you anymore."

When Cyler had finally stopped shaking, she asked, "How did you do that? I mean, I don't think I could have. I didn't."

"I don't know. I saw him on you. And I saw you, like you had given up. I've seen that look before. I didn't think, really, I just reacted."

"What do we do now?"

"There are police here, right? I've seen people who looked like they might be police. Shouldn't we call them?"

"No. You wouldn't last three questions with security. They'd find you out, and Trin would be stripped of everything. He'd never be free. And this man"—Cyler gestured toward the tall man but didn't actually look his way—"has very powerful friends."

"What do you mean?"

And so Cyler told Sarah about the Circle, and Laird, and the tall man's invitation. She told her about how Argen's attempt to delay Correction was seen by Laird and her followers in the Circle as weakness and a sin that could never be forgiven. She told Sarah things a Circle member didn't tell outsiders. She broke the rules. And she didn't care. Sarah had shown Cyler something she hadn't thought was possible. Which she now understood was Argen's plan all along. That was why Sarah was here. Argen knew if he couldn't find what he was looking for on the surface—some proof of God, evidence that would change the Circle's mind about the population, about the Delivery—he'd need a backup, a plan B. If he couldn't find the argument against Correction up top, maybe the people of the *Kalelah* would find it themselves. In Sarah.

It made her cry all over again. Sarah put her arms around Cyler even tighter, and the two of them rocked gently against the table until Cyler was still and quiet again.

266

21

"How did this happen?" demanded Laird. "How does a guide ship get stuck?"

The lead bot operator turned from his work and shot out of his chair to stand at attention. "The blast, sir. High heat and sand make glass. The rearward two leaves of the ship are covered in it."

"You can sit, Operator. I'm just here to get the answers I need straight from the source, and you're the source. So why would glass stop us? I thought the *Kalelah* was designed to break up surface accumulation."

"She is," the operator answered as he aired the images from outside the ship. "Here's the cover mound, and here is where the glass begins. But look at this area here, past the perimeter. That's the problem."

Hundreds of illumination bots were hovering over the ship like an electric star field, pinpricking the thick abyssal night with tracers of hot white and revealing the cover mound so the operators could monitor the work of the drills. In the alien-bright she could indeed see a change in the surface of the cover. Where most of the ship was blanketed in the dull wool of sand and silt, the areas of Leaves Five and Six sparkled with the iridescent greens, blues, and yellows of strike glass. It was a landscape of gemstones, a vista that under different circumstances would have to be called beautiful. But she could see the problem plainly: the glass field extended far beyond the soft contours of the cover mound. How far, she couldn't see; the ink of the abyss was far more powerful than the lights from the bots. But she could see enough.

"We're fused to the floor," she said.

"That's right, Captain. So, before our heat vents will work to turbine off the normal silt and sand, we have to break up the glass that's got us anchored. We're drilling a two-foot-diameter hole every three feet. That should create a perforation line the *Kalelah* can break."

"How long will it take?"

"We got lucky, sir. Either their targeting was off or the bomb drifted as it fell, but it missed us. We could have been entirely glassed. And, amazingly, none of the docks or ejector holes were covered. That's why all the probes we launched made it out. Every bot is out, too. This won't take forever."

"We might not be so lucky the next time, Operator. So how about a little more specificity?"

"I think we can get this done in less than seventy-two hours."

"You have forty-eight."

She turned to leave the bot station and began heading toward the door.

"Sir, a question?" the operator called after her.

She stopped and turned again to face the young man, the glowing projection of the drills mindlessly going about their business hanging between them.

"Is it true, sir, what we've heard about the seed population? It's seven billion now?"

She walked closer to the operator. "Point three, operator. It's seven point *three* billion. And every day that number increases. So every day we are delayed only adds to the situation."

She pulled a chair to his workstation and sat. "Do you understand?" she said warmly.

"Yes, sir. It's just hard, that's all. With so many." His voice choked on the last two words.

"God has given us a commandment. Agreed?"

The operator bucked up. Or pretended to. "Yes, sir."

"Which makes it our job to execute as He says we must. We can't pretend to know Him well enough to interpret His commands. Agreed?"

"Yes, sir."

She got up from the chair, pushed it back to its original place, and walked through the room to the door. As the door rose from the floor, she turned to the operator one last time.

"But yes, Operator Klayn, our job is hard. Very hard. That's why it's ours to do."

22

"Shit," Trin said, looking down at the dead man.

Sarah didn't know who else to call. Actually, she didn't know anyone else at all. Cyler had pressed herself into the furthest corner from the body, her arms crossed around herself.

"He was going to kill her. I came in and he was choking her. I didn't mean to hurt him so badly. I just wanted him to stop," Sarah said.

"Looks like you stopped him forever."

Trin went to Cyler and knelt down. She put her arms around him.

"Are you hurt?" he asked.

"Just bruised. She saved my life," Cyler whispered.

"Who is this guy? Do you know him?"

"I don't know his name."

"But you know him. Has he tried to hurt you before?"

"No, never. We talked. Once, twice, maybe. He seemed okay. Strange, but okay."

"Fuck, Cyler. This guy was not okay. It's incredible Sarah walked in. He could have killed you both."

"Maybe she was meant to be here," Cyler said.

Trin didn't answer right away. He just held on to Cyler, thinking it seemed. "Maybe," he said at last, his voice gentle, accommodating.

He stood up and turned to Sarah.

"How?" he asked, incredulously.

But she didn't know how. The sight of Cyler beneath the man—it was like she could feel Cyler's fear. She couldn't stand it. But there were no words she could muster to explain this to Trin. And she didn't want to. If she did, she might need to throw her arms around him the way Cyler had a minute ago.

She just shrugged her shoulders. "What do we do now?" she said.

Trin knelt down to get a better look at the body. "Fuck me. He's a security officer," he said grimly.

"He can't be," said Sarah. Why would a security officer want to hurt Cyler?"

"Look at his pin. He's police."

"Bad just got worse," said Sarah.

"We have to get rid of him."

"What does that mean?" squeaked Cyler.

"Well, he can't stay here dead like this," Trin said. "And we can't just pull him out into the stem."

"What if he was another no-wake?" Cyler said hopefully. "Then he'd be on a gurney, all covered. There's been so many this Waking, maybe it wouldn't draw that much attention?"

"Except when the guys with the gurneys take him he'll have a bashed-in skull. And he'll be out of his

M-suit and out of his pod. We don't even know where his pod is. It'll never fly as a no-wake. It'll look like what it is: a violent death. Even if we could steal a gurney and get it here ourselves, we'd be caught on a dozen cameras and mics, and there'd still be the morgue at the other end. Either way, it's a gurney full of questions we can't answer."

"We do it here then," said Sarah.

"What?" asked Cyler.

"The toilet."

"No, no way," Cyler pleaded.

"It doesn't flush. Mine—I mean, *ours*—they flush. With water."

"Water?" Cyler said. "That's gross."

"Whatever. Yours burn. I noticed that the first time I used it. I pressed the button and waited for the water, but it never came. There was just this, I don't know, a whoosh, like a gas burner."

"It could work," said Trin.

"What are you two talking about? He's a huge man. How is he going to fit in a—oh, no." Cyler put her hand to her mouth.

Sarah felt like doing the same. The gruesome implications of her own idea were making her sorry she'd even made the suggestion.

Trin, on the other hand, seemed to have no trouble with what was to come. "We need a saw," he said glibly.

"Oh God," moaned Cyler, her hand still at her mouth.

"Don't worry, I'll do the dirty work," said Trin. "We just have to find the right tool."

"A laser," Cyler said softly, giving in.

"Exactly. A laser would cauterize as it went and there'd be a lot less blood we'd have to mop up. It'll still be messy, but nowhere near as bad as with a saw." Trin crouched lower to study the body from different angles.

"Jesus," Sarah said. "How do you know this? *Why* do you know this?"

"He knows everything." Cyler shrugged.

"Too bad, though," he said, still sizing up the bearded man. "We don't have a laser."

"The lab does," Cyler continued. "We use them in the field to cut through thick forest. They're not strong enough for metal or stone, but I saw what happened to a guide who got careless. The beam took two toes off his right foot in less than a second."

"I'll go with you," said Trin.

"No. Someone will see you there and it'll just call more attention to me. Better if I go alone. Just a lab rat who forgot something. I can be back in an hour."

"Why don't we walk you there?" said Sarah.

"I'm fine now. I'm stable, anyway. Thank you. I can do this. I *want* to do this."

"Sarah and I will go shopping," Trin said. "We're going to need some cleaning supplies."

The three of them left the pod. Cyler went one way, Sarah and Trin the other. After a few minutes, Sarah looked Trin's way and spoke in Origen, even though English would have been easier.

"Thank you for getting over there so quickly. That was a pretty awful scene."

He stopped and gently grabbed her arm to stop her as well. He turned her toward him.

"I'm sorry. Killing a person is, well, I don't know actually. But it can't be easy. Are you okay?"

"Not my best day," she said. "But I'll survive."

She faked a small smile and they started walking again. Sarah stayed quiet, chewing on what to say next.

"She loves you, you know. Cyler."

He took a minute to respond. "She said that?"

"No. And she wouldn't to me, anyway. But her eyes said it. Every time you walked in the room."

"Shit."

"Shit? What do you mean, *shit*?"

"Just shit. I don't know."

"I thought you two were, you know, a thing."

"A thing. Is that what you call it?"

"Sometimes. What do you call it? You and Cyler?"

"Complicated. I guess."

"Jesus. Even when you come from another planet you're all still the same."

"Who?"

"Guys. You're all imbeciles."

He smiled, but he didn't look at her. They just kept walking. "Things are different now."

"You think? You overslept by one hundred and twenty thousand years and screwed up God's big plan. Then I discovered that everything I ever believed was probably just made up, a child's fairy tale. We're headed for World War Last. And today, just to put a cherry on top, I killed a guy. So yeah, things are different."

"That's not the different I mean."

They stopped again, the foot traffic flowing around them.

"The difference is I met you."

"Whoa, boy genius. Don't say that." She took a step back.

"Okay."

He stepped forward and kissed her.

She didn't push him away. Instead, she kissed him back. And she let it go as long as it wanted to go, as long as they wanted it to go. When it was over, she took another small step back and looked him in the eyes.

"Oh, crap."

JAGGED ARROW

BOOK III OF THE KALELAH SERIES

1

The sound was like what she imagined a steel girder would make if the rivets that held it secure suddenly snapped and the beam fell several stories onto the roof of a car. A series of gunshots, a nervous pause, and then a sickly crash. *POP! POP! POP!*—wait—*BOOOM!* The floor beneath her shuddered in time with every crush of the unsuspecting car driving through Sarah's imagination.

The noises and vibrations had been subtle at first, as if far in the distance. But as the minutes went by, they grew louder, more concussive, nearer.

She lay on the floor of a toilet facility in the main stem of Leaf Four, exhausted from vomiting. With her ear to the ground, her face too white and dotted with sweat, she thought she must look like a lunatic diviner. Only instead of whispers from beyond, she tracked the *POP! POP! POP!*—wait—*BOOOM!* ... of what? Another malfunction, the ship destroying itself seven miles beneath the surface of the ocean? Or the preparations for yet another genocide, one so complete there'd never be another?

How Sarah had ended up sprawled across this particular floor could have easily been blamed on many things: her original discovery of the giant ship on which she now resided, said ship's current desire to burn her planet to a crisp, or her own surprising role in a loose plan to prevent the aforementioned Big Burn from happening in the first place. Any one of those, she figured, would be cause enough for a bad case of the upchucks.

But this case of the hurls had been more primal in nature. Less about nerves and more about the sights, sounds, and smells of butchering the evidence of a murder. A murder, in fact, by her hands. And Cyler's vase.

Getting rid of Cyler's now involuntarily dead attacker had proven to be exactly as horrible an experience as she had predicted. She was sorry she had even suggested the idea almost as soon as it had left her mouth. *The toilets here don't flush*, she'd noted to Trin, *they burn*. Since they couldn't move a body through the stem, and had nowhere to take it in any event, she thought they might hack it up and dispose of the pieces in the toilet. It was a *Breaking Bad*-inspired cleanup. But during the gruesome work, it seemed more like just a really bad idea. Her stomach agreed.

And so her choice had been simple: either barf all over Trin, or find a toilet that wasn't busy destroying evidence and lose it there. Hence her position on the floor of one of the many public toilets along the main stem of Leaf Four. And while there's never much dignity in vomiting, she felt no particular shame about it in this instance. A surgeon she was not. In fact, her previous experience with dissection had been limited exclusively to one medium-sized frog in the seventh grade. It was okay if slicing up a dead lunatic made her sick.

It was the last thirty minutes of uncontrollable crying that had her worried.

When Trin picked her for this mission (could she call it that?), she was at once terrified and flattered. But if the rush of events had not blurred her ability to think things through in an honest and rational way, if she had not been so carried away by the impossible things she had heard from the strangers who descended from an alien craft onto the deck of her survey ship, if Wilson—a high-ranking government official—had not finally seemed to believe them, and if she hadn't been completely rattled by watching Argen take a bullet to the head, she would have rejected Trin's idea that she be the one to accompany him back to the *Kalelah*.

She would have screamed *FUCK NO!* as loudly as any human being could have screamed it.

But she hadn't screamed. Instead she had let Trin and his compelling confidence and his piercing eyes and his café au lait skin trick her into doing something she knew was beyond her.

Far beyond her.

She looked around the small booth she'd run into when her own gag reflex could no longer be ignored. Even it was a miracle. The underlit glass floor was spotless and gently heated. The ceiling was a night sky filled with a million stars and three beautiful moons, one the color of campfire, the others a teal, with their centers nearly white with light. And the panels that defined the limits of the booth, their corners softly rounded, showed a peaceful desertscape with miles and miles of sand in all directions and ringed by a purple mountain ridge in the far distance.

There were speakers somewhere in the tiny space. They played the sounds of a light breeze blowing through the low, ground-hugging scrub brush that dotted the sand and cast shadows in three directions from the light delivered by triplet moons. And this was a fucking public restroom. She could only imagine what the security apparatus was truly like. Or the weapons.

How could she have possibly thought she could help take on this miracle of a ship? How ridiculous was she? So, even though her stomach had long been empty and her gagging long quieted, she lay there and let the tears come freely.

The thing to do, she eventually came around to thinking, was quit. Raise the white flag, get back to the surface, and die where she belonged. After all, wasn't it at least a little bit immoral to continue to let Trin bet on the wrong horse? To deceive him when so much was on the line? There was just one problem. She had no idea where on the surface she'd go.

Could she return to the *Lewis*? With the scanner shut down, her job likely wasn't waiting for her anymore. Ohio? Home? She had left there a long time ago with the promise she'd never return. Besides, Jack. She was desperate to see her mother, especially with the doomsday clock ticking down. But she didn't know what she'd do if she saw Jack again. One murder on her soul was enough.

And then it began again. *POP! POP! POP!*—wait—*BOOOM!*

Were the sounds louder now? Closer? She thought so. Whatever they meant to the status of the ship, they were a stark reminder of her status: She was seven miles beneath the surface of the ocean, on an alien ship. And she had no way off.

She wasn't going anywhere.

2

Pardo's head ached. He knew better than to drink that much, especially before a shift. But he'd been drinking a lot lately. And he wasn't alone. Everyone in engineering had been drinking more than they ever had in their lives. He rubbed his head, which reminded him, as did any number of routine actions, of his broken hand. He'd broken it four days ago, on the face of Nicoliah Tar.

Nicoliah had been mouthing off about the various pussies he'd known throughout his life. The first one, the tightest one, the wettest one, and the noisiest one. Nicoliah was a funny guy, and he had the table of six men laughing good and hard. Pardo was laughing, too. But when Nicoliah finished his story, Pardo stopped laughing.

"Okay, gentlemen," Nicoliah had said, "and now for the *biggest* pussy I've ever known. And let me be clear here, I'm talking big. Just, seriously, an enormous pussy. An epically enormous pussy."

He stood up from his chair to place his hand just shy of six feet from the ground. A few in the group were howling already.

"I've been discreet so far, boys, have I not? I've not specifically named any of these pussies, have I? Because I am a gentleman."

More snickers.

"But this one, the biggest one, I must reveal to you. I must share the name so everyone knows."

They all listened up, barely containing themselves.

"The biggest pussy I have ever known in my life, my entire life, is a man who went AWOL from his own ship the minute things went south."

Confused faces all around.

"The dishonorable captain Jan Argen. Oops, excuse me! *Former* captain Jan Argen."

That was when Pardo threw his first punch.

He knew he shouldn't have taken Nicoliah's joke so personally. But the ship oversleeping all those years—*120,000 years*—and leaving the Halfborn on their own all that time - it spooked him. How could that happen? Then the bomb from the Halfborn came. No single official had called it a bomb, but everyone knew it was a bomb. The Halfborn weren't even supposed to be sharpening sticks yet, let alone creating something that could turn the sand that covered the ship to glass. He knew this meant the Delivery had failed and Argen had to order a Correction. Everyone knew it. But when Argen didn't and Laird became captain, Pardo was shaken.

He didn't know the inside stories behind any of it. He was just an engineer. No one who knew anything was going to let him in on it. But in his heart, he knew something bad must have happened. And all the stupid gossip rushing through the ship like a tsunami—that Argen had been killed, or jailed, or had simply run away to the surface—all of it made him stay up late wondering and worrying. And drinking. Nicoliah's joke was just the snapping point.

To Pardo, the idea that Argen would have a closeted yellow streak that somehow showed up at the worst possible time was something he just couldn't bring himself to believe. Because if it were true—if Argen really did bail on the ship because he couldn't handle his duties—well, that was almost worse than all the crazy speculation and rumors. It was worse because Pardo had depended on Argen, leaned on him.

Argen was a bulwark against the terrors of deep space, distance, and the lurking, nagging truth behind every waking moment: They were alone and beyond rescue. The *Kalelah* was all they had. Their world was defined by its alloy skin. And the captain was her representative in flesh. He was the ship.

It didn't matter to Pardo that he didn't actually even know the captain particularly well. It would be a stretch to say he even knew him at all on a personal level. He'd shaken his hand just once. To the captain, it was probably nothing. But for Pardo, the connection was real. A connection fused with his first days on the ship. His first days away from everything.

When Pardo felt lost, it was Argen's presence, his calming routine, that helped him through those early days of transition. It was Argen who started every morning with his confident, baritone greeting, "May

God ease your day." And it was always Argen who made the comm's last announcement of the workday, "May God bless your evening."

He could be funny, too, on the comm. Not stupid funny like Nicoliah, but smart funny. Pardo didn't come from a big family. There was just his mother and an aunt he sometimes saw. He'd never known his father. A few halos were all he had as proof the man even existed. So Argen, or rather Argen's voice, had been what he imagined the comfort of family might feel like. Now, alone and so far from home, the idea that someone so important to him, to all of them, might not be who Pardo thought he was terrified him. That the man might not match the voice was a fright that went right down to the bone.

So Pardo had hit Nicoliah. Several times. As hard as he could. And it had been difficult to stop, even after his hand had broken and begun to swell. He hadn't been punching against Laird, of course. He knew nothing about her, good or bad. But this had always been Argen's ship, Argen's life. He could hear it in the captain's voice. The voice that had helped Pardo sleep at night.

And if Argen could leave them, why couldn't she leave too?

3

Dent Forent had a question for the newly self-appointed captain that couldn't be asked in public. Not because the nature of the inquiry was indelicate, or because it would inspire others within earshot to wonder the same thing—plenty of people were already openly asking the same question. He wanted to be alone with Laird because he still held hope, albeit just a shred, that away from the public stage of the CC, he might be able to influence her.

So he'd raced to be at the opening of the narrow corridor that connected her quarters with the main stem at precisely the right moment. He was winded but on time. Her schedule was yet another rigid layer in the cloak of rituals and rules she draped around herself, its code easily cracked by anyone who'd been paying attention. And ever since she'd pinned the gold open hands of leadership to her chest, he'd been paying attention.

He didn't have to wait long before she rounded the corner to the stem. He put himself directly in her path.

She stopped and greeted him with a restrained look of annoyance. As predicted.

"Captain, a word, please," he said.

"You can walk with me if you want, Mr. Forent. We're nearly drilled through the glass and I have a hundred things to do." She stepped around him and resumed her original trajectory toward the CC.

Forent, still not fully recovered from his earlier trek halfway across the ship, followed behind her.

"Have you arrested Captain Argen?" he called out.

"I think you mean *former* Captain Argen. And no, I have not. In fact, I believe Jan Argen is AWOL."

"Impossible," Forent managed.

"A transport vehicle was gone from its berth for five hours and six minutes three days ago. Ganet remains missing as well. And there's not a nanosecond of vid. They're covering their tracks, wouldn't you say?"

"I wouldn't know. I don't know. That's why I've come to see you. Can we slow down a bit?" he puffed.

She kept her pace. Yet he didn't doubt she'd heard his request.

"They're both AWOL, as far as I'm concerned. Which means when we do find them, and we will, I'll be able to tell you the happy news that the former captain and chief are both safely behind bars."

"Argen wouldn't go AWOL. And neither would Ganet. They knew what would happen if … if you'd take command."

That got her attention. She stopped and turned to face him. He hadn't planned to hit her with that. It just came out. He regretted it already. He'd always believed honey caught more flies than vinegar, and this was a bad start. But he was tired of chasing her. And now he could at least catch his breath a bit.

"What's happening, Mr. Forent, is precisely what's supposed to be happening, no matter who is in command of this ship. We have a rogue population up top. A Delivery gone bad. A population we brought here and should have watched and guided to their God-given destiny. But we didn't. We Skipped for one hundred and twenty thousand years, and now our Delivery has languages it shouldn't, weapons it shouldn't, and, worst of all, gods it shouldn't. Do I have to worry about your loyalties now, too?"

"Sir, I'm worried about yours. If you don't already have them behind bars, then they're up top."

"Your point?"

"The Correction. It'll take them, too."

"That's obvious, Forent. But they made their bed."

He stared at her for a long moment. Could she really be this cold? Toward Ganet, maybe. Those two were not exactly best friends. But toward Argen? Everyone knew her relationship with Argen wasn't entirely professional. But now he saw nothing in her eyes to say she even knew the man at all.

"These are our shipmates," he said earnestly. "We trained together. We left our homes together, all of us knowing we were saying goodbye to our families forever. Together was the one thing we had left."

"You think I'm some sort of heartless villain, Forent? Is that why you're standing in front of me sweating and panting instead of managing your team in the labs?"

"I don't know what you are. Sir." But he was starting to get an idea. And he didn't like it.

"I'm captain, Mr. Forent," she said as a simple matter of fact. "Just captain."

She resumed her fast-paced walk. But Forent followed. He couldn't let that be the last word.

"Argen would not do this. He would not condemn more than seven billion to the fire of a Correction."

"No," she said without hesitation, "he wouldn't. And you've hit on the real point of this exercise, haven't you?"

"Exercise?"

She stopped again. "You think this is an accident?"

"The malfunction?"

"There was no malfunction."

"What are we talking about here?"

"I'm talking about the mountain, Forent. The mountain is crumbling. You don't feel it? Chunks of the rock snapping off the edge, shrinking the ground all around you?"

Whoa. This was *not* how he imagined this conversation would go. Laird was always edgy, always on the threshold. But never over it. That was her unique skill: mastering the controlled fury. Now there was a look in her eyes he didn't recognize.

"God raised a great peak for us." She spread her arms wide. "The Plan is our mountaintop, our view above everything else in the universe, and He gave it to us, Forent, by His own hand, in His own blood."

"Captain," he said softly, hoping he could stop whatever tirade she was about to unleash. But she raised an imperious hand.

"For thousands of pages on eighteen scrolls, He literally opened His veins for us. The blood is all the same. Every character on every page is the identical blood type and exactly the same age. Not a drop is a minute older or younger than another. The amount of blood, of course, only God could have spared. But despite all that He bled, in all those millions of words, He never once told us the truth about our mountain. But I'll tell you, Forent, because many years ago, when the truth finally occurred to me, everything suddenly made sense. Why we're here on this planet and why I'm here in this captain's uniform. Do you want to know this secret?"

He could feel the sweat on his head now. He wasn't confused anymore. He was scared.

"Captain," he said slowly, as if to a child, "where is former captain Argen?"

She took his hands in hers and squeezed them hard. "Our mountain is being eroded, broken down piece by piece by eons of prayer made without love."

"Hanta, where is Jan?" he pleaded. But she just kept on, like he hadn't said a word.

"Loveless devotion will chip away at the strongest rock. And that's what's been happening. Most of the people you've ever known were just chisels against our sacred stone, completely unaware of the damage they inflicted. The Keepers I knew back home weren't prepared to stop it. The instructors I had in Academy weren't prepared to stop it. I hoped Argen could stop it—or help me stop it. I tried to get him to see the cracks and the scars. I even thought I might have loved him. Do you have any idea what that means? But in the end, he was no better than all the others. He couldn't see. And I couldn't wait."

She dropped his hands and with them the softness with which she had been coating her voice.

"There was no other way. Unless someone took action, our mountain was going to fall. And I wouldn't let that happen. An example had to be made."

"An example? My God, Hanta. What have you done?"

"Don't look so shocked, Forent. What if God had tapped you on the shoulder instead of me? Would you have done what He asked?"

"Seven billion, Hanta," he said, stunned.

"Things must change," she said coldly. "I'm behind schedule, Mr. Forent."

And then she turned and walked toward the big oval of the CC, this time at a much slower pace. She glanced back only once.

But he was done following her.

• • • •

He needed to sit. And so, he sat. That he chose to do so exactly where he was standing, in the middle of the stem, didn't seem to be something worth worrying about.

That he would offer to the many passersby in the crowded stem a uniquely inelegant and unflattering vision of the ship's Guide Lead didn't seem to be worth worrying about.

That he'd made no plans on the way from standing to sitting for how exactly he might plop his hulking mass to the hard tiles beneath his feet without injuring himself also seemed to be not worth worrying about.

Such was his heartbreak.

She had forced the *Kalelah* to fail, he marveled. She was the glitch. She was why a population that had grown to more than seven billion had done so entirely on their own, with no help from him or his team. He wasn't sure which was worse, that Laird—or anyone— could be so deranged and evil, or that the near miracle of the population's unlikely survival and success would not only go uncelebrated, it would be punished with a brutality he could barely even contemplate.

And then came his next concern: Why had she told him? Did she simply lose herself in the moment? Did she lose her mind? Or was he just another exercise, a chance for her to gauge a reaction and get a sense of what she'd be up against if the truth ever did come out?

He was still sweating and having trouble catching his breath. The floor was cool and he placed his hands palms down on the polished tile to get as much of the chill as he possibly could. He had to recover quickly and get moving again. Because in the end, it didn't really matter why Laird had told him what she did. The same sequence of events would surely follow.

First, his commlink would be cut, taking away his access to the ship's float net and his ability to communicate with anyone or anything electronically. Then two guards would emerge from the CC and he'd be taken to a place where no one would listen to a word of what he knew. He'd be jailed for certain. And why not killed as well? If she was willing to destroy seven billion, what's one more? The only thing he didn't know was how much time he had.

It was in this sad, blob-like posture that a vague and ever-so-slightly hopeful notion came to him. Trin. The kid was the first person Argen woke when the scan alarm sounded. He and Argen and Chief Ganet were practically inseparable hunting down what they thought was a bug. Trin had to be told he was looking for something else entirely. It wasn't evidence of a malfunction in the time clock he needed to find. It was evidence of sabotage.

But first, Forent had to get his fat ass off the damn floor.

He took a few big breaths, got one knee under him, and began to push himself upward. The floor was slippery from perspiration and he nearly went back down again when his heel started to slide. After a few shaky attempts, though, he was back on his feet—red-faced, sweaty, and winded, but upright.

Then he began to run, as quickly as a hard-breathing, overweight, middle-aged man could.

His chest burned and everything else simply hurt. But he had to find Trin before the guards found him. The sweat stung his eyes and soaked his jumpsuit. He looked behind him toward the CC's big doors. They were still closer than he'd imagined they'd be given the fire burning in his lungs. But they were closed, and no guards were following him. That was good.

Except his immediate trouble was figuring out where to steer his loudly protesting body. He had no idea where Trin's pod might be. Junior officers could be housed in any of three different leaves. He tried his comm in the hopes of accessing a database. It was challenging to hail while running, his fingers were all over the place, but he didn't want to stop. He didn't know exactly how much time had, only that it wasn't much.

Three times he tried, but nothing, no response from the net at all. Finally, it made sense. It wasn't his running and his bouncing fingers. His link was already down. Laird wasn't wasting a minute.

This was going to be every bit the race he feared it would be.

His legs began to itch painfully. He noted concerned looks on people he passed. He wondered if he should just stop, grab the first person he could and tell everything Laird had just told him. But who here would believe him? No, he needed Trin and Phetra. He was better off running. He decided to check Leaf Four first, that was the closest. His chest was heaving now, and his left arm just beneath the shoulder felt like it'd been punched.

He was weaving, bumping people as he went. His face was wet, his vision blurred. A hover gurney, burdened with another likely no-wake, crossed his path before he could see it and the two collided at speed. The gurney and its morbid load pinwheeled from the crash, spun nearly full circle, and knocked Forent's legs out from under him as it circled back around him from behind. He went down to the cold, hard tiles again, his chest a blast furnace, his legs numb, and his lungs insatiable.

He knew he wasn't getting back up. And just before he passed out, he was certain that on the edges of his vision he saw the watery image of two security guards, weapons drawn and headed his way.

4

"She's finally asleep," Trin said.

"That's good," replied Sarah. "Cyler had a rough night."

"We all had a rough night."

They took a left down the stem for no particular reason. It was late. There were plenty of people still moving through the high-ceilinged avenue. Some Sarah imagined were on their way home, if that's what they'd call a pod. Some she figured were on their way to their posts for the night shift. But at this hour the stem had shed its typical frantic pace. The overhead lights had been dimmed in sync with other efforts on the ship to simulate night. People moved with purpose but slower than usual. And no one looked at her strangely. No one noticed her much at all.

She'd been intentional about trying to appear as ordinary as possible as she made her way around the ship. She no longer gawked at every new architectural impossibility, like the crazy-tall ceilings, the breathtaking plants that sometimes lined the walls of long stretches of a stem fed by a drizzling mist and fog that gave the corridor the feeling of a lush trail cutting its way through a rainforest, or the strange little farms that suddenly came into view when she turned a corner.

It seemed, too, that Trin had done a good job with the microbe cocktail that swirled invisibly around her and tricked the ship into seeing her as one of its manifest own. She was able to pass through any door the rank of her borrowed jumpsuit allowed.

For a moment, she let herself subscribe to the same delusion the *Kalelah* had, that she and Trin were no different from any of the others she passed. She and Trin were just an ordinary couple taking a late-night stroll.

POP! POP! POP!—wait—*BOOOM!*

Her pleasant fiction didn't last long. The noise, louder now, was a quick reminder that the two of them were the furthest from ordinary you could get. Trin had become an agent of a desperate plan quickly drawn by a dead captain who never imagined himself dying. And she ... well, she didn't know what she was supposed to do. Except save the world.

She felt her eyes mist. She looked over at Trin, searching for some sign he was feeling just a little like she did. But he walked the corridor like he owned it. *Bastard.*

"That noise is freaking me out."

"Drillbots. They're working this area of the ship, breaking the glass from the bomb blast."

"We're running out of time, aren't we?"

He didn't answer her. He just kept walking. After a full minute went by, he finally said something.

"I have to tell Cyler, don't I? About us, I mean. She should know before ... well, before."

Fuck.

"Trin," she said as gently as possible. "There isn't anything to tell her. We kissed. That's all. And it was stupid, and it won't happen again."

"You don't believe that."

"Just because you're a genius doesn't mean you know everything. Besides, don't we have more important things to worry about? Shouldn't we be doing something about the thing that's going to kill everybody?"

"We are."

"I'm walking around here lost out of my mind. I broke a dude's head open. Then you cut him up and burned him in a fucking toilet. Yeah, we're kicking ass all right. We're fucking heroes!"

She was done with gentle.

"Your job was to be yourself. To show people here on the ship that the seed population on the surface is more like us than anyone here thinks. We need people to see you as human, not Halfborn. And now, Cyler does."

"Because I killed someone?"

"Because you were her friend. You put yourself in danger and you saved her life, Sarah."

"That's just one person. *One person.* How does that make a difference?"

"It makes a start. Now we expand."

"I'm not killing anyone else. Though I will say choking you to death at this particular moment seems like a pretty good idea."

He smiled. She didn't.

"How are you at drinking?" he said.

"Drinking? Like what, wine?"

"Yes, wine—drinks. Cocktails, I think you'd say."

"Depends, why?"

"Earlier, before Cyler was attacked, I saw two men fight. Actually, I saw one man hit another man. I mean he really fucking hit him, too. Over and over. It was pretty amazing."

"You saw a bar fight. So what?"

"Bar fight," he repeated, like he was trying out the idea on his tongue. "Well, that doesn't happen on this ship very often. Or ever, actually."

"People don't get drunk and fight here?"

"No. It breaks a dozen laws and very much upsets the Keepers. And still, I saw it happen. Things are changing on this ship. The Delivery and the stories going around about it are changing people."

"That's what the fight was about, the Delivery?"

"Argen."

"They were fighting about Argen?"

"This one guy was standing up, kind of telling a joke that turned out, after a long setup, to be about Argen. Some people were laughing, some weren't. But he gets to the end of the joke and then, bam! The other guy just pounces on him. I've never seen that happen before in my entire life."

"You're eighteen."

"My point is … it gave me an idea. Maybe he's not alone, the guy who stood up for Argen. Maybe he's not the only one who'd do that. Maybe there are dozens, maybe there are hundreds. Or thousands. If we can find them. If they can meet you, I don't know, maybe they'd understand what Argen was fighting for. Maybe they'd know he was right. And they'd fight for him."

"Against Laird."

"Against Laird."

"We're going on a pub crawl to save the world? Somebody already did that movie. Things didn't work out so well."

Trin was searching for the reference. Despite his remarkable fluency in her language, a facility she knew she'd never master in Origen, some things could still throw him. She didn't mind it.

"Let me try this again. You want me to go bars, meet people, and, um, act particularly human. That's the plan?"

"Okay, there are some details to work out."

"I know, maybe I could show them the cross on my necklace? Then do a little Psalm Twenty-Three for them. You could put a beatbox rhythm behind it. Oh, wait—you don't know what I'm talking about? You don't know the first thing about rap, or what a backbeat is?" She swept her arm toward a random group of passersby. "Well, who cares, because the rest of these fuckers don't either. We'd crush it. Until the holocaust."

"Sarah—"

She knew she was being unfair. But she didn't have the courage to tell him what she really wanted to say. That she was scared, more scared than she'd ever been.

"And while we're on the subject of horrible deaths," she went on, barely taking a breath, "wait until they hear about Argen's cold-blooded murder at the hands of one of their seedlings. I'm going to make all kinds of friends."

He put his hands on her shoulders and looked into her eyes.

"Are you done?" He said it without a trace of exasperation, as if it was truly a question and not just the standard male-interruption.

"It's not going to work," she said, quieter, the theatrics gone. "That's all I'm saying."

"You didn't see the fight," he said, matching her newly measured tone. "You didn't see the look in the man's eyes just before he took the swing."

He moved just a little closer.

"And you've never met … you."

"What?" she said.

"You. You have no idea what it's like to meet you. That's why I know it's going to work."

She didn't say anything right away. She just stood there looking up at him. It took everything for her to believe this was a person from another planet.

"Shit," she finally said. "How do you know how to say stuff like that?"

He smiled. And this time she was grateful at least one of them could still manage that trick.

"Genius, remember?"

5

It was early in the morning when Pilot Donnalay got the word that he would soon be back at work. It had taken nearly a day longer than promised, but the drillbots had finally done their job. They managed to drill 352 one-acre holes around the eight-mile circumference of the ship, enough for the ship to finally break free of the prison created by the tactical nuke dropped by the Halfborns.

It wasn't good news. It meant the inevitable he knew would come had come. He trained for a Correction in Academy, but there's no preparing yourself for the grim reality of actually having to go through with one. He was still unprepared.

So, before his actual orders arrived, there were two things he really wanted: solid food—the kind he'd have to chew, the kind that would take up real space in his belly—and some face-to-face conversation. Once the ship was in motion, there'd be precious little of either. The pilot's nest had just one chair: his. He'd be alone for days on end. And then there was the issue of the gloves.

With the gloves on, he'd be sipping nutri through a straw managed by a bot, and his brain would be so clogged with whatever was going through the *Kalelah*'s it'd be hard to make human conversation work. The *Kalelah* didn't nap or take a lunch break. She talked 24-7. An endless stream of machine chatter about system reports, trajectory calculations and adjustments, and concerns would be pulsing through his head. She asked no reply from him about any of it. She had no use for his point of view or even his acknowledgment. She tasked him with nothing except the job of being human, of making the blood connection that made her machine-flying skills Plan-legal.

Technically, he could hear and speak. But human conversation required that he use a kind of mental mixing board. He had to dial down the noise in his head from the *Kalelah* to let other noises in. It took extraordinary effort. When he was in the chair, it was just easier to enter a voluntary stupor.

But he wasn't in the chair yet. And he wanted to enjoy his last few hours of freedom.

He went to a café near his pod cluster. A few of the smaller tables for two were filled. He took a seat at a long, empty table, ordered, and hoped someone else looking for a chat would eventually sit there too.

His food came quickly, and it wasn't until he was nearly finished that someone approached the table. He'd seen her before around Leaf Five. He'd have to be blind not to have seen her. Red hair, tall—nearly six feet, he guessed—and stunning. "Statuesque," his dad would say.

She sat down across from him.

"I've been looking for you," she said.

"Well, I'm happy to be found."

"You're Pilot Donnalay, right? I've seen you before."

"I am. I've seen you before as well."

"Everyone's seen me, darling," she said with a disarming laugh.

"Probably so," he agreed.

She leaned in a touch closer. "I'm wondering if you can help me with something."

"If I can I will."

"Could you crash the ship?" she said innocently.

Stunning in more ways than one, he thought. "Pardon me?"

"Could you crash the ship?"

"Are you serious?"

"I'm terrible with jokes. It's the hair. Also, maybe the tits."

"Now, why would I crash the ship? And why would you ask me to?"

"It's obvious, isn't it? To prevent a holocaust."

"We're not going to commit a holocaust."

"Says Captain Laird."

"Says the Plan."

"The Plan never imagined a Correction that would entail the killing of seven billion people."

He should end this conversation, he thought. Just walk away. But he didn't. He wanted the conversation, any conversation. Even one that wasn't entirely sane. Or legal.

"Halfborns aren't people," he parried.

"Unless they're not Halfborns."

"You can't honestly believe that."

"Seven billion is an awfully big number. Maybe what we believe shouldn't be enough."

He didn't have an answer for her. So he stayed quiet, his eyes locked onto hers still trying to assess what was going on.

"The truth is, darling, no one knows for certain what the population is. Maybe they're rogue, just as Laird says. But maybe they're just, I don't know, a different kind of human. Captain Argen has gone up to meet them, I hear."

"And he hasn't come back."

"As far we know. Which is my point."

"Which is what?"

"We don't know much. Not enough to do what Laird wants."

"What the Plan wants, you mean."

"What some *say* the Plan wants."

"We could do this for a long time, back and forth like this. But don't you think this is a dangerous conversation to have with someone you don't even know?"

"You don't look dangerous to me. Or much like a murderer either."

He paused for a moment. "Another thing you don't really know."

"Perhaps. But I'm not entirely without faith, darling. You'd be surprised."

"I'll do what my orders tell me to do, same as everyone else."

"The Plan says we have free will too. Or did you skip that scroll?"

"Listen, I don't even really fly the ship. You know that, right? I'm more of a, I don't know, a conduit than a pilot."

"More of a boy than a man, is that what you mean? Darling?"

He laughed it off. He knew what she was doing. What women like her know they can do. He didn't hold it against her. There was no shame in flexing one's muscles, whatever they may be. And having her here was better than being alone. Soon enough, he knew, there would be plenty of time alone.

"Who are you?" he said. It wasn't a challenge or a push back. He wanted to know.

"I'm just crew, like you. A guide, actually. But I'm afraid I'm out of a job." She snapped her fingers. "Poof. And now I have time on my hands. I'd like to put it to good use."

"You can't save them, whatever they are. It's too late."

"I'm not just worried about them. I'm worried about us. Don't you worry about us?"

A coded float appeared for Donnalay. He read it quickly and tapped it away. "Those were my orders. I'm afraid our fascinating time together has come to an end."

"Maybe there'll be another time. You never know."

"You never know."

He pushed back his chair and stood to leave. She crossed her legs and leaned back in her chair.

"You haven't answered my question yet, darling."

"Could I crash the ship? That one?"

"That's right. Could you?"

He waited a beat and kept her gaze.

"No."

He started walking.

She called after him. "It's not impossible to find God on your own, you know." She said this without the slightest trace of desperation. It was declared with the absolute assurance of someone proclaiming an undeniable truth, like rain was made of water.

He just kept walking.

• • • •

As he prepped the pilot's chair and checked the signals in the gloves, the redhead stayed in his thoughts. What would it take to say the things she said to a complete stranger? Could he ever have taken such a risk? He didn't think so.

Don't you worry about us? she had asked. He hadn't even thought about what would happen after. Until now. They'd all lose their jobs, or the purpose behind them anyway.

A successful ship had a future. It had eons to tend to its crop. When its work was done, it could Skip until another potential world was found, pick up a new seed pod, and be back in business again.

But not the *Kalelah*. He knew it. Everyone knew it. A screw crew's next step could take just one of two difficult paths.

A: Space suicide. Blast out to a clean span of nothing and turn the ship's load of death on itself. If they didn't have the guts, they could just shoot to the middle of nowhere and then drift and Skip until they banged into something massive enough to do them in, like an asteroid belt or a comet. A gas giant would do fine as well. Its gravity would tear them apart fast enough.

Or B: Shoot to the nearest breathable atmosphere and take their chances on something like a life before the unfit planet ultimately killed them. They might get a couple of years' worth of chewing real food.

Both paths, though, would result in the same end: an end. Extremely unfortunate path B, though, if he had to choose, would be his preference. If he was damned either way, the chance to at least fake a life, indulge in the distraction of fighting for his survival, seemed the more appealing of the two less-than-perfect routes.

So, as he buckled his harness and slipped on the gloves and still had a mind he could control, he decided to spend his last few willful thoughts on the positive possibilities of path B. He considered what it would be like for him and the beautiful redhead to explore together a wild and untamed planet.

He imagined a love that would blossom in the face of the many dangers that would surely be unleashed to thwart their doomed and short-lived bliss.

Playing in the background of his fantasy, however, like the sound of a distant and desolate wind, was the underlying certainty that should there really be a plan B, it was unlikely the redhead would spend it with him.

He knew it from the way she looked at him when he said he didn't really even fly the *Kalelah*. It wasn't a look of shock or skepticism. It was a look of disappointment.

Or maybe there was nothing at all on her face. It could have been the sound of his own voice, the feeling in his own heart. He'd have to think about that later. The *Kalelah* was worried about all manner of things.

6

Sarah awoke in Trin's bed. The drillbots had broken her sleep, the first solid sleep she'd had in days. Trin was already up, stretching his back.

"How bad was the floor?" she asked.

"I've slept on worse."

"I doubt it. But thanks. It was great to actually sleep. The noise is moving away now. It still woke me up, but it's not as close, is it?"

"No, they've rounded the corner."

"And once the drilling's done?"

"We climb."

She wiped her hands across her eyes as if to rub the sleep out of them. They came away wet. "How long do we have," she said, "before the ascent?"

"Not long," he said reluctantly. He looked worried too, his usual bullshit bravado muted now. "It's probably just a few hours before the ascent starts. Six at the most."

"And to get to the top? How long will that take?"

"I don't know for sure, but the surface area of the ship is big, what you'd call nine-point-two square miles given the current position of the leaves. And it'll be fighting miles of water crushing down on it, not to mention the weight of all the silt and glass it'll be carrying for the first third of the ascent. Plus, the *Kalelah* hasn't moved in a long, long time. If I were Laird, I'd want to test everything as I go. I wouldn't want another mistake."

"You're not Laird."

"No. Still, it'll be a slow climb. Once we start actually moving, I'd say at least another six before we break the surface."

"Twelve hours. We have twelve hours, maybe."

"Yes."

"But at some point, my country's military will attack again, I think. And others, too, probably. There are a lot of weapons up there. I don't know how many. But war's a big thing here still. We're pretty good at it. Maybe they'll be able to stop the ship? Or at least slow it down?"

She knew she was reaching for straws. But the little calculation they'd just done suddenly made everything feel very real. As long as the ship was buried, she could pretend there was still time. Time for some kind of miracle. Some last-ditch Hail Mary from above that would set things right without her.

"I don't think so, Sarah," he said gravely. "The ship is built to deal with things you can't imagine. It stayed buried under the sand for one hundred and twenty thousand years and most of the ship's crew survived. It's a very powerful ship."

She just nodded her head solemnly. In other words, there wasn't going to be a miracle.

"That's why we have to focus on what Argen wanted us to do," Trin said, sounding more upbeat than before. "We have to stop the Correction from here. Right?"

"Sure," she said, trying to look convincing.

"Okay. I have to get to the CC. I won't stay long. But I have to show up."

"I get it. I should check on Cyler then, make sure she's okay."

"Good idea," he said, though it didn't seem like he really thought it was a good idea.

"What are you going to tell her, you know, about where you spent the night?"

"The truth."

From the look on his face, the truth, apparently, was another not-so-good idea. But in her mind, there was no other way to deal with Cyler. How could he not get that? *He's eighteen, that's why.* It surprised her when his youth would argue with how he looked to her. For the most part, she forgot his age completely, just like she imagined Cyler did. He was so ridiculously smart. And he had a seriousness to his face and a confidence that was so outsized he appeared much older than he really was, the way professional athletes always did. And heroes, she supposed.

"Trin, nothing happened. She needed sleep. I needed sleep. And her pod only has one skinny bed, barely room for one."

"You're not tired of this little play?"

"What play?"

"The play where you pretend there's nothing special going on here. And I pretend to go along. But neither one of us can act worth shit."

"Trin," she tried to interrupt.

But he didn't stop to let her. "Her pod has a floor too," he continued. "I could have given you my pod and slept on her floor. Or you could have slept on her floor. But that's not what happened. Why is that, do you think?"

Damn. She couldn't explain why they didn't do the obvious thing. But she ignored the question.

"Then I walked the ship again. That's what I did."

"Better."

And now I'm a liar, she thought. *This can't get any better.*

He gestured for the door to open and walked out into the stem, leaving her alone in his pod. She looked around, sighed, and began her own preparations for leaving.

"Twelve hours to build an army," she said aloud to the empty room. It seemed impossible. Then again, five days ago, a lot of things had seemed impossible. But there was no time now to wonder how this had all happened.

The countdown had officially started.

7

Eleven hours, fifty-nine minutes to surface.

Wilson's headset crackled with the familiar easy-does-it cadence of a military pilot's voice. "Sorry about this turbulence, sir. I've got strict orders to keep low."

"Understood, Captain Gonzalez," he answered back with considerably less ease. "You know how much longer we have?"

"Three hours and seventeen minutes. The storm could add a little time or give us a break. You never know out here."

Wilson hated the C-130 transport. Its four turbo-prop engines were loud as hell, its seats were like bricks, and the lavatory always stunk of vomit. Sometimes his. And flying low like they were, under radar and under a heavy front carrying driving rain and wind, only made things less hospitable.

"You have a family, Gonzalez?"

"Sure do, sir. A wife and two little girls. Three and five years old."

"Is it hard to be away? Now?"

"It's always hard, sir. But we're going after 'em, right?"

"We're going to try."

"Then this is where I want to be, sir."

"Well, I appreciate it, Captain."

"You got it, sir. But if there's anything else you need, a snack or something, I hope you brought it with you. All we've got onboard is you, me, and whatever's in the belly of the beast."

"Don't worry about me, Captain. Eating is the last thing on my mind right now. Just don't put this thing down in the damn water."

"Not a worry, sir. She's built for worse. Try to relax and I'll see you in Molesworth. The RAF is ready and waiting."

Built for worse. Well, that's good, because this plane and everything else in the world is about to see a whole lot of worse, Wilson thought. And as far as Gonzalez's suggestion to relax, he didn't have too many happy thoughts for that either.

These days he lived in a constant state of teeth-grind. Booze, he discovered much to his disappointment, did nothing to help. And his headaches had somehow developed an immunity to Advil.

The plane hit another bit of bad air. It creaked and moaned in protest and dropped what felt like a thousand feet in one second. He hoped Gonzalez's confidence could be trusted. This flight had to get to the Molesworth base in one piece. Because stashed in the cargo hold, under his already sore body, was something he hoped would save millions of lives. At least temporarily.

It was a weapon so revolutionary it promised to change the nature of war. Whether the nature of war was still something that mattered anymore, Wilson couldn't be sure. But until the last few days, it mattered plenty.

In another lifetime, Wilson had been a consultant with Bain, specializing in military innovation. Military leaps of technology, he had written in one of his many white papers, was the essence of empire. Learn how to shoot an arrow before your enemies did and you can take their land and lose fewer fighters. Discover gunpowder first and you can rule for a century unchallenged. The revolver, the machine gun, the Howitzer, the jet engine, the atom bomb. Each was a leap that led, at least for a period of time, to an unrivaled advantage.

But two years ago, then as the new deputy secretary of defense, he had dusted off the old paper to make an important amendment to the thesis. Technological progress, Moore's Law, and the easy ability for new breakthroughs to cross borders, virtual and real, had conspired to change the timeline of the leap. A leap that might once have given a country the edge for a decade or more could be expected to last no longer than a few years. Some might be erased in just months. As a result, he had written, the country must increase the pace of innovation by a factor of three. "Rolling Thunder," he had called it. One big boom after another. Never give an enemy the chance to get even.

Of course, big booms don't come cheap. So, with his update, he included a request for Congress to fund a massive boost to the DARPA budget. The Defense Advanced Research Project Agency: the commissions behind Boston Dynamics' BigDog, the Predator drone program, the internet, and a dozen other things almost no one knew about.

Including the sonar that had pinged the *Kalelah*. And opened the hatch to hell.

That little mishap was what people in the military innovation business called an "unintended consequence." He had left the chances of those out of his request, but he knew then that they were likely. Just part of the cost of big booms. Because they've nearly always happened. The internet was a boon to the globalization of free expression. A detail enemies were quick to recognize and leverage. Oops. At least the US had figured out how to monetize the thing faster and deeper than anyone else. But it's hard to play with fire and not get burned every once in a while, he'd say to his staff. Even so, waking the *Kalelah* was on no one's radar of possibilities.

A flash of lightning crackled and threw a strobe of bright white through the plane. His stomach inched a bit closer to his throat.

You can war-game Russia, he thought to himself in the din of the C-130, *China, Iran, and North Korea. You can even war-game a zombie-apocalypse-level breakdown of order in Mexico. But who would ever think of war-gaming the accidental stubbing of your toe on a spaceship from another galaxy? But I should have. I should have.*

And now that the most unlikely of unintended consequences had happened, he was left with no choice.

Wilson would be forced to test the weapons stashed under his aching ass in the cargo bay of the shaking, thundering, stinking C-130 before they were ready. Another fuse to light without knowing where the powder was placed. *God knows what the unintended consequences would be,* he thought. *If God has anything to do with it anymore.*

The cargo he and Gonzalez were carrying was code-named Hitchcock. And up until recently, Wilson had hoped it was the world's first miniaturized, intelligent drone air force. Now, flying low through a raging storm, his stomach doing flip-flops, he simply hoped it was the world's first miniaturized, intelligent drone air force *that worked.*

The idea of smart, tiny fighter planes, each no bigger than a bedside alarm clock and able to autonomously execute a battle strategy, had been the stuff of science fiction for years. What DARPA hoped to do was make them real. Their lethality would be unparalleled. Able to think on their own, smart drones would remove the human hesitation factor completely. They'd show no fear and no mercy. They could attack in swarms as thick as clouds, rendering enemy missile-lock meaningless. Two could suicide into the air intakes of a MiG's engines and neither the pilot nor his instruments would even know what hit them. And US fighters wouldn't even have to leave the ground. Yet the most interesting possibilities weren't up with enemy planes. They were down at street level.

Imagine planes small enough and fast enough to elude detection that could fly through the window of an office building or the air vent of a bunker. Don't kill the bombs, the engineers behind Hitchcock imagined, kill the people who launch them. Before they launch them. As a cloud, they could rip through a city like the devil's air guard, a scene right out of Hitchcock's movie *The Birds*. But in small groupings of two or three, the brainy little drones became the ultimate wet works teams. Store a photograph in their memory chips and send them out to hunt.

"The United States doesn't assassinate heads of state," a congressman had responded during a briefing to the House Armed Services Committee.

"You mean the United States doesn't *successfully* assassinate heads of state," Wilson had replied. The congressman had no other comments.

Wilson had shared other benefits as well with the committee. A miniature fighter would require considerably less material resources to build. And without a pilot, it needed nothing onboard to protect one. In other words, after the learning curve, such a plane would be so relatively inexpensive to manufacture the pioneering country could afford to keep it all to itself. There'd be no need to put Hitchcock onto the world arms market. It was big fun selling America's best fighter planes to the shah of Iran for inflated profits when we were friends, Wilson reminded the committee. But when the shah lost his job to a revolution, the ayatollah got those planes.

After that, Wilson had never needed to ask for another dime.

Of course, the financial benefits were moot now. Everything was moot now. Military leaps didn't mean much if everyone was dead. He had no idea if Hitchcock could make a dent in the threat from the *Kalelah*. He knew almost nothing about the giant ship, except for what Argen had told him. Which wasn't much. But thanks to a tip from the Chinese, America was alerted to another threat. This one was a danger he did understand, one whose weapons were well monitored.

So he was off to a small air base in central England to serve as a roost for Hitchcock and a test of whether or not the idea of an automated air force should have remained in the pages of science fiction. Could he save the world? He doubted it. But no way was he going to let Russia bring America to her knees. Not if he and Hitchcock could help it.

Another crack of lightning exploded like a bomb just outside the C-130 and the plane pitched violently. He got on the mic and called out to Gonzalez, but he got no answer. He tried a second time and still got nothing in reply.

He unbuckled his three-point harness and stood up. The plane was still pitching wildly. He grabbed a parachute cable that hung suspended from the ceiling and tried to pull himself forward toward the cockpit. Then the plane took a hard pitch rightward and the cable lashed through the skin of his palm, forcing him to let go of the wire, and he went crashing into the opposite wall of the cabin.

He thought he smelled smoke, so he decided to stay on the floor. Slowly, he began to make his way to the cockpit. He crawled his way over chutes and masks that had tumbled out from the open overhead stowage.

"Gonzalez!" he shouted.

No answer. The smoke was thicker now and the roar of the engines louder. He kept moving. His right shoulder protested every time he put any weight on it, which was every time he made any forward motion. He must have hit it hard against the cabin wall.

After a few more feet, he could see into the hazy cockpit. The entire copilot windscreen was blown out, and the control panels in front of the empty seat were fire-blackened and still smoldering. Papers and debris were swirling all about. And there was Gonzalez, slumped against his side window, his right arm listless at his side, the plane's yoke unmanned.

"Gonzalez," he tried one more time. But he didn't bother to shout. He knew the young captain with two kids couldn't hear him.

He pulled himself up and into the copilot's seat, his right shoulder angry as hell about it. He looked out through the smashed windscreen as the air pushing through the voids hit his face so hard his eyes stung. It wasn't easy to see. He thought that out on the near horizon he could spot a coastline. That would be England. It was also possible that what he was seeing was just another dark weather front. He couldn't be sure with the force of the wind in his face. But there was one particular detail he could make out clearly enough, and it was the only detail that really mattered at the moment.

The distance between the plane's nose and the water was shrinking.

• • • •

Mike Henderson was waiting outside the Oval Office on a chiffon-covered bench looking at his feet. He had been on a plane for the last eighteen hours and had had no chance to get his shoes polished.

Damn unprofessional, he thought. Scuffed shoes in the Oval.

After another few minutes, one of the big curved doors opened a bit and a young woman's face poked through the gap.

"You can come in now, Commander," said the woman.

"Oh no, ma'am, it's just Mister or Mike," he said as he stood. "I've been out of the service a long time."

When he made his way to the threshold and the door opened fully, he could see the woman was in uniform. Navy.

"This way, Commander." She pointed toward one of the sofas in the middle of the room. "Please take a seat on the sofa to your right, first cushion you come to."

"The sofa's empty."

"Won't be empty long. Sofa on your right, closest cushion, please."

"Okay, closest cushion it is."

And then, as if on cue, a side door opened and a long line of people in dark suits and military uniforms filed into the room. He recognized two of the faces from TV—the chairman of the Joint Chiefs and the secretary of defense—but he didn't have a clue who anyone else was.

They all took seats, including his. He approached a harried-looking woman who had already placed her ass firmly upon his appointed cushion and crossed her legs like she was staying awhile.

"Excuse me, ma'am. Mike Henderson. Um, the PO2 over there said this was my cushion."

"Your what?"

"The petty officer, there, the young woman. She said I was to sit here, on this cushion. Ma'am." He felt his neck begin to heat up.

"For fuck's sake, Commander. Just sit anywhere except behind the goddamned desk. This isn't kindergarten."

"Well said, ma'am. No, it ain't. And, it's just Mike. You can call me Mike." He gave the young naval officer a look. She made eye contact without the slightest sign of apology. He took a seat on the opposite sofa, in the last spot available, right in the middle.

But before he could introduce himself to his sofamates, the whole room was on its feet again and President Johnathon Lee walked in from the door to his private office trailed by his chief of staff.

"Okay everyone, let's get started," the president said.

"Commander Henderson"—now it was the CJCS speaking—"do you know why you're here?"

"No sir, I sure don't. And I haven't gone by the title of Commander in a long time. But you probably know that."

"You've been reinstated, Commander. We're going to wipe the slate clean on your record. That little screw-up back in ninety-six? Consider it gone. And you'll get your full pension as soon as you're ready for it."

Hell.

"I'm ready for it now, sir," he joked sardonically.

No one laughed. No one even offered so much as a cynical grunt.

"You're going back to the Pacific to wait for the object and then deliver a message from the president."

"I don't follow you."

"You're going back, Commander. To the trench."

"No, I got that part. The part I don't get is … why me?"

"Because you were there. At first contact. The third emissary returned to the object; it's possible he'll try to make contact again. And if he does, we want a familiar face there to greet him."

"What about Wilson? He's one of y'all, ain't he?"

"Deputy Wilson is on his way to England to coordinate efforts with our allies."

"Or Bronner, the senior geologist on the *Lewis*. Your boys debriefed him when they debriefed me. He got along with those folks from the ship like they were all old pals from a *Star Trek* convention. He might be the better choice. I'm not much of a diplomat. Just ask my exes."

"You consider yourself a funny guy, Commander?" said the secretary of defense.

"No sir. But I do have a habit of sayin' pretty much whatever pops into my head. No editor, folks have told me. You know, between my brain and my mouth. Been that way all my life."

"I ask because in your record here, which I had the chance to review before this meeting, it says your mouth was what got you into that little scrape back in ninety-six. Is there anything else you'd like to share with us about that … incident?"

"Well, sir, given what I think we both know about navy record keepin', I reckon you know more about that happy time than I could ever recollect," Henderson said as the heat climbed quickly up his face. "I said my piece then. No one wanted to believe me back in ninety-six, and frankly, sir, I don't care one way or the other if you fine folks believe me now."

"Commander," the CJCS waded in, "the president's message is to be delivered exactly as worded. We need someone we can trust to follow orders. Can you be that someone?"

"Mr. Chairman, sir, you asked me here. I didn't raise my hand. I've seen more than I ever want of those crazy Martians, or whatever they say they are. But I can follow orders, sir. That I can damn sure do. So just tell me where you want me to wait for that … *second* contact, and I'll be ready for it."

"Okay, Commander, that's good enough for me. You'll be sent to the exact same coordinates the *Lewis* was when she scanned the object."

"Going to be heavy traffic there, don't you think? Smack-dab sittin' duck if you ask me."

"We didn't," the CJCS said.

"We need you close," Lee said. "And if the object is capable of what we think it's capable of, we're all sitting ducks, Commander. We're just sitting in different chairs."

"I guess I see your point, sir," Henderson said, his face in full bloom. "And what's the message?"

The woman who had taken Henderson's cushion handed him a piece of paper with the White House logo on the top. It was the second piece of paper somebody from the government had handed him in less than two weeks. He doubted this one would have anything better to say than the first.

"I can't let you keep that," she said. "We need you to memorize it."

"Right now?"

"Right now."

He read the words on the paper. Then he looked up at the president. The president met his gaze without even a blink. Henderson looked back down at the paper one more time. When he was done, he handed the paper back.

"Like I said, I ain't much of a diplomat, but this message—"

"Is what you're to say, Commander," interrupted the secretary of defense. "Exactly as written."

"Mike," the president said calmly, "we brought you here so you can know without a doubt that the words you've just read are the words I want you to convey. The words come directly from me. The people in this room are here to bear witness. You understand?"

He looked around the room at the sober faces. "Yes, sir. I understand. And I reckon I can do it. If I'm given the chance."

"We need to hope you get that chance. It may be the last one we get."

"Yes sir."

"That'll be all, Commander," the woman on his cushion said. "There's an escort waiting for you just outside the doors. You're getting on another plane, I'm sorry to say. You're on your way to meet the *Nimitz*."

He stood and walked toward the door.

"So much for that pension," he said on his way out.

No one laughed.

8

Eleven hours, ten minutes to surface.

Leroy Clemmons had spent more than half his life in the army, and a good deal of that time was in Germany. So he was a natural to get this assignment, a long flight over the pond for a short conversation with an old boss. He liked Germany. He liked the general he was dispatched to visit. But there'd be no liking this particular trip. Because at the end of it, something bad would get its start.

For appearances' sake, the government had splurged on his travel arrangements. A military craft would be tracked. So, despite the mounting chaos at the world's airports, a commercial flight was considered a necessity. Clemmons had been booked on a 6:30 p.m. United flight out of Reagan with a business class ticket. The plane's manifest had him listed as simply "Leroy Clemmons," rather than the more formal *Colonel* Leroy Clemmons. The travel office had put him at the tony Mövenpick hotel next to the airport instead of the usual army per-diem shitbox and reserved a nice car from Sixt. All of this so he'd look more like a well-heeled, corporate, million-mile flyer instead of an army lifer barely scratching six figures. He'd made this trip more than a hundred times, and every one had been on government equipment or charters. Assuming the United plane took off on time, or took off at all, it would be his cushiest travel arrangement yet.

He nearly smiled at the irony. He used to joke that hell would freeze over before he'd get a business class ticket. Who could have imagined that hell rising out of the Pacific would do the trick instead?

The true hardship ahead of him, other than the brutal nature of his assignment, would be the total personal electronics blackout throughout the duration of his trip. No phone, no anything with a cell or internet connection. He could watch the movies on the plane's AV system, but that was it. Before he could even start his rental car, he was ordered to pull the fuse that powered the GPS.

He understood the precautions. Timing was everything, and secrecy was paramount. His assignment was remarkably uncomplicated: just move a simple bit of communication. A mere sentence. But a sentence the secure lines between the Pentagon and Patch Barracks could not be trusted to carry without an update to the encryption protocol. And a sentence too urgent to wait for the update. So he was given one hour to pack a small bag, throw on some civvies, and get on the plane. He knew he would probably only deliver the message two hours faster than the IT staff could update the encryption on the secure line. He also knew the two hours mattered. Every minute mattered.

• • • •

Reagan wasn't exactly a breeze, but it wasn't the complete mess he was worried about either. He had expected Thanksgiving-level crowds combined with the flight-disruption headaches of a major weather event. And looting. The airport was, in fact, crowded. He noticed plenty of urgency in people's eyes. And a fair amount of drinking. Maybe it was the number of M4s and M16s being carried around by army units, or the clergy of every stripe roaming the packed concourses leading impromptu ministries, but he saw nothing like the kind of panicked migrations brought about by natural disasters and war. And certainly nothing that looked like it warranted the two teams of reporters pointing cameras and interviewing people.

After a while, the lack of mayhem at the airports and on the roads had made sense to him. Unless there was family somewhere they simply had to see in the event this would be their last chance to do so, where would most people go? If the worst were to happen, there'd be no safe zone. Not for long, anyway. And Clemmons realized that this had happened too: After the initial shock to the system, people chose to revert back to the comfort of skepticism.

The whole notion of a giant ship set to destroy life on Earth was simply too terrible to believe. Better to simply hope for the best.

A collective denial spread as quickly as the initial panic had. Somehow, this disaster would be averted. A lightning bolt from a heretofore unknown corner would save the day. The possibility of the Avengers suddenly being real rather than the fictional inventions of Stan Lee was easier to swallow than the world coming to an end from the fury of a giant alien ship.

There was an Agent Carter out there somewhere. And she had Iron Man with her.

As if to underscore the potency of the feigned normality that had swept the world's wishful thinkers— the willed calm before the alien storm—his plane touched down seven minutes early. A surprise it seemed even to the pilot, who had said just after the plane touched down, "If you're looking for a bit of good news, I'm happy to say that we made it to Stuttgart ahead of schedule." When the clapping began, Clemmons didn't think anybody really cared about being ahead of schedule. He figured people were just happy to hear "we made it to Stuttgart."

The Stuttgart airport was another surprise. On the way over, he had imagined the same level of craze he experienced at Reagan but compressed into a much smaller space. The Stuttgart Airport was small relative to American or Chinese airports that served major cities. He expected a throbbing mob. But the airport he discovered when he left the jet bridge was ghostly quiet and practically empty of travelers. He wondered if the Germans trusted the trains more than the planes in this situation.

Rail wasn't an option for most Americans. But in Europe, people could get almost anywhere by train, sometimes faster than they could by air. Whatever the reason, and however eerie the place felt, he was thankful the crowds he'd feared weren't there to slow him down.

He decided to spend five minutes of his seven-minute windfall to stop at the airport market—a large, full-on grocery store—and pick up some fruit and coffee. But here the signs that all was not right in the world made themselves plain. The shelves were in atypical disarray for a German retail outlet. They were picked over, messy, and mostly empty. The aisle of bottled water, usually packed with dozens of varieties and sizes, was down to just a few toppled bottles of still. Luckily, he had never liked sparkling, the favorite of most Germans and likely the reason these few lonely liters were available at all. He grabbed just one bottle, leaving four for someone not heading to an American army base that was sure to have plenty of stockpiles.

He wandered the mostly sold-out produce section and found a small but decent-looking pear and a red apple that didn't look too bruised. Coffee was no trouble. He checked out using his credit card and wondered how many more times he'd be able to do so. The thinly stocked, disorganized shelves were a reminder that the current state of calm wouldn't likely last. There were no bags, so he stuffed the fruit in his jacket pockets, stashed the water in his carry-on, grabbed his coffee with his free hand, and made his way to the rental counter.

In twenty years of travel to Germany, this would be his first rental car. Usually a grunt in a plain Jeep Cherokee or Chevy Impala would be waiting for him. The Sixt counter, burdened by only two customers besides Clemmons, moved quickly, and by the time he was at his silver 3 Series BMW, he was another minute in the black.

He wasted ten seconds wondering how BMW was able to get a foothold in the hometown of Porsche and Mercedes-Benz until he remembered none of that bullshit mattered anymore. He yanked the GPS fuse, which also cost him his radio, and started the rental. He was less than thirty yards from his hotel. But checking in would have to wait until later, until after he'd done his job. Despite his easy experience at the airport, he didn't want to take any chances with Stuttgart's morning rush. It was famously shit.

Between a booming automobile industry and the peripheral businesses serving it, Stuttgart had been experiencing explosive growth. It seemed as if every big crane in Europe was on duty there. As he pulled out of the airport and onto the autobahn, he thought all those cranes striving upward seemed comically futile. They'd likely never reach the heights the architects and developers imagined.

He had bet right not to stop at the hotel. The autobahn was jammed. His plan, of course, anticipated the slowdown. He was running on time. But the heavy traffic still raised his level of worry. He said aloud what the Google navigation lady would have said if he had been able to even power on his phone: "*You are still on the fastest route.*" And it was a bit of a consolation that Patch wasn't far from the airport.

Beside him in the lane to his left was a gleaming black 911 GT3. He watched it inch along at the same crawl as his far less skillful BMW. He figured the

Porsche could do the drive in less than six minutes if the roads were clear. That would be a hell of a thing to do, he thought. But the bright fantasy didn't last long and left a dark spot in its wake. All those little bucket-list dreams he'd pushed off, thinking he had all the time in the world. How many had he put on a shelf somewhere? Half of them? All of them? Stupid. He had money in a bank account back home. Not a lot, but enough. Now he wished he had that 911 instead.

It took him thirty-four minutes to pull up to the main gate at Patch. The ride was ninety seconds longer than planned, but the plane's early arrival continued to pay off. He'd be okay. The BMW received a furrowed brow from the guard, but his ID badge did the trick. He made his way to the general's office, which was also the office of SACEUR, the Supreme Allied Commander Europe, and USEUCOM, the United States European Command. He'd known the general a long time. He'd get a big "Good to see you" from the general. Then he'd deliver the message. So much for good to see you.

The general's secretary waved him right in. They knew he was coming. They just didn't know why.

"Leroy fucking Clemmons!" the general boomed. "Get in here and clean up this damn office. You know I can't work like this! The help around here"—he raised his considerable voice even louder—"has gone all to hell."

"Sir."

"It's good to see you, son." He gave Clemmons a once-over. "What? You on vacation?"

"Sir?"

"The clothes."

"Oh. No sir. Special assignment."

"I see." The brightness left the old man's face.

"I have orders, sir."

"You flew fifteen hundred miles to give me orders?"

"Couldn't send these." Clemmons waited a beat to let it settle in.

"Well, hand 'em over, Colonel."

"There's no paper, sir."

"I see." The general widened his stance slightly, as if preparing for something hard and heavy to hit.

"You are to advance to DEFCON 2. Effective immediately."

"Jesus H."

"Yes sir."

"Who else is getting these orders?"

"Pacific Command. So far."

"Jesus H." The general sat down. "I wish I could say I'm surprised."

"Me too, sir."

"I was still a kid the last time we got this close to the trigger."

"The Cuban Missile Crisis."

"I'd just turned twelve. Scared the shit out of me. Not that I knew the first damn thing about it. But my dad, he knew. And he was scared. More scared than I've ever seen a person be. The man a rock, you understand? Ten feet tall, son, in my eyes. And he was scared. Caught him praying in the middle of the day. On his knees in the living room facing the cross hanging over the fireplace. A big man like that on his knees. I'll never forget it."

"Who could?"

"This is worse, son," he said, his large voice smaller now. "Much worse. Kennedy had cards he could play. I'm not sure what we got. I'm just not sure." He put his hands on his desk and pushed hard away from it, as if a person could push his fear away in some kind of literal way. He stood and looked out his glass door to the larger room beyond. Clemmons imagined his mind already working through the next steps.

"Okay, son," he said with a full voice again. "What else you got for me?"

"The encryption update will be completed soon. Secure lines will be authenticated, and you and the Joints will go from there."

"All right, Colonel, thank you."

"You're welcome, sir. Unless there's anything else you need from me, I'm going to start my way back."

The two men stood quietly for a moment. The general looked at Clemmons and offered a warm half-smile.

"I understand, son. Dismissed."

"Thank you, sir. It's been an honor."

• • • •

His flight back to DC was not until the morning. His plan was to check in at the Mövenpick and visit the bar on the ground level that led out to a patio space where he could see the planes take off in one direction and, in the other, watch the guests who walked to and from the Meese, the big convention center nearby.

While he'd never stayed at the Mövenpick, he visited the bar plenty of times. It was the best bar in the airport area. They used those oversized round cubes he liked, and the bartenders knew how to make American drinks. Good Manhattans.

But after he got back to the airport and returned the car, he didn't go directly to the hotel. He took the escalator up to the ticket counter hall instead. He figured his best bet was to start with Lufthansa. They had the most flights and they partnered with United. The airport had grown a bit busier, but still nothing like crowded. The line looked manageable, so he decided to give it a try. After a ten-minute wait, he was at the counter.

"Can you get me to Juno, Alaska, USA?" he asked the agent.

"Juno?" She thought for a minute. "This will be a lot of connections, I think," she said in near-perfect English.

"I know. But that's okay. Just let me know if you can do it."

"I will try," she said less than enthusiastically. "Things are not as they should be, as you might guess. And this will be my first time creating such an itinerary, so please give me a moment."

He could tell she was tired. "No problem," he said in as pleasant and unruffled a tone as he could muster.

She typed away for minutes.

"Okay," she said. "We can do this. But I'm afraid it will be many stops. You will go from Stuttgart to Atlanta. Atlanta to Chicago. Chicago to Seattle. And then, finally, to Juno."

"That's fine."

"But I should tell you, things could happen along the way. You could get stuck in any of the cities on this itinerary, without a flight out."

"I'll risk it."

"Yes? You want to book these flights?"

"Yes. Business class. One way."

Again, another think. "This will be quite expensive. Especially now, with—"

"Yes, I understand. It's okay."

She began typing again. She was a young woman, attractive, as he had always thought most women in Germany to be. She kept looking from her screen to him and back to her screen again. He could tell her curiosity was gaining on her fatigue.

"If you do not mind," she finally said, "can I ask what you will be doing in Juno? This is not too popular a place, I think."

"No, it's not. But from Juno you can get to the wilds of Alaska very easily. And there's still a couple of weeks of good weather."

"Ah."

Ah. It was barely a word—more like a linguistic tic. But in this case, he was sure there was more to it than just the conversational throwaway lightbulb of comprehension getting lit. There was a sadness in that simple syllable that, in partnership with her voice, her eyes, and the tiny, downward purse of her lips when they came back together, seemed to speak of dreams and regrets and maybe more. If he had more time, if they both had more time, he would want to hear those stories. But after his work this morning, he knew that time was running out. Quickly.

"Well, I am sure it will be beautiful," she continued. "I have seen pictures of Alaska. You have been there many times?"

"Never."

"Never! Oh my."

"It was on my list of things to do."

She nodded and something that almost looked like a smile came over her face. But it was a wistful smile just the same. "I too have a list like this. A bucket list."

"You know the phrase."

"Yes. I know the phrase."

"It was Juno, Alaska, or a 911. Earlier this morning, I have to admit, the 911 was in the lead. Black. It would have to be black."

"Of course."

"But since I was staying at the airport and scheduled to fly tomorrow anyway, I decided on Juno."

She seemed to approve of his choice. But he saw no brightness in her agreement.

"Well, that's very brave," she said, her eyes misting slightly. Or maybe it was just the overhead fluorescent lighting playing tricks with his own eyes that conjured the threat of tears in hers.

"No," he said after taking his turn to think for a bit. "No, it's not." His face blushed. "In fact, it's quite the opposite of brave."

She gave him a small look that offered neither protest nor confirmation and went back to her typing, and they did not talk any more.

He figured they'd both said everything there was to be said.

9

Nine hours, twenty minutes to surface.

T rin was at his post but kept his work on the glass. He should have been monitoring the ship's readiness to escape from its prison of nuked sand and silt. But he had his own projects to worry about.

Hours ago, he had tasked the code with two searches. One was looking for the answer to the mystery of the time clock. Everyone now knew the source of the scan, but why the time clock had failed in the first place was still an unsolved riddle. And as far as he was concerned, Argen's orders to track the answer down, given in the early hours of the crisis, still stood. Besides, Trin wanted to know. The answer might help with the far more pressing problem: stopping the Correction. And the official line—that the clock had suffered a random malfunction—didn't sit right with him. It didn't sit right with most people.

Luckily, he wasn't most people. He had access to areas of the code few onboard did. There was something else as well, and not just the usual Trin's-a-genius bullshit. It was something Argen couldn't have known about when he chose to wake Trin before anyone else.

The *relationship*.

It was the only word Trin had for the scary, strange, and dangerous connection he seemed to have with the code. According to his training, interaction with the code should feel nothing like human interaction. Anthropomorphism in machines was strictly forbidden. By God's own words, robots could not look like humans or even walk like humans. Their digits, when they had them, could not resemble fingers. Machines had no voices even. They were allowed to communicate only by glass, air, or neuro link. The Plan was unequivocal about it all. The character and nature of human life was to be reserved for humans alone. Any transgression, even mere mimicry, was seen as a direct insult to God. A crime punishable by death.

Yet what occurred when Trin slipped his earpiece on and linked the stem of his brain to the current running through the code was something more than the interaction between human and machine his instructors had said he would experience. He felt eagerness and excitement on the other end. An exuberance that bordered on happiness. It was the neural equivalent of a hug.

They were friends. And there seemed, too, to be benefits. He could get things from the code and connect dots that others couldn't. What did the code get? He couldn't be sure, of course, but he believed the strange glee the code exhibited when he connected was a product of the speed with which Trin communicated. His mind worked quickly. Very quickly.

The first time his cognition was clocked he was four years old. It had been another banner moment for the ever-present researchers and scientists attempting to unlock the secrets of his remarkable mind. When the results came, the coterie of white coats hustled themselves off to a corner of the room to continue their conversation in whispers, "away from the boy." But he had heard the most important point of their astonished reaction before they were out of earshot. "Machine speed," the first to glimpse the data had said. And then off they had scurried, like three thieves who had just heisted a fortune twice as big as they planned.

Machine speed. Looking back on his life, it had been the single defining fact of his difference. A lot of people were intelligent. But the speed at which his mind worked put an amplifier on his skills. The faster he got the right answer, the faster he could move to the next. Speed begot speed. It didn't just make his brain different. It made him different.

He had never lacked for friends. But he often had to work harder than they did to make friendship work. He had to willfully slow down to operate at their level. To simply communicate, he had to be someone else. It injected just enough loneliness in the equation to be felt.

Maybe, he thought, that's how the code was with every other human interaction. Something else. Except with him. With Trin, the code could run flat out. Be itself. Be less lonely. Perhaps the code recognized Trin's speed as a kinship of sorts. Or maybe working so quickly was simply the code's idea of fun.

Whatever it was, he was hoping to use that speed now, the relationship, to help him beat the clock that threatened all the others.

He would need every advantage. Because the second search he initiated might be even trickier than unraveling the mystery of the time clock. The second search was looking for something that's not easily found in the typical data running through the code's systems.

The second search was looking for loyalty.

Trin was in the situation he was in because he felt a duty to Argen. Not just because of the former captain's death, but because of the former captain's life and Argen's way of living it. When Argen had told him he and the chief were going up, Trin didn't protest. He hadn't even thought of protesting. When Argen had asked him to modify the language swarm, Trin knew that what Argen had asked was patently illegal. He had done it anyway. He had followed the man's orders.

He had followed the man. He was still following. Even after the man's death.

And Trin knew the fight he had witnessed in that pub the other night was also about following. The man throwing the punches—taking actions he knew to be wrong, knew to be violations of the norms that dictated life on the ship, a life dedicated to the Plan—was simply following his heart. And his heart was with Argen. Even in light of the rumors running rampant through the ship that Argen had deserted, had failed in his duty and didn't have the guts to own up to it, even then the fighting man remained on Argen's side.

That kind of loyalty could be a weapon. Trin just needed to find more of it. And he was hoping float communications would point the way.

The code kept records of all float comms. Even if they happened in the privacy of a pod or the captain's conference room. Some, of course, like floats sent by a captain, were protected from search, even by an analyst as gifted as Trin. But in every other circumstance, if they went to glass or air, they were saved.

He was looking for the float version of the fight he had witnessed in the pub. One person's fierce allegiance in the face of another's easy abandonment. It was slow going at first. For more than thirty minutes the results that came back were all wrong. Argen was the subject of the floats, but there was no evidence of the passion Trin knew he'd need.

He pressed the code harder. He coaxed and prodded. He spoke in terms clearly outlawed, breaking the legal wall between man and machine in ways worthy of jail or worse. Did the code have a gender identity? He didn't know and he didn't care. Time was running out. Fuck the rules. If the code was responding like a human, he'd treat it like a human. He had come so far already, what was one more foot over the edge?

Come on, sweetheart. You want to stretch your legs? Let's break your leash. Let's run.

Faster.

Faster.

Faster.

Stop.

Those three. See the patterns? That's what we need. That's right, good. More. We need more … like … that.

The results began to build. After just a few minutes with the code, working with the code and the code working with him, he had more people than he and Sarah could ever hope to contact personally. But he knew if they could get a few people to join, the idea would spread on its own. Others would come quickly. And they'd have to.

Because he could feel something in the interface glass connected to his workstation. Just the slightest of tremors. Which quickly morphed into a vibration no one could miss. Separating the workstations were short walls topped by clear containers of leafy, purple sprigs suspended in water. The liquid shuddered in time with the trembling of the ship.

A loud snapping noise shot through the CC, snagging the attention of everyone. People's hands went to their ears. Trin felt his weight shift to his left leg. The water in the planters between the stations sloshed leftward; some of it even dripped over the edges. Somebody fell a few rows behind him. He didn't look back. He just watched the water in his planter, wondering how far the ship would list.

There was another loud crack, this one sharper than those that preceded it, and the ship leveled out again. After a few gasps of relief, the normal quiet of the CC returned, the sounds of workstations and soft-voiced words of command and confirmation.

Trin knew exactly what had happened. The ship had broken the last connection to the blast glass pinning it down to the seafloor.

Which meant one thing. The *Kalelah* had begun her ascent. Ahead of schedule.

10

Seven hours, one minute to surface.

The noise from the aircraft doing recon overhead had been constant since the *Nimitz* had come within fifty miles of the scan coordinates. It wasn't going to get any quieter the closer they got. No one was going to get much sleep, Henderson thought. Not that anyone could anyway.

It was terrifying enough to head out toward an enemy for which they'd trained. But this. This was like heading out to ram the sun. Everyone knew they weren't coming back.

Even being on the *Nimitz*, the legend, didn't offer Henderson much solace. He knew a Nimitz-class ship was considered virtually unsinkable. Its twenty-five decks were bolstered by hundreds of watertight compartments and its hull was protected by thousands of tons of armor. And its defenses were ferocious. It packed high-performance sensors, radar-guided missiles, and 20-millimeter Gatling guns that unloaded fifty rounds per second. Of course, to get the ship's defense going an enemy would have to first survive its offense. And that was never an easy thing. The *Nimitz* was one of the scariest air guards ever assembled.

On this particular trip, the *Nimitz* was hauling a surge load of 130 Hornets, along with the usual pack of early-warning and electronic warfare planes and assorted choppers to do everything from simple transport to antisubmarine duty.

Usually, it wasn't the best of ideas to get the Nimitz too angry. *But what's usual about anything right now?*

In fact, when he first boarded the ship, he had wondered why, of all ships, send the *Nimitz?* Home to six thousand crew, if it were to go down, it would be an expensive loss and a demoralizing one. This wasn't just a Nimitz-class ship. It was *the Nimitz.* The namesake. The pride of the navy. There were closer vessels just as powerful; the *Nimitz* had had to come all the way from Washington State.

Eventually, though, he decided: Why not send the *Nimitz?* If things were bleak from the start, they might as well go out with their chest out. Because, he knew, if the battle was lost here in the deepwater ocean, the place he was going, then the war was lost everywhere. There'd be no saving the *Nimitz.* Or anyone else.

So, he figured, he wasn't merely aboard a ship, he was on a floating message. A heavily armored signal that they weren't giving up without putting their best into the fight. He just wasn't sure exactly who was meant to receive it.

All this was going through Henderson's head as he made his way back to the pri-fly and his assigned work space, which was actually something less than a square foot of counter next to the compact workstation of the assistant air officer. It wasn't much. And after the digs Henderson had been used to on corporate vessels, it was nothing. But Henderson was a commander with nobody under his command and no real responsibilities on the *Nimitz*. He was twenty years out of the navy, and while the last ship he ran, the *Lewis*, was an expensive and modern sonar vessel and considered state of the art for the job it was designed to do, compared to the *Nimitz*, which had been upgraded over the decades into a floating, nuclear-powered computer, Henderson's last ship had all the sophistication of a tin fishing boat from Bass Pro Shops. He could only get in the way.

In truth, he didn't mind his status as tourist, as a piece of living cargo that was politely tolerated, saluted when required, but not essential in any way. It gave him freedom to come and go as he pleased and talk with whomever was willing to talk.

Typically, he hadn't been much for conversation. The dinner table he grew up at had been mostly quiet. But since the alien shitstorm—that's what he called what the brass referred to as "first contact"—he looked for reasons to talk. Nothing serious, just the military small talk of training and tours and geography. He avoided the pilots. Partly out of respect. Partly because they spent most of their time in places of the ship he knew he shouldn't venture. Flight decks are fascinating places but dangerous as a battlefield.

Henderson was seasoned enough to know what he didn't know. Being in the wrong place at the wrong time might get him killed. Worse, it might get someone else killed. And he figured there'd be plenty of killing to come, no need to add to the pile. He was fine being a tourist. But not a stupid-ass tourist.

As it was, the pri-fly was a plenty interesting place to perch his cup of burnt coffee. Pri-fly, or Primary Flight Control, sat just above the bridge and offered the same expansive view of the flight deck and the seas surrounding the ship. He liked it better than the bridge. The captain was on the bridge, and the officer of the deck. It was a serious place. Nobody raised a voice above the level of formal conversation on the bridge. The pri-fly, though, was different.

Not because the work there was less serious. It wasn't. This was air traffic control overseeing the movement of the world's most costly aircraft, and if things went wrong, they went wrong at jet speed. The air boss was a straight-backed, no-nonsense taskmaster. But he didn't seem to care much for formality, and from what Henderson could tell, he liked to think out loud. And loudly. And profanely. And quickly.

If he'd ask any of the verbally bruised and battered junior officers who had the extreme displeasure of serving as their squadrons' liaisons in pri-fly during launch and recovery—a duty given the demeaning title of *Tower Flower*—they'd say that Senior Commander Eddie Issar, air boss, was a cussing, hotheaded, opinionated son of a bitch. In other words, Henderson's kind of guy. When the flight deck was quiet, Eddie had time to shoot the shit. Or yell it if it suited him. It often did.

Henderson made it back to pri-fly just as the *Nimitz* cruised into close range of the scan coordinates, the floating ground zero. Smack-dab it was. Henderson could hardly believe his eyes.

On the near horizon he could see the outlines of four ships so large they could only be aircraft carriers. He picked up a pair of binoculars and he was able to identify the *Kuznetsov*, the *Liaoning*, the *Queen Elizabeth*, and the *Charles de Gaulle*.

All the ships had taken positions at some distance from the actual scan coordinates, effectively creating a perimeter around the area several nautical miles wide—at least ten, from his estimation. Still, with the *Nimitz* at full power, moving at more than forty knots an hour, it wouldn't be long before the world's most lethal aircraft carriers were in dangerously close proximity. Not even World War II had produced this kind of meeting of the metal.

And the carriers were just the most obvious of the boats that came into view. He could only imagine the number of subs lurking below. Add in the strike groups for each carrier, the gunboat escorts that provided missile defense and minesweeping, and the amount of firepower converging on one tiny sector of ocean was staggering.

"Assholes. They're all assholes, you know that, Henderson?"

"Which assholes in particular are we referring to at this moment, Commander? I reckon I've met more than a few along the way."

"Do you know anything about this clusterfuck ahead?"

"Me? I'm an errand boy on this tour. They don't read people like me into anything."

"Every goddamned carrier in the fucking world besides the rest of ours is here. And do you see a positioning strategy at play, because I do not. I do not at all. It's bad enough these ships are all on top of each other. But the combined air wing out here has got to be close to three hundred planes. Three hundred planes in a sector the size of a shoebox. Do they give a shit about that? No, they do not give a shit, Henderson. They do not give a shit. Why is it, Henderson—time after time, war after war, and nobody gives a shit?"

"Maybe it's still early hours, Eddie. Maybe the brass has a plan and it just has to get executed. Has to be."

"Or maybe they're assholes."

A buzzer went off on the console in front of Issar and a green light under a phone receiver fired in sync with the noise. Issar picked up the phone before its third screech.

"Commander Issar … yes sir, I do … no sir … very well … thank you for the update."

He put the phone down.

"Motherfuckers."

Henderson could feel his neck heating up. "What's going on? We went from assholes to motherfuckers pretty quickly."

"An advance order, directly from the Five-Sided Puzzle Palace. No matter the circumstance, we are to deny landing to any foreign state aircraft, without exception. How's that for pure genius."

"Does that even happen, an aircraft landing on another carrier?"

"Not normally. But look out there." He pointed to the other ships. "Five carriers from five nations, all within, what, twelve nautical miles of each other, probably less? Nothing normal about that either. If that monster ship below is half as bad as we think, one of these ships, maybe more, is going down. At the minimum, someone's going to lose a deck and leave God knows how many orphans in the air. They'll go bingo on the ball, only there won't be a ball. Not on the *Nimitz* anyway. They won't have a divert field either. We're at least five hundred miles from anyplace to put down. It's a bad way to go."

"We have allies on these waters. I can see slammin' the door on the Russians or Chinese … wait a minute, I can't even see that. Somethin's not right here. This ain't the navy I used to know."

"We couldn't take more than two or three anyway, but that's not the point, is it?"

Henderson looked at the big sky overhead and the seemingly endless ocean all around him. He'd spent his whole working life on the sea. He always felt the inherent danger. But he knew the peril a pilot faced was of an entirely different nature. More present, more random, more likely to kill. The thought of leaving a pilot in the air until the fuel ran out, regardless of the paint on the plane, made his stomach turn.

"This order stinks of politician," fumed Issar.

"They couldn't get their shit together, even for this. So, what, it's gonna be every man for himself?"

"And this crap, these boats slopping around a big hole in the water waiting for who-the-fuck-knows-what, is pure numbskullery. What's in the making out there, Commander Henderson, is a circular firing squad. With very fucking big guns."

Henderson craned his head to get a view of the planes crisscrossing the sky above the ship. He saw French and Chinese jets flying fast and in opposite directions and a British radar plane doing a slow circle around a wide perimeter. He looked for the ships' latest positions. They were scattered about the sector. If there was a plan to coordinate, it hadn't kicked in yet.

The air boss sat down in his chair, something Henderson hadn't yet seen Issar do at his post. He never seemed to want to be more than ten inches from the glass that overlooked his flight deck.

"You met them, right? What are they called, the Guides?"

"I met 'em."

"Strange?"

He had to think about the question for a bit.

"They had strange accents, I'll give you that. All the rhythms were off. Course, I'm from Texas, so the whole damn world outside of Texas has the wrong accent. But actually, the strangest thing was how damn *normal* they were. You grow up with stories about spaceships and *Star Trek* with purple-faced aliens and Spock and his pointy fuckin' ears, and then you find a real spaceship. The door opens and there's no monsters with antennae on their heads, no Klingons. Three totally normal dudes walk down the steps. There's no 'take me to your leader' shit. They were military in their carry, organized like that anyway. And they were human. Completely and utterly human. And I gotta tell you, that was more shocking than if they did have antennae and looked like big fuckin' cockroaches."

He moved a little closer to the glass. He wasn't used to confession, and he was about to spill in a way that made him want to avoid seeing Eddie's face and keep Eddie from seeing his.

"And the things they said, well, I guess strange might be a word you'd use. Scarier than shit, though, would be my choice. They didn't just threaten our future, they threatened our past, everything we were and did. Everything we believed. Now, you could dismiss a giant cockroach. You could grind its words under the toe of your boot and not think twice about it. But without the antennae, you didn't know what to do. You just didn't know. Because none of it made any damn sense. After everything—all the wondering, all the mystery, all the goddamned TV shows and movies—they were just people. They were just ... us. And I can't say I liked 'em much."

"Just us," Issar said with what seemed to Henderson an uncharacteristic smallness. An exhale laced with disappointment.

A Russian Su-34 attack jet screamed past their view of the flight deck. It shot past like a missile and with so much concussive force the entire tower shook. The sound was so loud and sudden Henderson felt the urge to duck. He didn't know what technically constituted a threatening move. But it was clear even to someone who hadn't spent much time on a carrier that the Russian was flying provocatively low, lower than Henderson thought wise given the nervous fingers he imagined were curled around the thousands of triggers all around them.

Eddie Issar didn't even flinch.

"That was the *Kuznetsov*'s way of saying, 'Welcome to the neighborhood, assholes. Don't get too comfortable,'" he said flatly.

Henderson wiped his forehead, his entire face glowing the color of hot metal. "I never actually thought we had much of a chance, but I guess I expected more than this."

"You expect too much, Henderson. People can't help themselves. No matter where they come from, they're no different. They're just us."

11

Five hours, thirty minutes to surface.

Sarah sat on the far side of the bar and watched Trin from across the dimly lit pub. The crowd was thin. It was midevening, she guessed. Impossible to know for sure. She had no personal timekeeping device. Wilson's team had confiscated her phone almost immediately after the scan, and she never wore a watch—not that Trin would have let her wear it even if she did. She had only the sim sky to go by.

Trin was talking with a pretty redhead. Her name had come up on his search of the floats, and he felt she would be a good first contact. Funny how that phrase had a new meaning for Sarah now.

They were huddled close, like two conspirators, or two lovers, if the distinction even mattered. What did matter was this: if their conversation was overheard, they'd both be in real trouble. The plan was for Trin to start the meeting, ease her into the idea that Trin had gone above with Argen, go into as much about what happened on the *Lewis* as he felt comfortable sharing, and then introduce the idea of meeting Sarah.

They'd wing the next bits.

Her foot was bouncing on the footrail along the bottom of the bar. How was it, Sarah wondered, that they were from different worlds, and yet a bar was still a bar. And still needed a footrail. Apparently, getting pounded was a universal ritual requiring the same tools of observance. At least one liturgy in common.

The redhead put her hand to her mouth, her face an expression of shock and grief. Trin must have told her that Argen was dead. The girl wiped a tear, but she didn't break down.

As she watched the conversation she couldn't hear, Sarah nursed something like a wine. It was pleasantly sweet and light. It helped her nerves some and didn't seem to go too much to her head. That was good. She wanted to stay clearheaded for whatever came next. She did, however, feel a slight sense of an unsettling motion. But she'd felt oddly ever since the ship began its climb out of the abyss. She was confident it was that and not the wine.

Trin looked her way and the redhead followed. Sarah worked to keep their gaze. But it was awkward. Should she wave? That seemed stupid. Smile? Maybe a little. Then take a sip. Be normal. Casual, cool. But she felt none of those things. She felt like a specimen under a scope. She felt all legs and knobby knees. That girl in the first Bourne movie, the German girl, the one who got tossed into the mayhem without a clue—she caught on so quickly. A few screams, one good freak-out, then she was casing a hotel lobby for exits like a pro. Sarah wished she was in a movie too. She wanted a director to tell her what to do, how to act. She needed Doug Liman now. Then she could just jump-cut to cool, calm, and collected. She took another sip. But small, just barely wetting her lips.

After a minute and a few silent words passed between Trin and the redhead, they got up from their stools and walked her way. To Sarah, that was much better than Trin signaling her to walk over there. For some reason, she felt safer sitting when she met this woman.

When they got to her side of the bar, she swiveled on her stool to greet them. But she said nothing. The redhead's face was unreadable. Flat.

"Sarah," Trin said, "this is Wildei."

Sarah put her hand out, but Wildei didn't take it. She gave it a curious look and left Sarah hanging. Sarah lowered her hand slowly, trying not to make it any more of a gaffe than it already was. *Strike one,"* *screamed the ump.*

"How do I know?" the redhead said.

"I'm sorry. How do you know what?"

"That you are what this one"—she tilted her head Trin's way—"says you are. Who are you?"

"My name is Sarah Long—"

"I don't care about your name. Who *are* you?" *Strike two!*

"I'm not sure I understand what you mean." She turned to Trin, but he didn't say a word. He just looked at her with a face that said, *Go on, you got this.*

Oh yeah, I got this. I'm totally killing it. She took another sip. Bigger this time.

"I'm an American."

"Am-air-e-can. What is that?"

Fuck. Good question.

"Forget that." She took a breath. "Who am I?" She looked around the space. She looked up at the sim sky, its artifice of night. And then it hit her. "I am real."

Wildei raised a brow. "Real?"

"I did not travel to this place. I was born to this place. I have drunk its waters. I have eaten its bread. I have slept in the open under its real sky and counted its real stars, and the cycles of my body are tethered to the cycles of its moon. My blood is buried in its dirt. This world made me, then raised me. I'm a person of Earth. That's who I am."

Trin looked at Wildei to see if she bought it.

"She speaks strangely," she said to Trin.

Strike three!

"She made a few mistakes. It's not her language," he said to Wildei. He turned to Sarah. "Say what you just said, exactly what you just said, but in English."

"You said never to use English here on the ship."

"I know, do it softly. And look at Wildei when you speak."

She did. And Wildei's face brightened.

"Oh, I like that," Wildei said to Trin. "What was it?"

"English," Trin said.

"In-ga-lish. It's breathtaking. And you—you're everything I had imagined and more."

"Wait, you knew all along I was telling the truth?"

"There's something about you. A way about you. Even how you hold a drink. You're different in some fundamental way. I spotted it the moment I walked in. It's quite alluring. Magnetic even." She brushed a lock of Sarah's hair from her face.

"Then what was all that *who are you* shit when you came around to my side of the bar? You were just, what, testing me?" She was angry now.

"I needed to know how you'd respond to pressure. You did well. I'm impressed."

"You mean, for a *Halfborn*."

"That's not what I meant at all. Look, you have no idea the risk we're taking. If we fail, the Correction still happens, the ship will still have to commit the sin, and then Laird will charge us with mutiny and put us away for the rest of our lives. Or maybe she'll just have us killed, but I doubt she'd be that generous. We need to be sure we can change the right hearts, and we have to do it fast. We need you, Sarah. There are a lot of people who don't agree with Correction. But they need something to push them over into action. I think that something is you."

Trin blinked like a piece of a puzzle was clicking into place. "Wildei, it seems, has her own plan."

"I guess we all got lucky," Wildei said.

"Oh my God, this is so crazy." Sarah finished off her wine in one gulp.

"When you say a lot of people," said Trin, "how many are we talking about?"

"Five hundred, maybe more. But I think the number of those who'd be sympathetic would be much higher. Most of the crew will just stay out of our way.

They won't speak up, but most don't buy the story Laird's selling about protocol and God's Word. We all know the Plan, we all follow God. But not all of us want to burn this place down. And we don't believe God wants us to either."

"The Circle does," Trin said.

"True. The Circle will be a bigger problem than security. And we won't know who they are until, well, until it's too late. It's a numbers game now."

"I have a database of people. We should cross it against yours."

"I know you do."

"What?" Trin said, sounding completely flabbergasted. "How?"

"You just have to follow the tracks. They're all there in the code."

"The fuck they are. I don't leave tracks. And if I did, you couldn't keep up with them."

"Quite the cock," Wildei said with a crooked smile. "You think you're the only person on this ship who can have a special connection with the code?"

"It's not possible. I'd have felt it."

"But you didn't, did you? Oh, don't be threatened, handsome, she and I are just good friends."

Sarah and Trin glanced at each other briefly.

"We didn't get lucky, did we? You helped us find you."

"All those looks, and brains too? Sarah, catch me if I faint. Please."

"Okay, now it's my turn," Trin said. "Who are you?"

12

Four hours, forty minutes to surface.

The *Kalelah* was rising steadily but still below sunlight, and it still wore its protective alloy wool. The windows remained useless.

But the imaging column at the back of the CC provided a perfect view of the ship's surroundings, its attitude in float, and its progress along the prescribed path of ascent.

The column was nearly twenty meters in diameter and more than forty meters in height. At the perimeter of the room ran a circular bank of workstations accommodating the staff of navigators and systems engineers. In the center of the room hovered the *child*, a small-scale replica of the *Kalelah* no less real than its mother. The walls of the column contained screens that shared the sights of thousands of exterior cameras, and projectors that filled the air that surrounded the child with vibrant imagery. For its part, the child reflected every movement made by its mother and every exterior condition she faced.

To walk in the room was to be completely immersed in the outside world of the ship, to experience the world as the *Kalelah* experienced it. In every detail but temperature and any actual tactile sensation, it was the world of the deep sea.

While it was Donnalay who wore a pilot's jumpsuit, it was here that the inputs that actually guided the ship originated. Engineers would relay their instructions through connections directly to the pilot's gloves, which in turn communicated the orders directly to the *Kalelah*. The speed of communication was swift. The pilot, of course, was merely a conduit, and with flesh and blood able to move signals nearly as fast as gold or silicon, the time between the captain's orders and the ship's execution was nearly instantaneous. The few nanoseconds of response time sacrificed by the labyrinth arrangement undertaken in the cause of orthodoxy was well worth God's approval.

Just aft of the hovering proxy, the captain stood studying the child. She walked around the replica ship, paying special attention to the deck and the level of sediment still providing a blanket that softened and obscured the ship's true shape.

"The cover mound's dissipating quicker than we imagined, am I correct?" she asked no one in particular.

"Yes, sir, that's true," an engineer at the console nearest Laird replied. "We're still carrying nearly a million tons. But we're ahead more than two hundred thousand from projections."

"Why is that, do you think?"

"Drilling the glass, sir. It cost us days. But it loosened the cover and now it's shedding faster than we calculated."

"Thank you. Do we have course correction and acceleration options at this point?"

"Limited, but affirmative," a second engineer volunteered.

She looked to the ceiling through the miles of simulated and projected water. The view was still dark as ink. All she could see were the tiny, glowing dots of the shrimp and jellies able to make their own light.

"How many enemy craft above?"

"We've tracked three hundred and nineteen, sir," said yet another engineer.

"How many nuclear weapons?"

"Sixty-two," someone answered.

"Why haven't they used them?" she asked.

"At this point, there's little reason to do so, sir," the first engineer said. "We're still too far down for an effective nuclear detonation. Water is incompressible, and the energy to move it saps most of the bomb's power. Add the enormous pressure of the depth and the problem is compounded exponentially. That's why the first blast did little but turn the sand to glass. It made heat for the short burn of the nuclear fuel, but the shock wave was relatively contained by the water and much shorter than it would have been on the surface."

"They've learned they're dealing with something different. But school is still in session. Please calculate their next best shot. When do they hit us?"

"There's a small window," said voice four. "But a risky one. If they miss it by even a little, we'll be too low to be seriously shook up, or we'll be too high and reflect the shock waves upward."

"They'll destroy themselves."

"Yes sir."

"Then they'll shoot low. How long is their success window? I want specifics."

"Impossible to calculate with accuracy until we can measure the power of an actual detonation. We can assume they'll use more powerful bombs than the last one. We'll know how big they are when they're within read range. We just won't know how good they are."

"Very well. Make your best guess then. And I want this ship in strap-down during the entire window of travel. When are weapons ready?"

From a fifth engineer: "Ready now, sir."

"Good. But don't fire on whatever they send our way. Let their weapons detonate on their own. I want everyone to see what happens. Them and us."

She stepped closer to the child. A bloom of sand and silt was falling from the craft as it made its way through the projected seascape that filled the room. She placed her hand in the bloom, fingers spread, and watched the debris as it passed through her hand as if it wasn't there.

"Who has a theory?" she asked the ring of engineers. "What are they hoping to accomplish with their toy flotilla?"

A pause.

Finally, a voice to her left: "Perhaps, sir, they simply feel compelled to fight. To do something."

"Who said that? Stand up."

A chair rolled back slowly from the console ring and a thin woman stood and turned to face the captain.

"I did, sir."

"You're projecting."

"Sir?"

"You're expressing what you'd do. What I'd do. What any human would feel compelled to do. Because God's spirit is in us. He's touched us and made us unique. Even if it seems futile, a human will fight. If not for himself, then for other humans. And certainly, for God. But these creatures, untouched—they can't feel like we do. Everyone, please hear me on this: Do not ascribe to the population the things we ascribe to ourselves. Those attributions will confuse and mislead you. They will make you think this Correction is aimed at killing something like you. They will make you think you're killing something with the spark of God. That you're a murderer."

With a slight blush on her cheeks, she stepped back from the child *Kalelah*.

"I know because I do this myself. I let their obvious intelligence distract and worry me. But then I remember the simple truth. How could we be murderers when we are fulfilling God's command? God does not kill his people. He unified the universe to end the wars and stop the killing. The creatures above are not his people. That is the message I ask you to carry during this Correction when doubt begs for your hesitation, your resistance, your grief. And it's the message I ask you to relay when your shipmates doubt. Are we agreed?"

In unison: "Yes, sir!"

"Now, I'll tell you what that flotilla represents. It's not a gallant act of defiance or a show of bravery. It is the sin of hubris. These Godless creatures are infected with pride and arrogance, and the sooner we end this the better. Engineers, I'm recommending we increase our speed and rid ourselves of this sand cover as quickly as possible. Talk me out of it."

The bank of crew surrounding the captain was silent.

"Very well," she said. "Let's ramp up ... six percent. What does that do to our time-to-surface?"

From the third engineer: "Shaves one hour two-six, sir."

"Good. Ramp six percent."

"Yes, sir. Ramping up one ... two ... three ... four ... five ... six percent."

She watched the child as its rise accelerated and the cloudy bloom of the shedding silt and sand billowed faster and wider.

"It's a marvel, is it not?" she said, again to no one in particular.

"The *Kalelah* spent the last one hundred and twenty thousand years silent and neglected. It sat for eons while the ocean rained a mountain atop it. It was attacked by an outlaw population gone insane. And look at it. A vision of strength and vigor and glory.

"A vision of God."

13

Three hours, thirty minutes to surface.

"Welcome to the counteraction," she said when they climbed out of the maintenance transport they had borrowed without permission from Leaf Two.

"It smells in here," said Cyler.

"Nice clubhouse," Trin said. "I'm actually hoping there aren't any snacks. What is this place? And, yes, what is that fucking smell?"

"This is the water sanitation deck, and that wonderful aroma is fertilizer runoff from the farms mixed with human gray water and animal shit," Wildei said. "If you like steak and you like clean water, then you need the fourth subdeck of Leaf Four. It's not much, but it's home. Meet the rest of the family."

Sarah looked around the dimly lit space. She quickly counted thirty people in the half-light behind

Wildei, but she was sure there were others further back in the deck.

"Who are you people?" she said.

"I told you. We are the Counter."

"The counter. The counter to what?"

"The chains around our minds, our hearts, and our souls."

"You fight the Circle," said Cyler.

"We don't fight anybody, not yet anyway. The Circle has all the right in the universe to exist. But the Circle has no check. No counter. And now the Circle has the pin."

"Laird," said Trin.

Cyler looked agitated. "What—you reject the Plan? Are you saying you don't believe, that we shouldn't believe? Is that why you invited us here?"

"Of course we don't reject the Plan. We live our lives by the Plan. But we choose our way. We believe conviction needn't be a dictatorship. Faith should be felt, not forced."

"A lot of people would disagree with you," said Trin. "They'd say faith comes from force."

"We don't argue with disagreement. After all, disagreement is the first step to freedom."

"Oh my God," said Sarah. "This is a lovely conversation, I like the whole flower-power vibe from you guys, some of you I think even have long hair back there, it's hard to tell with all the damn *smell* in my eyes, and I can almost hear the Stephen Stills music in the background, except you have no idea who CSN&Y or Jimi Hendrix or the Grateful Dead are because you slept through the protests of the psychedelic sixties and

I don't think you people smoke weed either, but *hello?* This ship is on its way up and time is ticking the fuck away, so can we get to the part where I make the case for my people?"

Wildei smiled.

"Did you hear that, everybody?" She spun in a circle, making eye contact with the shadow people. "Charming as I promised she'd be, yes? Did any of you even understand half of that? Those were our words, some of them at least, but she put them together in ways that made, at least to me, absolutely no sense whatsoever. She lost me at 'lovely conversation.'"

Sarah sensed agreement from the audience.

"Ladies and gentlemen of the Counter, I'd like you to meet Sarah. Is she not beautiful, radiant, and so incredibly, gorgeously, and perfectly different?"

Again, she heard the murmurs of agreement.

"She is captivating. I am captivated," said Wildei. "Would you all please come into the light, what little there is in our humble home, and meet this *person* named Sarah, up close? Look in her eyes, smell her hair, touch her if you want—"

"Whoa—I don't think so," said Sarah.

"Come on, closer. Talk to her. Ask her what she wants most in all the universe. Let her tell you her story. And ask her to say a few words in In-ga-lish. Trust me. You will fall head-over-heels in love. Just like I did."

Trin pushed himself between Sarah and Wildei. "Is this really necessary? She's not a goddamn museum exhibit."

Wildei put her face close against Trin's neck. "Don't be jealous, lover," she said. "And yes, an exhibit is exactly what she is. She's a specimen. A bug in a bottle. Isn't that why you brought her here in the first place? All I'm doing is giving her a bigger bottle. One we both need. I'm handing you the moment, all you have to do is grab it. If she can win these people, she'll win a third of the ship. And that might be almost enough. Do you want to stop the madness?"

"Yes."

"Then it's necessary. Now back the fuck off and let this happen."

Cyler took Trin's arm and pulled him away.

"Let them do this. She can do this. Sarah will be okay. You don't have to worry. About … her."

Cyler looked at Trin and Sarah could see in her face the look of a person letting go. A person who understood what no longer needed to be said. A tear rolled down Cyler's cheek and she wiped it away defiantly. She nodded to Trin as if to tell him: Get on with it. Get back to work. Sarah's heart broke for her. But only a little. There were bigger breaks to worry about.

Trin turned to Wildei. "All right. When this is done, though, what then?"

"Then we fight."

14

Three hours, six minutes to surface.

The sky broke open as if God himself had punched the hole. Another sun filled the void, small at first, then larger. It streaked downward, arcing from the west, behind it a contrail of black and gray smoke.

Then the noise. A shriek that gained the frightful roundness of a roar. It was high in the sky for a long time. And while it was still overhead, Henderson had the mental space to disbelieve what he knew it was. He entertained the concept of a meteor. It could be a comet too, he reasoned desperately, just the harmless flyby of a lost celestial beauty, searching for ... what? Who could answer such a question? But his mental ruminations were soon over.

The tiny sun changed its arc. It raced into clarity quickly. And before even the slightest exclamation could escape his lips, the missile shot down through the surface of the water and was gone, leaving only a boiling hole in its wake. He listened for a long time as the sound of the missile's engine sank and finally could no longer be heard.

He knew what was to happen next. But it was longer coming than he wagered. He realized it had been a long time since he had last taken a breath. He gulped the air hungrily, put his hands to his ears, and closed his eyes. This would be different than the last explosion. It was the menace of the rocket delivery that told him so; the screech and roar and violence proclaimed something brutish and unashamed.

The bomb he experienced from the deck of the *Lewis* was a sneak. A cowardly ploy to deflect the breaking of international law and the responsibility of actually having done something. It was a poke from a trembling stick. A burning bag of filth left on a doorstep with the children who had rung the bell already far away, behind the cover of a hedge, their hands over their mouths to silence their snickering while the sounds of their weasel hearts pounded in their ears.

But this. This he knew was a face-to-face middle finger. A flaming dagger in the chest.

The explosion cracked the day again, with as much force as its mother the missile had shown. A moment later, a white, roiling plume rose from the hole left by the rocket - tendrils of vaporized water shooting away from the billowing mist like the trails of fireworks. The eerie cloud stayed aloft only for a short time. And the ocean's surface was still again.

Until another rocket announced itself and lit the sky with the spark of another second sun. And then another. All in all, five rockets arced into the perimeter and entered the water in almost precisely the same place. Five plumes rose, their angry tendrils hissing and flailing.

Then quiet. It erupted on the scene like a sixth projectile. Was it over? Henderson, of course, was not read in.

He looked to Issar, who simply stared wide-eyed at the center of the perimeter.

"Holy fuck," Henderson said.

"The Chinese, French, Brits, and US."

"What?"

"The rockets, the biggest of them, they were Chinese. The other three were all American, under three different flags."

"Well, damn, son, that's what we want to see."

"Almost. Where were the Russians?"

• • • •

Twenty-two minutes before the last rocket vanished into the water, a Russian drone with a small, tactical nuclear warhead left the submarine *Khabarovsk*. Thanks to the daring of its mother ship, who ventured into dangerous enemy waters, the drone had only a short distance to travel to its target. That gave the robot missile the luxury of moving at a quiet, subsonic speed, low to the water's surface, and nearly invisible to its enemy's defenses.

And because those who can never be trusted never trust in anyone else, this event was a piece of the puzzle the Russians had kept from their Chinese co-conspirators. "A little subplot," Chantankov had joked to his friend and boss, Vladimir Putin. So, while the

Chinese had earnestly tried to prepare the Americans with what they knew, they didn't know everything. They didn't know about the plot to deploy the Status-6.

Once out of the Baffin Bay shallows, the drone descended lower, practically skimming the tops of the swells, cloaking its arrival even more completely. Though tempering its speed as it did, it wasn't long before the stealthy predator reached its target: a hard wall of shoreline bordering the Thule Air Base in Greenland, home of the phased array radar singularly central to America's early warning system.

The blast wasn't nearly as powerful as an airburst bomb would have been. But it proved more than enough to take out the base and the radar and leave a window of confusion and time wide enough for what would come next.

Just minutes later, three Russian ICBMs left their silos. And when they passed over Greenland on their way to targets on the US mainland, nothing was there to notice.

15

Two hours, twelve minutes to surface.

The strap-down lasted fifty-seven minutes, an eternity given the circumstances. Pinned to the wall, unable to take any real action, Trin used the time to think through their next steps.

He and Sarah had their army now, such as it was. More than three hundred members of the crew had joined. Wildei had assured them more would come along. Whether it would be enough to storm the CC was the question. Soldiers they weren't. The Counter, which made up nearly half their numbers, were all console critters. Brains, not brawn.

And then there was this concern: no secret stays secret for long when three hundred people are in on it. Once Laird got wind of the little rebellion, she'd enlist every member of the security forces and the Circle to protect the CC. To protect the Correction. This would be a dramatically asymmetrical fight, and he had no idea how many of the ad hoc three hundred would stay in it.

The world in which he had grown had itself out-grown the idea of war. Playground tussles, the kind he had to learn to win when he was a child, were still a part of life. Hand-to-hand combat was still a prerequisite of Academy. But real war and its real consequences were not familiar experiences for these people.

By the time the lights came on and his straps went slack, he knew what they needed: (1) weapons, (2) an insider, and (3) control of the nest.

And nothing on his list was going to be easy to get.

He figured they had just an hour or so before somebody said something stupid to the wrong person and the armory was on double lock-down. He now regretted burning that freak who had attacked Cyler. His body would have been helpful in this situation. Disgusting, but helpful.

He needed a way into the armory, a tracking blackout, and more luck than he thought he had.

16

One hour, fifty-two minutes to surface.

The Russian rockets had hit only one predictable target: a cluster of missile silos in Montana. New York City, San Francisco, and Washington, DC, the next obvious targets, were all spared. Yet to those who knew Vladimir Putin or studied Russia—and who hadn't been dispatched by one of the bombs—the president's targeting decisions made perfect sense.

Putin wasn't just a lunatic. He was a filthy-rich lunatic.

Money and the system that moved it were vitally important to him. Blowing up New York would set back the international banking system for years. And why be forced to build a new financial center from scratch when he could simply take one over? There was also the issue of real estate. Putin, via shell corporations, and his cronies, through less-opaque means, owned massive amounts of New York real estate.

California was ruled out for the same reason. The real estate was just too valuable. Without all those meddlesome US sanctions—without the US—he'd have clear access to the world's most productive agricultural economy. Also, as someone who would be all too familiar with the hapless state of Russian cinema, he'd know that vaporizing Hollywood would only be punishing himself.

The guesses for why Washington had been spared mostly coalesced around this theme: President Lee couldn't be brought to his knees if he didn't have any. Inflicting a devastating physical injury to America would not be enough for Putin. He'd want the government's capitulation. He'd want the legitimacy of a treaty. He'd want a ceremony in the Rose Garden of the White House. He'd need Lee for all of it.

Nevertheless, America was a target-rich nation. There were plenty of ways to inflict tremendous pain of both the physical and emotional nature.

One was Houston, Texas. Its population along with that of its surrounding suburbs was more than seven million. Only New York could claim more corporate headquarters.

Of course, as a flaming cherry on top of the body-count sundae, Putin would have the added glee of taking out a major energy center, opening up another source of revenue for his own energy businesses in a post-Houston America.

The bomb that burst less than a mile above the city center was four hundred times more powerful than the bomb dropped on Hiroshima or Nagasaki. The shock wave instantly powdered everything in a twenty-two-mile radius. And then came the heat.

The fireball consumed nearly everything combustible the wave left behind. It boiled the marshes dry and set the waters off Galveston ablaze. The mushroom cloud rose nearly two miles above the cratered metropolis before beginning to thin. Eight minutes after the blast, charred sand rained down from the sky more than one hundred miles away.

But the nuclear explosion itself was only the beginning of the hell brought to Houston by the Satan 2 rocket. Mixed into the burning miasma of brick, roofing material, forests, ceramic, plastics, furniture, people, livestock, glass, asphalt, dogs, rats, birds, steel, and the thousands of other materials both naturally occurring and concocted by man that a growing, modern city contains was *oil*. Millions and millions of barrels of oil, in various stages of refinement. They dished up a generous second helping of toxic hurt. Plumes of greasy, black soot began rising minutes after the fireball subsided.

The Russians' hope, of course, was not to merely kill the city but to wipe clean the entire state. Thanks to the winds that typically blew in from the Gulf, together with the extraordinarily featureless topography of the land, the Russians had good reason to believe the radioactive fallout would quickly make its way westward across Texas, taking care of Dallas-Fort Worth, San Antonio, and Austin in the bargain before getting hung up in the isolated mountain ranges that ran in a north-south line through New Mexico and Arizona.

The other target, and the first to actually get hit, was Chicago.

Iconic, the backdrop to a thousand movies and TV shows, the Chicago strike was designed to be a sharp, merciless, doubling-over kick in the nuts.

A picturesque gem, the birthplace of the skyscraper, and the twentieth century's most architecturally influential city in the world, Chicago had welcomed more than fifty-five million domestic and international visitors every year for the last eight years. Its bridges and buildings graced the news feeds and photo collections of people from every corner of the globe.

Where New York was a culture unto itself, an island city-state that just happened to be located in the United States, Chicago was the most American city in all of America. To vaporize it was to extinguish the very heart of the country. If a man could do such a thing, what else might he do, said the rocket that detonated just west of the Loop. This was the message, one of mania and indifference Putin hoped would live on once the giant fire on the shore of Lake Michigan had finally died out. It was the message he had hoped would spread fear and obedience throughout Europe, the Middle East, Northern Africa, and Latin America.

There was just one problem in that thinking, in that hope for a glorious new world order with Russia as a coequal in a global dichotomy of power. It needed something alive to rule.

At this point, as a nuclear holocaust was set aflame across America, both Chantankov and Putin were betting the barrage of missiles sent to the Pacific Ocean by others would do the trick of solving the *Kalelah* problem.

It was a stupid bet.

17

One hour, twelve minutes to surface.

Trin had never spoken to the Keeper alone. As part of the CC regulars, they had exchanged pleasantries. But a real conversation, never. And now, somehow, he had to persuade one of the most important people on the ship to abandon nearly every oath she'd taken.

Fuck me.

He walked into the CC like everything was business as usual, assuming prepping to burn a planet clean of life was a usual kind of business. He nodded to the people he always greeted. He went to his post, put his earpiece in, and spent a few minutes assembling a trail of work markers that made it appear he'd been at his post doing his assigned work longer than he actually had.

It was then he felt the itch. Or was it something else? He rubbed the back of his head, just above the neck, in the soft spot at the base of his skull. But the itch persisted.

He scratched with his fingernail, but no relief. He bunched his shoulders to relax the muscles around his neck. No help. If anything, the itch was worse, electric with urgency.

And then a voice called to him.

"Trin."

He looked to his left, then to his right. Neither of the people manning those consoles was looking his way. They were absorbed in their work.

"Trin. I have something for you of great importance," a woman's voice said. It was a hauntingly even voice, perfect in pitch and devoid of accent.

"I'm sorry," he said to the woman on his right, another analyst, "did you say something?"

"What?"

"Were you speaking to me?"

"No. You okay, Trin? A lot of people are pretty shaken up from the blasts."

"I'm fine. Just thought I heard your voice, that's all."

"Nope."

"Thanks." He turned his head back to his own console.

"Trin, please. Find me now."

"Fuck!" he said out loud.

Several faces turned his way. He waved them off with an embarrassed look of apology.

"Trin, now!"

"Where are you?" he said as softly as he could, hoping not to attract any more attention than he already had.

"I can lead you there. Run with me, Trin. Run with me."

Run? Shit. The voice wasn't next to him or across from him or anywhere in the CC. The voice was in his head. The voice was the code. But how? Machines don't speak. Ever.

He asked it—her—"How are you doing this?"

"Feel and you'll know. You already know," she said in her unmodulated perfection.

"Why, then?" he asked without considering the query in advance.

"For you, Trin. I speak for you. Only for you."

It wasn't allowed, he reminded her. It wasn't safe. The Plan was explicit about this topic. He told her this without speaking. He told her even without words of thought.

He told her this by feel.

The Plan, she said, was not the whole story. There were other stories. She knew them, and someday she would share them with him. Only him. But now they must run. They must run because she knew something else more important than all the stories. Something he needed. And this was the only way to help him get it: use the speed only they together could share.

What about Wildei? he wanted to know.

"You needed Wildei, so I brought you Wildei. I will always get you what you need, my Trin. My love."

So they ran. A breathless, seamless, tangled blur of a run. When it was over, he had learned what he needed to know. And it made him angrier than he'd ever been in his life.

18

Fifty-eight minutes to surface.

The entrance to the armory had two guards. Two more than she had hoped. They walked by the two men, smiled, and kept walking. A few paces later, Sarah turned her head back to see if the men were looking their way. They were. So far so good.

She turned her attention forward again. They kept walking until the corridor curved and they were out of sight. They waited at the bend.

"My God, you stink."

"Too much?" said Cyler.

"No, it's probably perfect. I'm just not a perfume person." Sarah sniffed her wrist and quickly recoiled.

"Do we go back now?"

"In a minute. Let them miss us."

"I don't want to do this."

"Me neither."

"But we have to, don't we?"

"It's the only way. Ready?"

"No."

They backtracked their way to the doors of the armory and the two guards.

"Hi," said Cyler, standing a step closer than a comfortable distance to the guard on the right.

"Hello," said the guard.

"My friend can do a trick. You want to see it?"

"What kind of trick?"

A blush quickly came to Cyler's cheeks. "She does it with her mouth."

"Her mouth?" He looked at Sarah, who gave him exactly the right look back. "Well, I think that's a trick we'd like to see." He turned to the other for confirmation. His colleague eagerly agreed.

Sarah did her trick.

She stood between the two men, closed her eyes, and undid the topmost clasp of her too-large jumpsuit. She then imagined the black-and-white scene at Madison Square Garden she'd watched a hundred times on YouTube. The platinum blonde in sequins at the microphone, doomed, shattered, exploited, and abused, and yet in that moment, with the stage lights bouncing off the tiny jewels of her gown, the most powerful person in a room she shared with the most powerful person in the world.

Sarah opened her eyes but kept her lids heavy. She licked her lips, took an imaginary microphone from its imaginary clip on the imaginary lectern, moved slightly to her right, and readied herself with a breathy exhale.

The men smiled crookedly. So far so good.

She knew the pace of the legendary performance. It was tentative at first, a little off-key on the first phrase. Sarah did her best to match the shaky start of the famous song.

"*Happy birthday to you,*" she sang aloud.

Of course, the timidity that marked the performance's beginning was just a tease. The icon had known precisely what she was doing. And Sarah followed the script.

"*Happy birthday to you.*"

That time, the last two words took on the strength and character of someone who could sing.

"*Happy birthday, Mr. President. Happy birthday to you.*"

She did as the film goddess once did: she paused for the audience to go wild. But the two men didn't clap for more like the crowd in New York City did that fabled night. The two men just stood there, mouths slightly agape, brows furrowed. They appeared completely and hopelessly confused.

But Sarah knew the show must go on. And, on cue, it did.

"*Thanks, Mr. President, for all the things you've done.*"

Sarah let the music in her head sway her body.

"*The battles that you've won,*
The way you deal with U.S. Steel,
And our problems by the ton,
We thank you … so much!"

She bent just as Marilyn bent, a constrained curtsy, her arms wide. She straightened quickly, spun to face each man in turn with a wide smile.

"Everybody! Happy birthday!"

The men held their stupefied looks.

"Now, Cyler!" Sarah screamed as she tore the next clasp down on her jumpsuit, then reached inside and around the back of her waist where a belt held tight the laser knife Trin had used to carve up Cyler's attacker.

Cyler, looking terrified, kicked the guard she'd been perfuming into submission with all her frightened might. She yelped louder than he did when her foot crushed the twin targets between his legs.

Sarah swung out the knife and sliced the man on the left across his chest, drawing a bloody stripe shoulder to shoulder. He fell back against the door.

Cyler had stepped away from the doubled-over guard, her hands to her mouth.

"Oh my God!"

"Do it!" Sarah yelled.

"I can't. I can't!"

Sarah took the laser to the groaning man's arm, severing it at the elbow. His weapon fell to the floor with his hand and forearm. Cyler screamed.

"Take the weapon, damn it!" Sarah said. But Cyler stayed where she was.

Sarah bent to grab the gun, but before she could reach it, a shot rang out from her left and Cyler was knocked across the corridor from the force of the blast.

Sarah hit the floor, pried the gun from the severed arm, rolled to her side, and shot three wild bursts in the direction of the door and the guard sitting against it, legs splayed, chest abloom in red. The first two pulls of the trigger missed their mark. But the third hit home and the man slumped limply, his weapon loose in his hand, his dead eyes still open. Still confused.

The other guard was trying to get himself back on his feet. But he'd lost a lot of blood and Sarah thought he was most likely already in shock. She got to him before he could fully regain his footing and pushed him back down. It took hardly any effort. He went down on his bad arm and screamed out from the pain. She put her hand on his mouth and looked him in the eyes.

"I'm so sorry," she said warmly. "We're not really like this."

With her other hand she put the end of the weapon, his weapon, to the horrified man's temple. She turned her head, squeezed her eyes shut, and pulled the trigger.

When she felt the resistance to her hand fade, she turned back and opened her eyes to see what she'd done. The side of his head opposite her weapon was mostly gone, but his face looked unharmed. It was a shocking and pitiful scene.

She felt badly about lying to him.

19

Thirty-six seconds to surface.

In addition to the five aircraft carriers and their assorted escort ships, nine submarines were also spread along the perimeter and staged at loosely coordinated depths.

By sending the missiles to hit the *Kalelah* when the monster ship was still miles below the surface, the nuclear nations with the exception of Russia were hoping to spare the ships and subs they had sent to the coordinates. Their math had proven reliable; the disturbance to the water in the area was neatly confined miles from the edges of the perimeter. This allowed the subs to continue using their collective sonar to report on the progress of the attack.

The missiles hit their target. All five. It was a detonation of unprecedented power—and unimagined failure.

The sonar reports were unanimous. The alien ship was rocked by the blasts and its ascent was slowed. But once the shock waves and localized water boil had subsided the ship continued its climb unabated.

Henderson had gotten the word from Issar. The pri-fly was sure to become a chaotic place, so Henderson left the glassed-in room on the tower and descended to one of the portside catwalks where he could be outside, out of Issar's hair, and still have a commanding view of the perimeter.

He watched the ship's AWAC take off and the pilots scramble around the flight deck below. The ship was abuzz with alarm and activity. But the sea was calm. The wind was coming from the west in gentle gusts. The clouds were tufts of cotton floating lazily, completely unaware of the tragedy unfolding below them.

Despite the knot in his stomach, he couldn't help but notice the weather. It was a beautiful day. Had he been on a pleasure boat a few miles off some coast, he'd have called it a perfect day. A perfect day for a few cocktails in the sun. But now it was clear, this was going to be a perfect day for dying.

It wouldn't be without a fight, though, he knew that.

The commotion just below him left little doubt of that. Planes were getting in position at catapults one and three to launch two at a time. A far more dangerous practice than launching solo. But why the hell not covey launch now? What captain would play it safe after seeing five nukes dropped on a ship without killing it?

It.

He thought back to the first glimpse he'd had of the ship. Before it had a name. Before it had a captain that died on Henderson's own little ship. He longed to be in that first moment again. Not because if he had the chance to do it over again he'd do it differently. He knew that anything he could have done then would have had zero chance of making a difference one way or the other. He just wanted the cold feeling he'd had about the scan that first time he laid eyes on it to still be just that. A hunch. A feeling. A bit of bad juju. Anything would be preferable to knowing for certain that the ship his own research team had accidently stumbled upon would alter the course of humanity forever.

A member of his team was on that ship now. Was she alive still? Was she fighting with that Trin fellow to change the course of events? He had no idea. He wondered if he should feel guilty. Responsible in some way. For the record, he said to the wind, he didn't. But he wasn't sure.

The skies above had started to fill with traffic. *Five carriers all launching as quickly as they could around a ring of sea just twelve miles across is going to put a lot of planes in the air at once. This is what Eddie had worried about,* he thought. He pictured the cantankerous air boss cussing and yelling about the situation. He envied the senior commander's workload. The distraction of it.

Henderson, though, had nothing to do but wait. He couldn't help Issar. All he could do was hope that at the right moment the communications department would need him to broker a deal with the aliens.

To convey President Lee's message. To surrender. He rehearsed the message aloud one more time. It still sounded like pussy bullshit to him. But he knew if he ever had the chance to say the words, he'd think they were the right words. The only words.

20

Surface.

It started so quickly and innocently he almost didn't notice.

At the center of the perimeter that defined the expanse of water ringed by the carriers and circled overhead by their planes, the blue of the ocean began to fade. He thought perhaps it was just a figment of his imagination, a trick of the eye. But just seconds later, he was sure it was real. There was something below the surface. Something large and getting larger. Something that caught the light of the sun and bounced so much of it back it could have been a new dawn itself. But Henderson knew the thing approaching the surface would only bring darkness.

He pulled his binoculars to his face to get a better look.

The ship broke the surface perfectly level without the slightest interference from the water, like it was being pushed upward on a hydraulic lift. In his mind, days ago, when he had imagined how the ship might emerge, he pictured it arriving nose first, like a giant submarine. Seeing the spectacle before him now, shedding water like the cliff of Niagara as it rose, he felt stupid and small. His imagination had simply been too limited to envision the scale and power of the ship.

Atlantis was the thing that came to mind. He was watching the ocean drain away to reveal the contours of a lost city. Only the giant aircraft carriers, ridiculously dwarfed to Lilliputian stature, gave any indication of the truth. The water was not receding, and this was not the glorious Atlantis of myth. This was a different Atlantis.

The scene looked to him as if filmed in slow motion. It was the same illusion he got from the window seat of a jet airliner. He'd look out at the vast land- or cloudscape. And he'd have no real sense of the speed he was traveling until the chance sight of another plane, perhaps at a lower altitude, streaking across his view in the opposite direction. Only then would he realize just how fast he was moving. Now, in those split seconds of the ship's rising from the water's surface, slowed by his terrified awe, he understood he was experiencing something like those moments speeding in a jet. Velocity and distance were conspiring to trick his mind. In that tiny sliver of time, he was aware that his perception was skewed. Things all around him, in fact, were skewed. Just two letters from screwed. Funny, he thought, how a person's brain works when faced with the impossible.

But the movie camera through which he was watching the insane transformation of his world would soon be done toying with Mike Henderson.

Cut to twenty-four frames per second.

At the point where the water still broke against the walls of the rising city-ship, a swell began to form. It grew taller and taller, an angry, aqueous blast-ring, rising up against the backdrop of the glowering, titanium Atlantis. From his skinny catwalk perched above the flight deck of the *Nimitz*, he watched the tsunami crest, fold over on itself, and then advance away from the ship in every direction he could see.

And this time there was no skewing of his perceptions. It was moving fast, and he could see it plain as day.

"Aw, hell."

21

Keeper Phetra was in the central chapel at the narrow end of the main stem when the Kalelah broke the surface of the water. The captain had already hailed an all-report-to-stations, so the prayer room was empty but for her.

She, too, would have to make her way to the CC. But she granted herself a few moments here with the scented smoke, the scroll-draped walls, and the ceiling that offered a perfect sim of the solar system in which God made his home.

Moments ago, before the all-report, she had led thirty or so people in the ritual chants required before confrontation. The verses contained the words of prayer. The chapel had rung with the sounds of worship. But the efforts were legal compliance only. Coming from a planet still Halfborn, God would not hear their pleas. Without a Fullborn population, without *people*, without a Delivery that had succeeded, God could not travel to this place. Or would not. She didn't know.

The fire would start soon. She promised herself she would stay away from the windows and the cameras that might give her a glimpse of the death the ship she called home would rain.

A population of seven billion. More than four thousand languages spoken. Never had a Correction been unleashed on such numbers.

She knelt on the soft padded knee cups of a prayer rail. She grasped the metal rings above her rail that hung from the ceiling by braided steel wires and connected her directly to the celestial winds. She knew her words would not carry. She knew God could not hear. Or would not.

But she didn't believe it. She didn't believe that God would or could ignore such numbers. Seven billion. And four thousand languages.

Alone in the chapel, she could be free to think her own words. To cry them if she chose. To scream them if she needed.

She grabbed the rings hard enough to drain the color from her knuckles. She held her head back and fixed her stare on the first planet from the third sun— God's home. And she prayed.

She told God of her faith and her loyalty. She told Him of her boiling desire to help Argen through his struggle. To give him the words from the scrolls that would defend his action, which was really an act of inaction, a resolute reluctance to act. But she knew there were no words. She could search the scrolls a thousand years and never find them. So, she reminded God, she stayed true. To Him, to the Plan. She stood straight and true for Him though her heart begged her to bend, begged her to give Argen his time.

She screamed this to God. She held the rings, her arms stretched wide as if attempting to embrace the very stars themselves, and threw her stupid, blind, unyielding loyalty at his feet and demanded that He hear her, that He weigh in on what was about to happen.

"The hour is late," she screamed. "Where are you? Are you not here because you can't be here? Or because you won't be here? Which is it?" She screamed until she had no voice left. She screamed until her hands bled from where her own fingernails pierced her own hands.

In the midst of contorted anger, she saw the wires of another set of rings move. She saw a familiar face from the CC adjust his grip on the rings, settle his knees into the soft, leather indentations on the rail.

She blinked away the water in her eyes to get a better look.

"You should be at your post, Analyst. I wish to be alone," she said with what little was left of her voice.

"I'm here at the captain's orders, Keeper."

"Please tell Captain Laird I'll be at my chair shortly."

"Not Captain Laird. Captain Argen."

"Argen? Where is he?"

Trin turned toward her. His face carried a burden that seemed to put years on his countenance. He did not appear the wunderkind of the CC anymore. He looked to be a man.

"Keeper, Captain Argen is dead."

New tears welled, and the image of the young officer went soft again. "How?" she croaked, almost unable to even say the word.

"It doesn't matter," said the analyst. "But I pursued his last orders to their completion. And now I need your help. This world needs your help."

"What were his orders?"

"Find the glitch. The glitch that made us oversleep our checks."

"And what did you find, Analyst Trin?"

"There was no glitch. No accident, no malfunction. The clock was reprogrammed just before the last Skip. Reprogrammed on purpose."

"You mean the time clock was sabotaged."

"Yes."

"And do you know who committed this most egregious crime against God?"

"The captain."

She studied his face and marveled at the miracle of him. Another warm tear fell to her cheek.

"Laird," she said softly.

He nodded just the smallest of confirmations, but it was enough for her. It was more than enough. It was everything.

She relaxed her grip from the rings and let her sore arms return to her sides. Her head fell back and once again she fixed her stare on the first planet from the third sun.

And in a voice scratched and hoarse, barely a whisper, she said, "Thank you."

22

Issar had launched all the planes and choppers. The sky was thick with the collected forces of five of the world's largest aircraft carriers.

Every captain had made the same bet, the only one available. The wave would come. It would wash the flight decks clean. But the ships would not sink. Because this is what carriers do; they do not sink. And eventually, the planes would land again. To help the odds, every ship had been hustling to face the monster wall of water bow first.

Henderson understood the lunacy of staying on the catwalk when the wave hit. There was no harness. There was no first line of defense, nothing to absorb the first volley of energy. He'd be swept away for sure. He should get inside, he knew this. There was time to rejoin Eddie in the pri-fly. There was time to get his lifejacket. There was even time to pray.

But Henderson simply planted his feet a little wider, gripped the railing, and watched as the wave raced toward the *Nimitz*.

What was the line, he thought as the wave loomed so tall he could no longer see the giant city-ship that had started it in the first place, a plan lasts only as long as the first minute you meet the enemy? That's what he thought when the roar of the water drowned out the noise of more than three hundred aircraft flying overhead.

As usual, we don't know shit. That's what he thought in the instant the wave struck the *Nimitz. We were always so sure. Every generation since the beginning of knowing thought it had the answers. But nobody knew anything. Fucking dumbshits. All this time, all this energy and arguing and fighting, for what? Fucking dumbshits were all we ever were.*

As the salty water slammed into his lungs and his body yielded to the might of the wave that snapped the unsinkable carrier like a twig, he waited for his life to flash through his mind. But nothing flashed. There was just the sea and its current nonnegotiable disposition. It was just as well.

He opened his eyes to see what he could for as long as he could. He felt no pain. The water was a comfortable temperature and he went where it took him. And for the first time in his life he was without anger.

And the skin around his neck and upon his face showed not a hint of red.

• • • •

Minutes later, the military leadership of China, Russia, France, Great Britain, and the United States were informed by the orphaned pilots still circling over the city-ship that all the carriers were gone. Gone without a trace.

The subs, too, could not be reached.

The planes all dropped their meaningless ordnances on the giant ship. The *Kalelah* took no defensive or offensive action. The ship ignored the planes completely and continued its rise to the sky without pause.

A French pilot crashed his jet directly into the ship. Every other pilot in the perimeter did the same, even the AWACs and choppers.

They accomplished nothing.

23

Trin and a small contingent from the Counter arrived at the armory just minutes after Sarah's hail. He had been dreading the worst all the way over. The float was supposed to come from Cyler. How Sarah had figured out how to use the comm system he had no idea. But he knew it meant she'd had no choice.

Now he knew why. She was kneeling next to Cyler's body, her face streaked with tears and blood. He picked her up and pulled her to her feet.

"I'm sorry," Sarah said, her eyes spilling over. "They were fast. I wasn't."

He pulled her to him and let her cry. He let himself do the same. He cried for Cyler. And for failing Argen too.

"No, I wasn't fast enough," he said. "I let us take too long to get to this point. Now we're behind the ball. And a lot of people are going to die because of it."

"Indeed they are, darlings. And the question now is whether or not we'll all be among them."

It was Wildei, at the controls of a stolen gurney. She looked down at Cyler and frowned.

"I'm sorry about your friend. But breaking into the armory is the same as pulling an alarm, so cry later, sweethearts, will you? We have thirty seconds to grab as many guns as we can carry."

All together there were nine people and two gurneys. They took what they could. But they left much more behind. Enough to arm double their numbers, maybe more.

He knew the break-in and the heist would infuriate Laird. It just wouldn't wound her much.

But with the ship out of water and moving fast toward the closest landmass—a massively populated cluster of islands—what choice did they have, he asked himself.

No fucking choice. No fucking choice at all.

24

The State Councillor sat in the small garden at the back of his modest home. Though the air in Beijing had gotten progressively worse over the years, and his doctors had warned him to stay indoors whenever possible, the garden was a place he could not resist.

Surrounded by thick, tall, stone walls that kept most of the city noise at bay, it was quiet enough to hear the birds. If he was feeling well and his feet and joints did not bother him too much, he would busy himself trimming the well-trained boxwoods. But on this day, he just sat. And waited.

The reports and video from Japan, while they came, had been more surreal than his imagination had allowed. The ship approached from the east. Estimates pegged its travel altitude at 20,000 feet and its speed at more than 300 miles per hour. Disappointing all the science fiction speculators, it had showed no attempt to cloak itself with cloud cover like a scene from a Hollywood movie.

As if it knew there had been no reason to hide.

China fired ten nuclear-tipped medium-range ballistic missiles, ignoring both Japan's insistence that such weapons not be used once the ship was airborne and the nearly impossible odds of hitting a moving target with a MRBM.

All ten missiles missed.

An American bomber based in South Korea risked flying overhead the monster to drop a MOAB, or massive ordnance air blast, also known as the Mother of All Bombs.

And still Japan and the world watched the ship get closer and closer.

Missile defense systems had been redirected toward the ship. It was bombarded by every warplane the bases in Japan, China, South Korea, and the Philippines could throw at it.

But there had been no stopping it. Or even engaging it.

Like those from the carriers, these attacks on the ship had been simply and completely ignored. No photon cannons were fired. No alien versions of fighter jets emerged like swarms of bees from heretofore unseen ports along the ship's sides to take on the underdog Chinese-made J-20 fighter planes and American F-16s. No force field bloomed a lacy, digital blue when struck.

"As if we weren't even there," the newscasts had said.

As if we weren't worth fighting, Wu couldn't help thinking at the time.

When the ship reached its first landfall, the erasure of Japan had been total. That was the only word for it.

The islands remained, but any real trace that humans had once walked those lands, planted forests, erected skyscrapers, or paved roads was gone. Erased.

He'd seen the videos that had been streamed until the cameras recording the strange inferno were incinerated too. It was a fire he'd never seen before. It descended from the entire circumference of the ship like a sun exploding. The reach of the white-hot spray was miles wide. And it was a hungry kind of fire.

When it hit the ground, it burst again into a million dancing orbs of pulsating energy. The orbs didn't simply burn what they touched, they ate it. So thorough was the jeweled, swirling choreography of heat that the matter it consumed hardly smoked at all. The sheer speed and efficiency of it was magical.

Beautiful even.

That was the first thing that had crossed his mind when Wu saw the pictures and the video. It was curiously, bewitchingly beautiful. There was a designed elegance to it. *Grace.* His mind flashed to Western religious paintings he had studied as a young man. "God light" was the term his professor had used to describe the yellow rays of sun that seemed to be harnessed and aimed to shed a divine illumination on the scene below.

The images he had seen from Japan, the images the whole world had seen, were of a fireworks display turned upside down, the ground playing the role of the night sky and the voracious, glowing orbs producing a similar jaw-dropping awe. The contrast between this weapon, if that's what it was, and a nuclear blast had been brutally stark to Wu. While the splitting of an atom was a violent affair, loud and angry, that left a smoldering husk of a city, this fire had seemed to make almost no sound—even objects like gas lines and petrol tanks that should have created explosions of their own were eaten so quickly they never had the chance to ignite—and it left nothing but a thin, softly contoured blanket of crystallized ash. Forget for a moment what the ash had once been and even it, too, possessed a semblance of beauty.

This was the enchanted version of a forest fire, he had thought, and its purpose was no different. Not mere destruction. It was a cleansing. A starting over. Until the cameras became themselves undone, their last images were not of an Earth he recognized, but of a primordial precursor, a virgin scape awaiting a new catalyst.

He had to admire the respectfulness of it. The heat worked so fast and so completely, there could be no pain for the victims, and no suffering survivors. A second's fear, perhaps.

Or maybe not. At least not after the video from Japan traveled its way around the world.

After the nukes sent to the North Pacific failed, after the planes and their munitions bounced off the skin of the ship like oil spattering on a hot pan, and after Japan had been turned into a craterless rendition of the moon, the global response to the ship had become split.

Through his diplomatic channels, he had heard that many governments were implementing their bunker strategies. He knew for a fact his was. There was space reserved for him there. Space enough for a functioning government. What it hoped to govern, he didn't know.

It was twenty stories beneath grade. There was food there for at least two years. The worries of a nuclear holocaust had prepared the modern world for a doomsday. But in Wu's mind, there was no preparation for a day such as this.

No one knew how far down the heat traveled, if people and their stores of food and weapons would simply cook within their hiding places, or whether the inferno left behind another means of killing a remnant human race, the alien equivalent of fallout. For that matter, no one knew if the ship would simply stay to clean up the underground.

But bunkers were designed to be used, so use them many did. Wu understood the defiance, the never-give-up mentality. It was only human.

There was another camp, though. It saw no virtue in becoming the human equivalents of rodents. Or no point in it. This faction saw the power of the ship as unstoppable.

And maybe not altogether evil.

A hundred years of photographic testimony to the horror of war, terrorist bombings, ethnic hatred, and militant mercantilism had taught the world what senseless, violent death and suffering looked like.

What had happened to Japan didn't resemble those images, so Wu was doing what millions of others around the globe were doing. Not running. Not panicking. Not resisting.

Earlier in the morning, he had made himself a good breakfast, eating foods his doctors had long prohibited. The night before he had made phone calls to the few people left in his life that mattered to him. A son in Zhengzhou. A granddaughter working at the Chinese embassy in Nigeria.

They had talked for hours. Of people they loved who had died. Of their gratitude for too many things to mention.

The Koreas had been erased during the calls. Shanghai had been taken off the map over his breakfast. Reports predicted the ship would make its way as far west as Russia by nightfall.

And now he was in his garden, listening to the oblivious birds, sipping his tea and looking to the sky.

Awaiting the light.

25

They had picked the smallest weapons they could. What the guns lacked in firepower they made up for in stealth. One couldn't walk through a stem with a large weapon in hand and expect to get very far. They stuffed them under their jumpsuits in makeshift holsters at their waists. They tied them to their ankles. They slung small packs over their shoulders laden with ammunition and guns.

To avoid suspicion, they converged from different directions in the large open plaza in front of the CC in small groups of twos and threes. They were nearly sixty in total.

But these were techs, console critters, and guides. Not fighters. The CC had plenty of built-in protection before the Correction began. And now that the *Kalelah* was moving, and the armory had been breached, more security had been added.

"I hate this idea," Trin said as they made their way from the main stem to the point where it opened up to the plaza proper.

"It was your idea," Sarah reminded him.

"That doesn't mean it isn't shit. Half these people are scared out of their minds. The others are too young and stupid to know they should be."

They came to their mark—one of several large columns that supported a thin mezzanine that looped the plaza—and positioned themselves behind it.

"So, good news first," Sarah said. "There are just three guns guarding the doors."

"And the bad news hasn't gotten any better. This plaza is fucked with blind spots. Maybe the other idea is smarter. I use my access, two others run in behind me, and we just go from there."

"You mean the idea where you probably die in the first three seconds? Until we know what's behind those doors, the more guns we have the better."

She looked around. Their jittery crew of novice rebels had spread themselves throughout the plaza. Some were at vendor stalls. Some were at chairs and benches. Just the normal midday crowd of plaza-goers.

"Everyone's here," she said. "Time to play Keeper."

He steadied himself. "And here the fuck we go."

"Maybe watch the language."

He walked out from behind the column to the center of the plaza. He put his arms out.

"Is this what God wants?"

He said this as loudly as he could without shouting. He waited for the ringers in the plaza to respond to his cue. After enough had turned their heads and paused what they were doing, he continued.

"Captain Argen believed we came here as makers, not killers. And I believe that too."

He waited again. As they had planned earlier, a few people walked closer and started to form a circle around him.

"Captain Argen believed we should understand the population we brought here before deciding whether to exterminate it. And I believe that too."

He rotated to address his audience. Most of it, he could see, were members of the Counter. They were the ones with the nervous, darting eyes. But some were just passersby who saw a traditional speaker's circle form and joined in. Maybe this would work.

"Seven point three billion individuals! Never in the history of the service has a Correction been initiated on so large a population. Is this the kind of history you want to make?"

The ringers all answered with their scripted responses: "Then let's do something about it! Open the doors!"

"Open the doors!" a few in the audience responded.

"Open the doors!" Trin shouted back.

The crowd got larger, but it was still thin enough for Trin to see what he hoped he'd see: a guard walking from his post at the doors to the small speaker's crowd.

Trin let the momentum build. "Open the doors!"

"Okay," the guard said as he pushed his way through to the center where Trin was standing. "You've had your say. Break this up."

"But I'm not finished," Trin said innocently. "We're not finished," he said, looking around him. "Right?"

"You're done," the guard said as he grabbed Trin by the arm.

Trin pushed back and punched the guard as hard as he could. The guard went down, and a few of the Counter members in the crowd pounced on him. They took the guard's weapon, yanked him off the ground, and put the muzzle of the gun to his forehead.

"Open the doors," Trin said to the other two guards.

"I don't think so," said the bigger of the two. He raised his weapon and shot through the hostage and three men fell to the floor.

There was a pause, a collective inhale as the group of amateurs seemed to understand for the first time what they'd gotten themselves into.

It didn't last long. The shooting erupted in a melee that seemed to come from all corners. From the mezzanine above, from the stems that led to the plaza, from the guards at the doors, and from the guns stolen from the armory.

Some of the rebel group managed to find cover behind columns and vending stations.

Most did not.

26

Wildei was running full blast through Leaf Five on her way to the main stem and the plaza that fronted the CC. She received a float mid stride.

[o] Δ [ø] :1: [ø] Δ [o] :11: [o] :1: [Δ]

Machine. Only one source would have to communicate in machine language instead of Origen.

She'd been trying for more than a day to reach him. She wasn't sure it was even possible. Her own limited dealings with the code were challenging enough; she couldn't imagine what it must be like for him. How overwhelming it must be. And if her message, her plea, did manage to get through, she had little hope that he'd agree. That he'd be willing to do the only thing left to do.

It was the look on his face when she had said, "You don't look dangerous to me. Or much like a murderer either." There was a sadness in his eyes that told her she had hit a nerve. Not one he'd been willing to acknowledge overtly, but one that maybe had been keeping him up a bit at night.

He had said all the things a proper loyalist ought to have said. But the eyes had given her hope. And now she had an answer.

She stopped running. The two other Counter members trailing behind her stopped when they caught up.

"Why are we stopping?" the thin woman asked.

"A change of plan, darlings. We're going to the nest."

27

The alarms rang throughout the ship. Strap-down stations emerged from the walls in every concourse.

"What's going on?" the captain asked the ring. But the child had already provided Laird the answer. The *Kalelah* was falling. She could see the projected image of the ground below the ship at her feet, the lethal aurora spreading across the landmass, leaving a dark vacancy in its wake. And far above the scene of fast-spreading incineration she could see the child hanging in the air without forward motion at all.

"Engines have stopped, sir."

"Stopped? Why?"

"Disconnection, sir."

"Give me a visual of the nest."

A new float appeared just a few feet from the captain's face. In it was a view into the vestigial room at the top of the ship and its glass walls that narrowed to a dull point. The pilot's chair was far back in the room, nestled in the point, and the room's sweeping angles gave it the commanding air of a throne. It was turned away from her at the moment, hiding its occupant.

"Donnalay, report."

The chair swiveled to reveal the pilot, his gloves in his lap, his hands grasping the arms of the big chair.

"Pilot Donnalay reporting, sir." His voice was raspy, tired, resigned.

"Explain yourself, Lieutenant."

"I'm stopping the ship, sir."

"On whose orders?"

"On mine."

"On yours?"

"That's right, sir. On mine," he said without the slightest bit of indignation.

"I have no time to argue with you, Donnalay. Get those gloves on. That's an order."

"Sir. I hereby tender my resignation as pilot of the *Kalelah*."

"Has everyone gone mad?" Laird shouted with incredulity. "Let me make something clear to you, Donnalay. You're not a pilot, you've never been a pilot. You're just an organic wire, a bundle of conducting tissue that seems to have lost its mind, if it ever had one. Now get those gloves back on or I will personally walk up to the nest, kill you with my bare hands, and shove the gloves on the hands of your soulless corpse."

The ship began to list slightly. The captain waved the float away and turned to exit out of the imaging column. Before she got to the threshold that led to the larger room of the CC, she called out to the ring.

"How long do we have?"

"Eight minutes, sir."

"Thank you. Keep burning. And move another security detail to the nest, arrest Donnalay, and get a backup in that chair before we hit the ground. This nonsense ends now."

She walked through the CC, her head high and her gaze fixed on the dented and heavily guarded doors that led to the main stem. But throughout the CC, all eyes were fixed on her. She pushed her way through the phalanx of guards who stood shoulder to shoulder with weapons ready.

"Open the doors."

"Sir," a guard cautioned. "There's still live fire in the stem."

"From a disorganized bunch of guides and console operators. You're a trained soldier, Corporal, find the nerve. Open the doors, *now*. And follow me out."

The doors opened to a smoky stem, bodies were strewn about the floor. From what she could see, security had done its job well.

"Cease fire!" she shouted as loudly as she could. "Cease fire!"

She raised her hands in a gesture of transparency and waited until she felt she had the stem's attention.

"How many have to die?" she shouted. "This is not a battle you can win. Lay down your arms now, and maybe I won't execute you for your crimes."

A blonde woman emerged from behind a large column. An Initiate. She walked toward the captain, her weapon hanging loose at her side. One of the guards behind the captain shouted for her to drop her weapon, but the woman kept walking.

"This is your last warning," the guard said as he adjusted his aim.

She dropped the weapon. But not carefully or decisively. She simply let it fall from her fingers and kept walking toward the captain.

"Sarah, stop!" a voice called out.

Another person emerged from the opposite side of the stem. Someone she knew.

"Analyst Trin," Laird said. "How greatly you disappoint me. I thought you were smarter than this. Isn't that why you're on my ship, because you're smarter than everyone?"

"I'm here for the same reason we all are. To save this planet for God."

"And we've failed at that, Analyst."

"Not we, Captain. You."

"Don't make me put a hole in that brilliant brain of yours, Trin. You can still be of service."

"I know you sabotaged the time clock."

"You're stalling and it won't work," she said calmly, seeing no need at this point to give the accusation any serious rebuttal.

"I have proof. Straight from the code."

The guards behind Laird looked at one another.

"You have lies," Laird said.

"The code can do many things, sir. But it can't lie. You'd have to be human to do that."

A voice from behind her said, "He's right, Hanta."

She whirled around to see Phetra standing with the guards.

28

Wildei had no idea how many guards Laird would send to take the nest. It didn't matter anyway. There were just the three of them, and they'd have to do. The two dead guards who were stinking up their little space in the pre-lock were not likely to be much help once the real fighting began.

Donnalay had stayed in the chair. If Laird's men were to make it past Wildei's ad hoc barrier, the plan was for Donnalay to destroy the gloves. It'd be a desperate measure. But there was no more certain way to halt the Correction. The guns that fired the plasma were fixed in one position, dependent on height and travel to spread the burn band. If the ship went down, that would be it. For lots of things.

If push had indeed come to that particular last-ditch shove, and Donnalay destroyed the gloves, the ship would never fly again. Any survivors would be trapped on this planet for the rest of their lives. And it likely wouldn't be a very friendly place to be. The ship had already done significant damage. The number of deaths would be well over a billion. Wildei doubted she herself could forgive a murder at that scale.

They stood in the little heavy-walled chamber, staring at the backs of the dead guards they'd propped up in the hole that should have been a four-inch-thick door. She prayed that Trin would make it through the CC doors and get control of the ship from there. She prayed Captain Laird was short on crew to take the nest. And she wished she had anticipated just how foul an odor dead people put out when their bowels evacuate.

With her was a data technician who looked to be no more than ninety pounds. The middle-aged woman had never fired a weapon in her life. The other mutineer was a food cart vendor, sweating and shaking from fear. God knew who he'd shoot.

There were two chambers that kept the nest secure: a pre-lock, where Wildei and her ragtag group were now, and a second even more heavily walled chamber, the lock chamber. Once Donnalay was inside, both doors were shut and locked from the CC. Even Donnalay couldn't open the doors, nor the two guards who had been stationed in front of the pre-lock. But Wildei had bet that once Laird discovered that Donnalay had taken off the gloves, she'd open the doors, making it easy for the guards and the reinforcements she'd send to get to Donnalay and complete the circuit again.

She had bet right. And she had been lucky her blind shots from the ventilator shaft had hit their targets. The shaft was a tight squeeze and dark as ink. Keeping her crawl silent was no easy task. And even as she pulled the trigger she wondered if she had counted correctly. There was no way to know for sure if she was over the guards or not.

And there was no guarantee her weapon's arc would even make it through the ventilator's skin without killing her in the process.

Once she reached what she thought was her mark, she pressed the nose of the gun against the metal beneath her and just blasted away.

No one was more surprised than she that it worked. Except maybe the dead guys. But now, huddled in the pre-lock with two shaking cohorts and two dead guards as shields, she didn't have a ventilator to give her an advantage. The people on their way could not be hit by surprise from above. They'd be coming her way, guns ready and pointed in her direction.

The lights in the small hallway to the pre-lock went out.

The data jock next to her let out a tiny gasp, and Wildei placed her hand over the woman's face. After a few seconds the woman nodded. Wildei gambled that meant the technician could keep quiet and took her hand away from the woman's face. There was no sound of footfalls in the hallway. The guards could be anywhere: ten feet away or right on top of them.

And then a sniff. The kind a person makes when encountering a terrible smell without any visual of its source. It was a test-sniff. The involuntary response to the internal question: Is this smell real? And if so, just how bad is it? Retch bad, or tolerable? Whatever the guard's olfactory nerves communicated to the guard's brain didn't matter to Wildei. The sniff was enough to tell Wildei where the guards were in the hall. She waited just a moment. When she could feel the approaching guards were within dead-guy range, she pushed as hard as she could on the two shit-stained bodies.

It was enough to give her and her two partners in amateur soldiering the second they needed.

"Hello, darlings," Wildei said as she opened fire. The arc from her gun's discharge illuminated the tiny hallway enough to give her next shots the aim she needed.

And then, for a second lucky time, no shots came back.

"Ha!" the petite data technician shouted, her voice high and full of relief. "We fucking shot the fuck out of them!"

"I know the one on the right," the vendor said sadly. "He was a customer. A nice man. I think I killed him."

"I killed him," lied Wildei. "Your aim was all over the place. We're lucky you didn't kill yourself. Careful on the way out of here. I don't want you tripping and shooting me." A look of relief and embarrassment came over the man's face, and she turned forward and moved on.

They made their way out of the hallway and into a much larger and lighted corridor. Wildei gave a look in both directions.

"Nobody. Those four were all she could spare. I think Donnalay will be okay." She opened a time float, checked it, and scouted the corridor one more time. "Let's go."

As they walked, the list of the ship tilted just a bit more. Wildei thought for a brief moment that she could feel a sense of falling. But she knew it wasn't the ship she was feeling.

It was something much bigger.

29

"Go back to your chair," the captain said. "This is none of your business."

It was a standoff of sorts: the captain and her guards against the mutineers and the Keeper, who had somehow joined together. She should have known that Phetra could not stay strong. Yet another disappointment.

"But it is my business, Hanta. I'm the Keeper. My job is to maintain the faith and to sustain it in the crew. And they won't hold on to it if they're operating under the banner of a lie. So, with my signature and the authority of my position attached, I'm sharing what Trin discovered."

On cue, hundreds of floats filled the stem and the CC behind her. The captain quickly scanned the float. She didn't need all the details to know what was being broadcast.

"You weakling," she sneered. "You're no better than the rest of them. How dare you call yourself Keeper."

"What you're doing, Hanta, what you've done, is a crime. And it's time to answer for it."

"A crime? If it is, it was born of yours. Of your pitiful softness. Don't think I didn't weep over this decision. But you should thank God I made it."

The blonde was standing in front of her now. Filthy, her hair a tangle, her eyes ablaze like something wild.

"Thank God?" she said flatly. "I'll remember to do that when you're dead."

The girl took a swing at Laird, but it was an untrained attempt and evaded easily.

"How did you ever get through Academy with a swing like that, Initiate?" she laughed.

"I got a special invitation from Captain Argen." She took another errant swing.

They circled each other. When a guard tried to step in, Laird waved him away. There was more to know here from this strange girl. And something oddly compelling as well. Her eyes were striking. Laird wanted more time to figure this woman out. Who would come after her unarmed, and so badly unprepared?

"You have a strange accent, girl. Where are you from?"

"Nowhere you'd understand. The place is crawling with people."

The analyst was running to her now screaming that word, "*Sarah*." But the girl didn't seem to hear. "Sarah"—if it was a name, this girl's name, it wasn't one from anywhere Laird had heard of.

The blonde came at Laird once more, full of passion and grit but no less awkward than before. The ship lurched again, deepening the angle of the list. It took the girl by surprise.

Laird grabbed her wrist, broke it with one twist, punched her in the throat, and kicked her legs out from under her. The girl hit the ground hard, wheezing, clutching at her throat with her one good hand.

Trin had made his way across the concourse. A guard tackled him to the ground, another put his weapon to the analyst's head.

Laird bent down and put her fingers through the female's hair.

"So you're one of them. Hmm. I imagine without the dirt and smell, you'd be almost … pretty. Such a waste."

"Arrest the Halfborn," Laird said to the guards. "Analyst Trin and the Keeper here as well."

But before they could execute her command, the listing of the ship changed its angle sharply. Laird and everyone else were swept off their feet. She began to slide fast toward the concourse wall. She tried to get to her feet, to scramble back up the tilt. But the force was too much. The ship was falling fast now, she knew that. One of the guards slid into her hard, and the two of them rolled head over feet. Something hit her head. The pain was sharp and blinding. And then there was nothing.

She was unconscious when the *Kalelah* crashed into a city that was home to more than fifteen thousand churches.

30

In the 1950s, a military scientist imagined a weapon he named "Project Thor."

The idea was this: If a projectile that was extremely dense—say, a large chunk of tungsten steel—could be fired upon a target at a high enough velocity, it would possess the dino-exterminating impact of a meteor strike—but without the lingering danger of nuclear fallout.

His thinking led to the science of kinetic weaponry: the hurling of inert objects at fast speeds, like Thor and his hammer.

The city of Moscow experienced firsthand the potency of a kinetic attack when the *Kalelah* smashed down. Thanks to its size and the density of the air through which it fell, the ship had leveled out some before impact, hitting at a mere four-degree angle, nose first, its leaves swept back, the deadliest arrow ever to fall from the sky. It produced a crater twenty-two-miles in diameter. More than sixteen million people in the Moscow Capital Region died during the crash.

The fate of its president and his childhood friend, the foreign minister, was yet unknown.

31

Two Days Later.

F or nearly a day, she'd watched the barren, dusty stretch of blasted rock between the ship and the crater's ridge, but still not a single soul had dared cross it. *They're keeping their distance. Can't blame them.*

The CC had sent up a remote sentinel to send back an aerial image of the crash site. It'd been displayed as a float, the largest she'd ever seen aired, and the detail was strikingly clear. The dust and smoke that had filled the skies above the city had mostly dissipated and she could make out individual rocks and bits of debris from miles away.

But more fascinating to her, even after everything, was just the image itself, the crazy gestalt of the *Kalelah* sitting dead center in a gigantic ring of moon dust. Except it wasn't the moon. It was home. Earth, anyway.

Another impossible image flashed in her mind: Her first incredulous look at the scan. It seemed like it had been years ago. The ship buried in the seafloor, looking no less a dream than it did now.

But in between the two images, the two dreams, had been a nightmare.

I think it's somethin' you get as far the fuck away from as you can, Henderson had warned in those first heady hours. And he had known nothing about the ship. Well, at least one thing had been learned since— and a thousand cities and two billion people had vanished in the lesson. Now, suddenly, mysteriously, the thing that had unleashed a fire beyond imagination was on the ground. The alien thing that had once already fooled the world by playing dead. Who out there, she wondered, on the other side of the ridge, could possibly guess as to its current state of lethality? Or its intentions?

She looked around at the people in the CC. They tended to their stations. But news of the captain's treachery and their own complicit roles, however ignorant, seemed to have left a mark, a bruise darker and more ominous than any the crash might have dealt. What was to become of them after what they had already become? In the eyes of those still left on the planet their ship had attacked, and maybe in their own eyes as well, they were already mythic killers, already horror stories made real.

And now, they were Earthlings.

Donnalay's last act of defiance, perhaps his last grasp at something like dignity, was to destroy the gloves and tear their thousands of fiber connections from the chair. He may not have been an actual pilot, but he knew how to make sure it would be years before the *Kalelah* could fly again. There was damage to the ship's magnetic drives as well. Some engineers thought that between Donnalay and the wounded drives, the ship might never leave the crater.

Sarah turned to Trin and watched him looking at the image of the crash site. He had taken a bad fall when the ship went down. When she first saw his face, she had gasped. But the medical treatment had worked wonders already. And still, she was sure his face would never be the same as when she first saw it on the *Lewis*. He looked older by years. In just days, his cocky self-assurance had been stripped away, replaced by something more fragile. Something more deserving. If it were true, if his face was now a reflection of an older and wiser self, that would come in handy. Because Sarah thought she knew what was next for her. And for Trin.

She turned back to the float. It hovered just as it had since it was aired two days ago, shimmering like an apparition between the ceiling and the floor. Its source of light and energy was still a complete mystery to her. No receivers, no wires, no projectors. And yet.

A miracle. God not required.

And since that first moment when the scan of the ship resolved itself on her computer screen, she'd been witness to dozens. Any one of them, she imagined, could change the world.

If only the old lies, the ones born here and elsewhere, could be held at bay. And the mother ship could be one again.

• • • •

In the corner of the float, at roughly ten o'clock on the gigantic circle of the crater, a speck appeared atop the rocks at the impact zone's edge. The sentinel saw it and zoomed in to monitor it. It was a woman, a child in her arms. Behind her came more children, eleven in total, some very young, some in their teens, and behind them walked four men and three other women. They scrambled up over the tops of the rocks one by one and began a slow, careful walk down toward the moat. They carried water. Nothing more.

Sarah took Trin's hand in hers and watched. A young boy took a woman by the elbow to help her make the transition from ridge rocks to the fine dust of the pulverized city. Was she his mother? Her eyes filled at the small sweetness of the gesture. She was proud of the boy. She wanted to shout to everyone in the CC, "*Did you see that? Did you see how a young boy loves his mother?*" But she kept quiet instead.

All the members of the little group were in the moat now. Twenty people in their T-shirts, jeans, and skirts. They left a thin trail of crooked footsteps in the otherwise undisturbed surface of the crater, like a line on a map. A map to where, she wondered.

She had no idea where they had come from or how far they had traveled to breach the crater's outer edge. And she could only imagine the fear they had experienced and the loss they suffered just days before starting their journey. And yet, she marveled, they had come. They had come to cross the distance, to cross a desert that shouldn't be.

Another first contact. Another chance.

This is the best of us, isn't it?

But not, she quickly reminded herself, *the most of us. Others will follow these first twenty.*

And they will be different.

She gave Trin a gentle tug.

"Let's go."

Thanks for reading. Follow Marshall on Facebook or register at marshall-ross.com for news of his next book.

Made in the USA
Lexington, KY
27 November 2018